Paper Lions

a novel

Sohan S Koonar

MAWEN**Z**I
HOUSE

We acknowledge the support of the Canada Council for the Arts for our publishing program. We also acknowledge support from the Government of Ontario through the Ontario Arts Council.

Cover design by Sara Koonar

Maps by Natalie Koonar

Library and Archives Canada Cataloguing in Publication

Title: Paper lions : a novel / Sohan S. Koonar.

Names: Koonar, Sohan S., 1950- author.

Identifiers: Canadiana (print) 20190072431 | Canadiana (ebook) 20190072555 | ISBN 9781988449777
  (softcover) | ISBN 9781988449784 (HTML) | ISBN 9781988449821 (PDF)

Classification: LCC PS8621.O64 P37 2019 | DDC C813/.6—dc23

Places described in this book are real. However, this is a work of fiction and resemblances to any persons are unintended.

Printed and bound in Canada by Coach House Printing

Mawenzi House Publishers Ltd.

39 Woburn Avenue (B)

Toronto, Ontario M5M 1K5

Canada

www.mawenzihouse.com

for Nadia

Map of Punjab – Basanti's Journey

x
Sialkot

Basanti's journey (1947)

• Amritsar

N

PAKISTAN | INDIA

Sirhind Canal

Raikot
Ludhiana
• Samrala
Doraha
Chandigarh•

P U N J A B

Map of Village – Raikot

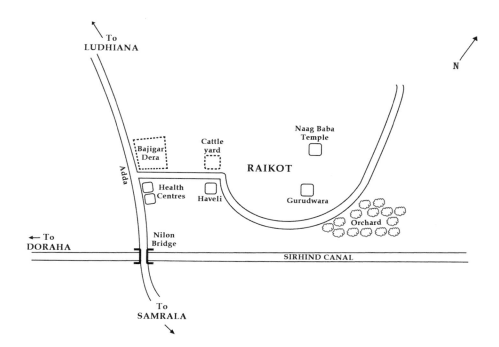

Characters

Bikram Singh
Lal Singh (Masterji) and **Maaji**, Bikram's father and mother
Guddi and **Pyari**, Bikram's sisters
Jagtar, Bikram's wife
Chand Singh, Jagtar's father
Beeji, Jagtar's mother
Darshan and **Sukha**, Jagtar's brothers
Sewa, Bikram and Jagtar's son

In Samrala
Mirza Gujjar, the dairyman
Pundit Gopal Sharma, matchmaker and astrologer
Golu, head of the gang of ruffians

Bikram's employees
Ramu, chef and household manager
Rakesh Kumar, publicist

Politicians
Aalok Nath, MLA
Prushotam Nath, Aalok Nath's son
Arjun Singh, MP

Ajit Singh
Inder, Ajit's wife
Siamo, Ajit's cousin
Satwant (the Captain), Ajit and Inder's son
Amrita, Satwant's wife
Sher Singh (the Jagirdar), Amrita's father
Jeet Kaur, Amrita's mother
Jorawar Singh, Police Superintendent, Amrita's brother

Kulbir Singh, Sub-Divisional Magistrate, Amrita's brother
Pinki and **Nikki,** Satwant and Amrita's daughters
Nasib, Ajit's son

Villagers
Baru Marasi, head of the cattle yard
Lalu, the bootlegger
Bhaga, the snake-catcher
Pushpa, a Brahmin elder
The Comrade, school headmaster

The Mukhia of the Bajigars (the Rustum)
Sehba, the Mukhia's wife
Rana, the Mukhia and Sehba's son
Basanti, Rana's wife
Changu, Basanti's father
Mata, Basanti's mother
Gulab and **Piara (the Little Dervish),** Basanti's brothers
Dadi, Basanti's grandmother
Laxman Das, Basanti and Rana's son
Naura, the Mukhia's second wife
Wazeer, Naura's son
Devi, Basanti's cousin, Wazeer's wife

At the dera
Shanti
Paso, Shanti's granddaughter

BOOK ONE

1937–1945

Bikram

"Wait over there," the ticket clerk told him with a gesture of his head when he announced himself. "The Manager Sahib will be interviewing the applicants this morning, and he's not in yet."

Bikram entered the waiting room of the bus station and took a seat. The room was large, with six rows of wooden benches filled with travellers—men and women, a few children, a couple of babies asleep in their mothers' arms. He could see the twin bays where buses parked to deliver and take on passengers; they were now empty. The clock on the wall behind the ticket clerk hung at a slight angle from the vertical. It read precisely eight o'clock.

"Hot tea!" A hawker, carrying a large aluminum teapot in one hand and a tray of clay mugs in another, meandered between the benches, stopping to pour for a buyer before accepting a coin with a practised gesture.

"Amla oil, beard wax, brushes and combs!" a second hawker shouted.

"Glass bangles, ribbons of every colour, kohl, talcum powder, face creams!" called another.

Bikram looked away from their eager stares, not to be trapped into purchasing something.

With a blast from its horn a bus lumbered into the bay and gave a shriek of the brakes before coming to a shuddering stop. The engine growled and died with a mighty gasp of acrid black smoke from its rear that filled the waiting room with an oily stench. Bikram covered his nose with the loose palla of his turban, as did many men, and the women coughed into the folds of their chadors.

Eight men and eight women disembarked first. The men, with hennaed beards, wore loose turbans, kurta-salwars, and rawhide moccasins with pointed toes. They were Muslims of the Gujjar caste. The women were dressed in shorter, more fitted white kurtis and bulbous black skirts that fell to their ankles. Their white chadors were wrapped tightly over their heads. They stood awhile, looking around, then the man who was their leader led them across the street to the tonga stand and they were soon seated, the men in one tonga and the women in another. From their clothing, Bikram guessed that this was a mourning party, probably on their way to a nearby village for a funeral. The other passengers had emerged and scattered.

Now the ticket window was besieged by a horde of men elbowing each other, shouting their destinations and the number of tickets they needed. A uniformed bus driver chewing paan watched with a grin and let a long stream of reddish spittle fly from his lips to land not far from people's feet. A coolie lit a birri and took a deep puff; thick, harsh smoke drifted across the room. An older Sikh glared at him and the coolie sauntered away.

"Last call for Ludhiana!" the bus conductor shouted. He blew his whistle, and passengers scrambled to get on, squeezing their bundles and cloth bags through the narrow doors. The driver climbed onto his seat and started the engine, but not before bowing to the idol hanging on a string from his rear-view mirror.

The clock read ten. Bikram knew that the ticket clerks shortchanged illiterate villagers a paisa or two per ticket, and he passed the time by adding up the number of tickets demanded. By eleven the count stood at seventy-one. Four paisa made an anna, and sixteen annas made a rupee, so the clerk had likely pilfered a full rupee in just one hour. *He must be sharing the loot with the station manager*, he thought. The clerk had looked familiar, and Bikram remembered where he had seen him before: at the liquor vend, sharing a bottle of country rum with his cohorts.

At noon, the waiting room began to empty. It was then that Bikram noticed a well-dressed youth accompanied by an older man sitting three rows down from him, clutching a large manila envelope. *Another applicant for the position?* Bikram fussed with the envelope on his own lap. He had graduated at the top of his class, first division. People had fêted his accomplishment and congratulated his parents. As a matriculate, he was qualified to move on to higher learning, and he was eligible for scholarships to pay his tuition. Little good they would do him, though, when his family could not afford the additional costs he would incur. And so here he was, praying for the position of a ticket clerk. Samrala was a small town and good jobs were scarce.

A breeze came in, bringing the aroma of onion fritters from the tea stall across the road. The other candidate's older companion abruptly got up and brought back a steaming bag of fritters. Bikram's mouth watered.

Just after two o'clock a well-coiffed man in a smart bush shirt and creased trousers came to sit beside him. "You are a candidate?" he asked.

Bikram quickly folded his hands and bowed his greeting. "I am, Sahib."

"Show me your certificates."

Bikram handed over the envelope and watched the slender fingers of the manager pull out the papers. After studying them the man said, "You are quite the scholar, Bikram Singh. You scored high in arithmetic."

"Thank you, Sahib."

"You were born in 1920, I see. Almost seventeen years of age?"

"Yes, Sahib."

"You qualify for the job."

Bikram stood up and bent to touch the man's feet in gratitude.

"Stop, stop."

Bikram froze.

"Sixty rupees, up front."

Bikram's spirits rose. "I get three months' wages as advance?"

The smile on the man's face turned into a smirk. "It will *cost* you three months' salary in advance. You pay *me* sixty rupees now, and you have the job."

Sixty rupees? His father had not spared him so much as an anna to buy a glass of lemonade with.

"I don't have sixty rupees, Sahib."

"Fine."

Bikram saw his hopes turn to ashes as the manager rose and walked over to sit beside the youth. He shook hands with the older man and exchanged pleasantries, and then all three crossed the road to the tea stall.

Bikram stood up slowly. His feet felt leaden. He shuffled out of the waiting room onto the road and turned towards the town's long bazaar. He stopped under the shade of the first tree and sat down on his haunches.

How will I tell my mother? He blinked as tears stung his eyes. She had sounded so confident, telling him again and again that he would get the job easily. All it required was an elementary school education, and he was a matriculate, after all. Little good that had done him. He swallowed the lump in his throat and sighed. Where was he supposed to get the sixty rupees?

The bazaar opened onto the wide, cobbled road that ran the length of Samrala and beyond, joining the cities of Ludhiana and Kharar. Bikram had first walked it as a wide-eyed ten-year-old when his father was transferred here from the isolation of a dusty, remote village in the interior. It had thrilled him with its hustle and bustle, and the din at its storefronts. The names of these businesses, in large painted signs over the doorways, in Urdu, Gurmukhi, and English, evoked far-off, exotic places: Lahore Utensils, Kashmir Carpets, Kabul Sweets, Bombay Fabrics. The local photographer displayed his latest portraits in the windows, photos of newlyweds in all their finery, stern-looking soldiers, staring families with frozen expressions.

"Bikram!" A former classmate, now working as an assistant to a tailor, waved from behind a sewing machine where he sat cross-legged.

Bikram waved back and hurried his pace.

Pungent aromas wafted from the coal-fired cooking ovens of Pehalwan Restaurant and Sweets. Men sat outside, stirring huge brass pots, browning onions, ginger, and garlic tadkas mixed with strong spices. The place was crowded with villagers enjoying samosas, pakodas, and tea. Bikram's hunger was now unbearable.

Another former schoolmate was turning the screw of a sugarcane juicer on the sidewalk, filling glasses with the sweet greenish juice. The constant effort rippled the muscles on his shoulders and arms, and his skin shone with perspiration. Bikram nodded and the youth barely acknowledged him.

Other schoolmates now worked in their family businesses selling cloth, tailoring, making shoes, repairing bicycles, hammering brass into pots, polishing furniture, hawking juice, and manning the tills of restaurants and shops. These were hard-working Hindus of various castes, from Baniyas down to the lowest. Muslims worked in the mercantile pursuits of their fathers, and also as hakeems peddling cures, and as barbers, butchers, dairymen delivering door to door, or trading in cattle, sheep, and goats.

Bikram was a Sikh, and a Jat, a respected caste, traditionally land-owning. But in that moment Bikram would have happily given up his status to be with his school friends doing any one of those useful jobs.

A block from his home stood a vegetable cart. Bikram's family owed the vendor, and the man had embarrassed his mother by loudly refusing her further credit. Just that morning, Bikram had proudly resolved to use his first paycheque to pay off the debt and make things right. Now he approached with lowered eyes, his shoulders tense, afraid the man might say something.

His own street was a dirt path. Imposing fired-brick houses with walled courtyards behind shiny steel gates were interspersed with mud-brick abodes, like the one his family lived in, behind rickety wooden gates. Each home had a pump in its courtyard for bathing, and soapy water ran out to the street and pooled in blocked drains on both sides.

His mother took one look at his face and sat down heavily on a cot under the roof of the verandah. His two sisters stared at him anxiously. He sat down beside his mother and dropped his head into his hands.

"The manager wanted sixty rupees as a bribe, Maaji."

"May he rot in hell, his body full of maggots!" she hissed.

Bikram's sister Guddi held out a tumbler of water.

"Thanks," he said, without meeting her gaze. "I'm hungry . . ."

Guddi returned to the outdoor kitchen and came back with two stale rotis and half an onion on a small plate. He took a sip of water with the dry roti and then a bite of the onion. It was pungent and stung his nostrils.

"I am down to two potatoes." Maaji sighed. "And I have barely enough flour to last the month. What will we do?"

Bikram's father came home late that afternoon.

"Biki didn't get the job," his mother said.

"Why?"

Bikram explained about the bribe, and his father shook his head.

"Let me join the army, Papaji," Bikram begged.

Maaji shook her head. "You are my only son. I won't let you."

"No one has to pay a bribe to join the army," he argued.

"Biki, tell your father he must go to the village and demand his share of the land from that odious brother of his."

"I will go with you," Bikram offered.

Papaji sighed. "Biki, you know how difficult your uncle is."

"Tell your father that my two curses are going grey sitting at home waiting to be wed."

The "two curses," Bikram's sisters, were both of an age for marriage. Pyari was sixteen, a year younger than Bikram. Guddi, almost nineteen, was the urgent priority, in grave danger of a life of spinsterhood. Yet Papaji could not raise enough money for even one modest dowry. Every moneylender in Samrala had turned him down because he had nothing to his name to offer as security.

"At least when your grandfather was alive we received enough grain and jaggery to last us the year," Maaji pointed out. "Remember the pinnis I made for your winter breakfast with the rich milk cake your grandmother sent every fall?"

"Hey! Pretty ladies!" Whistles and laughter. The rude calls were coming from the gate.

Maaji rushed the girls inside and closed the door. "Bastards!"

The town bachelors—known as "the dandies" because of their natty turbans and closely trimmed beards—were led by Golu, a local ruffian always in and out of jail for assault. People called men like that "number ten criminals" after the section in the penal code that dealt with repeat offenders. It was rumoured that Golu was a member of a notorious gang of dacoits, armed robbers. He and his gang had been seen more and more often on their street lately, whistling and singing lewd songs to the young women.

"I'll fight them," Bikram snarled. It was what a brother should do.

"Let it be," Papaji told him. He pretended to read the newspaper, so he could hide his face.

A few anxious minutes later, the dandies' voices could be heard receding down the street.

Maaji folded her hands in prayer and lifted her face to the heavens before unlocking the door so that Guddi and Pyari could join them in the kitchen.

Papaji put down his newspaper. "We will go to my brother on Sunday."

༄

The family's ancestral village, Mirpura, lay six miles south of Samrala. Bikram had fond memories of summer holidays spent at his grandfather's spacious brick house, with its huge courtyard and cattle barn. Grandma fed him tumblers of milk, bowls of yogurt, and dal swimming in butter. He would join his cousins to bathe at their well, and they would choose teams to play kabaddi for hours in the village common, while his sisters flew on swings under banyan trees.

First his grandmother had passed away, and then a year later his grandfather. And that was when the problems had begun. The house and the land now belonged to Bikram's father and uncle, who lived there with his wife. His uncle farmed and reaped the profits, but he would not acknowledge Papaji's claim to the land. He would not offer him rent or payment, would not even allow his name to be put on the deed. Family visits stopped, and so did the gifts of grain, sweet jaggery, and milk cake. Bikram's uncle would bring his harvest to the grain market in Samrala but he never visited. Not even for a cup of tea.

"Mirpura," the tonga driver announced, and he pulled on the reins.

Bikram and his father stepped off and headed for the gates of their ancestral home.

"Lal Singh!" Auntie shouted at Papaji, pulling the gates open. "What a surprise!"

Bikram bent to touch her feet, and she pulled him up and hugged him.

"Look at you. Thin as a reed. Don't they feed you?"

"Living in town is expensive," Papaji said.

Auntie's daughter bent to touch his feet and he offered his blessing. "Live long."

As Auntie led them through the gates and past the cattle yard, Bikram noticed an impressive horse, a mare. He nudged his father, to be sure he saw it too.

In the courtyard, his cousin, glancing shyly at Bikram, pulled a cot into the shade, covered it with a sheet, and asked them to sit.

"Where is my brother?" Papaji asked.

"At the well. They are watering the sugarcane," Auntie said, and smiled.

"I will fetch him." The cousin hurried towards the gates.

Bikram noticed the buffaloes tethered at the feeder nearby. Looking at the large udders of the female, and thinking of all that nutritious milk, he imagined how tall and strong his male cousins would be now. It was two years since he had last seen them. They were older than him.

Auntie served fist-sized pinnis with tea.

"You bought a mare?" Papaji observed.

"For your niece's wedding. It came at a good price."

So they were already collecting their daughter's dowry with the income from Papaji's lands, Bikram thought, and bile began to rise in his throat. Uncle arrived and Bikram stood to touch his feet. The man towered over him, his waist even thicker than the last time they met. Papaji embraced his brother and they smiled at each other.

"You will stay for lunch," Uncle announced.

Papaji waited until after the midday meal before broaching the subject of the money he needed for his own daughters' dowries.

"I can't help," Uncle said. "We barely make it here. The crops fail or the fields get flooded." He shrugged. "At least you earn a steady wage as a teacher. And you have never offered to help me."

"I can barely feed my family," Papaji told him. "Guddi is almost nineteen. I have to get her wed. I need my fifteen acres."

"To mortgage it?"

"What else?"

Bikram saw fire in Uncle's eyes. "I will never allow that, Lal Singh. Never!"

"Then help us wed my sister!" Bikram shouted.

Uncle glared at him.

"You have already bought a mare for your daughter," Bikram put in.

"And that pains you?"

"No. I want Guddi to get a mare in her dowry, too."

"I am not stopping you. It's the tradition. Buy one."

"With what?" Bikram shouted. "You are usurping my father's land. Stealing our birthright."

"You cur!" Uncle roared. He stood up and seized Bikram by the collar, lifted him up, and dragged him to the gate.

"Brother, take your hands off my son. He only speaks the truth."

Uncle shoved them both onto the path and slammed the gate in their faces.

When Maaji heard how they had been thrown out disgracefully from their ancestral home, she swore.

"May he perish, may his family perish, may God bring him down with leprosy! The rotten man. How dare he lay a finger on my son?"

"Enough," Papaji begged.

Guddi rubbed Papaji's back and muttered encouragements. Pyari sat beside him and put her arms around him.

"May his house burn down!"

"Shut up! We own half of it!" Papaji rarely raised his voice, and Bikram was startled.

From the street, a whistle, followed by raucous laughter. Again, Maaji hustled the girls inside. Papaji sat with a pained look on his face, and Bikram felt his jaws clench.

"*Come to me on a starry night, my beloved.*" The words from a famous couplet floated over the courtyard. "*Rouse my passions with the touch of your fingertips.*"

A gate smashed open and the singer's words seemed to die in his throat.

"Golu, you bastard! Come here!"

The booming voice of Mirza Gujjar the dairyman made Bikram jump to his feet and race into the street. Papaji and Maaji were close behind. The huge dairyman stood holding an unsheathed sword as Golu and three of his buddies cowered against a wall. Mirza's four adult sons stood beside him, similarly armed. Other neighbours stepped out of their gates carrying weapons as well.

"This is my street! No one brings filth onto it!"

"We were just passing through," Golu insisted pathetically.

Mirza Gujjar hit him with the blunt hilt of the sword, eliciting a howl, before pounding Golu with his bare fist. His sons moved menacingly towards the other dandies, who shrieked and fled down the street.

"Stay away, you filthy dog!" Mirza Gujjar kicked Golu in the ribs, making him roll over a few times.

Bikram watched open-mouthed as the town bully whimpered in fear, covered his head with his hands, and curled into a ball.

Mirza Gujjar bent down and lifted him up. With Golu's bug-eyed face close to his he snarled, "Next time, I will kill you. Do you hear me?" He shoved him away, and Golu scrambled to his feet and ran down the street towards the bazaar, his messy turban bobbing on his head.

Maaji fell at the dairyman's feet. "Thank you, thank you."

He lifted her up gently and smiled. "They will not dare to come back."

Papaji folded his hands in gratitude.

"Your daughters are my daughters, Masterji. No need to thank me."

Bikram bent to touch the good man's feet.

"Live long, my son."

People stayed in the street to talk about the big event, their faces alight with excitement. Bikram felt the blood rush to his face and his heart pounding; a great burden had been lifted from his shoulders.

After supper, Maaji made a decision. "Biki, tell your father to go visit the Brahmin matchmaker," she announced. "So far we have not had a single proposal for Guddi, we cannot wait any longer. Hopefully Gopal can help."

Papaji reached under the cot for his shoes. "Follow me," he said to Bikram.

As they walked through the market, there was a spring to Papaji's step, he almost seemed taller. All this thanks to Mirza Gujjar. They made their way down a narrow street and came to an iron gate. A plaque on the wall read "PUNDIT GOPAL SHARMA: ASTROLOGER."

A plump man welcomed them into the front room of the two-storey house. The top of his head was shaved, and the hair he had left fell in a long rat's tail. He offered them a cot to sit on and then took a seat across from them, smiling benignly.

"What can I do for you this evening, Masterji?"

Papaji cleared his throat and began haltingly.

"I have no money, no chattels."

The matchmaker nodded.

"My daughters finished primary school. They can read the scriptures and write letters."

"I see."

"I need to find a match for the older one. She is almost nineteen, so you see I am desperate, Punditji."

"You are of what caste?"

"We are Jats."

Gopal nodded with approval and scratched his shaved head. He appeared to go deep into thought.

They waited.

"There is a match. The father is a numberdar in Khurd village— owns forty acres of productive land."

The lines on Papaji's forehead deepened. A numberdar was a tax collector, a position he would pass on to his sons. This family did not sound like a match for Guddi. Too rich.

"His five daughters are married. He has but one son. Twenty years of age."

"What is the catch?" Papaji blurted.

"Look, Masterji. The numberdar does not want a dowry, and a simple temple ceremony will suffice."

Bikram held his breath. It sounded too good to be true.

"And the boy?" Papaji asked in a low voice.

"The boy was born with a club foot and survived a bout of smallpox."

That night, Papaji waited until the girls were asleep in the room they shared with Maaji. Their door was closed. Bikram sat silently as Papaji told Maaji the details of Gopal's recommendation. Her jaw dropped and she blinked back tears.

"So . . . that is our only option?"

"Yes." Papaji put his hand on her knee and looked at her.

Maaji returned his stare and Bikram lowered his eyes. Sweet, beautiful Guddi, with her head of long curly hair, fair skin, and Maaji's fine features, deserved better.

Maaji spoke. "The boy will inherit his father's title and forty acres of land that can be tilled by sharecroppers and provide a good living for Guddi. And you said the numberdar has a pukka house and a pukka barn as well, and was able to marry off five daughters?"

"You are not thinking of marrying Guddi off to this disfigured cripple?" Bikram said.

In the dimming flame of the oil lamp, Maaji's face looked impassive. She sighed.

"I most certainly am. It's a rich house she is going to."

She held her son's gaze until he lowered his, and an overpowering sense of shame enveloped him. He felt the sting of tears. He had let his loving older sister down. He felt like a piece of dung, and he wished the floor would open up and swallow him whole.

Guddi's wedding was a less than joyous occasion. The groom's family gave the impression that they were condescending to allow Guddi into their clan, and Bikram saw a pained expression cross Papaji's face more than once. Guddi herself was trying to put a brave face on things, but there were tears all around when she left with her new husband for an uncertain future.

A week later, Bikram was walking through the bazaar and saw the dandies sitting at a table outside the liquor vend. Golu saw Bikram, too, and the young men got up and began to follow him.

"Slow down, now. Where will you run to?" one of them shouted.

Bikram looked around desperately for a familiar face, someone who might come to his aid. No gates of residences opened onto the bazaar, so it was a place where men argued, fought, called each other dirty names.

He felt a hand on his elbow and turned around. The thugs stared at him, smirking.

"We saw your monstrosity of a brother-in-law all gussied up as a groom at the temple," Golu sneered.

"Leave me alone."

Golu looked around. "I don't see that interfering Muslim neighbour of yours anywhere here."

"You should have given your pretty, pretty sister to Golu," one of the men said.

"Yes, and I would have made her moan with pleasure."

One of the dandies began to groan and thrust his hips, drawing smiles from the men who were sitting outside a tea stall.

"How's she ever going to love that cripple? Tell me, Bikram!"

Another leered. "Pyari is still free. Send her to me tonight and I will build a house for your father."

"I will take her," Golu smiled. "From behind. Doggy style."

Bikram turned and pushed past the thug blocking his way.

Golu followed him, grunting and limping and pulling scary faces.

"Now remember to send Pyari tonight!"

Bikram ran, their taunts ringing in his ears.

"Run, you turd, run, run. We will all be here, waiting."

"I am joining the army," Bikram announced as soon as he arrived home.

Maaji glared at him. "No, you are not."

Gopal the matchmaker was sitting beside Papaji, going over the accounts from Guddi's wedding. He had lent the family three hundred rupees to buy a simple bridal ensemble and a bit of jewellery for her dowry. The payments would be deferred until Bikram found a job, but the interest was already adding up at two percent per month.

The taunts of the louts still torturing him, Bikram said, "I can no longer bear it. I will join the army."

"No." Maaji stood up, hands on her hips.

"Let him," Gopal interceded.

"And let him get killed? My only son?"

"Bikram finished high school, he is a matriculate. He scored a first division. He will be recruited as a non-commissioned officer."

"Officer?"

"Yes, sister."

She frowned. "A captain?"

"No. He needs two more years of college for that. But a sergeant, yes."

Maaji sighed. The word "officer" intrigued her.

"How do I go about getting recruited?" Bikram asked.

Gopal smiled. "Simple. Show up at the Clock Tower Army Recruitment Office in Ludhiana on the morning of any weekday."

"I can take the bus tomorrow."

Gopal scratched his head. "Masterji, if you can get a high-up government official to write a letter of recommendation for Bikram, it will greatly enhance his chances of earning a sergeant's post."

Papaji stroked his beard as Bikram watched and waited. Much depended on what his father said next.

"One of my students is the son of Ajit Singh of Raikot, the Zaildar."

"Zaildar Ajit Singh," Gopal exclaimed. "He will be the best person for a recommendation."

A zaildar, whose duty and privilege it was to collect revenues from the residents of many villages, was a man whose opinion would carry a good deal of weight.

Maaji sat down beside Papaji. "I will write a letter to the Zaildar tonight and send it tomorrow."

"Remember, sister," Gopal added, "the army will give Bikram uniforms and shoes, keep him in barracks, and feed him well, including a ration of rum. He can save and send you most of his salary. I hear it should be at least thirty rupees a month, and it will rise each time he earns a promotion."

"Ten rupees a month more than I earn as a teacher," Papaji said.

"Do it." Maaji smiled, shaking her head in approval.

You are a godsend, Gopal, Bikram thought. *A true godsend.*

Pyari came to sit beside her father and put her arm around his waist, resting her head on his shoulder.

"I will see to it that you have a proper wedding and a handsome groom, my sister," Bikram promised.

Ajit

The noon sun had warmed the spring air, and Ajit stopped his mare to remove his woollen coat, first unslinging his shotgun and his bandolier and hanging them for a moment from the saddle horn. His coat folded and stuffed into the saddle bag, he enjoyed the relief that the breeze brought. His mare pawed the hard dirt path.

"Sat Sri Akal, Zaildar!" A man cutting alfalfa shouted the traditional greeting across the field. The Zaildar dismounted as the man approached. The shiny metal of his well-honed scythe reflected the sunlight in short bursts that made Ajit squint. They shook hands.

"Good crop," the Zaildar said, pointing to the knee-high grain.

"Here I have a good crop, thanks to the well, but my other plot is in higher, sandy soil and will barely repay the seed."

"Nature did not co-operate this winter," Ajit agreed. The rains had been sporadic and short.

"When will they dig a channel from the Sirhind Canal to bring water for our parched fields?"

Ajit had heard this question repeated in all the villages he had visited, where half the land remained without irrigation. *They* were the authorities who controlled the canal works. And Ajit was one of *them*.

"Last time I asked, they said it would take another couple of years yet."

"Zaildar, I beg that you keep hounding them. We need canal water here. Otherwise I am going to have to let my other plot lie fallow."

Ajit sighed. "Believe me, I will do my best," he promised. *After all,* he thought, *fallow land is not taxed.*

Ajit Singh was on his quarterly tour of the fields that lay under his fiefdom. The forty villages covered over a hundred square miles, with borders at the Sirhind Canal to the south, the Machiwara-Navan Shehar

Road to the east, and the Ludhiana-Samrala Road to the west. The northern edge almost reached the municipal boundary of Ludhiana, which housed the district administration and courts. It had crossed Ajit's mind to buy a motor car to get around, but it would have been useless on the washed-out dirt paths in the monsoon season. In any case, he preferred travelling on horseback. It felt more traditional.

Every village had a numberdar who reported to him. The numberdars collected taxes door to door. Some rode to his property in Raikot to deliver the monies, others waited for him to pass through. They were his eyes and ears. And though Ajit knew they saw him as a powerful man, he was very conscious that he himself reported to a British official, the District Collector of Ludhiana. As zaildar, Ajit was just another rung on the Raj bureaucratic ladder.

He'd been travelling almost a week now, and a week in the saddle seemed like long enough. It was time to return home. It was nearly dark when he rode into his estate and gratefully handed the reins of his mare to the caretaker of the cattle yard. Crossing the wide path to his haveli, he enjoyed a familiar feeling of contented pride.

"Bapuji!"

His son Satwant hailed him from the rooftop before running down the outside staircase to hug him. This boy, too, was a source of pride.

His son handed him an envelope. "My arithmetic teacher, Lal Singh Sir, sent a letter home with me for you."

"Later. Let me wash and change first."

Inder, who was resting on a cot under the verandah, looked up at him and smiled. His wife had a languid beauty and elegance that always soothed him. He smiled and nodded to her before climbing the staircase to his rooms on the second floor. "Draw a bath for Ji," he heard his wife tell a servant girl.

Satwant followed, carrying his father's shotgun and bandolier, and hung them on an iron keela in his room.

"Do you want me to clean the barrels, Bapuji?"

Shaking his head, Ajit sat on the cot to pull off his boots and peel off his socks. The cool floor relieved the aching in his feet, and he spread his toes wide before pulling off his shirt and undershirt and then standing to drop his pants. The clothes lay on the floor for the servant to pick up for the next day's laundry.

Satwant was still carrying the letter from his teacher. "Masterji Lal Singh just married off his daughter to a cripple, Bapuji, a man from Khurd."

"Khurd?"

"Yes. In a small temple ceremony. He is a Jat, you know. Masterji is. But he did that anyway. Could he not have found her a better husband?"

Ajit recalled hearing about the wedding. He knew this man, the numberdar, who had been desperate for a good bride for his only son. The bride came from a poor family, he had heard.

Satwant sat on his father's desk chair. "Why would anyone give such a man their daughter, Bapuji? Isn't it cruel?"

"We can discuss it later, son."

The wide verandah was lit with a gas lantern and they sat on chairs around a rectangular wooden table to eat. Ajit's wife and son sat on either side of him.

"Is Siamo back?" he asked.

"She is. She should be out shortly," Inder replied.

Siamo was his cousin. Widowed at an early age, she had been left at his gates by her father, who had lost his own lands to drinking and gambling and had no intention of supporting a dependent daughter. Ajit and Inder had taken her in, and she was like a sister to him. She had helped them raise their only child. The boy adored her. And why not? She doted on him as if he were her own.

"Bhua!" Satwant shouted, using the term for a father's sister, and Ajit turned to see Siamo's stocky figure approaching them. Her usual toothy grin had been replaced by a pinched look.

"Everything all right?" he asked as she sat down heavily beside Satwant. The boy started pouring dal into a bowl they would share. Even now, at thirteen, he still ate from the same plate as his aunt.

"How was your visit?" he asked as she slowly chewed a bite of roti. She often paid a visit to the family of her late husband.

"Not good." She sighed.

"What happened?"

"Oh, nothing I want to talk about at dinner." She fed Satwant a piece of roti.

"Now you are worrying us," Inder said. But Siamo was not going to say a word more.

Satwant was terribly curious about the letter from his teacher, which his father still had not opened. But he waited until they had finished eating and the servant girl was clearing the table before insisting, "Bapuji, read the letter now, please."

"All right." Ajit tore the envelope open and pulled out a folded sheet.

"Out loud, Bapuji."

He read in silence.

> My respected Zaildar Sahib,
>
> My name is Lal Singh and I am Satwant's mathematics teacher. I humbly ask for a favour that you provide my matriculate but unemployed son, Bikram Singh, a letter of recommendation. He wishes to join the army and I am told that your support will get him recruited as a Non-Commissioned Officer.
>
> I am a poor man, and a second wage will make a great difference in our lives. I have one younger daughter still to wed.
>
> Your humble servant,
> Lal Singh

"You read it," he said, handing the letter to Inder. She read it aloud.

"I was sure this was going to be about something bad you did in school, Satwant," she teased.

Satwant made a face.

"My Satwant is a very good boy," Siamo said, hugging him.

Inder folded the sheet, put it back in the envelope, and handed it to Ajit.

"Are you going to help Masterji's son, Bapuji?"

"Of course. It is a reasonable request. I will write a reply that you can take back to him tomorrow."

"I hope he doesn't have to sell his younger daughter to some other cripple," Satwant said.

Inder turned to Ajit. "What is he talking about?"

When the story of the unfortunate marriage had been told, Inder glared at her son. "We do not make fun of people who have suffered from a birth defect or a deadly illness. You must promise never to use that term *cripple* again. Promise me, Satwant."

"Yes, Maaji. I'm sorry."

When at last Inder had taken Satwant upstairs to go over his home-work, Ajit looked inquiringly to Siamo, who now looked even more pale.

"Nasib has polio," she blurted.

The words exploded in his head. Polio was a dreaded, often deadly disease. Almost every village had lost someone to it, and even those who survived it were generally left lame.

"He will live, but no one knows if he will ever walk again. Poor child. Only five years old." Siamo folded her hands and uttered a silent prayer.

He thought of the little boy whom he had never seen and could only imagine. An urge to saddle his mare and ride out to hold Nasib in his arms overtook him, and he saw Siamo look at him with alarm.

"There is nothing anyone can do but pray and hope for the best."

Ajit felt utterly helpless. A great guilt burdened his soul.

"I must bring him home."

"Now is not the time." Siamo's voice was tremulous but firm.

"Why not?"

"You know very well why not! How will Inder and Satwant react?"

"I am torn inside, Siamo."

She lowered her eyes, and he saw the glint of tears.

"Why did this have to happen to him?" she asked. "It should never have happened."

Her words did nothing to ease the terrible pounding in his chest. Nasib needed him, and he could not fail the boy. Heaving himself off the chair he stood for a moment, then turned and walked out through the gates in the dim light. He crossed the path to the cattle yard, lifted a saddle, and turned to carry it to a fresh mare.

Siamo's figure loomed in the dark, hurrying towards him.

"Bir. Stop," she hissed, addressing him as brother.

"Step aside. I must do this."

"No. Put the saddle back, please, I beg you. Let your mind settle."

He stepped forward, and Siamo, too, took a step closer. They stood a foot apart from each other. Then he felt her hands on his chest gently pushing him back.

"Siamo?"

"Brother, think of the consequences. Things are bad enough as it is. You will only make them worse."

His wife and son's banter floated from an upstairs window of the haveli. He felt a tremor in his limbs. The truth of Siamo's words began to settle on him.

She took the saddle from him and walked back into the darkness of the barn to lay it on its stand. Her footsteps came closer and he felt her hand close around his elbow. He let her guide him out of the cattle yard back to the haveli gates and give him a gentle shove.

"Go to your room, brother. Pray for Nasib."

She walked him to the outside staircase. He managed to get to the top and turned. Siamo stood like a sentinel at the bottom. He sighed, stepped inside his room, and managed to find the box of matchsticks to light the lantern. His fingers trembled as he adjusted the wick before opening the cabinet door and reaching for the bottle of rum.

"Oh." Inder stood in the doorway, and he averted his eyes from hers. She closed the door, and he was alone.

It had happened the summer when Inder took Satwant to spend a month at her parents' village, and Ajit stayed home. Ajit's life was interrupted by a visit from Palo, the youngest sister of Siamo's late husband. Palo had visited Siamo a few times before when she was a little girl, and he'd paid her no mind, but now she was a coltish sixteen-year-old, beautiful and bubbly. And he was smitten. Palo would follow him around the grounds as he supervised his workers and tended to his livestock. She would listen to his stories, ask his advice, speak flatteringly of his strength and handsome appearance. He felt like a much younger man when she was around, alive and attractive. One day, when she asked to borrow a book of poetry, he chose a collection of romantic verse, and on the frontispiece he wrote a sonnet of his own, declaring his love.

What had he done? He'd made a terrible, embarrassing mistake. Would she mock him now or, worse, pity him? But that night at supper, with her eyes holding his in the lamplight, she began to rub his toes under the table, and his heart beat so fast that he could hardly swallow.

They made love every day for a week, sneaking unseen into the storeroom or the cattle barn. Once they even dared to meet in his bedroom on a moonless night, Palo having made her way noiselessly up the staircase. Those were the happiest moments of his life, and when Palo's father came to fetch her, Ajit stared stonily as she passed through the gates, turning once to show him a look of desperate pain.

Drowned in the sorrow of separation, he realized just how much the poets he read must have suffered the pangs of unrequited love to have penned such truthful verses. Three months later, when he returned from a tour of the countryside, Palo's father was waiting for him in the cattle yard. When they were alone and out of earshot of the caretaker, the father spoke.

"Palo is pregnant with your child."

Ajit's first reaction was to offer to take Palo as his second wife. But that was a risk. Marrying a relative, no matter how distant, and especially one who had just spent two weeks at his haveli, would cause a scandal. It would bring shame to his name, outrage Inder's brothers, and destroy his marriage. His biggest fear, though, was for Satwant. What would he think of his father now?

He begged Palo's father to allow him a week to come up with some sort of a solution. He took Siamo into his confidence, and it took her a few days to overcome the shock.

"I never suspected a thing," she said.

She became the go-between for Ajit and Palo's parents. Ajit provided money, and Palo was sent to live with a distant uncle until the birth of the child. The plan was to give the baby up for adoption. But when he learned it was a boy, Ajit wavered.

The family named the baby Nasib. Fate. Once he no longer needed suckling, Nasib was brought back to Palo's parents to be raised. Palo was married off to an older man, a childless widower. She left for her new life without ever again seeing her childhood home.

Palo's father was stoic in the face of questions about her whereabouts and about the boy. He also kept his word and never mentioned to anyone the name of Nasib's father. Ajit honoured the agreement by staying away, and not asking where Palo had gone. He knew that he could not trust himself and would certainly try to see her. It was enough that her father had chosen not to kill her for the indiscretion and the shame she had brought on his family.

Still, Ajit thought about her every day, and regretted his shameful weakness, which had led him to fall head over heels for her, lose his mind in the lustful, reckless pursuit of her. He found solace only in the fact that their union had resulted in their son, a boy he could not publicly accept as his own but whom he was determined to care for.

Siamo became the surrogate parent, the indulgent aunt. She went to visit twice a year with money and clothes and brought back news of the boy. They began to talk openly about Nasib, even in front of Inder, who had the impression that something untoward had happened to the child's parents and the poor boy was an orphan being raised by his grandparents. Being a pious, kind-hearted person, Inder added gifts, mostly clothes, for the unfortunate child.

And now the news that Nasib had polio shook him to the core. Would the day ever come when he could bring his son home, where he truly belonged?

༄

As he'd promised, Ajit wrote a letter for the son of Satwant's teacher, recommending him for recruitment as a non-commissioned officer. More than that, he offered to introduce father and son to the recruiting colonel and put in a good word in person. He felt sorry for the man who'd had to give his daughter to an undesirable groom. And, perhaps more to the point, as a zaildar he was expected to bring in a certain number of new recruits for the Royal Indian Army, and he got a stipend for it, too.

They had arranged to meet one morning a few days later at the recruiting centre in Ludhiana. Ajit was approached by a slightly built fellow accompanied by a younger man, both of whom looked appropriately apprehensive.

"Zaildar Sahib."

The older man turned out to be Masterji Lal Singh, and the youth with him bent to touch Ajit's feet.

"My son, Bikram Singh."

Ajit folded his hands and smiled, and looked up at the clocktower. There was time enough for a cup of tea before the recruiting office opened.

"I hope your travel to the city was pleasant?"

"It was, Zaildar Sahib," Lal Singh responded. "Bikram was very excited to come to Ludhiana. It's a bustling place."

"Indeed, it is. Over there." Ajit took Lal Singh by the elbow and guided him to the tea stall across from the traffic circle.

"We had breakfast before we left this morning, Zaildar Sahib," said Lal Singh.

Ajit ordered tea and a plate of biscuits anyway and gazed at the youth, who looked rather nervous, with his hands pressed between his knees. He smiled and gave Bikram a pat on his shoulder.

"Don't worry. The army has a routine they follow when recruiting. A doctor will check you for any disability or disease and will make sure you meet the minimum physical requirements. Since we are trying to get you recruited as an NCO there will be a language and arithmetic test. You brought your certificates?"

Lal Singh pulled out a brown envelope from the cloth bag he had brought.

"Good. Enjoy your last days as a civilian, Bikram. You will be in uniform soon."

The boy smiled. "Thank you for promising to introduce me to the Colonel."

They made small talk until Ajit spied a uniformed soldier unlocking the door and heard the approaching roar of the Colonel's motor car.

When the Colonel stepped out, Lal Singh glanced nervously at him. "A white officer? British?"

Though the British had ruled India as a colony for well over a hundred years, Ajit understood that it was still not usual to see them in the towns and villages of Punjab.

"He is a good man. I have dealt with him since he was transferred here a few years ago. Speaks good Urdu." Turning to Bikram, he smiled. "Relax."

They made their way back across the street to the recruitment centre, where they were brought to the Colonel.

"Ajit Singh." The Colonel removed the pipe from his lips and nodded, and Ajit felt properly acknowledged as a man of considerable local importance and influence. Then he looked at the youth. "Are you the candidate today?"

"Yes, Sahib." Bikram bent to touch the Colonel's feet.

He stepped quickly back. "No, no, no, my son. We do not do that in the army. Come to my office."

At the door, Ajit stopped Lal Singh.

"Wait outside. I will join you shortly. This could take all morning."

The clerk began the paperwork and checked the certificates.

"Good marks!" he exclaimed, and Bikram beamed.

The Colonel asked Bikram to go through the door to another room for the medical inspection.

"The Doctor Sahib will be here soon."

"I will wait outside with the father," Ajit said, and shook the Colonel's hand before leaving.

He found Lal Singh on a recreational platform built around a tree by the clocktower, and he took a seat beside him. He asked the teacher about Satwant's studies.

"Your son is a gifted student," Lal Singh said. "Very well-behaved and attentive. His homework is always completed and on time."

"I can thank his mother for that."

"You are a fortunate man to have an educated wife."

"She is a good mother," Ajit said.

"Satwant takes after you. Same profile, features, mannerisms."

"You are very gracious. I think he takes after both his parents. Gets his sensitive nature from his mother." And Ajit wondered what Satwant got from him.

They sat in silence for a long moment before Ajit stood up.

"Masterji, I am going to walk to the courts. I have some work there."

Lal Singh nodded.

It was almost noon when Ajit returned, and Lal Singh was sitting in exactly the same spot, gazing at the door of the recruitment centre. A small line of prospective recruits and their companions had formed in front of it. Ajit sat down just as Bikram came out, followed by the Colonel.

"Meet Havildar Bikram Singh," the Colonel said with a smile.

People turned at the booming, accented voice. The tall Englishman had a commanding presence and cut quite a figure in his immaculate uniform.

"Congratulations." Ajit turned to shake Lal Singh's hand.

"He passed with flying colours, but he has to get spectacles. He's a bit nearsighted, won't be assigned to a combat regiment," the Colonel said before leaving.

Bikram bent to touch both men's feet. Ajit intoned a blessing.

"I do not know the words to thank you enough, Zaildar Sahib," Lal Singh gushed.

"You raised a fine son, Masterji. He earned the rank of sergeant himself."

On their way to the bus station, Ajit stopped at an optician's shop.

"I must buy you a gift, Bikram."

"You have already done so much for us," Lal Singh protested.

Glasses were expensive. Good ones could cost a month's wages. Ajit was feeling generous and guided them to the optician.

"Let's get you fitted, Bikram."

"You bought Masterji's son glasses, Bapuji?" Satwant asked.

Ajit smiled.

"Now you must buy me a gift too."

"What?"

"A bicycle, Bapuji, so I can ride to school and not have to take a tonga there."

"You can ride a bicycle?"

"Yes, Bapuji. My best friend lets me practise on his every day."

"How about a mare instead?"

Siamo came to sit beside them on the verandah.

"He will get a mare in his dowry, Bir."

"That's years away!" Satwant pointed out.

"Get him a bicycle, Bir. He is old enough to be trusted to ride alone to Samrala."

"What if I buy you a bicycle, and you ride with me on my tour on one of the mares?"

Satwant jumped up. "Yes, yes! During summer holidays!"

Inder smiled. "You know, Satwant, that you will inherit the title of zaildar from your father, just as he did from his father."

"Time to start your education outside of school," Ajit added. "A zaildar has a lot of responsibilities. It is important that you start learning them now. I will teach you how to be a proper and good zaildar."

Satwant's expression turned serious and he nodded sagely.

"How fast they grow up, Bir." Siamo smiled. "I remember changing his diapers like it was just yesterday."

"Bhua!" Satwant grimaced.

One sunny day in early spring, as Ajit stood at the gate of the haveli overlooking his lands, he saw a tall man he did not recognize coming up the road. Unsure of what this portended, he thought of having his shotgun brought to him, but as the man got closer he could see that he was not armed. In fact, the stranger raised his arms in a gesture clearly designed to put Ajit at ease. And when he spoke, his accent betrayed his faraway origins.

"Your home is palatial, Malik, and your yard must hold dozens of cattle."

Ajit smiled. The title *malik* both honoured and amused him. He understood the man to be one of the nomadic Bajigar people, and in their language, Gauri, the word suggested a king.

"It was built by my great-grandfather," he explained.

"It looks like a fort."

The enormous haveli never failed to impress. Ajit nodded once again, seeing it through a stranger's eyes.

"Malik, my kabila is stopped along the road. I seek permission to camp on your fallow land."

"The piece that lies at the corner of the path and the paved road?" Ajit asked. It was where the Adda was, where the bus stopped to pick up and drop off passengers. Vendors gathered there to sell their wares.

"The same, Malik. We are tired after a long journey and our animals and children need to rest for a couple of months."

The ancestral home of the Bajigars was in the deserts of Rajasthan, but they left when the Mughal Emperor Akbar the Great pressured them to become Muslims. Since then they had lived as nomads, vowing to return when they could live under their own rule. But the world had moved on; their territories were now home to other tribes, and under British authority. Recognizing that their dream of return was hopeless, the Bajigars were beginning to find new places to settle. The government encouraged the idea, seeing it as a move towards stability, hoping that the Bajigars would eventually send their children to school and integrate into modern society.

Ajit could see an advantage for himself as well. It had been difficult lately to find enough labour to work his fields, and a third of his land lay fallow this season. The Bajigars were good workers—the men could till and plough, the women pluck cotton and shuck maize.

"I will come with you and meet your clan."

They walked along the path towards the Adda, Ajit wondering about the man's physique. The Bajigar were renowned for performing songs and dances and feats of gymnastics—or Baji. The men he had met were slim and wiry, yet this one had a barrel chest, and even under his flimsy dhoti Ajit saw his thighs were like tree trunks. His chiselled face sat atop a thick neck.

They found members of the clan sitting in a long row with their camels and goats under the tall, broad sheesham trees that lined the roadway. The women held infants and had their older children with them.

"How many families?" Ajit asked.

"Two dozen, Malik."

"Who is the headman?"

"I am the Mukhia."

The Mukhia was the head of a clan, Ajit knew, and a Raja was the head of the tribe.

"You look young to be a mukhia."

"My father and older brother died in an accident. I was elected three years ago."

"My condolences."

"Thank you, Malik."

The two-acre plot of level ground had a half dozen shady trees and was close to one of his wells. Ajit had little use for the land, which had once been rented to the public works department to store sand, gravel, and stones during the paving of the Ludhiana-Samrala Road. The ground was now hard and dry, but ideal for the Bajigars to build their flimsy reed huts for shelter. Ajit agreed that they could stay.

The Mukhia divided the land into lots, measuring them with his steps, and setting aside a common area. Within hours the families had claimed their spots and tethered their animals.

"My wife, Sehba, and our son Rana, Malik."

The slight woman, her face veiled with a dupatta, bent to touch his feet. The little boy followed.

"Live long," Ajit blessed them.

A tinkling bell made him turn to see Satwant grinning at him from atop his shiny new bicycle. He was returning home from school in Samrala. Ajit waved him over and introduced him to the Mukhia.

"You are a wrestler, no?" Satwant asked.

"Yes, I am, Chhota Malik. You are very observant."

"Ride?" Rana asked, pointing to the bicycle.

Satwant picked him up and placed him on the seat, then took him for a ride around the plot. He was immediately besieged by a dozen other children begging for rides.

"Your son is a very patient young man, Malik," the Mukhia observed.

"And now very popular, too!"

"He is kind, like his father, generous and gracious. May the gods and goddesses bless you both for your kind hearts."

"Mukhia, I need field hands starting tomorrow."

"Malik, you have answered both my prayers. Land for my people to camp on and jobs to work at."

"Wonderful."

"Malik, how much land do you own?"

"Three hundred irrigated acres."

"Malik, you have been greatly blessed."

Within a week, the Bajigar clan had constructed huts framed with branches from the orchard and dry reeds cut from the canal. The women had dug clay from the village common and fashioned earthen stoves, called chullahs, with them. Sehba organized two dozen of them to pluck cotton, and the women's quick fingers harvested five acres per day, making Inder happy. The main hall of the haveli was half filled with cotton balls stacked up to the ceiling, and the courtyard echoed with the women's musical voices every evening after the day's pick was weighed by Siamo and the workers awaited their evening meal. Inder was generous with portions, knowing that this might be the Bajigars' only meal of the day.

Ajit's indentured field hands were delighted with the additional help to harvest, and the children of the dera, the Bajigars' camp, made quick work of the roots left behind by pulling them out, shaking off the dirt, and carrying them in bundles on their heads to be used for fuel. Soon the fields were cleared for the winter planting of wheat, rye, black beans, and mustard.

"Fifty acres of sugarcane, Malik, should keep us busy the whole winter," the Mukhia said with laboured breath. He had just performed a hundred push-ups.

"You will stay for the winter, then?"

The Mukhia, who had already started doing deep squats, just grunted.

Ajit saw Satwant staring in awe at the man's rippling muscles. His son was clearly impressed by such discipline and endurance.

"You know, Bapuji, the Mukhia drinks a small bucket of goat's milk in one go?"

"Is that so?"

A tall, slender man with a shaved head and an impressive moustache had come to stand beside them. The Mukhia had earlier introduced him as a childhood friend, Changu.

"You must congratulate me, Malik," the Mukhia said now. "Changu has promised his daughter Basanti's hand to Rana."

Satwant looked incredulous. "How old is she?"

"Two years, Chhota Malik."

"And engaged already?"

"She was promised at birth, but it took me this long to buy the silver rupee to present to the Mukhia," Changu explained.

"Congratulations to both of you."

"Malik, have you received the silver rupee for Chhota Malik yet?" the Mukhia asked Ajit, continuing his squats.

"No way!" Satwant said. "I have to finish school, and then four years of college first! Right, Bapuji?"

"We will see, son. We will see."

Bikram

Two years after joining the army, Bikram found himself on a steamer pulling away from a dock in Calcutta. The ship's destination was the port city of Chittagong, close to the Burmese border with India. He had never sailed before, or even seen the sea, and soon he was retching over the railing.

A sailor in a grimy singlet grinned. "Steady now."

"Drink tea only," advised another.

Britain had declared war on Nazi Germany that September, and the Royal Indian Army was called upon to send troops to various parts of the globe. Bikram's first postings had been for basic training, and then, because of his poor eyesight, he was selected for administrative positions in accounting and supply. But now that Japan was more aggressive in the region, Chittagong had been established as an important supply depot, and Bikram had been sent to work in the Quartermaster General's office there.

The two-day journey tested him as the ship navigated the choppy waters of the Bay of Bengal. Finally their destination appeared over the horizon and a swarm of seabirds cawed shrilly, circling the ship and escorting it to port. A few miles inland from the port and the army camp stood the city of Chittagong, and beyond that were hills stretching far and away towards the Himalayas.

Bikram watched in awe as a tugboat pulled the steamer gingerly to the concrete dock, which was teeming with uniformed soldiers, sailors wearing caps, and coolies in dhotis, their bare, dark torsos glistening in the sun. Orders were barked, a plank lowered to the pier, and Bikram gingerly descended with a wide stance.

"Sea legs, Sergeant. You'll be all right by tonight."

Bikram managed a weak smile.

Next, he lined up and waited to present his papers to an officer seated behind a rickety table under a cloth canopy. Already he felt as though he were wilting in the unexpected heat and humidity.

"Bikram Singh," the officer, who was British, mumbled, turning the papers over.

"Yes, sir."

"Assigned to the Quartermaster General?"

"Yes, sir."

"Welcome to Chittagong. That way."

Bikram picked up his duffel bag and wove his way through the piles of boxes, crates, and bags, past the line of waiting lorries, towards the gleaming roofs of a half dozen Quonset huts set a hundred yards from the port. The silvery glint of a plane landing in the distance caught his eye. Lines of tents stretched into the distance. The size and chaotic energy of the place was astounding, nothing like the orderly army camps he had lived in thus far.

He presented himself to his commanding officer, a Major McKie. It had become apparent that the British held any rank that commanded meaningful authority in the Indian Army. In this case, though, Bikram suspected that it wasn't so much the rank that mattered—it was the fact that huge amounts of money and goods changed hands that made this a job for an Englishman.

The man himself was not especially impressive. There was something a bit lax, or maybe just weary, about his demeanour. But what the officer lacked, his office made up for. It occupied the front of a huge Quonset hut, and it had to be at least a hundred feet long, twenty wide, and fifteen high.

"You'll do fine, I'm sure, Sergeant Singh," the major said. "Just follow orders, stay out of trouble. You might even enjoy your time in Chittagong." And with that, Bikram was dismissed.

"Tent number nine." A harried clerk waved over a coolie who bowed and grabbed the duffel bag. "Follow him, Sergeant."

"The NCOs are assigned to the first ten tents, Sahib," the coolie explained as they walked inside the meticulously laid out tent city. "Four to a tent." They stopped outside a tent with its sides rolled up, and the sight of metal cots drew a sigh of relief from Bikram. He'd been worried that he might be sleeping on the hard ground during this assignment.

The coolie placed his bag on the only bare cot. "I will go fetch your bedding, Sahib. Make sure you sleep under a mosquito net. This is malaria land."

Bikram unpacked and sat down on his cot, unsure what to do next. But he was saved when his tent mates appeared, having just finished their shift.

A slight, darker-skinned man smiled and offered his hand. "I am Thomas."

"Bikram Singh."

A lighter-skinned and taller man with a bushy moustache introduced himself. "Call me Khan. Everybody does."

"Pathan?"

The man nodded. "Punjabi?" he asked.

Bikram smiled. "Of course."

His eyes widened at the sight of the third man—a gigantic Sikh with a huge head and a gap-toothed grin, sporting the worst-tied turban he had ever seen and a roughly trimmed beard.

"Mangal. Pleased to meet you."

Bikram was practically brought to his knees by the steely grip of the fellow's huge hand.

"Careful now." Thomas intervened and the big man relaxed his hold.

"Sit down, Bikram." Khan patted him on the shoulder.

"I am from the Bet," Mangal offered, referring to the wetlands along the mighty Sutlej River, north of where Bikram grew up.

"My home's in Samrala," Bikram answered, holding his aching hand under an armpit.

"Oh, a city boy."

"It's a small place."

"I've been through it. Ate the best fritters ever at the bus station there."

"Married?" Thomas asked.

Bikram shook his head.

"We are bachelors too."

Bikram discovered that he was the youngest of his tent mates. They were stores-keepers, assigned to manage the Quonset huts where goods were received, sorted, and shipped out.

"I am the new accountant," he said.

They quickly exchanged glances and smiled.

"In that case, let us welcome you in style!" Mangal grinned, and Thomas and Khan let down the rolled-up sides of the tent, leaving the entrance open. In the dim light he looked at his watch: six PM. Chow time.

Mangal pulled out a bottle, and when Bikram saw the label his heart skipped. Scotch whiskey? Native servicemen were allowed a regular ration of rum, but only the British officers were allowed whiskey. He watched in trepidation as the giant took a long swig and then offered the bottle to him.

"No shit-tasting rum for us," Mangal said.

"Where do you get it?" Bikram asked.

"Well, you might say it walks out of the storeroom when no one's looking."

"How do you account for it, then? Someone must notice it's missing."

Thomas guffawed. "Spoken like a bean-counter."

But Bikram was terrified by their blasé attitude. They were pilfering the stores. *What else do they steal?*

"Look, Bikram," Mangal said, "naturally there is some spoilage and some breakage in every shipment. This bottle is technically broken. Do you see what I mean?"

Bikram swallowed the words that rose to his lips under the searching eyes of his tent mates. He knew he had to make a choice—to throw in his lot with them or blow the whistle on their larceny. Joining them would make him a thief, but turning them in would make him a rat. And what if their commanding officer, McKie, was in on the game? What would happen to him then, after all that had been done to get him his commission? Was it really such a big deal, he asked himself, a few "broken" bottles and other petty thefts?

He took the bottle, raised it in a salute. The liquor went down smoothly.

"Good?" Mangal asked.

He nodded and handed the bottle to Khan.

Bikram was far from home, but his family's troubles were never far from his mind, and they weighed heavily on him. Gopal the match-maker had found a good, educated, and handsome match for his younger sister, Pyari. Papaji had performed the engagement ceremony with money that Bikram had sent home. But there were more expenses ahead. The groom's parents were well-to-do Jats and expected a fine wedding with an appropriate dowry. Gopal estimated that the cost would be fifteen hundred rupees. The sum would have to be bor-rowed, and at an interest rate of almost 25 percent, it would take years to pay off on Papaji's wages of thirty rupees a month alone.

Papaji wrote Bikram gut-wrenching letters asking for help. His tent mates could see that something was troubling him. One day Thomas told him, "You grind your teeth all night. And you thrash around on your cot."

"What is eating you, Bikram?" Khan asked, but Bikram didn't answer.

"You are like a little brother to us," Thomas said, and sat beside him, putting an arm around his shoulders.

"Just tell us what's eating you up inside," said Mangal, handing Bikram a glass of whiskey.

Bikram took a sip, then more. Thomas topped the glass up. The whiskey went down smoothly and spread a comforting warmth in his stomach. The feeling gradually rose into his chest, up his neck, and filled his head. A giggle escaped his lips. Words tumbled out of his lips, sounding like an echo, and he felt as if he were watching himself get drunk. Time passed in a flash.

"Bikram?"

Light filtered through the canvas and he sat up. It was dawn already. Mangal patted his shoulder. "You feel all right?"

Bikram blinked and groggily swung his legs off the cot.

"Steady now."

"Here, drink this." Thomas handed him a tumbler of cool water.

It dawned on Bikram that he must have passed out the night before. This had never happened to him. He worried what his tent mates would think of him now.

Later that day, Mangal came to see him in his tiny office crammed at the back of the Quartermaster General's.

"You owe fifteen hundred for your sister's wedding," Mangal

murmured, once the assistant was out of earshot. The office felt a lot smaller with Mangal's bulk crammed into it.

How does he know?

"And you need five hundred for the lawyer to get your father's land back."

"I do?"

He could not recall telling Mangal and the others anything of the sort.

"We are glad you told us. Me and the boys talked. We are going to give you the money. Get rid of your debts and get your father a lawyer. Or you can skip the lawyer, and I can get my brothers to take the land back for your father."

"You don't know my uncle," Bikram blurted.

"You don't know my brothers."

Bikram had little doubt that Mangal's brothers could do what he promised, but what would happen after they returned to their village in the Bet? What if his uncle decided to strike back at his father? Papaji was a meek man, and brothers killed brothers over inches of land in Punjab. He thanked Mangal, but explained that he could not put his father in harm's way.

"We will do it your way, then."

A rush of emotion overwhelmed him. "How will I ever repay you guys?"

"We will show you a way."

What way? There was a way?

"We will talk later. The four of us," Mangal said.

Sitting out on the beach that evening where they wouldn't be overheard, Bikram's tent mates agreed that each of them would put up a third of the money he needed.

"No interest, and pay us back when you can," Khan said.

Bikram was stunned; he wondered how long it had taken for each of them to save so large a sum. They all made the same salary as his. He had just received a raise of five rupees per month as a war bonus.

"I will collect from Thomas and Khan and write to my brother to go deliver two thousand rupees to your father as soon as possible," Mangal offered.

"You have that kind of cash at your home in the Bet?"

Mangal just grinned.

Bikram felt a rush of affection for his three friends. "You know that it will take me years to pay you all back," he said.

The other men burst out laughing.

"Now," said Mangal, "listen carefully to what we have to tell you."

Bikram listened in stunned silence as Mangal laid out the full extent of the scheme that his tent mates had been running: stealing all sorts of goods and resources from the army and selling it to smugglers and black marketeers. Right under the nose of their commanding officer.

"Major McKie approves?"

"He is as crooked as they come!" Mangal said as they huddled closer. "He gets half of the money we make, and we divide the other half three ways. Four ways, if you're going to be involved."

Bikram was aware that the war was taking resources out of India and there were shortages in the bazaars, of tea, coffee, sugar, cooking oils, petrol, tires, lubricants, any kind of liquor, cloth, and medicines. His tent mates had built a tightly controlled network of black marketeers and smugglers all the way to the hills, where the tribes thrived on growing opium. They could pay in cash, gold, and precious gems.

Mangal assured him that they adhered strictly to a code of honour.

"What if we are caught?"

"Court martial, followed by a firing squad."

He thought he was going to have a heart attack. But Mangal grinned.

"The CO is with us, and with you cooking the books it gets even better. In the crazy hurly-burly of war, who's going to bother to inspect us in this hellhole by the sea? Plus, we are pilfering only a very small percentage of the goods."

"And reporting it as spoilage and breakage. All perfectly reasonable," Khan added.

"It's not as if we're stealing tanks and guns," Mangal pointed out. "After all, the British have been looting us Indians for generations. Isn't it time that we looted them back? Bloody bastards."

"So," Thomas asked at last, "are you in?"

All three men were staring at him, waiting for his answer.

He knew that his family was depending on him. Pyari was his priority, and he was not going to let her down. His uncle needed to be taught a lesson. And his parents deserved to walk in the bazaar without cringing. In that moment, Bikram felt that, after his family, all his loyalty was owed to his new friends. No one else had ever shown him such kindness. Who else would have given up so much to help him? What was he to the army and its British officers? Just another Indian being thrown into the war.

Bikram nodded.

"You swear?" Thomas demanded.

"I swear."

Mangal let out a huge sigh.

"We have been losing money every single day since you arrived, Bikram. The scheme works best if you co-operate."

⚭

Bikram soon realized that with his cut of the earnings he'd be able to repay his new friends within a month or so. It boggled his mind. The Quartermaster General's depots in Chittagong held goods worth hundreds of thousands of rupees, and the turnover was getting faster and more frequent. The depots supplied most of Burma in the east and on into Thailand and Laos. Ships full of goods regularly sailed for Singapore and Malaysia.

A few weeks later, he received a coded letter from Papaji.

> *My dearest son Bikram,*
> *We are all well and pray for your health and happiness. Pyari wants you to know that she has recited twenty verses a hundred times each of your favourite prayer. I pray that it gives you peace as it has lessened our terrible burdens.*

He was grateful that Mangal had taken the precaution of ensuring that his father knew that all mail was censored by the army postal authority.

Two months later, his father wrote again, describing how well Pyari's wedding had gone. Papaji went on to say that he wished they lived in a bigger house, one that could accommodate guests. Bikram estimated that with his new source of income it would be easy enough to buy a decent plot of land, build a spacious bungalow on it, and furnish it. Everything he was doing was worth it if he could make his parents happy.

But he still had trouble shaking off the feeling that stealing was a sin.

Another letter arrived from Papaji.

> *Dearest Son,*
>
> *We are all well and pray this finds you in good health. I am so happy to tell you that I have accepted an offer of marriage for you brought to me by Gopal. As soon as you inform me of the date of your next furlough I will set the date of your wedding.*

Now he had another goal, something to look forward to! He shared the good news with his friends and they raised their glasses well into the night.

Mangal seemed genuinely happy for him.

"You will return a real man, Bikram. I pray she is beautiful and sexy and you plough her virgin soil hard."

Ajit

Ajit began to take Satwant with him on many of his official trips, touring the villages together on horseback. The father looked on in amazement one day when his son jumped off his mare to help a man struggling to raise a heavy bundle of fodder onto his head. Satwant loped across the field and helped lift it properly and steady it with both hands as the surprised man thanked him profusely.

Ajit thought his son was showing all the qualities of a good future zaildar.

Satwant had a facility with words and could carry on friendly conversations with the villagers. He would ask about the crops, the rains, the health of their families, putting the men and women at ease. He showed respect for the elders, bending down to touch their feet and receiving their blessings humbly with folded hands. The numberdars who reported to Ajit were charmed, as were their womenfolk, who gathered around the fresh-faced young man seated on a cot in their courtyards. "So handsome," was a common refrain. One elderly woman dabbed a pinch of soot on his forehead to ward off evil.

Ajit gave his gun and the bandoliers to Satwant to wear across his chest, the fatherly indulgence lending a warrior's look to the son. Satwant sat taller and straighter in the saddle, puffing his chest out in joy and pride. They stopped by a pond swarming with geese and Ajit let the boy fire a single shot, then watched him jump off his startled mare and run to collect the bloody trophy. There was a grace to his movement, an ease, and a feline, surefooted economy that surprised him. He had always thought of Satwant as a coddled scholar. It came as quite a surprise when he discovered that his son had made the school's volleyball and field hockey teams.

I must pay more attention, he told himself. His son was growing into a man right before his eyes.

And he thought of Nasib. Polio had left him with a pronounced limp. He had heard from Siamo that Nasib was taunted and bullied by the older boys at school, and it was all Ajit could do to keep himself from riding to the child's village to put the fear of God into the ruffians. He was proud of Satwant, but his heart ached for his younger son, and he could not bear to be reminded how he was failing him.

"Here." Satwant tossed the bird into the outstretched hands of a herder tending his flock of goats and sheep in a grove of acacia trees.

"Bless you, Chhota Zaildar!" the grateful man shouted as his billy goat, with a majestic set of horns, pawed the ground and snorted his aggression to the mares.

Satwant grinned at the animal's antics before turning his horse back onto the path.

Before returning home to their haveli, they stopped in a small, dusty village of mudbrick homes. The numberdar there, a nervous man with a creased face, greeted them and sat them under the shade of a tree in his courtyard.

"I have not been able to collect a penny, Zaildar." He wrung his hands.

This was the second year that this numberdar had failed him.

"Look here." Ajit glared at the man. "I do not want to be forced to take stern action."

"Zaildar, we have little irrigation here and barely survive with the crops we are able to harvest. You will not find a paisa in cash in the entire village. I beg you to understand our plight."

"I will be forced to take away the title of numberdar from you and call in the authorities to seize grain and cattle from the Jats in lieu of cash."

Ajit could see his son was alarmed. But there was something to be learned here.

"Zaildar," the man pleaded, "I will fall at your feet. Place my turban on them. You must not humiliate me thus."

Ajit stood up and started for the gate. Satwant followed. The numberdar ran behind them and took off his turban in a gesture of utter humility. Satwant took the turban and tried to put it back on the man's head.

"Father! Please show some mercy!"

"You have been warned," the Zaildar shouted at the numberdar as people came onto the street to watch. "Listen to me, all of you. Pay your taxes within this season or see your homes raided by police."

A woman began to keen, and Satwant turned to her. "Please stop crying, grandmother. I will plead with my father."

Taking Satwant by the arm, Ajit pushed him towards their mares. They mounted and rode out of the village. Ajit was silent and grim-faced.

Satwant started to argue. "Look at this soil, Bapuji. It is barren land."

Ajit kept riding and cantered the mare.

"Bapuji, please listen to me."

Ajit pulled on the reins and brought his mare around to face his son.

"Being a zaildar is not an easy job, Satwant. If I let this village off, the rest will start pleading poverty and stop paying taxes. I will lose my title. What then?"

"But there are exceptions!" Satwant argued.

"In taxes, there are none. You know that there is a war going on, and the government is pressing me to collect every single paisa. They pay, or they watch policemen strip them of their possessions."

Satwant had tears in his eyes. He had been coddled for too long in the haveli.

"Wipe your face, boy. Toughen up if you want to follow in my footsteps."

Satwant wiped his eyes with the backs of his hands.

"One more thing. After today, you eat from your own plate and Siamo eats from hers. Time to grow up. You are not a child any more."

He turned to avoid his son's eyes.

They had taught Satwant the virtues of a Sikh. And the duties, to protect and defend the weak and the helpless. And wasn't that what Satwant was doing now? Standing up for the numberdar and the peasants of the poorest village in his zaildari? Ajit thought back to the many acts of kindness his son had performed at the haveli and in the village. Giving away his used books, clothes, and moccasins. Helping charwomen lift baskets of refuse onto their heads. Carrying the bags of an elder from the Adda to the village. Letting the boys from the untouchables' street fly his kite and, much to Siamo's chagrin, letting them join him on the haveli's roof in kite fights.

Lately Satwant had become interested in the lives of the Bajigars, and he had learned their names and their history. Only the previous day Siamo had put her foot down when he told her that he wanted to learn to play the drum.

"You are a Jat, not an entertainer. Respect your caste."

"Why can't I be both?" he had argued.

"Because!" Siamo blurted, her fists clenched.

"All right, Bhua, all right. I will be a good Jat."

Satwant was sixteen years old now and awaiting the results of his matriculation examinations. In a few years he would start taking over the management of their substantial estate. Kindness and piety only went so far. Cold-heartedness and brutality were important attributes too, Ajit thought, especially for one born to the ruling class. That status had been earned for him by his tough, flinty ancestors, men who had won vast grants of land from grateful kings and fought in holy wars against tyrannical Mughal emperors, saving millions of Hindus from being forcibly converted to Islam.

Satwant would have to become hardened to the realities of life.

When they reached their haveli, the caretaker of the cattle yard unsaddled the mares. Ajit gave Satwant a quick hug and patted his back before following him to the gates.

Back at home, one of the first matters that needed attending to was a request from the mukhia of the Bajigar. Much to Ajit's delight, the nomadic tribe had chosen to stay on his land; they would build their community and also work his fields.

The Mukhia asked Ajit if they could trim some acacia trees to build a thorny fence around the dera. "It's the pariah dogs, Malik. A pack stole two newborn goat kids last night. The women are terrified lest they harm a baby."

"Yes, of course, please go ahead."

A few weeks later he heard drumbeats coming from the Bajigar settlement. Satwant rode out on his bicycle to see what was going on.

"The Mukhia won a match against a champion wrestler at the Machiwara fair, Bapuji," he reported to his father when he returned. "Changu is celebrating with his drum, and the kids are going crazy, dancing up a storm."

Like everyone else he knew, Ajit took a great interest in the wrestling matches, marvelling at the power and skill of the contestants. He decided he would go himself to congratulate the victor.

The Mukhia, who had been sitting among his admirers, rose to greet him.

"Congratulations!" Ajit called. He soon found himself sitting with the other men on a cot, passing a hookah around.

"Malik," an elder spoke up, "if the Mukhia could get the support of a wealthy patron like yourself, who knows how high he might reach?"

The Mukhia cleared his throat. "Malik, the truth is I need a sponsor so I can challenge Dalwara Singh at the Baisakhi festival in Samrala."

Ajit thought about this. "Dalwara is the Rustum, unbeaten for a decade."

"I know, and his sponsor, Mohamad Khan, permits him to wrestle only challengers with other rich sponsors."

"True, the bets are usually for very large sums."

In a wrestling match the biggest bets were placed by the sponsors; there was no point in a sponsor letting his fighter go up against a wrestler without considerable wealth behind him.

"I believe I can beat Dalwara if given the chance," the Mukhia said.

Ajit liked the idea. To be the sponsor of the regional champion, a Rustum, would bring him a great deal of prestige and respect. Look at Mohamad Khan. A Pathan of royal lineage, he had fallen in life and become a mere merchant—wealthy but not much respected. But when he became the sponsor of a Rustum, everything changed for him. Thanks to Dalwara Singh, Mohamad Khan's regal image had been restored.

A silence had fallen over the gathered crowd as they waited for his response. It would be a risk, of course, but what man worthy of the name ran from that?

"Yes, I will go and negotiate with Mohamad Khan."

"Bless you, Malik. Bless you!" the people called out.

Mohamad Khan welcomed him at the gates of his magnificent three-storey mansion in Samrala. Ajit was shown into a grandiose receiving room, exquisitely furnished, where he was served lemonade in a crystal glass and imported biscuits on a porcelain plate. Ajit kept his face blank and showed no sign that he was impressed.

They made polite small talk for a while, then got down to business. Word had got around quickly that Ajit was now the sponsor of the rising star in wrestling, the mukhia of the dera on the Zaildar's lands at Raikot.

"I must warn you, Zaildar Sahib, that wrestling is a gambler's passion. My Rustum has not been beaten in eleven years."

"The Mukhia is a skilled and athletic young man," Ajit replied.

Mohamad Khan took out a small notebook and studied it.

"The bet on Dalwara Singh's last fight was five hundred rupees."

"I can match that."

"You will have to double the sum, since the fair is in my hometown."

"Oh?"

"You are doubtful, Zaildar Sahib. Well, I understand. No need to lose a thousand rupees on an upstart."

"I have full confidence, Khan Sahib. I will bet a thousand rupees." With that, he even surprised himself.

"In appreciation of your first entry into our very exclusive club, I will handicap it by putting up double that amount."

Ajit was amazed.

"You will pay two thousand against my bet of a thousand?"

The Khan smiled. "Dalwara has made me a lot of money. I can risk a little now and then."

The Baisakhi fair of Samrala was legendary for its wrestling matches. Grapplers came from great distances, accompanied by their ardent fans. The third day of the fair was reserved for them, and thousands of men and boys came to watch. The matches started at one in the afternoon. Marshals with bamboo staffs held the baying crowds back, and uniformed constables stood by with rifles slung over their shoulders. It was all very exciting. Ajit had attended since he was five years old.

Drummers circled inside the grand akharam, a patch of land that had been ploughed well and deep to loosen the dirt upon which mighty men came to beat their opponents' ears to a pulp, mangle their limbs, and break their bones. It was a miracle, Ajit thought, that Dalwara still walked without a limp and could bend all his joints fully. He met Mohamad Khan under a large silver umbrella set up for shade and placed in his hand his envelope containing a thousand rupees. And there stood Dalwara, wearing the Rustum's highly starched black turban with the tall plume, and a long palla spread over his right shoulder. Two men massaged his thick legs.

In the akharam, smaller, agile men made quick work of their opponents, pinning their shoulders to the ground. The crowd roared and rewarded the winners with coins as they walked the circle, led by drummers singing their praises and exhorting the fans to be generous. The contests were grouped by size and weight of the wrestlers, and the ferocity of the bouts went up as the event progressed during the two hours in the dry heat of the mid-April sun.

"Hear ye, hear ye, hear ye," the barker announced at last. "Now for the final bout. Rustum Dalwara Singh."

The crowd, sun-dazed and eager for blood, went crazy.

"Rustum Dalwara Singh against the Bajigar, Mukhia Rana of Raikot."

There were boos, and in response the men from Raikot and from the Bajigar deras rent the air with their screams.

The Mukhia loosened up by running on the spot, his oiled skin glistening in the sun, while Dalwara slowly took off his turban and handed it to an assistant before folding his hands to mutter a prayer. Then with a loud yell he charged, clapping his thighs. They circled each other in synchrony, beating their chests and thighs in unison to Changu's drumbeats.

When they stopped, the crowd fell silent. Facing each other with knees bent and arms extended they inched forward, their eyes darting to thwart a sudden move. Their fingers locked, bodies collided, and each strained mightily to crush the other's hands, emitting fierce grunts and snorts. They broke off to circle once again. Dalwara's nostrils flared as if he were out of breath already. There was a dismissive curl to the Mukhia's lips that gave great hope to Ajit.

The slap of their torsos coming together was like a thunderclap,

and each tried to get a headlock on the other. Sweat poured over
their bodies, naked except for the tiny, tight loincloths that barely
hid their manhood. They ducked, they feinted, they landed elbows on
ears, chops on throats. The moves and countermoves drew gasps and
groans, and time stood still. Beside Ajit, Satwant hopped and jumped,
mimicking the combatants, beads of perspiration glistening on his
face, his eyes aglow, his teeth bared.

Then, before Ajit could blink, the Mukhia dropped to his knees and
grabbed his opponent's legs. With a mighty grunt, the Bajigar lifted
the flailing Rustum in the air before slamming him onto his back.
The crowd came alive with the electrifying double leg drop. Ajit saw
Changu jump into the air like a gazelle and beat his drum a dozen
times before landing on his feet. His heart raced. He was breathless
with excitement. Satwant jumped on his back, and together they
danced and screamed for joy.

"The new Rustum, Mukhia Rana of Raikot!"

The words were like a musical thunderbolt. Changu led the Mukhia
around the circle, his drumbeats feverish, his song of victory loud. The
wrestler's reward came from the spectators, and now men were lavishly bestowing rupees and coins on the victor. Mohamad Khan made
his way over to Ajit and they hugged, patted each other on the back,
and shook hands.

"Congratulations, Zaildar Sahib. It was a legendary bout, and I
am a proud loser. You picked your Rustum well. May he rule for a
decade."

And he handed him a thick envelope.

At the Bajigar dera the celebrations reached a joyous peak. The coun-
cilmen of Raikot were all present, toasting the victor. Changu beat his
drum deliriously. The women danced a gidda, twirling and laughing,
and the children joined in. Ajit had brought Satwant with him, and
the boy wore a smile from ear to ear.

The Mukhia, now wearing the Rustum's black turban, stepped
grandly out of his hut to the cheering of his people. He bent to touch
the feet of the elders, men and women, and received their loud blessings. Last, he stopped before Ajit.

"Malik, you are my king, my god."

"No, Rustum, you are the king, and God is the one and only God. He blessed me with you, and the honour we earned together today."

"I will serve you well, I promise you, Malik."

Ajit had thought about his next words, and now they flowed easily from his lips.

"In honour of Rustum Mukhia's legendary victory I wish to make an announcement," he began. Changu stopped the drumming. "I deed this plot of two acres to the clan and reward the two thousand rupees of my win to Rustum Mukhia to help all of you build permanently on this land you now own."

∽

"I like the girl," Inder said to Ajit. "She is a perfect match for Satwant."

She had just returned from a visit to the home of the Jagirdar of Palampur, a man of wealth, with much land and many tenants. Sher Singh had sent a proposal for the marriage for his youngest child and only daughter, Amrita, to Satwant. It was customary for women of the boy's family to go see the girl for themselves, just as the men of the girl's family had come to visit the haveli and speak with the boy.

"Bir, you should see their compound. It is like a palace." Siamo said. She had accompanied Inder on the visit.

"Our haveli is like a palace too, is it not?" Ajit replied. "Exterior walls three feet thick, doors and windows three inches thick, ten-foot courtyard walls—"

"Let's talk about the matter at hand." Inder had no patience for her husband's boasts.

"Sher Singh has asked that we perform the engagement on an auspicious day, as advised by his Brahmin, in two weeks. Just enough time for us to make arrangements and send out invitations to our relatives."

Siamo joined in excitedly. "Bir, they are going to be very generous with the gifts, and later with the dowry."

"Can we put material considerations aside for the time being?" Inder asked crossly.

Ajit was more sympathetic to Siamo. He knew that she had endured poverty, whereas Inder had never known want or privation.

"Continue."

"I proposed that the wedding be held four years from now. Amrita is very much a girl still, two years younger than Satwant."

Ajit nodded his agreement.

"Bir, the two are made for each other," Siamo enthused. "Amrita is so beautiful and well-mannered."

Ajit could not have wished for a better match for his son: the beautiful daughter of a man even richer and more influential than him.

"You saw the brothers?" Ajit asked.

"They are both tall, strapping young men. One is studying to be a lawyer and wants to become a judge, and the younger one is an athlete and studying to become a police officer."

It was important to Ajit that Satwant would have the protection of strong brothers-in-law, being an only child and son. Satwant's soft nature worried him. In the Punjab, a land boundary dispute could erupt any day, and one needed the backing of brothers or brothers-in-law to fight disputes. For a Jat, land was life and sacred. He'd had to call upon Inder's brothers when one of his own kin had challenged him over water rights from a shared well. The sudden appearance of five armed men on horseback had done wonders to resolve the argument in Ajit's favour. His kinsman had apologized on the spot, and no one had troubled him from that day on.

Two weeks later, Satwant's engagement ceremony was conducted under a vast canopy raised for the occasion and decorated with colourful bunting. Sher Singh arrived with his party of seven men in two cars. It was a special treat for the children of the village, a rare chance to gaze at the shiny vehicles up close.

Men and women filled the courtyard, seated separately on either side of the dais, where Satwant sat cross-legged, wearing a red turban and a suit of golden silk. His handsome looks drew sighs and prideful glances from the women of his kin. Siamo fluttered around him, adjusting his palla over his lap, tugging the back of his kurta straight, wiping the beads of perspiration on his forehead with her chador, patting his cheeks fondly. Inder hung back and veiled her face in the presence of elders and the village council, the panchayat.

The rituals were performed under the guidance of Brahmins. The Jagirdar placed seven mohurs of gold in Satwant's palla, blessed him by placing his right hand on his head, and fed him a piece of sweet ladoo. The men of the girl's side followed suit, substituting paper notes for the gold coins. Then they produced seven brass trays laden with coconut and dried fruits, folded their hands, bowed, and took their leave. They wouldn't accept so much as a drop of water, despite Ajit's pleadings, old-fashioned men sworn never to partake of any refreshment in the future home of a daughter.

"Let the celebrations begin!" Siamo shouted.

A troupe of Bajigars, who had been waiting at the gates to entertain the guests, entered the courtyard to the beat of Changu's drum and began to dance. The women wore their finest clothing, multi-hued garments hand-sewn from a patchwork of different fabrics. Their close-fitting kurtis topped their ghunias, skirts tied with a cord at the waist and flared to twirl attractively over their bare feet, which were red from the application of henna. Their oversized silver earrings, anklets, and bracelets glinted in the sun, and their long ribbon-tied braids swayed like snakes dancing to a charmer's flute. They began to beat the hard earth with their heels as the drummer skilfully set the tone and the pace, giving them a rhythm as they twirled and clapped their hands above their heads. The vibration from their heels striking the ground, the beat of the drum, the rhythmical clapping, and the ululating had the onlookers aching to join in, and Ajit felt a rare urge to let go and burst into a dance.

Two girls, about the age of five or six, with broad smiles on their faces and eyes alight, moved to the centre of the stage and danced with such abandon it took his breath away. Coins flew through the air in appreciation as cries of applause urged them on. It was a magical moment indeed. He had never seen such natural skill in children so young. The girls jumped and twirled as their colourful skirts ballooned and braids arced and their bodies swayed to the hypnotic beat of the drum. When it finally slowed and stopped, Ajit saw Inder rush to take the duo in her arms as the crowd clapped and hooted. Bajigar women bent to quickly gather the coins from the ground, bowing and scraping in gratitude.

Satwant stepped forward to give the two girls a rupee each. He pinched their flaming cheeks, making them giggle, and they buried their faces in his mother's neck.

"The one on the left is Basanti, Changu's daughter, promised to my son, Rana," the Mukhia told him. "Her cousin Devi is promised to my nephew, Wazeer."

He learned that the families were on their way far to the west with their clan to work digging canals.

"They will return in time to be wed," the Mukhia said, and he smiled as Ajit handed him a glass of rum.

Bikram

It took a personal appeal to Major McKie to get a two-month furlough after almost three years of Bikram's posting in Chittagong.

"Sahib, if I do not go and get married soon, my engagement will be cancelled."

Now he just had to live long enough to enjoy his wedding.

There was no reason to feel that the war would be over any time soon, in spite of the fact that the Americans were in the fight now, after the Japanese bombing of their naval base at Pearl Harbor. It was too soon to say what kind of difference they might make, but at least it was a hopeful development. Bikram followed the progress of the war in any newspaper he could get his hands on, and he knew that Germany had invaded the Soviet Union, while fighting continued back and forth across the western front. During a briefing he learned that the Japanese had already conquered Singapore and now were knocking on the borders of Laos and Burma. Consequently, the Quonset huts constantly received supplies that were quickly shipped out to the troops. And so there was a lot of money to be made. But Bikram was scared of getting caught. He knew there was no backing out. He occasionally got the hint that if he tried, his partners and Major McKie would find a way to silence him. He didn't see any way to extricate himself from the scheme now. If he blew the whistle, he would take his friends down with him. He owed them his loyalty. And yet he was beginning to think maybe the loyalty, like the guilty conscience, was all on his part.

Chittagong was generally considered a safe posting, out of the way of the real action, but it was getting perilously close to the range of Japanese bombers. The army conducted air raid exercises, and the mournful sound of sirens was nerve-racking. There was live fire from the concrete pillboxes guarding the port. Exploding shells fell into the open waters of the sea and sent plumes high into the sky.

As the date of his furlough neared, Bikram worried. All his paper currency was in tins fitted with tight caps and stored in a hole dug in the dirt floor of the tent. Should he take it with him? Was it safe to travel with so much? Or should he leave it behind and risk it getting mouldy underground?

"Take it all with you. You must," Mangal said. "Buy strongboxes in Samrala. Lock it up and bring the keys back with you. Trust no one."

The money filled two large duffel bags, which Mangal helped him carry up the steep plank of the steamer. Then, giving him a hug, Mangal whispered, "Fuck your new wife hard. You hear? Who knows when you will get a chance again."

The trip home took six days of sleepless sea and train travel. He kept the duffel bags close to him, and his heart raced any time a military policeman poked his head into his compartment. He prayed that nothing untoward would happen that might result in a search. It made him wonder if all that wealth was worth facing a firing squad for.

"Khanna Station." The announcement was like music to his ears. He was not much more than an hour away from Ludhiana now. He took a tonga home.

At the gates of the spacious courtyard of the new home that Papaji had rented, Bikram was mauled by his sisters Guddi and Pyari, then hugged by his parents. Maaji wept tears of joy seeing him with a man's build and full beard, and she clung to him.

"Your room is the one upstairs." Papaji helped carry his luggage up the exterior brick staircase. He was glad to see the sturdy door and windows with thick iron bars. The room was airy and looked comfortable. It was early spring and he was grateful for the absence of flies and mosquitoes, and that he would sleep indoors. He bathed, changed, ate a hearty meal, and begged to be allowed to sleep for as long as he needed.

The next day, his sisters watched wide-eyed as he counted a thousand rupees into Maaji's palm to pay for his engagement and wedding costs. He gave them each a hundred rupees to buy new clothes for themselves and their children—Guddi had a son after two daughters; Pyari had a son and was pregnant again.

The name of Bikram's bride was Jagtar.

"Your in-laws are of good lineage but lack the means to give you a suitable dowry," Gopal explained. "Your match, however, is perfect for you."

Bikram was told that Jagtar's father was employed as a land surveyor in the Sub-Divisional Office in Khanna, and he was disappointed. He felt he deserved better. He was now a sergeant-major, two steps below the highest rank for an NCO, that of an honorary captain.

"It was the best proposal I received," Papaji said, and he reminded Bikram of the days of their own financial straits.

The wedding was a simple affair. Only thirty men made up the wedding party and rode the bus he hired to Khanna. Uncle had not been invited; Papaji had hired the lawyer and commenced a lawsuit against him, but he was contesting it at every turn. The wedding party was received without much fanfare and participated in a simple gift-exchange ceremony. They were served decent meals under the canopy, seated on thick sheets on the floor of the local serai, since the bride's family lived humbly in rented rooms that would not have been adequate. Bikram had hired traditional singers to entertain, and he was glad to have bought enough country rum for the occasion.

The Ceremony of Bliss was held the next day before dawn at the local gurudwara, a trio of hymn-singers reciting the four verses. The bride was dressed head to toe in red and her face was veiled, so Bikram could not see it, but he got the impression that she was lithe and graceful. After the ceremony, he received blessings from his father- and mother-in-law.

There was a showing of the modest dowry, its centrepiece a sewing machine and a set of gold jewellery for the bride. And then afternoon tea was served. Finally it was time for Bikram and his new bride to depart for his parents' home. As often happened in weddings, the bride wept, and as they climbed aboard the bus, her family too cried and clung to her. At last she was pushed up the steps by a stout nain, the traditional female companion of a girl going for the first time to her matrimonial home.

It was midnight when all the rites and rituals of welcoming his bride into the family home were completed, and his sisters led her up the staircase to his room, which they had decorated with bunting and streamers. In keeping with tradition, they charged him a few coins to let him through the doorway and giggled their way down, singing a bawdy song.

Bikram closed the door and turned to see Jagtar in the light of the lantern, sitting demurely on the edge of the cot in her red satin wedding ensemble, her face covered and her hennaed hands folded in her lap. He walked over and bent down to pull back the veil and gave a small gasp. She was beautiful. More than he had dared hope. Fair of face and fine of feature, her long neck sloped onto slim shoulders. He lifted her chin, and she held his gaze with languid, almond eyes, then demurely lowered them. She smiled, and her generous lips opened slightly to reveal even, white teeth. He pulled her up into an embrace and their eyes locked as he felt her hard breasts pressed to his chest. Holding her by the waist he began to kiss her, lightly at first, but then he found his breath quickening and his stiffness pressed against her. He blindly searched for the cord of her salwar.

"Blow the flame out, Ji," Jagtar whispered, her breath hot on his ear.

Life in the army had exposed Bikram to the flesh trade. New recruits would go together to visit the Randi Bazaar in Lahore, walk its streets, and gaze up at the garishly dressed women standing on balconies, calling out. Novice soldiers dared each other, and some did climb up the narrow stairs, but he did not. For him, in those days, every paisa was precious and to be saved. Later, in Peshawar, he had accompanied his barrack mates and visited the city's red-light district. The variety of women there was astounding. Fair-skinned, with grey or blue eyes and brown or golden hair, they had been brought from the gloriously historic cities of Kabul, Balakh, Bukhara, and Tashkent. Their rates were too high for him. In Chittagong, Khan and Thomas would sometimes go to a crumbling mansion where delicate Oriental girls catered to their vices, but not before the price was paid to the elderly matrons flanked by unsmiling pimps. It was rumoured that foreign spies had infiltrated the brothels to collect information, and the place was often raided by military police. "Boast and die," Mangal would say.

Watching the perversions in that musty mansion behind faded curtains in fetid rooms had turned him off. Now he had Jagtar, taut, smooth-skinned, and firm. She smelled heavenly, of rose attar and talcum powder. For three straight days he could not get enough of her, making love all hours of the day and night while his parents carried on a semblance of normality downstairs and in the courtyard. He couldn't wait for his bothersome sisters and their children to go home again, and he gave them each a sack full of presents. They left singing his praises.

"You must take Jagtar to visit her parents," Maaji reminded him one day. It was an ancient ritual: shortly after the wedding, the bride made a visit to her paternal home.

He rented a tonga to travel to Khanna, and when they arrived at his in-laws', he was shocked at the conditions in which her family was living. Since the wedding festivities had been held at the serai and the gurudwara, Bikram had not actually seen his wife's family home. In a crowded tenement, the family was jammed into two dingy rooms with stained ceilings and crumbling plaster walls. Jagtar sat with her mother, Beeji, and Bikram sat next to his father-in-law, Chand Singh, on a covered cot. Chand Singh's two sons, Darshan and Sukha, squatted on their haunches on the bare floor. The sons still wore their finery from the wedding, the kurtas now crumpled and dirty. Both were bare-headed and sported loose topknots.

Bikram was curious and asked many questions. He learned from Chand that they had pinned their hopes on their two school-going sons and prayed they would finish college and earn well-paying jobs.

"He is poorly paid," Beeji said of her husband. "But for the odd rupee a Jat places on his palm in bribery, we would not even be able to afford this home."

"I am actually the assistant land registrar. I certify all the documents when people register land or buildings they have purchased," Chand explained.

That got Bikram's attention. "So, you know the local prices well."

"I can value any property to within a paisa."

"If I gave you twenty thousand rupees, what could you buy with it?"

Chand gave him a quick glance, and it crossed Bikram's mind that they all seemed to have a cunning, alert look to them.

"I have never seen that sum in cash in my life."

"Just for argument's sake," Bikram insisted.

"It would buy this entire tenement."

"It is crumbling."

"It sits on more than four acres of very desirable land. The owner earns a horrendous amount in rents."

"If you had that money, and only that much, would you still buy this tenement?"

Chand nodded his head. "It borders the Grand Trunk Road that runs from Kabul to Delhi. Someday it could be torn down to build shops, warehouses, or a cinema. Khanna is a growing town and slated to become a district."

Someone knocked on the door, and Beeji rushed to answer it. She opened the door just enough to squeeze through it. Bikram could hear sharp words, spoken behind the door by a man.

Chand looked nervous and blinked as they heard Beeji pleading. Jagtar's cheeks flushed, and the boys stopped chomping on the stale ladoos.

Bikram stood up and opened the door. A man who looked like a merchant stepped back and mumbled an apology.

"What is he owed?" Bikram asked Beeji in the stern voice of a military officer.

"Bikram Singh, please come back in." Chand grabbed his arm and tried to pull him into the room.

"Tell me," Bikram demanded of the merchant.

"I am the goldsmith. They owe me three hundred rupees."

Bikram pulled his wallet from his pocket and counted out three hundred-rupee notes. He handed them over to the jeweller. The man folded his hands, smiled, and bowed before turning around and hastily walking away.

"Darshan," Bikram called out.

"Yes, Jeeja."

"Here, go fetch some tea from the bazaar. My throat is parched."

The youth grabbed the rupee note and, with his brother trailing behind him, ran out.

"Bikram Singh." Beeji had sat again. "We are poor. We could not save enough for the wedding. I am ashamed that we can't even entertain you properly."

"How much in total did you spend on the wedding?"

They looked away.

"Tell me."

"About a thousand rupees," Chand said.

Bikram counted seven more bills and held them out. The two elders looked wide-eyed at them.

"Take it. I have a lot more of these."

Jagtar started to cry.

"Here." Bikram stuffed the bills into Chand's shirt pocket.

Beeji sat back and let out the longest sigh Bikram had ever heard. "Waheguru, Waheguru, Waheguru-ji." She intoned the name of God with folded hands.

Chand looked as if he were about to pass out.

Bikram rose to comfort Jagtar and took her in an embrace, a bold act in front of her dazed parents. She clung to him and cried her eyes out.

"Listen, Ji," Jagtar said in a small voice as they lay in each other's arms that night, back home. She had given herself totally to him, allowed herself to be fully undressed in the light of the lantern, but only after checking to make sure that the windows and the door were shut tight. He delighted in stroking her naked parts.

"What?"

"Do you really have twenty thousand rupees?"

"Huh?"

"Tell me, Ji."

"I might."

"I don't believe it."

He raised himself on an elbow and ran a finger along her arm.

"Want to see it?"

That cunning look flashed in her eyes.

"If I show it to you, will you do it again?" He gently put a finger in her mouth.

She nodded, her eyes holding his. Her lips puckered around the finger.

"All right."

He got up, pulled the trunk he'd purchased from under their cot, and unlocked it. She sat staring at the bundles wrapped in wax paper and tied with string. Taking one out, he threw it to her.

"Open it."

Her eyes widened as she spread the notes on the bed and counted them. "Hundred-rupee notes," she whispered.

Bikram noticed her nipples hardening and her lips swelling, and a moan escaped her open mouth. He took out another bundle before opening a heavy tin can and laying out the shiny gold coins.

"Oh, God," Jagtar gasped, her voice husky.

He thought she might faint.

"How did you . . . ?"

He told her.

She was silent for a long moment.

"The total in here is over two lakh."

"Two hundred thousand—"

He put his hand over her mouth. "Hush."

"You haven't told Papaji or Maaji?"

He could feel her body trembling. He explained the reason.

"My father is going to have a seizure when he finds out the sum, Ji."

"Your father looks like a worldly man, Jagtar. Can I trust him?"

Jagtar wrapped herself around him.

After that revelation, Jagtar seemed eager to visit her parents again. "It's time to do business, Ji," she said.

When they arrived in Khanna, her brothers were sent off to watch the matinee at the cinema, and Jagtar got straight to the point.

"Ji has twenty thousand rupees, Bapuji. He needs your help to invest it." As Bikram had instructed, she did not reveal the true extent of his wealth.

Chand sat with his mouth hanging open, and Beeji swallowed hard. Her eyes darted from Bikram to Jagtar, and then to her husband. Her lips moved silently. He knew that she was intoning the name of God, Waheguru.

"Take your time, Bapuji," Bikram said.

After what seemed an inordinate period of silence, the elder asked,

"I was told at the time of my first meeting with Pundit Gopal Chand Sharma that you earned a wage of thirty rupees per month. How did you come to possess so much money, then?"

"Fortunate circumstances." He took a risk and told his father-in-law about the scheme at the Quartermaster General's office in Chittagong. There was something in Chand's eyes and expression that made him add a lie. "It is not all my money. Our leader is a vicious man, Mangal Singh. He can be very vengeful if crossed."

Jagtar frowned. "You did not mention that."

"So you need to establish trust with me?" Chand asked.

"I need to do that. There could be a lot more money than you have been told."

"I will do my absolute best and work hard to buy you the best properties."

"My partners will be very happy to hear that."

Beeji cleared her throat. "Bikram Singh, we come from a great lineage. Jagtar's great-grandfather was a zaildar. Unfortunately, he was a vain man and squandered his lands and title. We are honourable people and would never betray the trust of our only daughter's husband. You can rest assured."

This cleared the air, and Bikram felt generously disposed.

"You can keep five percent of the funds you invest as your commission."

Chand choked up. "I was so worried about how to pay you back for your help, Bikram Singh. You took such a burden off my shoulders. I will do all for free."

"All right. No commission on the first twenty thousand, then."

When he'd first arrived in Chittagong, Bikram's only worries had been to make sure Pyari had a proper Jat wedding and his father got his ancestral property back. He'd thought maybe he could go so far as to build a nice brick house for his parents. But the good fortune that had come his way now exceeded his humble fantasies—unimaginable wealth, a beautiful bride, and the perfect father-in-law, a man who was uniquely positioned to help him build a solid portfolio of properties. Bikram lay awake sorting out his thoughts. According to Chand, political speculation was causing uncertainty in the property market.

India was on the brink of being granted its independence from Britain. The Muslim League had issued its Lahore Resolution in 1940, asking for more autonomy for Muslims within the new Indian state, and the feeling was that this was going to end with the demand that a separate country for Muslims be carved from India. Needless to say, this was causing a lot of consternation and worry.

Ludhiana was not a Muslim majority district, so even if a Muslim territory were created Ludhiana would almost certainly remain a part of Hindu India. But local Muslims, particularly merchants and wealthy families, were starting to hedge their bets. They were quietly putting some of their lands and buildings up for sale, in order to buy property in Muslim-majority areas and cities to the west. That way they would have a foot in both territories. Chand, as an assistant land registrar, was privy to this information. And, as he explained, uncertainty was just another word for opportunity.

"They are desperate, and no one has the cash. You could buy them out very cheaply, and with the utmost secrecy and discretion, Bikram Singh."

Chand had a list with more than enough properties for the investment of two hundred thousand rupees. Plots of good land. Rural acreage bordering the towns of Samrala and Khanna that would become urban in a decade or so, with warehouses, shops, and tenements fetching good rents. Bikram's first priority was to buy land suitable to build a bungalow for his parents, and he purchased a corner lot from Mirza Gujjar, the dairyman. Their happy faces were a satisfying reward for the gut-wrenching worry of previous years, the need to pay a bribe just to get a low-paying job, his uncle's hands around his throat as he was being shoved out of his ancestral home, the town loafers outside the liquor vend harassing his family with impunity. These things were never going to happen again.

No one raised an eyebrow when he started spending. His family had a rather anonymous existence in Samrala, and their neighbours were all preoccupied by their own concerns. Mirza Gujjar never once asked about the cash he was paid for his plot.

"I have been trying to sell it for years," was all he said.

The day Bikram rewarded Chand and Beeji with the purchase of an older two-storey house on a shady street in Khanna, Jagtar made such passionate love to him that it left him breathless. Later, back in Chittagong, when he received the good news of her pregnancy in a letter from Papaji, he came to believe that their child had been conceived that night when they had tried to consume each other, exhausting themselves.

Money—handling, counting, and stacking it—aroused Jagtar in a curious way, and he was the beneficiary. Her passion took him to heights of pleasure and satiation that he could never have imagined in his wildest fantasies. He craved the look that came into her eyes when they lay together and talked of owning this or that, and how it hardened her nipples, swelled her lips, and brought goosebumps to her skin.

"You have done such sewa for my parents, Ji, given them so much."

He decided on the name Sewa, meaning selfless service, if their child were a boy. Sewa Singh. It sounded nice. Humble and worshipful. The idea that he'd performed sewa helped to satisfy his conscience. He could always make amends, build a gurudwara in gratitude to Waheguru, and give some of his riches to the poor at an opportune moment. He decided one day he would donate a tenth of his wealth in tithes.

That was all that was required of a hardworking and devoted Sikh.

Ajit

Satwant broke his heart.

He'd secretly written the entrance examinations at the Military Academy in Dehradun, passed them, and signed up to train as an officer. Without seeking permission from his parents.

Inder was in silent shock. "Why?" Ajit demanded.

"I have learned a lot in two years of college, Bapuji. This is the path I've chosen."

"But you are an only child, an only son," Siamo said, tears streaming from her eyes.

"I have the right to choose my future."

"You are in line to be a zaildar." Ajit wanted to shake his stubborn son by the shoulders.

"I do not want to be a tax collector who has to harass poor people, threaten and punish them. I no longer find it desirable for me."

"Oh, God." Siamo struck her forehead with grief.

"There is a nasty war going on," Ajit said. "Once you become an officer, you will be sent God knows where to fight. Did you not think about that? Or what your parents will have to endure? The torture we will suffer?"

"Bapuji, I did it as a devoted Sikh. It is our duty to serve our country, and the best way is to fight to defend it."

Satwant had filled out into a grown man, taller than his father, with broad shoulders and a nice beard. He had learned to tie his turban well. Ajit looked at his handsome features and his heart rose into his throat at the thought of him leaving to join the army.

Siamo sat down heavily on the floor, alarming Satwant. He pulled her up and gently wiped her tears as her chest heaved and her body shook.

"Don't worry, Bhua. I will be safe. I promise you."

Stupid martial notions. Ajit had sent his son to school to study history, political science, civics, the arts, to learn to be a wise man making his way in the world. Someone had brainwashed his son in college.

"At least I am not becoming a freedom fighter and taking up arms against the British," Satwant said.

Ajit had to agree—that was worse and sure to lead to tragedy. Freedom fighters were avenging the terrible atrocities committed by the British against Punjabis. No one had forgotten the Amritsar massacre of 1919, in which British troops fired on a crowd of ten thousand men, women and children—some of them peacefully protesting colonial rule, others simply celebrating Baisakhi, a spring festival. Hundreds were killed. But the desire for freedom had not dampened. The Sikhs were collecting a lot of martyrs this way. Bhagat Singh and Udham Singh were the two most admired. They'd been hanged. And was this the right time, while the whole world was at war, to be spitting in the face of a great empire? They might be simply overthrowing one master to take on another, and worse.

Ajit felt a bit of relief. "Who talked you into this?" he asked.

"I was counselled by the Colonel."

That bastard. He knew that Satwant was Ajit's only heir. He would go the very next day to confront the old man. Give him an earful.

"Bapuji, if the Japanese end up conquering India, we will be a lot worse off than we are right now. You should read what atrocities they wreaked upon China, Korea, and Singapore. They cannot be allowed to occupy India. People will be killed by the millions. We will end up in perpetual slavery."

"Go speak to your mother. What is done is done. Explain yourself to her."

Slowly climbing the staircase to his room, he heard Satwant begging his mother to listen to him.

Ajit marched into the recruiting office in Ludhiana to give the Colonel a piece of his mind, but he came away feeling chastened.

"Yes, I did encourage your son to take officer training. So? You yourself have encouraged dozens of other men's young sons to join the army, and drawn healthy stipends for doing that, Zaildar," said the wily old Englishman. "Remember Sergeant Bikram Singh? Was he not the only son of his parents? Where was that fatherly concern when you herded him through that door?"

Was Satwant's decision a matter of karma? Ajit's only comfort was that the Colonel had promised to secure for Satwant a non-combat posting. Now, wandering through the bazaar in Ludhiana, he spied an astrologer sitting on a gunny sack on the curb; in front of him burned a stick of incense. Ajit had never had his palm read—he was not the sort who was eager to know the future, in case he didn't like what he heard—but given his uncertain circumstances and troubled mind that day, he decided to take the chance.

The astrologer, a Brahmin with a tonsured head and a forehead lined with ashes, looked up and gestured for him to sit on the ground before him. Ajit looked around first to see if there were any men he knew nearby.

"Tell me the details of your birth." The astrologer picked up a well-thumbed notebook and a small pencil.

Ajit recited the facts as best as he could and watched the lines and symbols the man drew on the page. The astrologer studied them for a long while before he said, "Show me your right hand." Ajit spread out his palm. The astrologer studied it, holding it in both his hands, turned it, twisted it, and spread it, mumbling to himself. Then he sat back and held Ajit's gaze for a disconcertingly long moment.

"You are carrying a secret."

"What?"

"You are carrying a secret."

"Like what?"

"A significant secret. It is troubling you."

Ajit said nothing.

"Your palm shows two sons."

Ajit nodded.

"One has a shorter life."

His heart stopped.

"Acceptance does not come easy to you. Know that fate has a way to make you bend to its will."

"You are confusing me," Ajit said, pulling his hand back.

"I only tell what I see. It is up to you to decide what is the truth."

"What do you see?"

"I see a tortured soul."

Ajit folded his hands, then gave the man a couple of rupees, rose, and walked away, disturbed. *Know that fate has a way to make you bend to its will.* He had for so long felt in charge of his own life, a wealthy man, a leader in his community, a strong husband and father. But was this notion of his own power and control simply an illusion? And if he was not the master of his own desires, of his own fate, why should he pretend to be the master of his son's fate?

When the day came, Ajit, Inder, and Siamo accompanied Satwant to the Ludhiana railway station, where Sher, the father of his betrothed, Amrita, and Sher's sons joined them. Satwant would travel to New Delhi and change trains for Dehradun.

Once they had settled around a table in the station canteen and ordered tea and pakodas, Inder enquired after Amrita.

"She will start at the Government College for Women here. She wants to study to be a teacher," Sher said with obvious pride.

"A college professor," her older brother said with a smile.

"Unlikely now, however," Sher said. "I propose that Satwant and Amrita be wed in two years when Satwant graduates as an officer but before he is posted to serve."

Satwant blushed as all eyes turned to him.

"What do you think?" Inder asked him.

"I will do what you ask, Maaji."

"I am going to enjoy planning your wedding, then." She smiled.

"Any special wish for the dowry, Satwant?" Sher asked. "A motorcycle?"

Satwant shook his head.

"I hear that you love riding. How about the best Marwari filly I can find? I could have it trained by the date of the wedding."

Satwant smiled broadly, but kept his eyes lowered.

"A Marwari filly, then."

He nodded his assent.

It was an ancient tradition among Jats to give a mare to their daughter's groom in dowry. Ajit had received one in his. However, the educated ones seemed to prefer motorbikes these days.

"I hear that the best fillies are to be found at the stables of the

Maharaja of Jaisalmer in Rajasthan," Sher said. He turned to Ajit. "Why don't we go there together and select one?"

"With pleasure." He realized then that Sher was not going to spare any expense.

Later, standing on the train platform, Inder clung to Satwant and wept inconsolably, as Siamo wiped tears with her chador. Ajit shook his son's hand and gave him a quick embrace. Satwant extricated himself to shake his future in-laws' hands.

"May Waheguru watch over you." Sher patted his back.

✑

Satwant graduated from the military academy two years later with honours, and became a commissioned officer in the Royal Indian Army. He was now home, much to the delight of his family, preparing for his wedding and awaiting his first posting. He was standing with his father in the cattle yard and admiring the spirited mare that had arrived as part of the substantial dowry Amrita had brought with her.

"I will call her Bakki," Satwant said.

"The mare needs to be exercised every day," Baru Marasi said. A Muslim, Baru was the village's horse trainer, and belonged to the Marasi caste of messengers and village criers. He also served as an animal healer. He was the tallest man in the village, strong enough to carry a sick calf across his shoulders.

Bakki stood a couple of hands taller than the rest of the mares, and men often stopped by to admire her. She was a beautiful bay, with a white star on her forehead and white-socked hooves, a long, black mane. Her unclipped tail swished to dismiss the flies from her back. She almost seemed to preen for her admirers, striking poses and snorting mightily while pawing the ground with an iron-shod hoof.

"You see her ears are longer than those of the other breeds," Baru noted.

Bakki posed with ears alert as if on cue.

"She hears you." Satwant smiled.

"She is a desert war horse bred to carry a warrior fully dressed in chain mail and armour, plus his weapons. Look at her muscular haunches and rippled back, the wide hooves and thick neck. Look at that chest! This breed has huge lungs so they have the stamina to go into battle. They're fast and agile. They can turn and twist and join the fight by rearing back and maiming foot soldiers with their forelegs. Just imagine one of those hooves striking your forehead. It would crack open like a melon. Common horses are bred just to pull carts and tongas. Bakki can walk, trot, canter, and gallop."

Even Bakki's saddle was magnificent. Sher had commissioned the best upholsterer and a silversmith to stitch and decorate it.

The wedding was three full days of drinking, feasting, and performances by celebrated singers and dance troupes. Afterwards, Amrita was brought to Raikot as a new bride in the golden-domed rath, just as Satwant's mother had been. In anticipation, Ajit had had it repaired and its wheels painted and top replaced with new fabric. It was pulled by his finest pair of white oxen, with silver-tipped horns. A troop of armed men escorted it.

The bride and groom did not emerge from their rooms for three straight days following their first night together. Siamo carried trays of food and jugs of buttermilk up the staircase. It irritated Ajit that Satwant was behaving like a randy billy goat.

"What do the women at the kitchen think of his shenanigans?" he asked Inder. "I am embarrassed."

"But you didn't let me out for three days either."

"What? I don't remember any such thing."

Inder sighed. "Just think about it, Ji. They are working hard to make you a grandson."

Siamo called from the gates, "Bir, send Satwant to the haveli to get ready."

The new bride had to be presented to the village deities. It was a strictly observed custom in Raikot, and failing to do so could bring misfortune on the new couple.

The first visit would be to the Naag Baba shrine, built to honour the cobra god who, it was told, had been born to a woman of the village as a twin to her human son. The legend was known far and wide, and people came in droves to celebrate at the annual fair held in the god's honour. Pregnant women came to seek good health and others came to pray for a child. It was said that those who came with true intentions left blessed.

The second stop would be at the tomb of the great Sufi saint Pir Baba Shah. One of Ajit's ancestors had deeded ten acres to the revered holy man and helped plant an orchard on the site, with a narrow well to water it. The Pir had lived there two centuries ago. His tomb stood in the middle of the verdant orchard, considered to be hallowed ground, and was worshipped by Muslims, Sikhs, and Hindus.

The third visit would be to the memorial built to honour their ancestors who had died as martyrs in the holy wars, the revered Shahids.

The pilgrimage would then end at the Sikh temple, the gurudwara, for the reading of the Ardas, seeking God's benediction. Inder had prepared a large amount of prasad, food to be given as a religious offering, which would be distributed throughout the village after the conclusion of worship.

Baru placed his hand on Satwant's head. "Bless you, my son. May Allah look kindly upon you."

Satwant smiled and patted Bakki's flank before taking his leave.

As Ajit approached the haveli, there came the sound of joyful singing, and he arrived just in time to see the procession of women of his household and kin singing and dancing, following Satwant and his unveiled bride. Inder, like other brides of the village, new and old, had pulled a dupatta over her face. Siamo, considered a daughter of the haveli, did not have to cover her face. He grinned at the cheek-splitting smile on her face and the joy in her eyes.

Siamo had not warmed to Amrita right away. For one thing, Amrita had been so bold as to ask her father's permission to be wed without a veil. Sher had asked Ajit and Inder for their opinions first, and he'd agreed only after Inder said, "God has seen her face. Why should she veil it in the presence of the Holy Granth, our living Guru?"

Siamo had frowned. "It is too modern. Next she will want to wear a frock, like a Memsahib."

"When did you ever see a Memsahib?" Inder asked.

"I have seen a few driving by in their cars."

"That's not the same."

But once Amrita arrived as Satwant's bride, Siamo lost all her misgivings and took the girl to her bosom. Amrita was humble and respectful, and she sought permission for the smallest of things. Siamo would hover over Amrita, making sure she lacked for nothing, learned the routines of the haveli, and did not perform any work. She would remind the girl constantly, "You are newly wed."

"I can do it," Amrita said.

"No. I will do it."

"But, Bhuaji, I can pour my own tea."

The women of the Bajigar admired Amrita too. Sehba, the wife of the Mukhia, came one day with the older women of the clan to bless the girl and offer her the gift of a pair of heavy, silver earrings.

"You are *our* daughter-in-law, too," they told her. "Satwant is like a son to us."

Amrita, charmed, bent to touch their feet. The humble gesture from a highborn daughter-in-law of the Malik earned her great praise.

"Live long, daughter. Live long and un-widowed."

They left singing the young bride's praises.

A crowd gathered each afternoon to watch Satwant take his daily ride on Bakki. Women watched from their rooftops. The village urchins had to be scolded to get out of the way so their running and shouting would not startle the young mare. It was a sight to see. Satwant sitting tall in the silver-trimmed saddle, holding the braided reins. Bakki snorting and high-stepping through the gates, prancing down the path to the orchard, trotting on command, and then bursting into a blur of hooves and dust as she galloped and shook the earth beneath her before disappearing past the trees, covering an almost mile-long distance in a flash. Satwant was a glorious rider, moving as one with his horse.

"Wow, do it again," a girl begged.

Satwant motioned for Rabi to grab her and lift her to the saddle. Rabi was the caretaker of the cattle yard, and Baru's cousin.

The girl clung to him. "I'm so high up, it's scary!"

"Lift me up, too!" came the cries from a dozen more children with arms raised as the first child was lowered to the ground.

Satwant shook his head with a regretful smile and turned the mare into the courtyard.

Ajit laughed. "You could spend the whole day giving rides."

"I know, Bapuji." Satwant was still a little out of breath from the ride.

Ajit patted his shoulder. He always felt overwhelmed with pride at
the sight of his son galloping the magnificent beast.

Rustum Mukhia had bested every wrestler he had faced in the district and earned accolades and rewards from his fans, who numbered
in the tens of thousands. The Raja of the Bajigar tribes had dubbed
him Lion of the Bajigars. When Ajit won especially large amounts on
his bets, he would share some of his winnings with the wrestler, and,
much to Ajit's delight, Rustum Mukhia was using his windfalls to construct an impressive brick dwelling. Others too started to expand their
huts, replacing the reed walls with mud bricks, hanging proper doors,
installing windows. Some of the huts were given a coat of whitewash
decorated with religious symbols. It was a sure sign of the clan's intention to settle permanently, assuring Ajit the labour he needed.

Satwant was given a posting outside the distant city of Peshawar to
the west, on the quiet India-Afghanistan border.

"It is a frontier posting for three years," the Colonel told Ajit.
"Hopefully the next one will be a peacetime posting to a cantonment
in the interior, and he can take his wife to live there with him."

Ajit felt a great weight lift off his shoulders. The worry that his
son would end up in a combat role had haunted him and Inder, and
given grey hair to Siamo. The two women had observed every holy
day, fasted, prayed, and performed pilgrimages to the Golden Temple
in Amritsar and to the goddess Naina Devi in the hills. They'd given
alms to beggars at the gates, and sought blessings from the ash-cov-
ered sadhus who came by with their dreadlocks and steel tridents and
alms bowls.

Satwant's two-month furlough passed in a blur and the time came
for him to leave. Sher and his family came to bid him goodbye at the
railway station in Ludhiana. They gathered once again in the canteen
and ordered a meal.

Satwant asked his father, "Bapuji, please allow Amrita to go stay
with her parents for a month." As head of the household, this decision
was Ajit's prerogative.

Ajit nodded. "She can divide her time between Raikot and her parents' home in Palampur."

No one seemed to have an appetite. Inder and Siamo did not touch their plates, and Amrita sat quietly crying, her head bowed as her mother patted her back.

"Take care, my son," Siamo said, repeating the words as if in a trance.

"Be safe always," Inder said.

"I will," Satwant said, his eyes on Amrita.

The Frontier Mail arrived in a cloud of smoke and steam and came to a screeching halt. Whistles blew, coolies shouted, and engines chugged.

On the platform there was a frenzy of activity. Coolies with luggage on their heads charged for the doors followed by anxious passengers. People elbowed each other, pushed and shoved. Satwant managed to board the second-class sleeper compartment and they waited for his face to appear at a window. He opened the window and leaned out, and as soon as he did, Inder and Siamo clung to him, their wails almost as loud as the engine.

As the train pulled away, Ajit caught a glimpse of Satwant waving frantically to Amrita, who stood on her tiptoes waving back, tears flowing down her cheeks.

They stood on the platform until the train disappeared in the distance.

Bikram

As the steamer pulled away from the pier and Bikram watched the shoreline of Chittagong receding for the last time, he thought of the many close calls in the last three years that had jangled his nerves.

Not long after he had returned to duty following his wedding, the Japanese advanced all the way to the Indian border and occupied the Sentinel Islands of the Andamans. Chittagong was then well within the range of Japanese bombers, and a strict blackout protocol made for long and anxious nights. Japanese navy ships prowled the waters of the Bay of Bengal.

"I am dying to crush some enemy skulls with my bare hands," Mangal said with a grin one evening, squeezing his palms together.

Then, one cloudy night, hearing the howl of the sirens, Bikram jumped out of his cot. Running towards the bomb shelter, he collided with the massive bulk of Mangal. He felt the giant's iron grip start to squeeze his skull. He began to panic.

"Mangal, it's me, Bikram. Let go! Mangal, stop!" Did he know what he was doing? Was he sleepwalking?

Mangal's hands fell, and Bikram could see in Mangal's dark face the eerie glow of his teeth.

In the morning, he heard that coast guard ships had seen lights on the rising tower of a Japanese submarine, and they'd raised the alarm, fearing a torpedo attack on ships anchored in the harbour.

Mangal had a crazed look in his eyes. "I hope they sink the damn thing with depth charges. I want to see blood and body parts float up."

Bikram never said a word about Mangal almost squeezing him to death that night, but he was never quite able to put the episode out of his mind, either.

Though he didn't see any fighting firsthand, Bikram did witness its effects on soldiers brought back from the front. Men with severed limbs, burned bodies, torn by bullets and explosions, awaiting transportation to hospitals in Calcutta. The news in the summer of 1944 of Japanese defeat in the desperate battles of Kohima and Imphal, just a few hundred miles north of Chittagong, was greeted with much rejoicing, and Bikram felt his jaws begin to unclench, the tension leave his mind and body. The war was in its final throes. In June, Allied troops had landed on the beaches of Normandy to begin the liberation of Europe. French and American troops had liberated Paris in August. Guam had been liberated in July. Germany and Japan were in retreat. And with the dropping of the atom bombs on Japan, the war was finally over.

The Quartermaster General's stores began to be emptied and the place decommissioned. The Royal Indian Army declared a surplus of personnel. Major McKie had been promoted twice, and he used his authority as a Brigadier to grant Bikram, Mangal, Khan, and Thomas an honourable discharge, citing fatigue, ill health, and so on. Bikram finally packed his gear and went up the ramp of the rusting outbound steamer. He had yet to see his son, who was now more than two years old. He carried a small black-and-white photo of the boy in his breast pocket and took it out often.

He was travelling with Mangal, and six days later, they stepped down onto the railway platform in Khanna. Mangal was going on to Ludhiana, and the two embraced.

"You are like a brother to me, Bikram. Don't ever forget that. Call on me if you need anything."

"I will," Bikram said. "Come and visit me anytime you want."

Bikram's tonga pulled up in front of the steel gates of his parents' new home in their old neighbourhood. Papaji opened the gates and immediately hugged him. Maaji ran towards him, followed by Jagtar holding the hands of a toddler. As soon as he could extricate himself from his father's embrace, he rushed to kneel before the boy and tried taking him in his arms.

Sewa kicked and screamed.

"I am your father," Bikram said, trying to calm the boy.

"Let him go," Papaji said, and Sewa climbed tearfully into his grandfather's arms.

Bikram turned to Jagtar and saw, through her translucent dupatta, the tears running to her chin. She bent to touch his feet. "Sat Sri Akal, Ji. Welcome home."

It was torture not to be able to hold her in his arms, but it would not have been proper. The neighbours started trickling in and he turned to greet them.

Mirza Gujjar's beard had turned snow white, but he seemed hale and hearty. "Look at the place, Bikram." The dairyman beamed and pointed to the bungalow.

A wide verandah with round columns ran the width of the house. Cushioned cane chairs stood under it. The courtyard was large and tidy. The windows had iron bars and screens. His first impression was one of pride and awe; he couldn't believe that he had been able to provide such a large home for his family.

"Thank you." He bent to touch the elder's feet.

"May Allah grant you peace and good health," Mirza Gujjar intoned.

Papaji helped carry his bags through the high double doors, and he walked under the cool verandah into the house. The hallway ran right through to the back, which had double doors identical to those in the front. The high ceiling was painted a brilliant white and the walls a light shade of yellow. All the rooms led from the hallway and were large. Papaji showed him to his.

Spacious, with windows on two sides, it was furnished with two wide cots and twin steel wardrobes that took up an entire wall. The floor was polished granite. He walked around to get a feel, opened a single door, and stepped into a washroom with its own hand-pump above a concrete tub.

"The privy is at the back," Papaji said.

Jagtar came in and Papaji left them alone, closing the door after him. She immediately flew into his arms. Their embrace got tighter and tighter until they were out of breath, and he kissed her long and hard on her mouth. His hardness pressed against her.

"Later, Ji," she whispered, her breath warm on his ear.

He did not want to stop his wandering hands.

"*Later*, Ji," she said again, promise in her eyes.

She wiggled free and opened the door of a wardrobe to select a towel.

"I will draw your bath."

Sewa sat at the dining table on Maaji's lap and ate from her hand.

"He belongs to them, Ji." Jagtar smiled, handing Bikram a platter.

He looked at the food. The rotis were buttered, the eggplant subzi looked dry, and the split lentil dal had no hint of a tadka of sautéed onions and garlic. It tasted of turmeric and salt. He asked for pickles to add some flavour, and Jagtar brought him a jar of lime in vinegar.

He ate a little and pushed the plate away. Maaji looked up and frowned.

"I am not really hungry."

"I made everything, and you love my cooking, Bikram. Eat more."

He did not have the heart to tell her that his palate had changed. The fiery curries of Bengal had made the simple fare of her kitchen taste bland.

Jagtar ate slowly and watched him as he pulled the plate closer and took a bite.

"Water, Ji." She handed him a brass tumbler and rose to pour from a jug. He caught a whiff of the essence of rose perfume and felt a jolt in his groin.

"Something sweet later?" he asked, holding her eyes.

She blushed a deep red.

"I made halwa and rice pudding," Maaji said.

"With sultanas?"

"Just the way you like it, my son. It is a good day to have you back under our roof with us. I thank Waheguru-ji." She folded her hands, and Sewa followed suit.

It made Bikram smile. Sewa buried his head in Maaji's neck.

"Go to your Papa," she said, but he only clung tighter to her.

"Give him time. This is the first time he has seen you," Papaji said.

"I don't believe it. I show him Ji's photo every day. He calls Ji his Papa."

"Say something, Sewa." Maaji sat him up straight.

"Scary man."

"Your Papa is not a scary man," Jagtar scolded.

"He is." Sewa pouted.

"Little ruffian," Jagtar said.

"Witch," Sewa said.

Jagtar sighed and shrugged. "He has a vocabulary."

Sewa slept with Maaji in her room, and Papaji had his cot in the gathering room. Jagtar closed the windows and locked their door from the inside. The room was well lit with a large lantern. Bikram's bags were still unpacked, and before he could get a hold of her she'd wriggled away and knelt on the floor beside them. She asked him for the keys. He sat on the cot and tossed them to her.

She opened the first bag and started taking out his clothes, piling them beside her.

"Where is it?" she asked.

"Where is what?"

"The bundles of notes and the tins full of gold."

He pointed to the long duffel bag. She opened the small brass lock and took out a folded summer blanket, some towels. Then her eyes shone and her lips parted. He could hear her breathing. She began to dig through the bag, and with a loud sigh she at last sat back holding two bundles wrapped in oilcloth. In a second, she had the notes out.

"Oh, the smell of money." She lifted them to her nostrils.

"They are musty."

"Not to me." She stood up and brought the notes, still tied with twine, to the cot.

He grabbed her by the arm and pulled her beside him.

"Ji." She presented him her mouth.

He began to caress and kiss her. She didn't release the bundles. Under him, she held on to the money as he made love to her. As his breathing grew deeper, beneath the essence of rose he could smell the musty notes as she wrapped her arms around his neck, moaned with closed eyes, and moved in rhythm with him.

After they'd finished and washed, Jagtar busied herself putting away his clothes in the wardrobe. She did not touch the duffel bag until she had finished going through all the clothes, sorted out the toiletries, and discovered the gifts he had bought for her and Sewa.

"Like them?" he asked as she felt the fabrics.

She nodded.

"Come on. Finish, then. I am ready for another go."

"Patience, Ji." Jagtar closed his wardrobe, the key still in the lock, and opened hers. It had drawers with locks.

Bikram watched as she took out each bundle of notes and laid it carefully in a drawer. He could see the goosebumps on her arms as the glitter returned to her eyes, and when she turned he saw her nipples were hard and pointy. He rose, put his hand between her legs, and felt the moisture on his fingertips.

"Please, Ji. Can't you see I am working?"

After she'd finished and locked the long, deep drawer, she gave herself to him.

"I missed this for so long," she whispered, her voice hoarse and husky.

"Papaji, can I explain some things to you?" he asked when they went out for a walk together.

"Something I should worry about?" Papaji stopped at the ring road and looked around.

"Let's sit under that tree," Bikram said.

"You are not in some kind of trouble, are you? Discharged from the army and all that?"

"No. In fact, the story is a happy one."

He slowly laid out the opportunity he had taken advantage of in the Quartermaster General's office "to earn a bit more." It was nothing unusual, just what they called "leakage," and it happened everywhere, he assured his father.

"How much did you earn?" Papaji asked. His face had fallen.

He decided to lie. "Just under a lakh."

"Rupees?"

Bikram nodded. Papaji squinted his eyes and looked away.

He realized then that his father was a man who had always led a simple life, and now he'd been told that he was living on the proceeds of his son's crimes.

"That sum is more than I earned in my entire life, many times over, in fact. What if you are discovered?"

"Not a chance. No one will ever know, and we left nothing incriminating behind."

"I wondered sometimes. The money you sent for Pyari's

wedding and the court case, then more for building the house and your wedding."

"What happened to the lawsuit?"

"I won."

"You have our land now?"

"I legally own it. But your uncle will not let me even step on it."

"He will not give up possession?"

Papaji nodded his head. "You know me, Bikram. I am not a violent man."

"I will settle our accounts, Papaji. You will see."

Later that day, when Bikram went to the bazaar to get his turbans dyed and starched, he passed by the liquor vend. A rounder and grizzled Golu was holding court. An open bottle stood on the rickety table he and his friends sat at.

I will settle with you, too, Golu, he thought. *You will find out just the kind of man I am now.*

He suddenly had a spring in his step, and an inspiration. He had an idea.

Bikram and Jagtar paid a visit to her parents, and Chand and Beeji greeted him like a long-lost son. They ushered Bikram into the gathering room, a large space with several cushioned cane chairs and side tables supporting brass vases filled with fresh flowers. He had noticed the rows of colourful plants running along the courtyard walls.

"I like growing things," Chand said.

"Still a Jat at heart. Can't stay away from the soil." Beeji beamed.

Chand and his wife looked younger. Their cheeks were fuller and their frames heavier. Both wore well-cut clothes, polished shoes, and tortoiseshell glasses. Chand's beard was neatly trimmed, and he wore a natty maroon turban that gave him the air of an aging dandy. He sported a heavy wristwatch and a ring with a huge ruby that he seemed to like waving around.

"You never wrote us to tell us that you were coming on holiday," Chand said.

"Ji is back permanently, discharged from the army under the surplus provision," Jagtar told them.

They exchanged quick glances before Beeji said, "But you are still young, Bikram Singh."

"I got what I needed from the army, and more. I am tired. I want to live with my family and watch it grow."

After they had caught up, enjoyed their treats and cups of carda-mom- and fennel-spiced tea, Chand stood up.

"You must be anxious about your business. Come to my office and we can talk in private."

"I will help you in the kitchen, Beeji." Jagtar began to clear the plates and cups.

Chand's accounting was pristine and precise. Bikram studied the meticulous entries in a thick ledger. All the sums seemed to be in order. He read the monthly rents and interest incomes from monies lent to local merchants; they came to over a thousand rupees per month, more than enough to keep him comfortable, fifteen times greater than his army salary. He owned tenements, warehouses, and shops in Samrala and Khanna. Almost a hundred acres of farmland abutting the municipal boundaries that Chand felt could become very valuable for future housing developments. "The population is only going to increase."

Chand pulled out the deeds from a heavy, steel strong box with a huge lock. Bikram studied them and was shocked. Each one listed him and Jagtar as the registered co-owners.

"I needed her to sign the purchase documents in your absence, Bikram Singh," Chand explained. "Her name had to be included."

Bikram nodded.

"Did you bring more money?"

"Yes."

"How much?"

"Two lakh."

Chand sat thinking for some moments.

"There are some excellent properties that kind of sum will buy."

Bikram looked up.

"For example, Mohamad Khan's mansion and Mirza Gujjar's dairy, plus a few more."

"What?"

"The market has been very active lately. Independence will come, and this idea of partition is not going away—a Hindu India and a Muslim Pakistan. As I told you, since Ludhiana is a majority non-Muslim area it will very likely remain Hindu. So Muslim landowners are selling here and buying in Lahore or Sialkot."

"Lahore will be part of this new Pakistan? The Sikhs will never agree to it. Lahore was the capital of the Sikh Empire under Maharaja Ranjit Singh."

"A hundred years ago. It has been under British rule ever since."

"And did the British not promise us Sikhs our own country?"

Chand gave a bitter snort and shook his head.

"No, it will never happen," Bikram said bitterly. "They will not sacrifice Sikh land for a Muslim state," and he handed the documents back.

"Say what you will, my son. The promises of the British cannot be trusted, could never be trusted." Chand locked the deeds away in a steel drawer.

"Tens of thousands of Sikhs died fighting their bloody wars. How can they forget our sacrifices?"

Chand swore in disgust. "Because we are not united. Right now, the Sikhs who belong to the Indian National Congress want to stay in India. The rest belong to different factions and cults, like the Akali Dal."

"What do you mean?"

"Well, the Akalis claim to be the true representatives of the Sikhs. But there are five different political groups who call themselves Akali Dal, each with its own leader, and they are all busy quarrelling with each other. The British understand the art of divide and conquer. Imagine if all the Akalis united in a common front. They would be undeniable."

Bikram sat pondering the information.

"Tell me more about this Mohamad Khan."

"A prominent merchant in Samrala, descended from Pathan royalty. He's a respected philanthropist and patron to many causes. I'm sure you have passed by his mansion. It soars three storeys high."

"And it's for sale?"

"Very discreetly, yes."

"Have you told Jagtar?"

Chand shook his head. "I have trouble enough trying to keep her mouth shut. You will have to tell her sternly to watch her tongue. She is like her mother. Boastful and a show-off."

Jagtar wanted to host a celebration.

"We have not done a thing to celebrate our son, the house, or anything else," she pointed out. "You were away. That's why. And I pledged a thanksgiving Path for you to return safe and sound to me."

As usual, Jagtar's idea was sound. The Path, a ritual prayer recitation, would enhance his local reputation as a pious man.

"Well, now I'm back. Select a date and I will make the arrangements."

"It will be a chance to invite all our relatives."

He nodded. "And a few friends."

They visited the bazaar together to shop, Jagtar veiled in her finery, Sewa on Maaji's hip, Papaji carrying empty cloth bags and a wallet stuffed with cash. They visited the dry foods store, the halwai's for the finest sweets, a greengrocer, and the cloth merchant. Finally they stopped at the juice vendor and ordered four glasses of orange juice. While they were fussing over their drinks, suddenly a hush fell over the bazaar, and Bikram heard the steady clip-clop of hooves approaching.

"Look at that, Maaji," Jagtar exclaimed.

It was the most splendid horse Bikram had ever seen. Huge, with large, alert ears, flared nostrils, and darting eyes. It high-stepped in the middle of the paved road as people made way. The rider sat tall in the glinting saddle, the strap of a double-barrelled shotgun criss-crossing a bandolier over his chest.

As he approached, Papaji shouted, "Satwant Singh. Is that you?"

The rider pulled the reins and looked towards them, and recognition dawned on his handsome face. He smiled, and gracefully swung off the saddle. He folded his hands and bent to touch Papaji's feet.

"Masterji, Sat Sri Akal."

"Bless you, my son. Live long." Papaji embraced him, and his face lit up with pride.

Men and women watched open-mouthed the elegant display of humility performed by the tall young man. It elevated the rider even further in their eyes. Maaji stood wide-eyed beside an equally stunned

Jagtar. Bikram felt his throat dry up, and he muttered a hoarse greeting when Papaji turned to introduce him.

"My son, Bikram Singh. Your father helped him join the army. Remember, you carried the letters?"

"I remember very well, Masterji. Sat Sri Akal."

Bikram returned the bow with folded hands.

"Come visit with us," Papaji said.

"Please forgive me, Masterji. I must reach Manki village before noon. I have an appointment there."

"Big horse," Sewa said.

"My grandson," Papaji explained.

Before Papaji could finish, Satwant had scooped Sewa up and swung him onto the saddle, holding him there.

Sewa clapped happily. "Look, I am so tall!"

A vision flashed before Bikram's eyes. A grown Sewa, handsome and tall just like Satwant Singh, riding an elegant mare through the bazaar in Samrala and everyone stopping to gape at him. It burned into his brain.

"Here you go." Satwant placed Sewa back in Papaji's arms, bent to touch his feet again, and turned to put his foot in the stirrup. In one graceful motion, he was seated tall in the saddle. He pulled the reins and the mare took a few steps back. He raised a hand in a salute and trotted his horse up the road.

The bazaar began to buzz again. The family drank their juice slowly, stunned into silence by the extraordinary event.

On the day that Mangal and his brothers roared into town in their motor car, their guns slung over their shoulders, half the bazaar quickly shut down. That's what Bikram heard. The merchants feared that a daylight robbery was about to take place and alerted the local police. Told where they would be staying, a nervous uniformed police sub-inspector came by to confirm, followed by a group of rifle-toting constables. Bikram assured them that Mangal was his guest, a fellow soldier visiting for the Path, and he invited them to stay and partake in the langar, the meal offered by the family to anyone who wished to eat.

Sewa stared at the big man. Mangal played hide and seek with him, and everyone gathered watched in amusement as he tried hiding his considerable bulk behind the columns of the verandah. Sewa was hugely entertained. He even let Mangal grab him and throw him into the air, catch him, and do it all over again. Bikram watched with a wry grin. Why had he not thought of playing some game with the boy?

After the langar, they waited for the neighbours to leave before giving out gifts to the relatives. Gold bangles and silk suits, turbans and shawls; the children got clothes and money. Papaji moved around, making sure that no one lacked for anything. Mangal had brought a case of army rum, which delighted all the men.

"I need you to stay," Bikram told the big man. "I asked you to come because I have a couple of problems to sort out."

"Sure."

"Tell your brothers to stay, too."

The next day, Bikram, Mangal and his brothers all rode to the ancestral home in Mirpura and knocked on the gates. Bikram's uncle came out and immediately stepped back, seeing the guns and the men carrying them.

"I am here to take possession of my land," Bikram said.

People started to gather on the path to witness the confrontation. Uncle's eyes darted from one kinsman to another, seeking support. When no one stepped forward, he folded his hands and pleaded with Mangal.

"I am an ordinary Jat trying to raise a family," he said.

"You are an arrogant man with a dung-filled skull who has tormented his brother for ten years and usurped his rightful inheritance, despite a court order. Your days of muscling in on your brother's share are over," Mangal spoke.

Bikram's male cousins came to stand behind their father, armed with axes and swords, and Mangal and his brothers broke out in laughter.

"Do you plan to lie dead on a burning pyre at the cremation grounds today?" Mangal asked.

His uncle's eyes widened, his body shook, and he waved his arms. "No, no, no. Please leave my sons out of it."

"In that case, I will grant you one week. Pay the outstanding rents in full to Bikram's father. Negotiate rent for future sharecropping of his land and for living on his half of the ancestral courtyard. Failing that, there will be no more notice, only mayhem," Mangal said.

"Bikram," his uncle beseeched, "please tell my dear brother Lal Singh I will visit tomorrow and sort out our differences."

Later that night, they found Golu holding court beside the liquor vend with the town dandies.

Mangal pulled a chair from a table beside theirs and invited his brothers and Bikram to sit. He ordered a tray of fried fish and pulled two bottles of army rum from a bag. He asked the nervous server for a jug of water and glasses.

He poured out the shots, then turned to salute Golu. The dandy bowed and raised his glass.

"Join me." Mangal patted the seat beside him.

"Sure."

"I hear that you are the strong man in town, and I am here to pay homage to you." Mangal poured him a shot.

Golu puffed out his chest, accepted the drink, and raised it in salute before quaffing it.

"Another?" Mangal asked.

"Sure."

"This one is to toast my friend and brother Bikram Singh. You remember him, don't you?"

Golu bowed to acknowledge him and raised his glass.

"You remember wanting to screw Bikram's sisters?"

Golu stared at the giant, his eyes widening. His dandy friends began to back away.

Mangal placed a massive paw on the man's shoulder. "I was told that you like limping and making scary faces. Golu's eyes bulged. "Do you?"

Golu started to plead. But in the blink of an eye, Mangal smashed Golu's foot with the heel of his boot and tore the dandy's cheeks with his fingernails. Golu screamed. Everyone watched, horrified, as Mangal lifted the screaming man like a rag doll and flung him across the road while the other dandies fled in panic.

"Listen here, listen all," Mangal shouted. "No one, and I mean no one, will ever trouble Bikram Singh or his family. If you dare, you'd better buy a shroud first."

BOOK TWO

1947–1951

Basanti

Basanti's father, Changu, and some of the other Bajigar men decided to take their families and travel west to Kila Tikka Khan, because there was good work there digging a canal. When that job was finished, Changu worked in the fields, at the brick kiln, or cutting wood.

The girls left their dera only in groups, to scavenge, to sing and dance, or to pluck cotton. Basanti and Devi were never out of the sight of their grandmother, Dadi, or some other elder. Dadi had taught Basanti how to dig grass by the roots with a trowel, beat the dirt off it, and bundle it in a gunny sack for the camel to eat, and that was her job today. Her shoulders ached, sweat rolled into her eyes, and she got blisters on her palm. While she was working, her little brother Piara waddled by, chasing a butterfly.

"Does he ever stop?" Devi asked.

They called him the little Dervish. Always exploring, following, darting here and there. Dadi was forever chasing after him in case he ran into the creek or under a cow. At night, he snored like an old man, even louder than Bhapa. Basanti was grateful that he shared a cot with her brother Gulab and not Dadi.

Piara was only two, and Gulab was supposed to be looking after him, but Devi was always too happy to play with the little boy. Whenever she called his name he came running into her arms. She wobbled on her thin legs trying to adjust him onto a hip before taking him away to keep him out of mischief.

Better her than me, Basanti thought. *He probably weighs as much as she does. Mata feeds him all the tastiest tidbits.*

When the gunny sack was full—it took them most of the afternoon—Basanti helped drag it back to the dera for the camel. Her father had warned her, "A lazy camel is a dangerous beast." She had heard enough horrible tales of camels biting and kicking, and she kept her distance from the animal, which stood tethered to a post.

Devi and Basanti were cousins the same age, twelve. And they
had been promised to cousins, too, the son and nephew of the famed
Rustum Mukhia, the Lion of the Bajigars, who was from a different
clan from theirs. Now that they had left the old village far behind,
they had a new Mukhia to lead them. But he wasn't nearly as exciting
as the Rustum.

Basanti's father often boasted of his friendship with the legendary
wrestler.

"I was the drummer who brought him luck."

"Yes you did, Changu," his wife would say with pride.

Now when they went out, the men stared at Basanti and Devi for a
lot longer than they used to. It made Basanti uncomfortable. She was
particularly bothered by the glare of the mullah who stood outside the
mosque in Kila Tikka Khan. His eyes seemed to go right through her.

One day, as they were walking they passed a group of village bachelors. The men were openly leering at them.

Dadi sighed. "Ill winds are starting to blow."

"Ill winds?"

"Bad times are coming, Basanti."

"Why do you say that?" It made her queasy.

"My heels are itching. We will leave here soon."

Dadi was revered by the clan. She knew all the old stories and the
healing arts. She could offer relief from stomachaches, fevers, cuts,
and bites. Basanti would help Dadi collect the herbs and barks she
used in her concoctions. She'd even heard people say that Dadi could
see the future, and Basanti did not doubt it. She had been under Dadi's
wing since she was little. She even shared her cot.

Dadi hurried their pace as the sun sank further into the horizon and
the light took on a golden hue. The rains had been heavy this season
and water stood in ditches everywhere. They were within sight of their
dera now and the silver streak of the stream. The sound of bells from
cattle returning from pastures to their pens floated in the air.

"Do you remember the long walk from Raikot, girls?" Dadi seemed
to be a bit out of breath now.

"A little."

"Three weeks, and you both complained the whole way."

"I remember being so hungry," Devi said.

"Are we going to walk all that way back?" Basanti asked anxiously.

One evening, Basanti's father returned to the dera looking unusually tired. There was an anxious look in his eyes. During the night, her parents talked in whispers. They sighed and tossed on their cot. Since they all slept together under the same roof, it made for a long, sleepless night for her as well. The next morning, the men stayed at the dera instead of going out to work. The Mukhia set a cot under the shadiest tree and his wife covered it with her best blanket. The men spoke in low voices, and the women seemed jumpy, and loudly scolded their children.

Basanti understood the reason for the commotion when the Chaudhry arrived. The Chaudhry owned the village and all the lands around it, as well as the seven neighbouring ones. People said his sharecroppers numbered in the hundreds. He had recently taken another wife, and Basanti and Devi had danced at the wedding, a grand affair. The Chaudhry's mother, the aristocratic, white-haired Begum, had rewarded the girls well for their performance, and the entire dera had feasted for three days there.

The Chaudhry was accompanied by the Mullah and followed by two men wearing bandoliers and carrying long guns in their hands. The Mukhia, carrying his traditional curved staff, greeted the guests nervously and sat the Chaudhry and the Mullah on the cot. Their guards stood behind them and stared at the people, who were sitting together on the ground. The Mukhia squatted at the Chaudhry's feet.

"The time I thought would never arrive has come," the Chaudhry said, after declining refreshments. "You must all make a decision today—to stay here or leave tonight."

"Those willing to accept Allah will be welcomed into the village with open arms," the Mullah said. "No harm will ever come to them, and they will live with us as equals in our new nation of Pakistan."

People turned to each other and spoke in whispers.

"Many are leaving," the Chaudhry said, "but I hear of massacres in the hills."

It sent a chill up Basanti's spine and made her want to pee.

"Tell us, oh Malik, you tell us what to do." The Mukhia bent down and held the Chaudhry's feet. It was a cowardly gesture, Basanti thought, and it brought grins to the faces of the guards.

Basanti glanced at Devi. The fear she felt was also in her cousin's eyes.

The Mullah smiled and nodded and combed his hennaed beard with his fingers.

"Convert and be safe. Utter the name of Allah now, I urge you."

The Chaudhry raised his hands and motioned the Mullah to be quiet.

"Do what you choose. Stay if you want, or go if you must."

Basanti's father stood up and joined his hands. "We will go, Malik."

The Mullah's eyes flared.

"You will put your women and children in danger. It is a hundred miles to the border as the crow flies. You will not make it alive. The countryside is filled with marauders." The Mullah was almost frothing at the mouth.

"I was born a Hindu and will die a Hindu," her father said.

She saw the Mukhia stare at him as more men stood up. The guards shifted their guns from hand to hand.

"You are madmen," the Mullah said contemptuously.

Children hopped into their mothers' laps and clung to them. Whispers of "Rama, Rama, Rama" spread through the clan.

The Chaudhry stood up and called for silence.

"All right, then. I will provide you with an armed escort to the border of my lands. Beyond that, may Allah smile benevolently upon you all and keep you safe."

When the Mullah marched over to her father she ran to him and held his hand.

"Changu, I beseech you. Convert. My son will take Basanti as his wife."

"She is promised."

The Mullah shook his head at her father, who stared defiantly at him.

"Then cut her hair. Dress her like a boy. The marauders might be fooled into sparing her."

Her father bent to touch the Mullah's feet, but he just shook his head and grimaced. He placed his palm on her head. "Khuda Hafiz, Basanti. Go with God."

Basanti wept inconsolably as Dadi held her arms and her mother snipped her long locks off at the scalp. Devi kneeled beside her, and then it was her turn to go through the same ordeal. When Mata stopped cutting, they fell into each other's arms, their chests heaving.

Gulab grinned. "You look ugly."

Dadi reached out and brought him to his knees with a stinging slap and he ran crying to their mother.

"Go help Bhapa load the camel, boy." Mata was in no mood to either console him or berate her.

Dadi pushed Basanti and Devi into the hut. "Come on, girls. Put on your brothers' long kurtas."

When Basanti took off her own kurti, her grandmother looked at her chest and nodded. "Good. They're barely lime-sized buds." Then she pulled one of Gulab's kurtas over her head. Finally Dadi gathered her girl clothes, folded them, and stuffed them into a gunny sack filled with bedding and blankets. "Take this out to your father."

Basanti obeyed, her eyes unseeing and her ears deaf to the cacophony around her.

Just past dusk, six armed men on horseback arrived. The clan formed a caravan and began their long walk under a full moon. Basanti understood that they were no longer welcome in their village because they were Hindus, and now that the land was called Pakistan and belonged to the Muslims only, they would have to find a new place to live.

Basanti's mother rode the camel, holding little Piara in her arms. Bhapa walked on one side of the lumbering beast and Dadi on the other. Gulab carried a short spear in one hand and a light axe in the other. He seemed to grow taller when he was handed the weapons. The silence of the hour was broken only by the cry of a baby or the howl of an animal prowling in the fields. Puddles glinted in the starlit night. The leader of the guards rode back and forth, urging a steady pace, and he allowed only one stop before sunrise. Basanti walked as if in a trance, lifting one foot after the other. When the camel in front of her lifted its tail and let loose a barrage of droppings she carefully dodged it, but she was tempted to stop and gather the dung to dry for fuel.

"What a waste," she thought.

Towards dawn they stopped at a small village, where the leader let
them water the animals at the well and fire up the communal tandoor
to bake rotis. The locals offered food left over from their dinners the
night before.

"This is where we turn back," the leader of the guards said.

Basanti saw fear fill her father's eyes. As they fled the dera, Basanti
had pulled the palm-sized idol of Laxmi from the shrine that stood at
the entrance and stuffed it into a pocket of her kurta. Now she began
to rub it through the cloth, muttering prayers. "Save us, dear goddess.
Save us, dear goddess. Protect us, dear goddess. Take a human form,
Laxmi Maa. Guide us to safety."

They formed their line again, but this time the Mukhia led the caravan, seated on his camel.

"Keep moving, now. Keep moving. This is no time to linger," he
exhorted.

Every time they approached a village, Basanti's heart rose to her
throat. People stood on roofs to watch them walk by. The streets
stood empty, gates closed. They passed through silently and without any trouble. She called for the goddess's benediction many, many
times.

Smoke rose from a village a short distance from their path. Blood-
curdling cries came, carried by the breeze. Dadi prayed loudly—
"Rama, Rama, Rama"—over and over. Other women picked up the
chant. Basanti tried, but no sound came from her throat. Even the
animals seemed to sense danger and needed no prodding.

They stopped beside a pond surrounded by huge banyan trees. A
man climbed a tree to keep watch while the animals were watered,
babies put to breast, limbs massaged, and food was served. Basanti
wasn't even aware she had closed her eyes until she came to with a
start.

"Riders!"

They rose as one and turned their anxious faces in the direction the
watchman was pointing. Basanti climbed up a tree trunk and saw two
men approaching fast on horses from the direction they had come. As
the riders came closer she saw their uniforms, and then their guns, and
then she quickly clambered down and hid behind Bhapa.

The first to reach them, a grey-haired man, dismounted and spoke to them. "Don't fear. We're policemen."

"I am very happy to see you," the Mukhia said.

"If you hurry ahead, you'll soon reach a refugee camp set up by the army. From there, you'll have an armed escort to the border."

"Will you take us there?" the Mukhia asked.

"No. We have to round up other refugees, those who are not travelling safely in groups. There are marauders in the area."

"Did you see the village on fire back there? What's happening?"

The man put his foot in the stirrup, nodded his head slowly, and looked away.

Soon they approached a large village, and they hesitated. Women in burkas stood on rooftops, and Basanti's father looked around in alarm.

"Where are all the men?"

"Salaam alaikum." The greeting arose from several throats, and in the half-light Basanti saw unarmed men come forward onto the path.

The Mukhia slid off his camel and approached them with folded hands. "We are poor Bajigars. I seek your permission to pass through your village, my Khans."

"I welcome you and your clan in peace. Please proceed," a booming voice replied.

The women disappeared from the rooftops as the men made way for them to enter. With sweat trickling down her spine Basanti urged the camel forward.

A gate creaked open and two women in burkas emerged, offering bundles of food. Other gates swung open, and soon the street was filled with their new benefactors. They were greeted with friendly cries of "Khuda hafiz," "Shukria," "Salaam," and "Namashkar."

"Carry on in peace," a man with a long beard shouted. "May Allah guide you home in safety."

Basanti bowed and bowed and bowed at every step and cradled the warm bundle of rotis she had been given. The sun sat just above the distant horizon and the light turned golden.

"Keep moving, now. Keep moving." The Mukhia was perched once again on his camel.

Basanti managed to pull a warm paratha from the bundle—it had a heavenly smell of butter—and she began to chew. The bread, with all its salty goodness, melted in her mouth. *Thank you, Laxmi Maa, thank you,* she repeated silently. Her legs became steadier and her vision cleared.

Just past dusk, after they had travelled another day, an authoritative voice pierced the darkness.

"Who goes there?" It stopped them in their tracks.

A light came on and Basanti saw a flat, round face and an olive-green hat.

"Soldiers," the Mukhia called back to them. "Gurkha soldiers. We are safe."

Cheers erupted, and the camels strained at the reins.

"Watch out."

An agitated camel brayed and stomped the ground. Someone screamed.

"Get it under control," the Mukhia ordered as her father raced past her.

She hung on to the reins of their own camel for dear life, glad for once that it was almost two days since their beast had been fed.

It took a while to restore order, and then a flashlight shone in her face.

"Thirteen."

She squeezed her eyes closed, then opened them to see Dadi's face glow for a moment, and she realized that the soldiers were counting them.

"Fourteen."

The rest was a jumble of more walking, following the lights of a motor car, and arriving at the camp just as the moon gave shape to figures. She ate more parathas dipped in dal, drank water from a goat-skin, and fell asleep.

She came awake when Dadi shook her.

"It's almost daybreak."

It was a vision that would stay with her the rest of her life. An elegant, uniformed Sikh stopped by on a white horse. His smile lit up his face and made her heart skip a beat.

"I am Captain Satwant Singh, the commander of the camp."

She gaped at him. Devi pinched her behind and said, "Look at him, gives me goosebumps."

"Captain Sahib." The Mukhia bowed with folded hands. "This is my clan."

"You are Bajigars?"

"Yes, Sahib. We come from Kila Tikka Khan."

"And you are the Mukhia, I presume. How many in your clan?"

He looked like a god. Towering over them. Seated on a muscled mount she feared could break out in a gallop any moment. It looked so powerful and impatient, raising and dropping hoof after hoof. The Captain barely moved. He had such kind eyes.

"Seventy-three souls, Captain Sahib."

The way he pronounced the title, the lilt of his voice lengthening the word, seemed to please the officer. "How many women and girls?"

"I will find out. I can't count."

"Come to my tent once you know. We also need everyone's name and age. Bring the heads of the families with you. I will be very happy to be reacquainted with the Bajigar people."

"Yes, Sahib."

He will hear my name and write it down, Basanti thought happily. Then, she glanced at Devi, with her shorn hair, wearing a kurta, and her heart sank.

"He thinks we are stinky boys," she whispered.

Devi's face fell and her shoulders slumped.

"Lift up the front of your kurta," Basanti whispered. "Show him you are a girl."

Devi elbowed her in the ribs.

"Ow!"

"Boys," the Captain scolded.

Dadi cuffed them both.

Basanti and Devi walked aimlessly around the camp. People sat beside their oxcarts under makeshift shades. Some people were baking rotis and boiling lentils on their fires, the aroma spreading in the still air. They passed a row of tents with their sides folded up; a few soldiers sat on iron cots cleaning their guns or smoking birris. One tent had a big white cross painted on it, and inside it were the sick and wounded,

people moaning in pain, holding limbs in bloodied bandages, leaning on sticks. A man in a grimy white coat was writing on a wooden
board. They came to a row of latrines, stinking, and ran away.

Two lorries rumbled in, belching thick smoke, and people gathered
around. The girls could hear moans coming from inside. A flap was
lifted and a stretcher lowered. Basanti closed her eyes at the grotesque
sight of a butchered body.

"Kill me," it begged. "Oh, kill me."

She ran from the gory scene with Devi at her heels.

They ran back to their camp and collapsed in a heap, holding each
other, sobbing.

"We move," the Mukhia said that evening.

"When?" her father asked.

"At daybreak. Now listen here, everyone. Just because we have the
army escorting us, that does not mean we are safe. There are thousands of refugees, and the Captain has only a hundred Gurkhas to
protect us. He told me to warn you to be vigilant and ready to repel
an attack. The marauders will sneak in at night as we camp in the
open to grab our camels. Kidnap our women."

"Rama, Rama, Rama," Basanti's mother cried out in a whimper.

"Any time we go through a narrow passage surrounded by woods,
houses, or crops, be extra vigilant. If we have to make a long line,
then the soldiers get spread out and can't protect us all. It becomes
every man for himself."

"Rama, Rama, Rama." The other women joined in now, praying
and rocking on their haunches.

"We will have to cut through villages and towns, and it will get
more and more dangerous the closer we get to the border. Just as we
are being pushed to leave this new Muslim nation, so are Muslims
on the other side being forced to abandon their homes to make new
lives here. And it seems that many of these Muslim refugees have suffered greatly. They want revenge, and they are willing to loot and steal
to win back what they've lost. They are inciting the locals against us
with their tales of woe."

They were just three days into their march when the Mukhia's
nightmarish scenario came true.

They were passing through a town on a long road hemmed in by walled courtyards. Basanti saw the Gurkhas kneeling and wondered why they were aiming their rifles at empty rooftops. Bhapa held the short spear in one hand and the axe in the other. Both Gulab and Dadi walked with their heads under the camel.

"Allahu Akbar!"

The cry froze her on the spot.

Men rose over the walls, their swords glinting. Then stones flew from the rooftops.

"Kill the Kuffars!"

Suddenly the Gurkhas were firing on the attackers. In the chaos of gunfire, slashing swords, axes, and spears Basanti knelt on the cobblestones holding the reins as their camel frantically shrieked and bucked. Screams and shouts filled the air.

"Piara!"

Mata was atop the camel, frantically waving.

"Piara, Piara, Piara!"

Something flashed in the corner of her eye, and Basanti turned to see a sword rising above Bhapa. Before she could scream, there was the pop of a shot and the attacker's face filled with blood. She turned to see the Captain wading through the melee, his pistol pointed forward.

"Shoot!" he roared, and the rhythmic, heart-stopping rattle of steady fire sent the attackers back over the walls.

"Move, move, move!" the Captain shouted.

Basanti spied a bundle lying beside her. When she turned it over she screamed. It was Piara, limp as a rag doll, blood oozing from his nose. She snatched him up and ran after the Captain's white horse, trying not to lose track of it as it weaved in and out of the chaos on the road. She ran with every ounce of strength she had, and finally caught up with him.

"My brother, Sahib. Save my brother! Please!" she yelled.

The horse stopped and turned. The Captain leaned down, grabbed her by the waist, and lifted her in front of him on the saddle. While he held her safely and she desperately clutched the bundle that was her little brother, they raced towards the lorry with the big white cross on its side. He gently set her down.

"Injured child!" he yelled to a white-coated man. Then, spinning his horse around, he rode back into the town.

"Jump in." The man reached down and pulled them up and into the slow-moving lorry. She struggled to gain her footing on the lurching floor, and reluctantly allowed Piara to be taken from her arms. "He will be all right here." The man helped her off the lorry, and more stretchers arrived.

Basanti ran back into the crowd, looking anxiously for her family, fighting against the people and the camels and the wagons that were moving swiftly past her towards safety.

"Mata!" she called. But every woman there, it seemed, was a mother, and they would look up at her and then clutch their own children even closer. Just when she felt there was nothing left to do but drop to the ground and cry, she heard her name being called. Her Bhapa pushed through the crowd and rushed towards her, and she held on to him for dear life.

That night, they made camp as far from the town as they could go. Those who were critically injured were taken to the hospital lorry, and they tended the rest of their wounded as best they could. Dadi treated wounds and made her healing concoctions. Sleep did not come easily, and the next morning the camp was quiet. Even the children were subdued, as though waiting for something to happen to make things normal again.

Finally, as they were going about their chores, they saw the Captain riding towards them, holding a bundle. He dismounted and held it out. It was completely shrouded.

Mata screamed, "My son, my son!"

The little Dervish was no more.

Mata howled her grief. Dadi beat her breasts and thighs. Other women of the clan joined her, raising their faces to the sky to keen. Bhapa took Piara into his arms, undid the shroud, stared at the face, then he knelt and laid the lifeless body on the ground.

"Wake up, you. Wake up, little Dervish," Gulab called. "I will never again complain about you." Bhapa picked up the bundle and cradled it in his arms for a while. Basanti clung to Devi, who cried the loudest, beating her face with her hands. "Piara!" He was her favourite and her shadow.

The Mukhia brought out a spade and the men crossed a ditch and began to dig under an acacia tree.

For days Basanti's mother did not eat or take even a sip of water. All she did was cry and blame herself for letting the little Dervish slip out of her hands as the camel reared and stones flew. Gulab went completely silent. All of them went over what happened, again and again.

"The man went to strike Bhapa with his sword. I saw it all," Basanti said. "But the Captain shot the man."

"Saved my life," Bhapa said, and he took a long puff from a hookah.

"Then I turned and saw Piara lying beside the foot of the camel."

"You grabbed Piara and ran after the Captain, Basanti," Bhapa said. "You ran like the wind."

It did not help. Piara was dead. She felt as though she had lost a part of herself.

They moved on. There was little to eat and a long distance to walk every day. Basanti's spirits flagged; she could feel how her hip bones protruded. Even the camel looked skeletal and brayed plaintively.

"We will only be safe among our own," Dadi said.

"I took this." Basanti dug into her pocket and pulled out the idol of the goddess Laxmi. She showed it to Dadi, who took it, rubbed it reverently, kissed it, and then passed it around to be worshipped by the others.

The Mukhia's wife gave her a cross look. "It belongs to me."

"Keep it," Basanti replied. "It did not save my brother."

"Stupid girl with a big mouth."

"Watch your tongue," Dadi snarled.

"How come *you* forgot our idol?" an elder asked.

The Mukhia's wife twisted her lips and lowered her eyes.

"Some great devotee you are," the elder said.

The Mukhia rose and slapped his wife on both cheeks. "You have but one job. Taking care of the goddess. We would be bereft of her protection but for Basanti."

Basanti turned to Dadi. "Remember you told me once that deities take human form to save people?"

Dadi frowned.

"The time I pulled those parsnips in the field."

"And the man caught you?"

"And wanted to chop off my hand. I was terrified. Then out of nowhere a godly man appeared and stopped my tormentor."

"I remember." Dadi nodded.

"You know what I believe?"

"What?"

"I believe the Captain is a deity come to life as a human. Who else could perform such heroic tasks day and night? Save us from evil?"

"Didn't save your brother." The Mukhia's wife sniffed.

"Saved you. Saved the rest of us."

When they at last crossed the border, it was just south of a place that was called Wagah. There was no line, no marker, but as soon as they knew they were on the other side, their fears disappeared. People sang.

"Jai Hind!" rose the cry from a hundred mouths. "Long live India!"

Men greeted them with blankets and packages of food.

"Everyone, please register with the authorities," said an official in shirt and trousers.

"Why?"

"For resettlement. To receive your due and be compensated for the loss of your lands and properties. You will be assigned properties of equal value. Properties abandoned by Muslims."

The clan rested in the shade of a mango orchard by a Sikh gurud-wara. It had a well, and they drew water for the animals. Basanti bathed for the first time in a month. She scrubbed Mata's and Dadi's feet with pumice stone and let them oil her scalp. She gazed at her image in the still water and sighed. Her hair had grown and didn't look quite so scraped to the scalp.

Now that they could be girls again, she and Devi put on their kurtis and ghunias before entering the temple courtyard to eat langar.

"My stomach must have shrunk!" She could eat only half the amount she usually ate, and even that made her feel bloated. She spied the Captain in the distance, seated cross-legged beside his soldiers.

"Dadi, can you take me to him so I can thank him?"

Dadi rose and she and Devi followed. When they reached the

Captain, Dadi bowed. "We want to honour you for your help, Sahib."
Both girls bent to touch his feet.

"Basanti and Devi, Sahib. My granddaughters."

"Basanti and Devi? Nice names for boys." The Captain grinned
and folded his hands. "I hope you find a peaceful place to live."

"We will always pray for you, Sahib. You are our devta." They
spoke as one.

Ajit

As the Zaildar, Ajit felt it was his duty to visit every one of the Gujjar and Baria households in the village. He wanted to reassure them that he would guarantee their safety if they decided to stay and not join their Muslim brethren in the newly formed Pakistan. He could sense their fear.

"We trust you, Zaildar. You have always been kind and fair with us. But there are some Sikhs in the village we can't trust, especially those we have had disputes with in the past. We are afraid of what they will wreak on us. The family has decided to take our chances in the new country." This was what he heard in all the Muslim homes, except for that of Baru Marasi. Every Jat had pleaded with him to stay, afraid that if the man who looked after the health of their cattle left, it would be disastrous. Cattle were the living wealth of land-owning Jat Sikhs.

"All my patron families are here, Zaildar. I have no dispute or enmity with anyone. Who's to say if I will find a similarly good situation in a strange place in Pakistan?"

Baru Marasi had two sons and no daughters. It was different for his cousin, Rabi, the caretaker of the cattle yard, who chose to pack up his meagre possessions. He had three young daughters, and some of the louts in the village had made lewd remarks to them.

"I will feel more secure in Pakistan," he said, but without much conviction.

The three months leading up to partition had been difficult. Ajit had read of bloody riots in Lahore in the west and Calcutta in the east. Conflicts between Hindus and Muslims had flared up like wildfires in Bengal, and battles between Muslims and Sikhs had begun in the greater Punjab. Women and girls were abducted and raped. Men were butchered. Urban communities divided and huddled behind fortified boundaries.

Ajit knew that the Sikhs were outraged by the Partition of India. The British had promised them their own state as reward for their loyalty in the past, but now had turned their backs. Satwant's posting to Peshawar meant that he was caught up in the movement of refugees in and out of Pakistan. He wrote that he would not be able to get furlough until after the Partition was complete. Ajit decided he would not go on tours for the time being. There were rumours of men organizing, and no one could tell what their intentions were. It was not the time to be riding around carrying quantities of cash.

Amrita was six months pregnant, and Inder and Siamo watched over her like anxious hens. Her father, Sher, came to visit. His younger son was now a deputy superintendent of police.

"Jorawar fears a bloodbath. Intelligence reports point to it."

Ajit sighed and wrung his hands.

"Trust no one, and stay at home," Sher said. "Keep your guns handy. Hire some Bajigars to guard the haveli and the cattle yard."

As the richest man for miles, Ajit had good reason to fear he would be a target for the dacoits, who might go on a looting spree under the cover of the mayhem that threatened to break out. Satwant's mare Bakki alone was worth a king's ransom. He decided to call on Rustum Mukhia.

"We will guard the haveli, Malik," the Rustum assured him.

Ajit managed a smile of gratitude. But the Rustum's wife, Sehba, looked distraught.

"We are worried, Malik. There has been no word from Changu or his clan. You know that Rana and Wazeer are promised to his daughter and his niece."

"These are bad times, Sehba. Let us pray and hope for the best."

His words were heartfelt, but he realized just how hollow they sounded. Those little girls would be lovely young women by now, he thought.

Waheguru, he prayed silently, *watch over the innocents.*

Over the next few weeks, caravans of loaded carts and camels began to pass through the village of Raikot on their way to Pakistan. The

Muslim women wore burkas and the men held spears and swords. He knew that they were trying to reach the security of the camps that had been set up to arrange their safe passage to the new border. The Gujjars and Barias, herders and farmers, left without notice one dark night, abandoning planted fields and ancestral homes.

Ajit walked through the five streets of the village, passing gates opening into empty courtyards. He remembered when he had played here as a child with his Muslim friends, eaten at their hearths and shared jaggery-sweetened hot milk from brass tumblers. He had received love from their mothers and grandmothers, who treated him as their own. What kind of strangers—Hindu or Sikh refugees, from Pakistan—would occupy these homes and cattle yards? Who would till the fields? Would they fit in with the villagers, or would they disrupt the way of life in Raikot? What strange customs or traditions and values would they bring with them?

Thoughts such as these would depress him. What came next was shocking.

Corpses were discovered floating in village ponds and wells, the bodies of murdered Muslims. Ajit spent days shrouding and burying them, as Baru Marasi uttered the Nimaz-e-Janazah, the funeral prayer. Across the distant fields at night came terrifying, tortured screams. News came from the grasslands of the Bet, where tens of thousands of Muslim Gujjars had lived peacefully raising cattle, that walls had been built with the skulls of those who did not escape.

Bloodlust had taken hold, and the province lit up with the flames of hatred, revenge, looting, and rape. Ajit knew that there were men from Raikot who took buses to the cities to join in on the mayhem. They returned in the dark of night, lest others see the loot they carried or their bloodstained clothes.

Jathas, armed and mounted militias of so-called Sikh saint-soldiers, were mustered under the auspices of the Akali Dals to protect the fleeing Muslims. But when stories of bloody atrocities committed against Sikhs by Muslims were heard, the Jathas rose up in a spirit of bloodlust and sought revenge. Soon, the mere sight of the Jatha was enough to inspire revulsion in peace-loving Sikhs.

Ajit could not bear to read of the unfathomable atrocities on both sides that the newspapers reported. The vacant looks on Inder's and

Siamo's faces greeted him after sleepless nights. Amrita was confined to an inside room of the haveli and allowed out, escorted, only to bathe or use the privy. The village's most competent midwife, a Muslim Gujjar woman, had left, and her place had been taken by one of her Sikh disciples. He worried, what if Amrita suffered complications during delivery?

The mere thought was too dark and frightening.

Amrita went into labour during an oppressively hot and humid night at the tail end of the monsoon. Under a full moon, Ajit sat on the flat roof outside his rooms and swatted the mosquitoes swarming around him. He could hear the shouts of the women and Amrita's screams below him. He prayed in silence.

Unexpectedly, Ajit heard screams coming from a different direction, from a distance. He jumped up and raced to the balustrade on the other side of the roof. The cries rose and fell in a way that was tragically familiar, and they seemed to be coming from the orchard of Pir Baba Shah, the Sufi saint. Was it possible that violence was being done there, on that hallowed ground? A long, sickening, high-pitched scream—this from a young girl's throat. It died suddenly, and gave way to the cries of his newborn grandchild.

He hurried down the staircase.

Siamo looked up. "It's a girl, Bir."

He sat down heavily on the top step. He had prayed so hard for a grandson. But Amrita and Satwant were young, there was time enough for more children. With the heart-wrenching scream from the orchard still ringing in his ears, his nerves shattered, he rose and went to his room and straight to the cabinet. He opened a bottle of rum and put it to his lips.

Bikram

It had started as a lark. Inspired by the sight of Satwant Singh riding his powerful mare through the bazaar, Bikram had bought himself a horse. He mounted the beast at Mirza Gujjar's dairy.

"You look like a Jathedar, a real commander," said Chand, his father-in-law, as Bikram walked the gelding in a circle. It was a docile animal and well broken.

"He is right," Papaji said.

Afterwards, as they sat in the gathering room to share a bottle of Solan whiskey, he asked Chand, "How does one become a Jathedar?" A year removed from the army, Bikram was deathly bored, and the idea appealed to him.

"I will go to Amritsar and convince one of the Akali Dals to appoint you," Chand said, and poured himself another shot.

"How much will it cost?"

"Let me worry about that." Chand burped and wiped his mouth with the back of a hand.

Mangal came to visit, and he was gung-ho about the idea too. He even bought a horse for himself so he could join. He had become a fixture in Samrala, and often stayed for a week or more at Bikram's home. Sewa followed him like a shadow. And the town dandies—with the exception of Golu, who had shut himself up in his house—liked to gather around him for drinks at the liquor vend.

When the Muslim owners of Frontier Transport left for Pakistan, Mangal coaxed Chand to help him buy the fleet of six buses. He took over the bus stop in Samrala and hired Jagtar's brother Darshan as the manager. This gesture endeared him to Jagtar and her parents, and she stopped complaining about Mangal's snoring, which reverberated throughout the bungalow every night. He contributed to the pantry and brought a cook from the hills, a man named Ramu, and convinced Maaji to use him. Ramu turned out to be a real gem, and Maaji abandoned the kitchen to him. It gave her more time to sit and gossip in the courtyard with the neighbourhood women. And Papaji suddenly discovered a taste for spicier dishes cooked in ghee. The meals became a boisterous affair.

Bikram wondered at the many facets of his friend Mangal. Charming and courteous to a fault with the women, humble and respectful with the elders, a tireless playmate for Sewa, a loyal ally to him. He had a commanding presence. Men greeted him with alacrity, while women gaped. Street urchins pestered him for change or candy and he obliged them. Constables saluted him smartly. But his mood could change with the wind, sending a shiver of worry through the men in the bazaar. And a roar from him sent even the pariah dogs scurrying into the alleyways.

Bikram was soon appointed a Jathedar by a fringe chapter of the Akali Dal. Its leader, a fiery orator, monopolized the press with his outlandish demands for a separate land of "the Pure," where only baptized Sikhs would be allowed to live. Sikhs who smoked, drank, or cut their hair would be ostracized and expelled. Bikram was a bit worried about what he'd got himself into.

"You just have to keep up appearances, is all," Chand said. "The leader is a flat-broke gas bag. He grabbed the five hundred rupees out of my palm faster than the blink of an eye."

"And do not drink or eat meat in public," Papaji said.

Bikram decided that he could live with that. He appointed Mangal as his second-in-command, and within a month they had a mounted Jatha of three dozen hardened Sikh men. Sukha, Jagtar's younger brother, joined them. Quite the orator, he harangued the men on the duties of a saint-soldier. To protect the weak and the vulnerable, no matter their faith. To live up to the principles and values of the Sikh faith. To do good and shun evil. To always speak the truth.

They decided to show the flag by making a tour of the surrounding villages. Muslims quickly got out of their way, but many Sikhs shouted greetings as they trotted by on their horses, dressed in the blue of the Akali Dal and holding long spears high in the air. As Jathedar, Bikram sat tall in the saddle, and revelled in his newfound importance.

"Mohamad Khan is getting desperate to sell," Chand told Bikram one day.

Bikram had passed by the three-storey mansion a few times but still wasn't sure if he wanted all the attention that would come with owning the iconic building. He decided to consult Jagtar.

"I can see it from our roof," she cried. "It's the tallest building in town!"

"Want to take a look?"

Chand arranged a private showing, after sunset, for Mohamad Khan was a discreet man. He greeted them at the gates and led them through the expansive cobbled courtyard, pointing out some of its features. "The peepal tree's waxy leaves shine like a million votive lamps on clear, moonlit nights. You can smell the aroma of the jasmine bushes. The planters hold a hundred plants each. We have marigolds, roses, you name it. There are two adjoining kitchens, one is halal, and over there are the servants' quarters."

His wife, the Begum, greeted Jagtar. Both remained veiled.

The verandah was wide and ran the length of the façade. A carved double door stood in the middle, and the windows on either side opened into the courtyard. Bikram was impressed by the elegance of the gathering room, furnished with imported furniture the likes of which he had never seen. Cushioned sofas and armchairs and glass cabinets full of lovely things. The floor was partly covered by a thick rug, and two large chandeliers hung from the high ceiling. They climbed the curved stairs to all three floors. The view from the third-storey roof, from behind the chest-high balustrades, was stunning: Bikram could see the lights of distant villages in all directions, and the town lay spread out before them.

There was no denying the quality of construction, and the thoughtfully designed layout that separated the women's quarters from the men's. The dining hall seated two dozen. The washrooms had indoor privies, just like the ones he had seen in the officers' quarters in the army.

"Did you see it, Ji? So, so elegant. So rich," Jagtar whispered as they lay in bed later. She was thrilled beyond belief.

"It's a lot of money."

"We can afford it. It's a once-in-a-lifetime opportunity. We will live in the finest home in town. Please, Ji? Say yes."

He caressed her lips and slid his finger in her mouth. She puckered her lips and sucked.

Bikram offered to buy the dairy, and Mirza Gujjar almost wept with relief.

"I will meet your price. You saved my family's dignity once. We owe you so much," Bikram said.

Chand was sure he could have negotiated a much better deal. But, sitting with him over drinks later, Bikram gave his reasons to his father-in-law. How Golu and his gang had terrorized his family, and Mirza Gujjar and his sons had stopped the gang from even entering their street.

"Today, I repaid a great debt."

Papaji nodded his approval. "Tell Sukha he will run the dairy."

After buying the mansion and the dairy, Bikram was down to fifty thousand rupees in cash. He had a lakh out on interest, and the monthly income from rents and loans more than covered his living expenses. Now he wanted a nice business to run.

"Become a grain merchant," Chand said. "You already own one of the biggest warehouses in the grain market here."

"It's rented out."

"The tenant is a Muslim. I can speak to him about you taking it over lock, stock, and barrel. It will give you a functioning business with bookkeepers, workers, equipment, and a roster of faithful clients."

It seemed that there was nothing Bikram could not have.

A fortnight later, Mangal threw the newspaper at Bikram. "Look at this. Read it."

TRAIN FROM PAKISTAN ARRIVES FULL OF A THOUSAND
DEAD AND MUTILATED BODIES

The headline jolted him. The details were gory and disgusting. *What kind of animals do this?*

"Damn Muslims." Mangal was frothing at the mouth, his eyes red with rage.

Bikram shrugged. "What can we do?" He did not believe that Muslims everywhere were to blame for this, and of course atrocities were committed on both sides, but it was dangerous to stand up to Mangal when he was in this kind of mood.

"Do? We can ride out and take revenge. Find us some Muslims to slaughter."

Bikram did not know what to say, but Mangal kept at him.

"What is the damn Jatha *for*, Bikram?"

"To protect the weak." Bikram's voice came out as a croak. The mere thought of spilling blood sickened him.

"Listen." Mangal grabbed him by the collar. "Tonight, we ride. And you are riding with us."

Oh God. Bikram swallowed, but his throat was dry.

"Don't go all cowardly on me, Bikram. Show some spine."

He badly needed a drink. The foolish game had turned ugly. He wished he could roll back the clock.

"Sharpen your sword." And with that, Mangal stomped out.

His stomach churning, Bikram quickly considered what might happen and weighed the risks. Thankfully, Mirza Gujjar and his family had already left, and so had Mohamad Khan, and most of Samrala's Muslims. The grain merchant he bought out had left the same night he was paid. Bikram heard of daily violence against Muslims in the bazaar, but there had not been any bloodshed yet in the town, and of course the police were out in full force.

Out in the countryside, however, it was a different matter. *Oh God.*

"Bring a change of clothes," Mangal whispered after supper.

Bikram felt sick and unsteady. The six shots of whiskey he had had would help.

Late that night the dairy compound filled with riders, their spears glinting in the light of the full moon. Bikram spied his brother-in-law Sukha saddling his mount. What was he doing here, the pious man? What did he think was going on?

The Jatha rode out in a long line, staying off the cobbled streets. They rode through fields wet from a recent rain, which muffled the hooves of the horses. An hour later, they crossed the long Nilon Bridge over the wide Sirhind Canal, flowing like a broad silver streak in the moonlight, and turned right towards a grove of trees in the distance.

Halfway there, Mangal pulled the reins and stopped to sniff the air.

"Cooking fires," he said in a hushed voice.

Sukha rode up to the front. "It must be Muslims camping in the Pir's orchard."

"What are we waiting for?" A man grinned.

"What are you saying?" Sukha asked.

"Let's go kill their men and fuck the women."

"Collect some loot," another said.

"No, no, no. We are saint-soldiers," Sukha insisted.

For a moment, Bikram felt relieved. It didn't last.

"Get out of my way," Mangal said.

"No. Please don't do this." Sukha begged with folded hands. "They are on hallowed ground. No one should shed blood on that soil."

Mangal shoved him off his mount. Sukha fell, then slowly rose up and spread his arms.

"You will be cursed," he cried. "The Pir will haunt your souls!"

Bikram felt a chill run up his spine. He wanted to vomit.

"Fuck off!" Mangal rode on.

"Jeeja, Ji!" Sukha appealed to Bikram. "Stop them. You are the Jathedar."

Bikram tried to speak, but his tongue was glued to the roof of his mouth.

Mangal turned and rode back.

"You speak a word about this, Sukha, to anyone, and I will personally slit your throat."

Mangal turned and rode away, leaving Sukha kneeling in the mud. Bikram followed his friend.

They dismounted at the edge of the orchard and, leaving the horses in the care of a couple of their men, slowly approached the light of the camp fires. The wet earth made their approach almost soundless. The camp was in a clearing around the large tomb of the saint. When they were close enough to make out figures in the dark, they stopped and spread out to encircle them. Now Bikram could see the sallow faces

of men and women gathered around the fires, and children lying on
blankets. There were probably forty or fifty people, altogether. Their
cattle stood tied to half a dozen heavily laden carts.

There was a moment of perfect stillness.

Then all hell broke loose. At Mangal's shouted command, the men
of the Jatha charged into the camp. With their long, deadly spears
they savagely attacked the Muslim men, who were overwhelmed so
quickly that they put up no fight at all. The women, screaming pit-
eously, were thrown to the ground, now slippery with blood, and
raped. The children were shrieking and crying, and Mangal and some
of the others kicked and savagely stabbed them, one by one extin-
guishing their cries.

Like a flash, one young girl erupted from a blanket and took off
into the woods.

"Get her!" Mangal shouted to him.

Unthinking, Bikram ran after the fleeing figure, his sword raised.

"Save me, Abba, save me!" the child screamed, darting desperately
through the trees.

Bikram caught up to her at the very edge of the orchard. As she
turned to face him, he swung his sword and sliced her head off at the
shoulders. Her body fell forwards, and he was bathed in her blood
from head to toe as it gushed from her severed neck. He dropped
the sword to wipe the gore out of his eyes, and he tried to clear his
bloody mouth. He tasted the salt and began to spit it out in panic and
desperation.

He fell to his knees, wrapped his hands around his head, and rocked
back and forth.

"What have I done? Oh, God, what have I done?"

They stopped at the canal to wash themselves. Only the men who had
stayed with the horses were unbloodied, and they sat holding the reins
on the sandy bank. Mangal flung his clothes into the rapid water and
waded hip-deep into it. He had found Bikram cowering over the dead
girl's body at the edge of the orchard and told him to get up, and
nothing more.

Bikram could see that he was the bloodiest by far. He peeled off his
clothes, removed his turban and moccasins, bundled them together,

and threw them as far away as he could. He waded in and began to scrub himself, lightly at first and then vigorously, immersing himself over and over in the silvery waters.

The ride back to Samrala was silent. His mind began to fill with scenes of the attack. The bloody spearing of the men. The rape of the women. He cringed at the cry, "Save me, Abba, save me!" still ringing in his ears, and the final scream of the terrified child a blink of an eye before he struck.

I never meant you any harm. I will never, ever hurt anything or anyone.

He shivered violently in the dank, warm night.

Basanti

Her clan stayed in the crowded refugee camp for almost a month. They were given rations and clothes by volunteers. There was little to do but look after their families' needs and exchange tales with other refugees about their experiences. Almost every family had a blood-curdling story to tell. Sometimes it was more than Basanti could bear to hear.

"I drowned my four daughters in the well rather than let them suffer at the hands of the Muslims."

"I cut my daughter into many parts, fearing that, leaving her whole, the Muslims might visit indignities on her dead body."

"I lost my husband in an attack, and two grown sons."

Their faces were lined, their eyes vacant. Many limped, leaning on sticks.

And every day, while she listened, Basanti thought of the broken body of Piara, the little Dervish.

One day, the Mukhia called a meeting.

"We have been assigned land to live on. Prepare to set out tomorrow."

"How far?" someone asked.

"About ten days on foot. We follow the Grand Trunk Road from Amritsar all the way south to the town of Doraha. It is only seven miles from Raikot, where your promised lives."

"I've been there," an elder said. "By the Sirhind Canal. It is a rail-way town. We should prosper there."

Any place that wasn't the camp sounded heavenly to Basanti, and they started packing under the flimsy tarp that had served as shelter for the past month. Mata stuffed their donated blankets and sheets into a gunny sack, Bhapa loaded the camel, and in the early morning they formed a caravan and began another long journey.

There were nights and days when they went hungry, and there were days when they feasted at a langar offered by Sikhs, or with Hindus at a pooja. They skirted the city of Ludhiana along its ring road and arrived at the bridge over the Sirhind Canal, and camped for the night on vacant land beside an old fort. In the morning, the Mukhia led the men across the bridge to the town of Doraha, to check the land and make arrangements.

Basanti was elated at the prospect of living by a town. The day was clear, and she climbed the tower of the fort with some others. Far to the east she saw the outline of snow-covered mountains, a scene to take the breath away. The land that was their new home was bordered by railway lines to the west and woods to the east. From where she stood, Basanti could even see the railway station. The canal lay to the north, just beyond a wide road running alongside it. Later a man came with a long, thin metal chain and measured a rectangular plot for each family. Bhapa took one on the far southeast corner, towards the fields and closer to the woods.

"A merchant will send oxcarts carrying bamboo to frame your huts with," the man said before leaving. They spent their first night under the stars.

Bhapa, Mata, and Dadi worked hard to erect the frame, then mix mud with straw and dung to plaster the walls. The next supply the oxcarts brought was dried reeds for the roofs. Basanti helped pound the dirt floor while a carpenter from the city hung the wooden door and two windows. It was the sturdiest and most spacious abode she had ever lived in. Mata set up the cots and unpacked the gunny sacks. Dadi built a mud chullah to cook outside over a wood fire. It became Basanti's daily duty to go to the canal to collect water. Near the canal it was slippery, and it was an ordeal coming back up, straining under the weight of the water in the large pot on her head. Happily, in due time a benefactor had a water pump drilled at the dera. And the Mukhia got permission to trim acacia trees and build a thorny fence as protection from jackals and other creatures.

Bhapa got work using the camel to haul groundnuts from the grain market to the oil mill. Dadi took Basanti and Devi to beg for pieces of leftover cloth from the tailors in the bazaar, which they used to stitch patchwork kurtis and ghunias. Their diet improved. Bhapa bought vegetables, lentils, and flour with the wages he earned. Mata shucked corn, cut sugarcane, and plucked cotton in the nearby fields, earning grain and jaggery. They drank tea every morning. Gulab was hired out to herd a Jat's cattle and graze them along the canal all day. He was fed three meals by his employer and began to grow strong.

They were also called to sing and dance in the town for special celebrations, and they would return with money, cloth, and sweets. But the men stared at them openly, even making lewd gestures, and that made them upset. Their mother made them promise never, ever to go into the bazaar by themselves.

One morning, a very tall Bajigar with broad shoulders walked into the dera and stood looking around the place. He was holding the curved staff of a mukhia. Dadi squinted, and then covered her head with her chador.

The man was Rustum Mukhia, and he was there to settle the bride prices for Basanti and Devi. After a meeting of the elders, the date was set. The double wedding would take place after the spring harvest two seasons hence, when both girls had turned fourteen. The bride price, paid to their fathers, was three hundred rupees each. Rustum Mukhia paid for his son, Rana, and for his dead brother's son, Wazeer, to whom Devi was promised. Fine suits of clothing and sandals would be presented at the wedding.

"Such good girls. And look at them," Rustum Mukhia said. "So beautiful. Like twin sisters."

They lowered their eyes.

"I hope their matches are as handsome," one of the elders said, after the guests had left.

"Did you not see the Rustum?" Dadi replied. "The boys are his blood. They have to be handsome, just like him. Big and strong."

That made Basanti blush.

That night, Mata served the leftovers of the feast that had been cooked for the Rustum. Thick lentils, cauliflower, rice, and halwa. Bhapa drank straight from a half-empty bottle of rum and burped loudly before taking out the bundle of notes and counting them again, his eyes catching the gleam from the embers in the chullah.

"Can you buy me a new suit of clothing, Bhapa?" Gulab asked, fingering the holes in his kurta.

"Add a pair of rawhide moccasins," Mata said. "And a dyed turban."

There was more joy just then than the family had known in a very long time, but no pleasure could ever again be untouched by the shadow cast by little Piara's death.

Ajit

The army automobile raising dust on the path brought Ajit running down the staircase and straight to the gates of his haveli.

"Satwant is here!" he shouted.

Satwant had been serving in the war between India and Pakistan over the state of Kashmir. Now that the conflict had ended, he had finally been allowed furlough. The driver cut off the engine and greeted the Zaildar before getting down to lift out the luggage.

Satwant, looking smart in his uniform, hopped out, and his father pulled him into a long hug. "Welcome home." The young man looked gaunt and tired, he thought, but also older.

Siamo's turn was next, and she ran her hands all over Satwant's face, crying tears of joy. In the courtyard, Satwant bent to touch his mother's feet, before hurrying into the haveli to find his wife. Except for a brief visit after Partition, he had not seen her since their daughter's birth.

Ajit and the two women waited outside in the welcome warmth of a brilliant winter sun. Soon Satwant emerged holding his fifteen-month-old daughter in his arms. "Look at her, Maaji. Look at those rosy cheeks." Amrita followed him, smiling proudly.

"She is beautiful," Inder agreed. "And gets into everything."

They had named the baby Paramjit Kaur, but they each called her by their own favourite pet name. Since she was the first-born, Siamo nicknamed her Guddi. Inder called her Pammi. Amrita used her full name only while scolding her: "We don't do that, Paramjit Kaur!"

The girl had only yesterday managed to climb the entire staircase to visit Ajit, one laborious step at a time, giggling and grinning all the way, while Siamo hovered a careful step behind her.

"My sweet Pinki." Satwant planted another kiss on a rosy cheek.

Another name? Ajit thought wearily.

"Pinki? What kind of name is that?" Siamo asked.

"Pink is English for rosy, and does she ever have rosy cheeks."
Satwant kissed one cheek again. And the courtyard came alive with
cooing and laughter.

Satwant carried Pinki whenever he got the chance, and spent much of
the day playing games with her in the courtyard. As soon as she lay
down for her afternoon nap, he changed and hurried over to the cattle
yard to saddle Bakki for a ride.

Father and son rode together through their fields and inspected the
sugarcane crop as it was harvested and crushed, boiled into jaggery, or
put through a centrifuge to extract brown sugar. The leftover molasses
was divided among the labourers, and he knew that it would be fer-
mented and distilled into country rum, an illegal but popular activity
in the village. The local bootlegger, Lalu, a kin of his, sold it in quantity for celebrations and weddings.

"I hope you retire from the army in time to take over as zaildar,"
Ajit said to Satwant.

"That will be a long time yet, Bapuji."

While he was home, Ajit tried to spend as much time with Satwant
as possible. It was their nightly custom to enjoy a few shots of army
rum before dinner in his room, since Inder frowned on drinking under
the verandah. Ajit wanted to know everything that Satwant had seen
and experienced in his duties. India's independence from Britain was
finally a reality, with all the chaos and confusion that anyone might
have anticipated. Partition and the resettlement of the refugees was
happening quickly and in an orderly manner, at least at home. All the
Muslim homes and fields in Raikot had been assigned to refugee Jats.

Satwant told stories about escorting refugees fleeing from Pakistan,
going back to find Hindu and Sikh girls and women who had been kidnapped, and escorting Muslim women and girls to Pakistan to rejoin
their families. Ajit suspected that the boy spared him many of the har-
rowing details, none of which would have been a surprise to him.

Satwant seemed to find it restful to spend time in the stables with
Bakki. But whenever Baru Marasi came by to tend the cattle, the discussion turned to the massacre of Muslims in the Pir's orchard, and the
story of the headless girl. The police had discovered the girl's body, but
they'd never found the skull. They'd had to bury the body without it.

Baru had planted an ornamental bush over her grave. "In case her head ever surfaces, I will know exactly where to dig to make her whole."

"I wish I had been here. I would not have let this happen," Satwant said, furious.

Baru shook his head sadly. "Those marauders did not care who they attacked in the dark. It was a violent time. Many an innocent Sikh life was taken, believe me. I heard horror stories from the Bet."

Rana, the son of Rustum Mukhia, was listening. He was sixteen and he'd been hired to help in the cattle yard, working to earn the bride price paid by Bajigar grooms. "Is it true that the headless girl is a ghost now?" he asked.

"She has appeared in my dreams begging to be made whole," Baru said.

"There are rumours in the dera of people who have actually seen her," Rana said. "My mother swears that the headless girl appears to her on full moon nights." The locals were great believers in apparitions.

"How old are you, Rana?" Ajit teased. "These are all old women's tales to scare children."

"Malik, I believe in them."

That night, Ajit thought about Nasib. His younger son was fourteen years old now, almost a man. What did he look like? He must have started a beard. Ajit thought of going to his village in some sort of disguise, to see him at least once, to put a face to the name. It would be better than lying in the dark and wondering. And why should he not? The same old societal taboos kept him from going. But sometimes the urge became almost unbearable.

He asked the only person he could talk to about it.

"And what would Amrita think of her father-in-law walking in with a son he has hidden for so long?" Siamo asked.

Once, only the feelings of Inder and Satwant had needed to be considered. Now Amrita, her family, and Pinki had been added to the list. The more the family grew, the more the prospect of his visit to see Nasib diminished. And so he did the only thing he could ever do. He prayed.

Bikram

Now that they were living in the glorious mansion that once belonged to Mohamad Khan, Jagtar relished her new role as the grand chatelaine. Only certain, very select people were invited inside her home. Others would be met under the verandah, and could only gaze longingly through an open window. Beeji, Jagtar's mother, often came to stay for a week at a time, citing the need to help her daughter manage the massive place. There were half a dozen servants to help her.

"I never, ever could have imagined such good fortune." Beeji was beaming, relaxing under the gaslight of a chandelier in the dining room.

"Ramu, bring more roti," Jagtar shouted towards the open window closest to the kitchen.

Ramu was just one of their many servants. A younger version helped in the kitchen and washed dishes. Four women came early every morning and worked till midday sweeping the courtyard, dusting furniture, mopping the floors, and cleaning the washrooms. A washerwoman did the laundry, hung it to dry, and ironed the clothes before leaving for the day.

"You should buy a car, Bikram Singh," Beeji said over lunch one day.

Bikram was annoyed by his in-laws' newly inflated expectations. Tongas and rickshaws weren't good enough for Beeji any more. And Chand turned his nose up at rum—only the best Solan whiskey suited his palate. That, and tender lamb.

"Yes, Ji," Jagtar chimed in. "It would be so dignified to ride around in a car."

Bikram glared at Sewa, who had littered the tablecloth with his food. "Teach your son some manners first," he said.

"I am doing my best, Ji." Jagtar pouted.

Four-year-old Sewa made a face at his father.

"Behave, you ruffian!"

Jagtar's eyes flared. "He *will* turn into a ruffian, Ji, if you keep calling him that!"

Bikram had never been able to become close with his son. He tried, but the boy took only to Papaji and Mangal. And he had his mother and grandmothers wrapped around his little finger. It was most infuriating.

"Sewa, tell your Papa that you will be on your best behaviour if he buys a car for us to ride in," Beeji prodded him.

"Buy me a bicycle, Papa. I will be a good boy."

"Selfish, selfish," Jagtar sighed.

These were the kinds of annoying conversations they'd had ever since moving into the mansion. Jagtar had let her new, elevated status go to her head, and she had become, if such a thing could be imagined, even more silly and superficial. Merchants and vendors in the bazaar now bowed lower and served her first, before other waiting customers. Jewellers brought their newest designs to show her. Tailors clamoured for her business. She even had a favourite shoemaker. They brought the bills to Bikram.

Jagtar had started feigning a city accent since she had begun to go with her mother once or twice a week on the bus to catch a matinee in Ludhiana. Beeji would tell the entire story of the movie they'd seen when they returned. It did amuse him, he had to admit, when she tried to act out a scene and he could see Ramu and his helper snickering behind her back.

"Prithvi Raj Kapoor, what a man, what a voice!" she'd say. Beeji was an ardent fan of the famous actor. Jagtar had yet to settle on a favourite star—it was an important decision for her.

Jagtar had bought a radio and set it on a table in the gathering room. When she turned it on, the servants would drop their ladles and brooms and huddle around the big, highly polished wooden box. Jagtar would then turn the volume up. It disturbed Bikram's afternoon naps, and he started climbing to the third-storey room to sleep. The breeze was cooler up there anyway.

It was there that he had his first nightmare about the massacre in the orchard.

It flashed in front of his eyes, in gory detail, as though he were right back at the scene. He was living it, hating it, but unable to change a thing. The spears glinting in the moonlight and the men going silently to their bloody, gruesome killing. The rapes of the screaming women. Mangal's brutal murder of the children. And the nightmare always ended the same way. A girl fleeing through the trees in the dark of night, crying to her God for help. His arms raised, the powerful swing of his sword. The shower of blood as her headless body met the ground, its salty taste in his mouth.

He awoke suddenly, gagging, retching, in a cold sweat.

He knew what they were whispering every day in the bazaar. That he had created his wealth by looting the fleeing Muslims. That he had been involved in some dirty, nefarious activities with his friend Mangal.

He had been told, straight out, by a reckless, drunken fellow, "They say that you killed hundreds, raped their women, drank their blood, and ate their flesh. They say that you still have uncounted bags of their gold in that big mansion, hidden in the dungeon."

He laughed all these stories off, but the words left him shaken.

"They will suffer, every one of those murderous bastards," it was said. "The Pir will exact a toll from beyond."

So far, nothing unpleasant had happened to him. On the contrary, his business was booming, he had more money to lend out, and his prestige had grown. Merchants folded their hands, vendors waved, and police constables saluted him, touching their batons to their heads. The sub-inspector of police, in charge of the local police station, would cross the road to shake his hand. Of course, he had sent a case of rum to the man's house when his son got engaged.

Bikram knew that the only way to quell the stories was to present himself as a good, civic-minded man, rubbing shoulders with the mayor and the councillors. He made a point of being seen in the bazaar dining with government officials, including the local magistrates, the civil surgeon, and the headmaster of the high school. He made generous donations towards religious festivals like Dussehra and Diwali, making sure that his name was read aloud as a benefactor from the stage daily before the week-long performance of the Ramayana. The audience greeted his name with enthusiastic applause. Surprisingly, no one seemed to ascribe them to a guilty conscience. The poor came to his gates seeking favours.

Yet the nightmares ruined his sleep and tortured his days.

⤳

Mangal got married and brought his wife to visit them. She was a village girl, garishly dressed and burdened with several pounds of gold jewellery. She was alarmed by the suggestion that she use the indoor toilet, which was unfamiliar to her, and Beeji had to take her to the fields after dark with a can of water.

Mangal doubled the size of the Frontier Transport bus fleet, and he began to buy trucks as well, which were being used more and more to transport goods in the country. He opened a truck stand behind the police station, and some of his cohort from the Jatha worked for him as drivers and assistants. They were hardened men who could be summoned in case of an emergency, such as a quarrel with an argumentative customer. And Bikram enjoyed the added benefit of a protection for him. In return, Mangal had made himself at home in the mansion with his wife, taking over a suite on the second floor.

Boredom began to weigh on Bikram once more as the grain business practically ran itself. His brother-in-law, Sukha, managed the dairy, which was thriving, and Chand took care of collecting the rents and interest on Bikram's properties. Bored, sitting cross-legged most of the day on the wooden diwan in the shop, his eye wandered. The new bride in the family of sweepers was rather attractive, and he found himself aroused as she swung her backside, bending and sweeping the courtyard. Jagtar caught Bikram watching her, and the startled young woman got a tongue-lashing.

"Watch your eyes, Ji," Jagtar warned.

Gopal the matchmaker came to visit, and Jagtar put on her annoyingly superior airs. Bikram and Mangal rescued the Brahmin by taking him on a tour of the mansion, and they stopped to talk while taking in the view on the third-storey roof.

"So, Bikram, Jagtar hasn't given you any more children," Gopal said, as soon as Bikram's wife was out of earshot.

Bikram shook his head ruefully.

"You have been home almost four years. Should have had at least a couple by now."

"Maybe she is barren," Mangal said, and smiled.

"Well, Bikram Singh, you are a rich man, and by rights you can demand a second wife. I have the perfect match for you."

"That will be impossible with Jagtar around," Bikram said.

Gopal sighed.

"You really want to get rid of her." Mangal grinned. "You know, she might just flip over this balustrade onto that cobbled street forty feet below. One dark night. It could happen."

The men laughed, but the Brahmin gulped and hurried away. The casually spoken words stayed with Bikram.

Basanti

Basanti walked into the woods with Devi, both barefoot and in their old clothes. Collecting fuel was a regular chore, but it always felt like an adventure. The trees rose high and dark above their heads, and there were fallen branches and tree trunks on the ground to skip over. They were glad not to be alone, for it was easy to get lost. There were no tracks, and sometimes they had to cross deep, rapid streams.

The farther they walked into the woods, the darker and quieter it became, until the only sound was the eerie calling of birds. Basanti had to remind herself not to think of the stories about demons and ghosts that Dadi and the other old women would tell around the fire at night. It was a bit scary, but it gave them a chance to talk alone.

"I hope Wazeer is nice," Devi said anxiously.

"Why wouldn't he be? He'll be charmed when he lifts your veil and he'll instantly fall in love with you."

"His mother is a widow. Do you suppose she's mean?"

"You'll find out soon enough."

"Basanti, aren't you curious about Rana? What if his feet smell, or he doesn't like your cooking, or he snores at night like your Bhapa?"

That made them both giggle.

"Rustum Mukhia said such nice things about us," Devi added. "They will be expecting angels!"

They entered a thick grove and began to collect fallen twigs, shaking off their dry leaves. Soon they had collected an armful each.

"I think that's enough," Devi said.

"No, look over there." Basanti pointed to a tall pile of drying branches. She raced over and pulled at one. "Come, Devi. You could at least help. The more we bring home today, the longer it will be before we have to come back. Pull." She grabbed another branch, and Devi joined in.

There was a rustle behind them, and they turned to see two uniformed men carrying bamboo staffs.

"What do you think you women are doing?" the taller one asked, glaring at them.

"Collecting wood for the fire," Basanti said.

"No. You don't collect wood on government property. This pile of wood has already been auctioned. You are stealing," the second man, shorter and stockier, said harshly.

Devi joined her hands as if to supplicate. "We did not know that."

Basanti added, "Please, Sahibs. We are poor children."

"Well, we caught you stealing." The tall guard was staring at her chest.

"What should we do with you?" asked the stocky one.

"Please, let us go. We promise not to do it again. Please."

The tall guard looked her up and down. "We can't just let you go."

"You don't look like children to me. You are fully grown women. Almost as tall as me. Adults who should know better." The stocky one was leering at them now.

"We are barely of age, Sahib." Fear gripped Basanti. The men were smirking. She'd seen that same look from men so many times before.

"You have to come with us to the Canal Bungalow."

"Why?"

"To be presented to the big Sahib, the canal officer. He is the only one who can decide whether to let you go or punish you."

"Punish?" Basanti's heart was pounding, and Devi looked as though she might throw up.

"You could be fined, or sent to jail," the guard explained.

Basanti bent to touch his feet, and he cuffed her on the head. Devi began to whimper.

"Move." The stocky guard prodded them with his staff.

"Follow me." The tall one started walking.

"Please, Sahibs. Please!"

"We won't," Devi tried.

The man turned and cuffed her this time, hard. "Shut up. Be quiet, and do as you are told."

They walked in silence. Basanti glanced around, hoping they wouldn't notice, and hoping against hope to see another scavenger or a herder who could help them. Soon they had left the woods and were standing in a clearing, where a low building with a sloping red roof stood.

"This way." The tall one led them down a path to the door.

"Please, Sahibs. I beg you!" Devi was shaking now.

The tall one held the door open and shoved them through. They stood on a cold floor in a large room with big windows. It had covered chairs set around a long wooden table. There were pictures of white people on the walls. Some wore crowns on their heads.

"Go in." The stocky man pushed Basanti hard, into a dark room. The tall man followed her, and Basanti felt herself being lifted and then slammed onto her back on a cot. His weight as he fell on her pushed the breath out of her. A scream rose in her throat as she felt him pull up her ghunia, and then something was pressing hard into her. His grunt met her scream as she felt her insides tear.

"Quiet." His hand muffled her mouth and nose as he thrust deeper and deeper into her, the pain impossible to bear. She felt him shiver, and then he pushed himself off, turned, and was gone.

She tried to grasp what had just happened to her. She buried her face in her hands and wept. She turned over to hide herself in the cot, let the throbbing pain break over her and tried not to think about dying. She lay like that, for how long she wasn't sure, until she heard someone else enter the bungalow.

"Bhagwaan!" The shout made her lift her head. "What happened here?"

An older Sikh with a white beard rushed to her and raised her up by the shoulders.

"God. Oh, God."

She sat up. Through the open door she could see Devi sitting in the hall, her head between her knees, her body heaving.

"Who did this? Tell me! Who did this to you?"

"The guards," she managed to say.

"Bastards. Animals. Monsters. I will make them pay."

He pulled her up by the arm and guided her through the door. Then he bent to raise Devi. It must have taken all his strength; he was a slight man. He led them, shuffling, into a room with a hand pump. She watched in a daze as he filled a bucket and handed her a cloth.

"Sit, wash."

Then he turned to Devi.

"Wash well. Then wash your faces, blow your noses."

She and Devi did what they could. Washing was cleansing, Dadi often said. They poured more water, rinsed the cloths, there was blood, and wiped and washed like fiends. Wept and whimpered.

"I am making tea," the Sikh said, and when he walked away they could see he had a limp.

Basanti reached out to Devi. She badly wished that she could have protected her. Their eyes met, and she saw her cousin's terror. *We must stand together now*, she thought. *More than ever.*

"Wash," she told her. "Cleanse away the filth." They frantically pumped more water.

The kind man led them to the kitchen. They sat down on the floor and he served them sweetened tea in mugs. He placed a plate before them. "Eat the biscuits."

Basanti dipped a biscuit in the tea. It filled her mouth with a sweet, buttery taste.

"Eat," the man said. "It will give you strength. Revive you."

"The guards?"

"I am the custodian here. I go to Doraha every week on this day to buy food and sundries. They must have known the bungalow would be empty."

"The guards . . ." Devi repeated.

"I will tell the canal officer about them. Tell him to punish them. Why were you in the woods?"

"To collect wood. For our cooking fires."

The man sighed, making a wheezy sound. "I will tie two bundles of wood I have so that you don't go back to the dera empty-handed."

Devi sat up taller and spoke with an air of injured pride. "I will tell my father what happened to me here," she announced.

The man froze. Blinked his eyes. Shook his head.

"Don't you realize what they've done? What evil they have committed?"

She shook her head.

"Those guards—they stole your virtue. Took your virginity. Do you understand?"

Devi collapsed again at this and began to weep.

"Girls. Think of what your fathers will do when you tell them that you are no longer virgins."

Basanti had heard terrible tales. Girls who were killed by brothers or fathers. Sold as whores to the brothel-owning Kanjar tribe. She looked over at Devi, sitting with her legs held tightly together. They would be declared unclean and exiled from the dera. Drowned in the canal. Or taken to that awful place called a Kanjar khanna. Forced to service men.

"Do not speak a word about today, my daughters," the man said. "Save yourselves to live another day. Put yourselves in the hands of God. May He take care of you, may He save and protect you."

They took the old man's advice and said nothing.

When she got back to the dera, Basanti lay on her cot feigning a headache and cramps. Dadi left her alone, and by the time Mata came home, tired from working in the fields, it was dark. When Gulab and Bhapa returned, Dadi made food and tried to make her eat. She refused.

"Let her be. Probably going through changes," Mata said.

Devi avoided her, and she understood why. It was too painful to sit and be reminded of their ordeal. The days passed in doing chores, cooking, and making baskets and palm frond mats and fans. Otherwise, Dadi left her alone and went to sit and gossip and share her hookah.

One day her period came.

She found Devi knitting a cord in her father's hut. She sat beside her and watched her nimble fingers fly through the threads strung on a wooden frame. When she tried to pat her shoulder, Devi stiffened, shaking her head with tears in her eyes.

"Talk to me, Devi. No one is listening."

"I have very bad thoughts, Basanti. Dark, dark thoughts."

"No, Devi. Please."

"I no longer want to live. Bear the shame. Relive the vile sin in my mind."

"Devi," she said in a soft voice. "Please, Devi."

Devi raised her head and her tear-filled eyes met Basanti's. "I look at the canal and I see my salvation."

No one could leave or enter the dera after dark without smashing through the thick fence of thorny branches. If Devi went to try to kill herself, Basanti thought, it would be when the dera was quiet during the afternoon, with the adults away, children and elders napping, and the gate open. She waited outside the kitchen every day and watched.

Sure enough, one quiet afternoon Devi hurried from her father's hut as if in a daze and walked quickly out. Her heart beating fast, Basanti followed her cousin over the dirt road, up the embankment, and caught her by her braids as she stumbled down the narrow path towards the water. She turned Devi around and held her in a desperate grip, an arm wrapped around her neck.

"Let me go. Let me go!" Devi struggled, but Basanti planted her feet wide and pulled her up the steep bank, off the path.

"There are people watching, Devi. They won't let you drown. You will end up making a wet fool of yourself."

"I don't care!" With a desperate heave, Devi freed herself, ran forward, and jumped into the canal.

Without a thought, Basanti too jumped into the cold, rapidly flowing water and immediately went under. Frantically flailing her arms, she managed to surface beside Devi, spitting water and gasping for breath, and she caught hold of her cousin's braid to pull her closer. A shout came from the shore, and two men scrambled down to the water and jumped in as she struggled to keep Devi afloat. Soon strong hands gripped her, and the other swimmer pulled Devi away. The girls were brought ashore and pulled to safety.

Devi retched, and a man slapped her back, making her bring up the water she had swallowed.

"Thank you, Laxmi Maa, thank you," Basanti prayed. Her wet clothes clung to her and she shivered.

Dadi's anguished face appeared in the crowd. "What happened?"

"Devi slipped and fell."

"And you?"

"I jumped in to save her."

"Stupid girl! You could both have drowned," Dadi said, and added, "and then your fathers would have lost both your bride prices."

They sat in Devi's hut, knitting salwar and pyjama drawstrings—which would later be sold—and discussing, in whispers, what had befallen them.

"We pray to Laxmi Maa. That's what we do," Basanti said.

"How?"

"Like this. 'Oh Laxmi Maa, listen to my prayer. Hear my appeal. Grant my wish. Protect me.'"

"That's all?"

"I think so."

"You think so? I wish we could learn from a Brahmin how to pray properly."

"No need. If it was our karma to learn from a Brahmin, we would not have been born as simple folk. It is our kismet to be illiterate, and that gives us the right to pray in simple words."

"You have so much conviction and strength," Devi said. "I wish I were half like you."

"We are Bajigars. We have brutal lives. We must have the strength to survive. To live and endure."

"But still, what should we do? Laxmi Maa is not going to turn us into virgins again."

"Learn to pass as one."

"How?"

"We will find a way."

Bikram

He watched Mangal's trucks haul Zaildar Ajit Singh's wheat to his competitor's warehouse, and saw the mounds being piled up in the market. Men worked like ants, bagging and weighing the wheat until late in the evening, and carrying the sacks into storage. Bikram wished the Zaildar were his client. But for some reason the man stayed loyal to the mealy-mouthed Bania.

He could tell that the Bania did not like him. For one thing, he was the first ever Jat Sikh grain merchant in the market, and Jats were not supposed to be in business. Their role was to wrestle with the soil and meekly sell their crops at the grain market at prices set by the greedy Banias. A month after the crops were in warehouses, the Banias doubled their prices for sale to consumers. The Banias then created shortages by hoarding, driving up prices, which the poor had to pay.

It was an unspoken conspiracy. Bikram did not complain because at the end of the day, he made money. He'd heard the rumours about him. *His father had nothing—Bikram Singh goes away to the army and now suddenly he's a rich merchant, taking our business? Such remarkable good fortune doesn't come to an honest man—is it true that he looted the fleeing Muslims?*

He didn't care what they said.

Sewa had started school. Papaji showed up each morning to walk him there and brought him home in the afternoon. Jagtar helped him with his homework before he was allowed to ride his tricycle around the courtyard. Neighbourhood boys came calling at the gates, inviting him to play, but he refused.

"Why don't you go play with them outside?" Bikram asked one afternoon.

"They play in the dirt." Sewa was a fastidious little boy.

"A little dirt won't harm you."

"They are rough."

"Well, then, that will toughen you up."

"I don't like fighting. Punches hurt."

"Someone punched you?"

"Yes. At school."

"Why?"

"Said I was the son of a bad man."

"Who said that?"

Sewa refused to say.

"Where did he punch you?"

"Here." Sewa pointed to his stomach.

"What did you do? Punch him back?"

"I cried."

"Did you tell the teacher?"

"Yes."

"What did the teacher do?"

"Nothing."

Jagtar kneeled to rub the little tummy. "Listen, Ji. You must go to the school tomorrow. Talk to this teacher. I don't want Sewa to be hit by a spoiled urchin again."

The teacher, an attractive young woman, came out into the hallway to speak with him.

"Sewa swore at the boy. Called him filthy names in front of the whole class. The boy gave him a shove before starting to cry himself."

"My son tells a different story."

"I was there and I saw it. It started with a fight over a piece of chalk. I must say that Sewa is frequently disruptive in class."

"Then use some corporal punishment on him."

"I send him to the headmaster's office."

"And?"

"The headmaster cautions him."

"And spares the rod."

"Sewa says you are the headmaster's friend, so he is never going to be punished. He is also very proud of being Masterji Lal Singh's grandson."

"I will speak to the little brat myself. Thank you, madam."

"Sat Sri Akal."
"Sat Sri Akal."
He folded his hands and tried to hold her gaze. She was standing close to him and, looking down her low-cut kurta, he could see the contour of her breasts. She had a beautiful face and was obviously single—there was no bindi on her forehead or line of sindoor in her hair.

She smiled, adjusted her light, colourful chador on her head, and turned back towards the classroom door.

Bikram was invited to a meeting called by the local Member of the Legislative Assembly, Aalok Nath, who was also the Minister of Public Works and Transport. A slight, white-haired man, bent with age and poor health, he was a long-time member of the Indian National Congress and a former freedom fighter who had been jailed many times by the British. Like his idol, Gandhi, he had held long fasts to protest against British rule.

Sitting several rows away from the stage, Bikram could barely hear what the old politician was saying. A microphone system had not been set up. Bikram was beginning to think he'd wasted his time, when he discovered that Aalok Nath's son, Prushotam, was an old schoolmate of his.

He mentioned this to Mangal, who was then trying to get more permits for Frontier Transport.

"Introduce me to the son," Mangal said.

They went to visit the MLA's modest two-storey home. Prushotam greeted them warmly and brought them into a room that had maps of Samrala and Punjab pinned to the walls. There was a photo of Aalok Nath standing beside the Prime Minister of India, Jawaharlal Nehru, another one with the Chief Minister Indian Punjab, and even one taken with Mahatma Gandhi. Bikram was very impressed.

"I hear you are thriving, Bikram."

"God has been very kind to me."

"So, what can I do for you?"

Bikram introduced his friend, adding, "He owns Frontier Transport, and he wants permits for a few more routes."

"Expand the empire," Prushotam said, and smiled. His plump,

pink face bespoke good health; his hair was fashionably parted; his white, homespun suit—the uniform of a politician—had been tailored for his ample frame.

"We came with the hope that your father might help."

"Leave the details with me," Prushotam said, "and I will get back to you."

A week later, Mangal sat on a chair in Bikram's gathering room and showed him a sheaf of official-looking documents.

"Routes?"

"Every one I wanted."

Bikram was flattered. "I did not realize that Prushotam liked me so much. What a good friend."

Mangal made a face. "He also took a bribe of a couple of thousand rupees. He came to the truck stop the day after we visited and told me his price."

"He what?"

"Charged a hefty sum."

"Son of a bitch. The bastard. Enriching himself on his father's influence."

"I asked for a petrol pump permit, too. Figured I might as well own one, since I am the biggest local buyer of the stuff."

"And?"

"Ten thousand rupees."

"For the permit?"

Mangal nodded.

"Are you paying it?"

"Already did. I want you to give me a piece of that land you own along the Samrala-Khanna Road to install it on."

Twelve thousand rupees in bribes in one day. Bikram was flabbergasted.

"You know he's going to inherit his father's seat one day," Mangal said, taking a sip of whiskey.

"God, no."

"My friend, everyone in town believes that Prushotam will be the next MLA for the Samrala constituency. I'm going to try and keep him in my pocket. I've got plans."

That night, when Bikram and Jagtar were preparing to go to bed, he told her the story.

"Is that so, Ji?"

"Yes."

"There is big money in politics." Jagtar's voice got suddenly huskier. "If you win."

"Listen to me, Ji. Think of running in the next elections."

Sukha decided to marry. His chosen bride was a girl who had been kidnapped by Muslims and brought back from Pakistan by an agency dedicated to reuniting families. She was deemed to have been defiled and had been rejected by her family. Sukha's pledge to accept her was read out at the local gurudwara and seen as an act of courage and piety by a Sikh. But it enraged his mother, and Beeji warned him not to enter the gates of her home with his shameful bride.

Bikram decided to stand by his pious brother-in-law. He remembered Sukha's face on that horrible night at the orchard: *We are saint-soldiers! Please don't do this!* Supporting him, he thought, might assuage his guilt a little. He told Sukha he would help him build a house at the dairy.

Bikram was the only family member to attend the simple marriage ceremony, bringing them gifts of clothing and jewellery for the bride, and he held a feast at the mansion.

Maaji escorted the bride to their new one-room home at the dairy. Later she told Bikram that it took a lot of cajoling to convince the bride to show her face.

"What a beauty! No wonder the poor child was kidnapped and held for a year by the son of a powerful clan leader."

"A child?"

"Jiyot Kaur is barely fifteen."

One day, Sukha's brother Darshan said with a grin, "Guess what? If you lift Jiyot Kaur and shake her, a basket of Muslim penises will fall out."

"Who said that?" Bikram snapped.

"Beeji," Darshan replied, a bit sheepishly.

"She actually said 'penises'?"

Darshan lowered his eyes.

"Beeji has gone too far!" Bikram shouted. "She is uncouth."

Jagtar heard this and asked, "Ji, how can you call my mother that?"

"She is cruel, greedy, cloying, just an obnoxious woman!"

"Ji, you are upset. Be quiet. My mother is not a demon. She is just a mother who wanted a normal bride for her son."

"Her son Sukha is a saint, a true Sikh."

"He is still her son, Ji. A mother has ambitions, dreams for her sons. Beeji wanted him to marry a virgin, not a tainted one."

It was the first time he'd come so close to striking her.

"Until she accepts Sukha's bride, your mother is not welcome in my home."

Jagtar started to cry. "How can you do that to my mother, Ji? How can you?"

"I will go one better. You have not given me another child. Maybe I will offer to marry a tainted woman like Jiyot Kaur. It will teach all of you a fine lesson!"

Jagtar started to wail.

Basanti

The hot winds of summer began to blow, creating dust devils in the dera. Basanti felt the excitement of her clan mounting as the day of the weddings—hers to Rana, and Devi's to Wazeer—approached. Since the Raja of the tribe had decided to attend—to honour Rustum Mukhia, the champion of the Bajigars—their Mukhia had decreed that all the huts should receive new coats of mud, the lean-tos would be thoroughly swept and cleaned, and the fence repaired.

Children received new clothes, women stitched kurtis and ghunias, and men bought new turbans in the bazaar and took them to be dyed and starched. A tattooist arrived to paint the symbol Om on her fore-head and Devi's and tribal dots on their cheeks. Dadi gave them dried acacia bark to chew, to redden their gums and lips, and Mata applied kohl to their eyelids. After washing and drying their hair, Devi's mother spent a day oiling, combing, and braiding.

Basanti looked into a square hand mirror and barely recognized herself.

"So beautiful, so beautiful," Dadi said.

They sat patiently for henna to be applied in intricate patterns to their hands and feet, and then waited some more for it to dry and set. They tried on their bridal ensembles of red-embroidered kurtis and ghunias, red chadors, and silver jewellery, all under the scrutiny of the women.

On the big day, the wedding party—men only—arrived from Raikot on oxcarts escorting the grooms who were on camels. Basanti watched from inside the hut as they were received and led into the centre of the dera to be honoured with garlands and gifts. Try as she might, she could not see Rana, for both grooms had silver sehras cov-ering their faces.

The women began to sing lilting songs; a loudspeaker blared

popular music. The children ran around chasing each other and generally raising a ruckus, even after the elders scolded them. Dadi bustled around, carrying her hookah, giving orders. Smoke rose from the cooking pits that had been dug for the feast.

Basanti sat beside Devi inside the hut.

"You are sure it will work?" Devi asked nervously.

She nodded. An older cousin had taught them a trick to make themselves bleed during their first coupling with their grooms. She swore it worked—she'd used it herself.

"Just don't panic at the last moment."

There was a commotion outside. "The Raja is here!"

It seemed as though everyone was rushing to the gate to greet the tribe's leader.

The tall man, holding a silver-tipped staff, was preceded by a drummer, whose beats rose to a crescendo as he proudly led the Raja into the dera.

"Will he give us gifts?" Devi asked as the Raja passed out of view.

"He would not come empty-handed, would he?"

"I am getting a headache from all this thinking and worrying."

"Lie down and rest. The ceremony won't start until after midnight."

That night they sat on covered ground facing their grooms across a ceremonial fire tended by a Brahmin, who chanted holy verses and poured drops of ghee on the flames, releasing billows of fragrant smoke into the air. He started the rituals and called on the girls' parents to participate. Through her veil, Basanti could see only shadows in front of her.

She was pulled to her feet and rose unsteadily, having sat cross-legged for so long. Someone handed her the garland of marigold flowers that she had helped string earlier.

"Hold it in both hands."

Another garland was placed over her own head and around her neck.

"Now, put that garland on the groom," Mata whispered, and helped her raise it.

There was applause, and she heard Devi being given the same instructions. More applause.

"You are wed," the Brahmin said. "Take the brides to their homes." Mata and Dadi guided her through the dark, back to the hut, and helped her change.

"Do it in the corner, I will cover it with ash," Mata said after she complained that her bladder was about to burst. "Then lie down and sleep. You won't be needed until the doli leaves in the afternoon."

Alone in the hut, she lay down, and listened to voices drifting through the open door and the windows.

As soon as the faint light of dawn broke, the women came to get her, and she hurried to the fields with them. They enclosed her in a circle by holding up sheets to let her undress and bathe at the pump. The cool water revived her, and Dadi helped soap her entire body while carefully avoiding wetting her hair. She returned to the hut to dress for her departure in the doli with her groom. *Leaving!* Mata wept as she helped her, and Dadi kept wiping her eyes. She wished they'd stop—if she herself started crying, would she ever stop?

And then they heard someone call out, "Here comes the Zaildar, the Rustum's malik. Look! He's riding his famous mare!"

Basanti had been told that the Malik would be escorting them to their new dera, which was on his lands. She rushed to the window to watch and gasped. The Malik looked just like an older version of the Captain. She tried to think back to the time when Dadi said they had danced at the Malik's haveli, but that was long ago. The Zaildar embraced Rustum Mukhia. They were the two tallest men there, until the Raja came and joined them—he was even taller. The people cheered to see three such important men greet each other.

When Basanti saw the saddled camel waiting to take her away she glanced over at Devi, who began to wail, and then she began to sob as well. She stumbled, and had to be quickly held up by strong hands. Someone adjusted and tightened her veil. She was lifted onto the saddle and a leather strap was wrapped around her hands.

At a command the camel began to rise, thrusting her forward and backward. She hung on for dear life.

"Rana, take the reins," a voice directed.

The camel began to move, and she felt her heart being torn from her chest as the women sang a mournful song of farewell, following her for the traditional number of steps. How many times had she walked behind a bride in just the same way . . . and now she was the bride! When they halted at the canal road, her camel moved on and their voices began to fade. She tried to turn and look back but it was impossible, for her chador was wrapped tightly around her head, so as not to slip and reveal her face to the men who rode in front on the oxcarts.

She felt the rhythmic sway of the camel and heard the teasing of the grooms who led them. The kinsmen were having fun, puffing on hoo-kahs. She could smell the smoke. Passersby shouted congratulations and the men in her party called back. She could not hear a horse's hooves and wondered where the Malik was. Had he gone on ahead?

They crossed a long bridge over the silvery canal just as the sun touched the horizon and she felt its golden glow.

When they arrived at their new home, Basanti and Devi were brought to a large square hut with whitewashed walls and blue window and door frames. It was lit inside with a big lantern hanging from an iron keela on the wall. They were seated on a cot strung with cotton, unlike the rough hemp they were used to, and presented to the women of the dera in the showing-the-face ceremony. Her mother-in-law pre-sided with an authoritative voice. A bunch of young girls stood close by and stared at them as a line of women went by. Basanti and Devi lifted their veils and bent to touch their feet, and they were presented with coins.

"Live long and un-widowed," was the repeated blessing.

Outside, where the men were celebrating, she could hear Rustum Mukhia offering drinks to his kinsmen. "It is the happiest day of my life," he repeated. "Drink."

When the ceremony was over, Devi was led to her hut by her mother-in-law, who was called Naura. Basanti followed her own mother-in-law, Sehba, to her hut. After the door was pulled closed on them and the windows shut, she took off her chador and sat down to eat. Sehba placed a brass tumbler of water by her feet.

"Take your time, Basanti. The men will celebrate late into the night."

She watched Sehba tie a string across the room and hang two sheets over it to divide the space. There was a cot on each side on which Sehba placed a bedding roll. Then Sehba told Basanti, "I am going to be just outside. Shout if you need me."

Basanti's hand went nervously to the large safety pin hidden in the folds of her ghunia. The plan was to insert it inside herself, spring open the sharp pin, and quickly prick herself a few times when the time came. There would be enough blood to confirm her virginity. She prayed that it worked, and that Devi, too, would not falter.

She sat on the cot with her chador over her and waited.

The next morning Sehba examined the rag. "You have a virtuous wife, my son!" she shouted. Basanti had wiped herself with it and then tossed it over the partition. "Go to sleep, you two." Her mother-in-law sounded pleased, and was no doubt thankful that she no longer had to stand vigil.

As for Basanti, relief washed over her, and she lay staring at the tin ceiling reflecting the light from the lantern. *Thank you, Laxmi Maa, thank you*, she silently prayed. The voices of merriment could still be heard outside, as could the booming voice of Rustum Mukhia.

Rana had rushed in all excited and barely said a word. His hands were busy, pinching, rubbing, and squeezing her body. He breathed noisily, and reeked of tobacco and alcohol. She'd put up the requisite resistance, which had only increased his ardour. A loud, tortured moan and he had collapsed on her. Now he lay still beside her.

After a long while, the door of the hut was opened and then slammed shut. She heard the heavy steps of Rustum Mukhia, and before long he blew out the lantern and the cot creaked under his weight.

His snoring became louder, and she covered her ears as Rana joined him.

How does the poor woman ever sleep? she wondered, lying wide-eyed in the dark.

Her thoughts were with Devi.

It took a full day before Devi confessed. The two of them had been left alone by their mothers-in-law, who were busy counting the coins received as gifts.

Devi never got a chance to use the safety pin. After waiting in the hut alone, she had dozed off and fallen into a deep sleep, tired from the night before, the long ride on the camel, and the showing-the-face ritual. She had not heard Wazeer return, followed by his mother, and awoke abruptly only when she felt him inside her.

As soon as he finished, Naura struck a match, touched it to the wick of the oil lamp, and passed Devi a rag and waited. When she got it back, she examined it.

"She's a whore."

The verdict brought Wazeer's weight on her and his hands around her throat.

"I am going to kill you."

Devi said she feared that these would be the last moments of her life.

Naura had pulled Wazeer off her, slapped her on both cheeks, and called her a whore again.

When Basanti asked Devi what happened after that, Devi sighed, swallowed hard, and looked at her with sad eyes.

"They hissed at each other so as not to wake the neighbours. Wazeer calmed down only after his mother told him that in the new India he could hang from the gallows for strangling his wife. Also, since they could not afford another bride price, he might as well accept a tainted one rather than go through life without one."

"He threatened to abandon you?"

"He threatened a lot of things. I'm afraid of him, Basanti."

Basanti hung her head. *Laxmi Maa*, she asked the goddess, *what sins did Devi commit in her past life to be punished thus? Why did you help me and not her? Why did sleep blanket her senses and leave her honour exposed in her hour of need?*

"Cheer up, girls. I know you miss your parents and clan. I did, too." Shanti, a warm woman with a kind smile, slapped their backs. "Now you are wed into this clan. Start enjoying your youth and your husbands." They were sipping tea in Sehba's kitchen mid-morning on their fourth day at the dera.

"My Rana is over the moon with Basanti. Their cot creaks all night long," Sehba said with a grin.

Basanti watched Naura's face. It turned from scowling to smiling. "Wazeer mounts Devi like a stallion. I have to cover my ears."

One must keep up appearances, Basanti realized. A dera was a small world, and Naura was not going to be out-boasted by Sehba. Clearly there was some tension between them. That gave Basanti a bit of comfort.

Devi buried her face in her chador.

"There is no shame in being the object of a husband's desires." Shanti laughed. "I wish I could say that. Mine no longer parts my legs."

"You liar, you," Naura said. "I can hear your moans from my hut."

"You mean the moans from my aches and pains. Here, look at my cracked heels and swollen feet."

"I hear that if you keep your feet up in the air, they don't swell." Sehba grinned.

"No wonder you have slender ankles. Mukhia must hold them up high a lot."

"Shanti, you are a shameless woman," Sehba said.

There was some truth to Shanti's teasing. Sehba did have her legs up almost every night, and Basanti had to listen to Rustum Mukhia's mighty heaves and his wife's breathless moans. And yet, with all their noisy coupling, all they had produced was the pigeon-chested, acne-faced Rana. How could that be? When Basanti had finally seen her husband in the light of day, she'd felt terribly disappointed. His cousin Wazeer had a brawny body and a handsome profile, despite his scowls and angry eyes that seemed to stare right through her.

Shanti changed the subject. "When are you going to take the brides to Raikot to present them to the village?"

"We should do it soon." Sehba looked at Naura.

It seemed to please Naura that Sehba was asking her opinion. "Let's take them tomorrow."

"Wear comfortable sandals," Shanti said to the girls. "It's a big village. Lots of gates to knock on. Tell your husbands to give you girls a night off to rest."

"Tell your husband to keep his hands off your saggy butt," Sehba said.

The teasing did not let up until an elderly man walked by and gave them an angry look.

"Lazy women," he said.

They wore veils and their bridal clothes, their feet in red sandals. A dozen women from the dera accompanied them and their mothers-in-law. Sehba stopped when they came to two large steel gates standing opposite each other across a wide path. "We will visit the Malik's haveli first."

The women led them to the gate on the right and started to sing and clap. A stout, smiling woman came to welcome them.

"The brides are here," she announced.

The haveli had a vast courtyard with high, brick walls. A long verandah ran along the length of the house, and women stood at the kitchen stoves staring at them. Two more came out of the haveli carrying laden trays in their hands.

"The Malkin, the wife of our Malik, and her daughter-in-law, Amrita," Sehba whispered in her ear.

"Lift the veils. Show us your faces." The Malkin smiled.

Basanti and Devi bent to touch their feet and receive their blessings.

"Live long and un-widowed."

Sehba pulled Basanti's veil back, and she stood with lowered eyes.

"Beautiful, my, my, so pretty." The woman who had opened the gate put a rupee note in her hand, and so did two more.

Now they turned to look at Devi.

"Are they sisters?" Amrita asked. "They look like twins."

Basanti admired the younger woman's outfit. Her V-neck kurti had short sleeves and shimmered down to her knees over a darker, bulbous salwar, whose stitched cuffs covered her sandals. She wore a set of beautiful gold jewellery, with ruby-studded bangles that tinkled every time she moved her hands. Even her chador had tiny sequins embedded in it.

"They are cousins, now married to cousins," Naura explained.

"Bring some cots," the Malkin said. The women who had gathered in the kitchen then arranged half a dozen cots in a semicircle. Basanti was surprised, since she had never before seen her people offered a cot to sit on in a patron's home.

"Sit, sit," the Malkin urged. "Boil tea and fetch biscuits. It's a day to celebrate," she shouted to a grey-haired woman.

"Imagine, they danced right here at your engagement to Satwant," Sehba said to Amrita.

"I remember," the Malkin said, smiling. "They stole the show."

"Who danced?" a tiny voice asked.

Basanti turned to see a little girl holding a rag doll.

"Pinki, come say Sat Sri Akal to Basanti and Devi," the Malkin said, and the little girl ran and jumped into her grandmother's lap.

The child was pretty, shy but curious, and she smiled before turning to hide her face.

They must have been halfway through the village when they saw a birdlike figure in a white chador hurrying towards them. It was the Brahmin elder, Pushpa.

"Sehba." The woman came to a stop before them. "What's going on?"

"We are conducting the showing-the-face ceremony."

"I see."

"Girls, show respect."

Basanti bent to touch the woman's feet.

"Show me your face."

Basanti lifted her veil.

"Very pretty, very pretty. You Rajput women are all pretty. No wonder the Mughals lusted after you. Sehba, did you take the brides to bow at the Naag Baba temple?"

Sehba looked uncomfortable and wrung her hands.

"You greedy, stupid woman," Pushpa said. "You dare run around with the new brides, collecting gifts from the Jats, and did not bother to first honour the village gods?"

Sehba hung her head low.

"Be warned. This will only bring bad luck. I warn you."

"I am sorry. I made a mistake," Sehba began to plead.

"Too late." Pushpa turned and stormed away.

Her stern words echoed in Basanti's ears for the rest of that day.

Ajit

The ploughing began in earnest on Ajit's lands. Four teams of oxen and both camels were led out of the cattle yard by six ploughmen at dawn and returned at dusk. Canal water now, at last, irrigated his property throughout, and he was renting half his land to sharecroppers. It took his own hired hands and animals a month just to prepare the soil for seeding the cotton, maize, millet, and a few more acres of sugarcane for the summer crop.

The first showers of the monsoons fell and the fields turned green. He hired twenty Bajigar men for weeding, and they had to be given three meals and tea twice a day. Ajit brought the refreshments himself on his good-natured mare. The job was somewhat beneath his dignity as zaildar, but he had a very special little helper. The mare also carried Pinki, who distributed the brass tumblers to the workers. Amrita would tie a cloth on her head to keep it covered in the sun, and Pinki kept her grandfather amused with her chatter.

"Tea is here!" Pinki called. This always brought smiles to dusty faces of the workers, who dropped their scythes and gathered around her.

"You are so pretty," a woman said.

"I know."

"Pinki, be humble."

"What's that, Babaji?"

He smiled and shook his head.

Then one day she announced that she would not go with him.

"Why not?" he asked.

"I want to help at the kitchen."

"But you enjoy going for rides!"

"The sun is too hot, Babaji. My head hurts."

He wondered what the little girl had found to do at home that was so much more amusing than a horseback ride. Until one day she came running up to him.

"Babaji! Look what Bajigar grandma Sehba brought for me." She held up a rag doll.

"That's so nice," Ajit said and knelt to examine it.

"And I played with Basanti, Rana's new wife."

"You did?"

"Yes, Babaji, she is so nice. She makes me laugh because she speaks funny."

Pinki tried to mimic her, and it made the women who were cooking laugh.

"And she is teaching me to dance!"

"Show me."

She began to hop around.

"That's not dancing." Siamo laughed.

"It *is*, Bhua."

"I think Pinki has a new friend now," Amrita said, bringing Ajit a glass of water.

Satwant had received a peacetime posting at Kanpur Cantonment. When he came home for a two-month furlough, the haveli lit up with his presence.

Pinki clung to her father, and he would not put her down even for a moment. They were finally separated at the dining table when Amrita took Pinki in her lap to feed her.

"I can eat by myself, Daddy, watch."

They watched as she tore off a piece of roti and curled it to make a spoon to fill with dal.

Satwant clapped in appreciation. Pinki looked around crossly and Ajit took the hint. "Shabash, Pinki, shabash." He too clapped, and the women joined in.

Pinki smiled.

"How's everything here?" Satwant asked.

"We are feeling almost lazy, now that we have a bit of a respite before the fall harvest and planting the winter crop," Inder said.

"And how's the zaildari, Bapuji?"

"As always. Independence has changed nothing."

"It has changed how people see things, though, hasn't it? It has taught us that the country belongs to us," Satwant said. "I mean, it always belonged to us, of course, but now it's ours to shape. Think of the future, Bapuji! Who knows what India might become in my lifetime, or in Pinki's?"

Ajit smiled. "You are so wise, Satwant, that sometimes I forget you're still young. Young enough to believe in change when power remains in the hands of the people who always held it."

"I expect that the new government will do away with feudal titles like yours altogether, Bapuji. Just look at how they seized and amalgamated the hundreds of kingdoms and principalities into one India."

"The rulers still get their stipends," he said.

"But for how long? I can imagine a better day, when the people determine their own fate. Can't you?"

This was what Ajit missed when his son was away. The conversation over dinner, someone to share news about matters outside the haveli or the cattle yard. Someone to debate with. He looked forward to the next two months.

Bikram

"You will find votes for Akalis in the villages," Chand said. "That's where most Sikhs live, and your strongest support will come from the Jats."

Bikram thought about that. In Samrala, half of the six thousand residents were Hindus, who would never support a Sikh religious party. And the town's Sikhs were educated and supporters of the sitting Congress members of the legislature. It made more sense to campaign in the villages.

He nodded. "You are right."

"My father is always right," Jagtar said proudly as she passed him the lamb curry.

Bikram had been assured by his Akali Dal that his candidacy would be successful. The leader had of course asked for a healthy financial donation to the party, and a pledge from Bikram to spend money on the leader's own personal campaign. The election was two years away, but the preparatory work had to be done now.

"Buy a car to visit the villages. Stepping out of a car will look more dignified than hopping out of a tonga," Mangal advised, loudly chewing his food.

Jagtar smiled, and her expression became dreamy. "Do it, Ji. I can just see you being fêted as an important man by the villagers."

"I can find you a second-hand one," Chand offered.

"Or I can get a newer car swiped off a city street in a far-away place like Calcutta or Bombay." Mangal grinned.

"No, no, no, Ji," Jagtar said. "If the police discover you driving a stolen car, your reputation will be ruined!"

"Just an idea," Mangal said, now cleaning his teeth with a fingernail.

"You'll certainly need a driver, though," Chand said.

Jagtar looked at her father. "What's wrong with Ji driving himself? You can drive a car, Ji. You told me you learned to drive a truck in the army."

"No, he has to have a driver. It's much more dignified."

"Another cost, Ji. Look at how easily they spend our money."

Chand glared at Jagtar, and he turned to Mangal. "You can lend me one of your experienced men, can't you?"

Mangal nodded. "I will get you a real Gursikh driver. One who has a long beard, ties a good turban, doesn't drink or smoke."

"There are drivers like that?" Jagtar asked, her eyes wide in exaggerated disbelief.

"Daughter," Chand said. "Let us men talk, please."

"This is my house. Don't you forget it."

She left the table and slammed the dining room door behind her.

They agreed that it made sense to start in the villages where Bikram was known as a grain merchant, or where family relations lived. What he needed was more information about their populations, and the caste breakdown.

"The untouchables will always vote for Congress. Gandhi's the one who enshrined constitutional benefits and job quotas for them," Chand muttered.

"Everyone is for sale for the right price, Bikram," Mangal said. "The low castes have all those government guarantees already, so we can get their vote by offering more immediate material benefits."

"What benefits?" Chand asked.

"Liquor, for one." Mangal grinned. "I can get excellent moonshine dirt cheap from the Bet."

"And what else?" Chand asked.

"Water pumps for their bastees. The Jats and Brahmins won't let them draw water from communal wells."

Bikram liked the idea. The lower-caste communities lived basically in slums, with no decent facilities. He could pitch water pumps as a public service, a sewa for the poor.

"How about you offer kanyadaan, also," Chand suggested.

"I pay for their daughters' weddings?"

"Sure," Mangal agreed. "You could organize mass wedding ceremonies, save on expenses."

Chand smiled. "The desperate parents will sing your praises. You could probably rope in some philanthropists and idealists to share the costs."

Bikram's ears perked up at the suggestion of partnering with rich merchants and zaildars. He thought of Ajit Singh in Raikot, and the idea of rubbing shoulders with his old benefactor excited him.

"Just before the election, we load trucks with flour and lentils and donate that to the poor," Mangal suggested. "Buy their gratitude, win their votes."

"You've been thinking about this, Mangal, haven't you?"

Mangal patted his shoulder before pouring a shot of whiskey. "I really want you to be an MLA, Bikram. It will make me very proud and happy. I'll do anything to see that it happens."

Bikram didn't know what to say.

"And don't forget the Bajigars," Chand added.

"Bajigars? Can they vote?" Bikram asked.

"Of course they can vote, and now that they are settled in permanent deras, they're easier to get to."

"How many deras in the Samrala constituency?"

"Dozens."

Bikram could feel his pulse quicken. Going on trips, meeting people, installing pumps, handing out food packets, plying voters with liquor. It sounded a lot more exciting than killing time all day at his shop.

"You must congratulate me today," Gopal said as Ramu handed him a cup of tea and placed a plate of sweets before him in the verandah.

"Congratulations, Pundit-ji." Jagtar smiled.

"Congratulations," Bikram said. "But what are we congratulating you *for*?"

"My son got a job as a court clerk in Samrala."

The matchmaker sat back, settling in to tell what he knew was a juicy story. It turned out that even though Gopal and Aalok Nath, the famous Congress MLA, were kin, Aalok Nath's son had asked him for six months' wages as a bribe.

"This is the new independent India," Gopal explained. "Power goes from the white sahibs to the brown sahibs, except that the brown sahibs have dung for morals."

Later, after changing for bed, Jagtar cuddled closer to Bikram.

"Listen, Ji. Did you pay attention to the pundit? When you're an MLA, you can be the one charging money to arrange jobs. Think, Ji, please . . . think."

He could feel her nipples harden against his chest. She cuddled closer and he put his finger in her mouth. She began to suck on it, and his hopes rose. It was going to be a great night, he thought, as his body began to tingle.

"You really like money, don't you, Jagtar?"

She took the finger out and whispered, "You know, Ji, what is my ultimate dream?"

"Tell me."

"To sleep on a mattress full of hundred-rupee notes."

Basanti

Before long, the beautiful wedding clothes, the jewellery, and the shoes had been packed away, and Basanti and Devi put on the faded and patched hand-me-downs of their mothers-in-law and went about barefoot. One tiresome day gave way to the next as Sehba and Naura gave the girls more and more chores to do. Devi cleaned the lean-to that housed Rustum Mukhia's buffaloes and calves; she thumped the dung into pies and dried them in the sun. Basanti milked the beasts twice a day and worked in the kitchen, kneading dough, boiling lentils, and making tea, and served the mothers-in-law, who now spent their days puffing the communal hookah and gossiping at the centre.

Some days it seemed like a full day's work just helping Sehba prepare food for the Mukhia. His mornings started with a bowl of yogurt, followed by a pinni, eaten with a jug of tea. At midday, he ate half a dozen rotis with whatever dal or subzi was left over from the night before, and a bowl of powdered jaggery mixed with butter, chased with almost half a bucket of buttermilk. At supper, he ate the equivalent of the midday meal, followed by a jug of warm milk sweetened with jaggery. He loved the gravy from stewed bones and rib meat that he saved from the carcass of a goat he butchered at dawn almost every day. He slurped the stuff noisily and sucked the marrow out of the bones, belching in satisfaction. He always seemed to end up with onion and coriander stuck to his moustache.

Basanti and Devi were rewarded with three meals a day, a sip or two of sweetened milk, a mug of tea, and the odd treat that the Mukhia brought after winning another bout at a festival or a fair. Basanti found him to be kind and generous, and he always asked after the young brides.

Rana left before dawn to work in the Malik's cattle yard and returned after dark to sit in the kitchen and sip a glass of milk with jaggery. He ate his meals at work and spent the nights mounting her or rubbing himself against her. Basanti had already come to hate him and his spidery ways, his breath coming in noisy, nasal screeches into her ear. They barely exchanged a word. If they were sitting together at the hearth he would ignore her and talk with his parents. And what did he talk about, more than anything? The mare named Bakki. He never stopped praising it. Rana cared for the beast more than he cared for her.

Rana arrived home late one night, unsteady on his feet and smelling of alcohol.

"Chhota Malik is home."

"Is he?" Sehba perked up.

"And Satwant gave you a few pegs of army rum," Rustum Mukhia said, and smiled.

The next morning, Sehba marshalled Basanti and Devi together with the other women and they set out for Raikot to work. On the way, a man approached them on horseback. Devi grabbed Basanti's elbow. "Look, look at the rider!"

Basanti looked up and couldn't believe her eyes. It was the Captain. The closer he came, the faster her heart raced.

Sehba ran to greet him. "Satwant!"

He stopped the mare and swung off to let himself be embraced by her.

"Girls, come forward and be presented to our Chhota Malik."

Basanti pulled her chador down to veil her face. Why did she have to be wearing such dowdy clothes when she was about to be presented to the hero of her life? Devi did the same, and they bent to touch his feet.

He stepped back, protesting, "It's all right. A simple greeting will do."

"You can pull your veils back. Satwant does not like the custom. His wife, Amrita, does not veil herself."

They did as suggested, and the Captain gazed at them, smiling.

"Basanti, on the right, is married to Rana, and Devi is married to Wazeer. You missed their weddings, Satwant."

The Captain leaned closer to them. "They are the same little ones that danced at my engagement?"

"You remember them?"

"How could I forget?"

"Sahib, you brought us safely from Pakistan," Devi said in a soft voice.

He frowned. "Oh, now I remember. You had your hair shorn to your scalps."

"We were disguised as boys, Sahib."

"And look at you now, both grown up into beautiful women."

Basanti lowered her eyes and felt blood rush to her cheeks. He sounded so sincere.

"Let me bless you both." He pulled rupee notes out of his pocket and gave them each one.

They bent to touch his feet again and he jumped back, startling the mare. It reared its head and neighed, making them all shrink back.

He turned to pat its neck. "There, there, Bakki."

"She is a frisky one," Naura said nervously.

"Rana never stops talking about Bakki, Satwant," Sehba said.

"And I am going to teach him to ride her."

Basanti felt the mare's energy and was awed by its elegance. She had never seen so handsome a horse. The saddle twinkled in the sunlight and made her squint.

"I'd better get going." The Captain gave Sehba a quick hug, as a nephew might hug a favourite aunt. Sehba glowed.

They watched as he swung onto the saddle, backed the mare, and turned it to ride past them. He kicked its sides and it broke into a gallop. Basanti suddenly felt a lot better and safer. Her Captain was back in her life.

"Give it to me." Sehba grabbed the note from her hand. "Look, a whole five rupees. Satwant is so generous."

Basanti and Devi were working together in the hut grinding grain, struggling to turn the heavy stone wheel of the mill. It was one of the few opportunities they ever had to speak privately, and when they could, they usually talked about their husbands, and what happened on their cots at night.

"Mine likes my virgin hole better," Devi told her, and tears filled her eyes. "You know . . . my bum. It hurts like hell."

"What?" Basanti stopped and stared at her cousin. Could a man really do that? She felt sick at the thought of Devi enduring such depravity. "Doesn't Naura stop him?"

"She giggles, the bitch. I hope maggots fill her intestines and kill her." Devi's voice dripped with bitterness.

"What?"

"She is a bad woman. Ever since Wazeer's father was killed in an accident, she's been filled with poison. He was Rustum Mukhia's older brother, and she thinks his son should have been made the mukhia here after his death, according to birthright."

"Wasn't Wazeer just a child when his father died?"

"He was. So, the clan elected the Rustum as their Mukhia."

"And she still resents him."

Devi nodded.

As voices approached, the girls began to turn the wheel. Basanti leaned closer as Devi hissed, "The bitch poisons her son with all kinds of stories about being denied their rights. Wazeer has problems with his head. He can't think straight. The pervert drinks, too. Gets bottles from the village bootlegger."

Basanti felt her head swim, and a helplessness invaded her soul. A wife had no choice but to obey and show respect for her husband and his mother, for the sake of the family's honour.

"You know something?" Devi had a gleam in her eye.

"What?"

Devi leaned forward and spoke in a whisper. "I will lift my ghunia anytime for the Captain."

Basanti felt her jaw drop.

"I am serious. All he has to do is wink."

"Devi! Are you crazy? How can you even think such a thing?"

"Oh, and you wouldn't do the same?" Devi asked. "I saw how you preened and blushed for him yesterday."

"I did not . . . And even if I did, what would he want with the two of us when he has such a pretty wife?"

"Men such as the Captain are like stallions. They need a different mare to mount now and then."

Innocent Devi, not so innocent any more.

"You are something else, Devi."

"At least now I have something to look forward to." Devi flicked a strand of hair from her flushed face.

"So . . . how will he know that you are willing to lift your ghunia for him?" She felt jealousy rise in her for the first time.

"I will find a way," Devi said, and began to turn the wheel again.

One day, the Captain strode through the gates of the dera, accompanied by a man with hair slicked and parted in the middle, carrying a thick book.

Sehba raced to greet them.

"Set a nice cot down and lay a clean blanket on it for them to sit on!" Naura shouted.

Devi leapt at the command.

Now Rustum Mukhia came out of the hut and hugged the Captain in a tight embrace.

"Welcome, Satwant. Welcome, Masterji."

Sehba turned to Basanti. "Put water to boil, quickly."

Basanti returned to the kitchen and packed kindling and sticks into the chullah. She blew through a bamboo pipe to start the fire; smoke came out and made her eyes water. When she glanced over the half wall of the kitchen, she was startled to see Devi standing by the seated Captain, talking to him. Her feet seemed to dance. Rustum Mukhia and two white-haired elders were seated on one cot, the Captain and Masterji on the other.

What are you up to, Devi?

Sehba brought out a large metal tray with her best china mugs and a plate of fist-sized pinnis, made of milk cake and sugar.

"Make a lot of tea. They are here to discuss something with my husband and the elders," Sehba said, and she left to go listen to the men.

Basanti felt pleased. It seemed the Captain would be here for a while.

Some time later, the man who had come with the Captain rose to make an announcement.

"We are here to register your children for school," he said, his voice ringing with authority so that it could be heard across the dera.

"School?" an elder asked.

"Yes, school. It is the law. All settled people must send their children to school."

"We are Bajigars."

"I said settled people. Bajigars are now a settled people," Masterji replied.

Basanti was craning her neck to look. When the water began to boil, she sat back to throw the leaves into the pot, adding brown sugar and milk as well.

"We have no need for school," the elder said. "Our boys have to work to earn a bride price, and girls have to learn crafts and cooking."

Devi came and grabbed the tray with the pinnis and tea, and quickly took it to the men on the cots. She bent to serve the tea, lingering before the Captain.

Basanti spied Wazeer watching her with red-rimmed eyes. "Watch your husband," she warned her when she returned to the kitchen.

"Mukhia, listen." Masterji took a gulp of tea. "As I look at you seated with your elders and holding that curved staff of a herder, I am reminded of Moses, the great prophet of the Jews. He led his people out of the yoke of slavery and on to a better place. Uplifted them. What are you going to do for yours? Keep them poor and illiterate? Or will you send your children to school to give them an education so that they can better themselves for the future? Join society as equals?"

"I agree with Masterji," the Captain said.

"There are fees, clothes, books, and slates to buy. We have no money," the elder said.

"I will pay for all of that," the Captain said.

"Tell me, Satwant, should I do as Masterji demands?" Rustum Mukhia asked.

The Captain nodded. "It is time to change from the old ways. Give your children a brighter future."

Rustum Mukhia considered this for a while, then said, "All right, Satwant. Masterji wins."

Masterji opened his book and took a pen from his pocket. "Present the children."

Devi turned to Basanti and smiled. "Oh, how I wish we could go to school."

"It's too late for us."

A little girl sidled up to the Captain. He lifted her onto a knee.

"What's your name?"

"Paso."

"What do you want to be when you grow up, Paso? A doctor? A teacher?"

"I want to marry you," the imp said.

The Captain burst out laughing and everyone joined in.

Devi sighed. "Now I am jealous of *her*."

A few days later, Rustum Mukhia returned to the dera limping and sore. He had experienced his first ever defeat, at the hands of a Jat who was younger and quicker. His cauliflower ears seemed to have been pulped in the bout, his shoulder pulled, and a knee twisted. Sehba laid him on a cot and applied warm compresses to the lumps and bumps. This defeat in the akhara was soon the talk of the dera, and people came by with long faces to console him.

He was no longer a Rustum.

"I have decided to hang up my langoti, Malik," he said when the Malik came to visit and sit with him. Basanti came to serve them tea.

"I think it is wise. You will soon be a grandfather," she heard the Malik say.

The Mukhia was bedridden for days, and Sehba spent all her time looking after him.

Basanti asked her, "What will the Mukhia do now?" Wrestling had made him one of the richest Bajigars. He had a brick hut, buffaloes, and a full pantry. She could not picture him bending in a field picking weeds like a labourer.

"He will set up a butcher's stall at the Adda and sell goat meat," Sehba replied.

"Get me a cup of mustard oil to drink, Sehba. I am dying of constipation," the Mukhia moaned, and she raced in again.

༄

The Captain returned to the dera with a tailor and a shoemaker. Sehba summoned the children.

The tailor took measurements for kurta-pyjama suits for the boys and kurti-salwar suits for the girls. The children had to wear Punjabi-style clothes in school.

"Uniforms are school policy," the Captain explained.

"Everyone must be equal," added the kindly and patient tailor.

Next the shoemaker traced outlines of the children's feet on paper.

Now the Captain drew close a large cardboard box he had brought, and from it he lifted a paper bag. He offered it to Paso, who reached inside and pulled out a wrapped candy. The children swarmed the Captain.

"Behave, behave!" Basanti tried to line them up.

"Listen to Basanti," the Captain said. "You must line up to get your turn."

As the children approached, he gave each one a candy, a notebook, a slate, chalk, a pencil, and a sharpener, which he showed them how to use. Devi was seated on the ground, as close to the Captain as she could be. Basanti cast her eyes around and saw Wazeer standing beside his mother, eyes locked on his wife.

Sehba came carrying a tray with pinnis and tea.

The Captain took a bite. "You make the best pinnis, I swear, Sehba."

"I made these especially for you," Sehba said with a bright face. "I have packed the rest for you to take with you."

The Captain split the pinni in two and touched Devi's shoulder. "Here."

When Devi looked up her chador slipped off her head, and she quickly pulled it back up. Her fingers seemed to linger against the Captain's as he passed her the treat. Basanti saw that her cousin's hands had a fine tremor, and her face was flushed. *So, this is the look of lust. Save us, Laxmi Maa*, she prayed, as her own emotions roiled her thoughts.

"You are so gracious, Chhota Malik," Devi said, softly.

"You too, Basanti. Have a half," he offered.

She had never tasted a pinni, made of milk cake and sugar and mixed with sultanas, dried fruit, and fennel seeds. She let the taste linger on her tongue. No wonder the Mukhia called them life-giving. Only women who had just given birth were offered these to eat, to restore their health and encourage their milk.

"We are finished, Satwant." The tailor began to pack away his equipment.

"Me, too." The shoemaker, an untouchable, had brought his own mug, and he packed it with his tools.

"When will you be back, Chhota Sahib?" Devi asked as the Captain stood up.

"Sometime soon, I hope."

"The dera lights up with your presence," she told him in her lilting voice.

Sehba took him by the arm towards their hut, and he went in to visit the Mukhia.

Wazeer, Basanti noticed, had not moved, and his eyes had never left Devi.

That evening, Wazeer came from the fields drunk, and Basanti watched him stumble past. A while later, screams erupted from Naura's hut.

"Bloody whore, show-off, touching hands!"

It was what she had feared. She had tried to warn Devi.

"I will teach you to flirt with the stupid Captain," Wazeer shouted. Basanti heard the sound of slapping, and Devi began to wail.

"What did he say?"

Basanti turned to see the Mukhia standing in the doorway, a bamboo staff in his hand.

"I never flirted with him," Devi screamed. "I swear!"

The Mukhia marched towards the commotion. Basanti pulled down her dupatta and hurried behind. Naura's door was flung open, and Basanti saw Devi lying curled up on the floor as Wazeer stood over her swearing and swaying.

"What did you say about the Captain?" the Mukhia roared.

Wazeer looked up and seemed to shrink back.

"Nothing, Uncle. I said nothing."

"You have a loose tongue, Wazeer, and one day it is going to cost you."

"Go away." Naura stood in front of the Mukhia and tried waving him off.

"Naura, watch your boy and keep him under control. I warn you, he is young and he's headed in the wrong direction."

"My son can do what he wants," Naura said.

"He's involved with a very dangerous man. Lalu the bootlegger is cruel. Wazeer is going to find out the hard way."

"So says the usurper of my son's birthright," Naura spat back.

Basanti took advantage of the confrontation to grab Devi and hurry her to her own hut. Sehba followed and helped her console and comfort Devi, with her bruised face and split lip.

Ajit

The two months of Satwant's furlough were pleasantly filled with visits from relatives, classmates, and friends. And every few days, Ajit and his son would ride out together to relive their trips to the villages of his zaildari. Men and women were drawn to Satwant wherever they stopped to rest. Satwant, having taken responsibility for the Bajigar children's education, would go to Samrala to buy cloth for uniforms and school supplies. When school started, he and the Mukhia led the Bajigar children into the village, boys and girls in separate lines, as people stood at their gates to watch.

Inder distributed a ritual offering of prasad when they stopped in front of the haveli's gates. Amrita had started teaching the alphabet to Pinki, who stood at the gates with her mother and grandmother, carrying her reader.

"Babaji, take me to school too."

"Next year, Pinki. You are too young."

Ajit too followed the children and watched them join the first-graders in the schoolyard and sing the national anthem. He could hardly contain his emotion at seeing the Bajigar children with freshly scrubbed faces and combed hair. Satwant came to stand beside him and put an arm over his shoulders.

"Look, Bapuji. Can you see any differences?"

Dressed in their smart new uniforms, their feet in rawhide moccasins, the Bajigar children looked just like the other village children. This was a singular moment in the history of the Mukhia's clan, a high point in the slow but sure integration of the nomads into settled society. But for Ajit, this triumph was tinged with sadness. Years from now, would there be any traditional Bajigars left, those who wore tribal clothes, spoke their native tongue, and followed ancient customs? Would anyone still perform Baji, or sing and dance at the village gates?

Satwant turned his head and smiled. "This is the new India, Bapuji. We are seeing its birth right here at this moment. It starts, appropriately, in a school."

The morning assembly over, they walked back home.

Satwant said, "Maybe it is too early to tell you this, but . . . I think you are going to be a grandfather again."

When Ajit saw Satwant off at the train station in Ludhiana, those words made the parting a little easier.

"Basanti, too, is heavy of foot, Malik," Sehba whispered to him as they watched Pinki trying to teach her the alphabet while they sat side by side on a cot.

"Congratulations. So, the Mukhia is going to be a grandfather too."

He saw Siamo amble over and sit at Pinki's side. "Teach me, as well."

"You are too old, Bhua," Pinki said without looking up.

Amrita put her hand to her mouth.

"Pinki."

"What, Mummy?"

"You are being rude to Bhuaji."

"School is for children," Pinki said.

"Basanti is not a child."

"Basanti is my friend."

"Saucy girl."

Pinki turned her attention to the hapless Basanti, who was holding a slate and chalk. "You made a mistake. *Ura* is drawn like this."

"I will try again." Basanti kept her head lowered, her head cover hanging just above her chin.

"You can't see is why." Pinki pulled the chador right off her head.

Basanti quickly covered her face with her hands as Sehba rushed to adjust the chador.

"You can't pull her chador off like that, Pinki." Amrita knelt before her and held her hands in admonishment. "Your Babaji is present."

"My doll doesn't veil her face in front of Babaji, and neither do you."

Ajit smiled at the girl's logic and decided it might be easier all around if he left.

Out on the path, Sehba caught up to him. "Malik, I was wondering if you could spare some cotton bushes for our cooking fires. I am short on fuel."

"Go ahead, take a bundle."

"May your courtyard sing with the voices of a dozen grandsons, Malik."

Later that day, when he returned from a tour of the fields, he saw Sehba walking briskly out of the cattle yard followed by Basanti, who, though clearly pregnant, was struggling under a huge bundle of dried cotton bushes. He almost began scolding the older woman but bit his tongue. It might not end well for the girl, and in any case, it was not his place to scold another man's wife.

"Sat Sri Akal." The headmaster of the primary school came through the gates of the haveli.

Ajit rose to shake hands with his friend, who often stopped by in the late afternoon to play a few games of gin rummy.

The headmaster was a committed communist who wore modest homespun cotton. But he had his vanities, and he liked to spend some coin on pomading his hair and polishing his shoes. Siamo claimed that she could see her face in the sheen of the Comrade's head.

"Did you read this, Zaildar? Another insurrection."

He showed Ajit the front page of his newspaper. There was a lengthy report on the uprising of the tribal Naga people in northeastern India.

"These people have been riled up by the white Christian missionaries, who have converted them from animism and fed them lies."

The headmaster had been born a Brahmin, but instead of tending a holy fire in a temple or creating an astrological chart for a devotee, here he was railing against Christian missionaries. All religion was anathema to him.

"What if the Naga have some genuine grievances?"

"About what? Having been barred from headhunting?"

Siamo came to sit beside them, and three-year-old Pinki followed, carrying her rag doll. Headhunting was not a subject to discuss in front of an impressionable child, and they fell silent.

The little girl tried to climb up on an empty chair.

"You will fall," the Comrade said.

Pinki gave him a sweet smile.

"Here, let me help you." Ajit lifted her up.

The Comrade dealt a hand of cards, and the girl reached out for Ajit's.

"No, no." He held them closer.

"Show me pictures," she said.

"Sit in Babaji's lap, then." Siamo got up, lifted Pinki, and plunked her in his lap. He had no face cards.

"No pictures," Pinki said.

"I can't play with you giving away my secrets."

The Comrade smirked. "You almost never win, anyway."

They played ten games, and the Comrade won six.

"You lost, Babaji."

"How do you know, Pinki?"

"Six is greater than four."

"By how many?"

She counted on her fingers. Her face crunched in concentration.

"By two."

He pulled her up and hugged her.

౿

The sound of an engine shutting off. A frantic banging on the haveli gates.

Ajit looked at the radium dial of his watch. It was four o'clock in the morning, two hours before dawn. Nothing good, he thought, ever happened at four in the morning. He got up, found his sandals, and gingerly made his way down the outside staircase. As he pulled the gates open, the sight of a uniformed officer standing in front of an army vehicle froze him. He had never before felt so much like a weak, vulnerable old man.

The young officer spoke quickly in a clipped voice. "Sir, it is my unfortunate duty to inform you that your son, Captain Satwant Singh, was martyred yesterday while fighting the Nagas." He saluted.

Ajit was light-headed. He stumbled. The officer held him up.

He was helped to a cot in the verandah, and men and women began gathering in the courtyard. He heard Inder's wail. Siamo and Amrita keened as they beat their thighs and chests. He couldn't look at them. It didn't make any sense. Nothing did. It had to be a bad dream, a very bad dream.

"Sir, please be calm."

Why did he say that? Wasn't he being calm? He stared at the officer, who had removed his cap and handed it to another soldier.

"How? How did it happen?"

"Sir, I do not know the details. I was informed by telegram and told to bring you the sad news. I am very sorry, sir. Very sorry."

He recognized Pinki's cry. He looked around in confusion.

His son was no more? "Oh God, Waheguru! No, no, no!" he shouted to the heavens. "I am ruined, I am ruined!"

Familiar voices spoke words of comfort in his ears. Warm hands embraced him.

"No, no, no! Not Satwant! Oh God, not Satwant."

He lost all sense of time. He found himself sitting with men on thick sheets laid on the floor, and their faces floated before his eyes. The Mukhia, Sher, the Comrade, cousins, neighbours, an endless stream. They knelt by him, took his hands in theirs, touched turbans with his, spoke the same words over and over.

"Courage, Ajit Singh, courage."

He too had said these words to others in their time of grief. Courage? It came nowhere near him. His insides were hollow, his brain frozen, his tongue paralyzed, his lips glued together. He felt his head nodding and eyes blinking with tears. He managed to pull a handkerchief from his pocket to blow his nose.

Baru Marasi bent and handed him a glass of water. "Drink it."

He shook his head.

"Take it." Baru opened his hand and put a small ball of sticky black opium in his palm. He kept insisting, until Ajit opened his lips and accepted it, along with a mighty gulp of cold water. Baru rubbed Ajit's back with his large, strong hands.

He began to feel detached. Voices became disembodied. He felt his body slump, and his eyelids became heavy. Someone lifted him in mighty arms and laid him on his side on a cot, then covered him with a blanket and slipped a pillow under his head.

He was neither awake nor asleep. He could still see and hear, but he could feel nothing.

"It is the worst that can happen to a parent," he heard, "to outlive a child."

"Waheguru, Waheguru, Waheguru-ji."

Bikram

The news had the town buzzing; in the town centre a man was reading aloud from a newspaper to others who had crowded around him.

"Naga rebels attack army post. Seven martyred, many injured."

"Captain Satwant Singh the first casualty of Naga rebellion."

"Full-scale fighting breaks out as army airdrops troops."

"'We will punish the perpetrators,' Prime Minister pledges."

"Sikh soldiers bear the brunt."

Back at the mansion, Jagtar looked stricken.

"Not that handsome young man."

He nodded.

"What a tragedy. I can hardly believe it."

"The life of a soldier is never safe, Jagtar."

"I can see him clearly, swinging down from that beautiful horse's back. And holding Sewa on its saddle."

Papaji came hurrying through the gates. Clearly he had been crying.

"Take me to Raikot. I must offer the Zaildar my condolences."

Bikram shouted for his driver to bring the car around from the new carport he had built in the courtyard.

They rode in silence in the backseat. Once the car turned off the paved road and onto the wide dirt path, a group of urchins chased it all the way to the steel gates of the haveli. Bikram and his father got out and made their way to the cot on which the Zaildar lay while dozens of men sat on the ground on gunny sacks and cotton sheets. A tall man served water.

Bikram went down beside Papaji and joined his hands before the Zaildar, who uttered a thank you. He listened as Papaji spoke the usual homilies and praised the Captain both as a student and a human being, a brave and honourable Sikh who made the ultimate sacrifice for his country. He saw the Zaildar blink his eyes, the tears trickling out.

"Courage, Zaildar, courage," Papaji whispered.

"Please sit." The tall man with the large turban and shaved cheeks pointed to a space among the gathered.

Papaji folded his hands and bowed. "Sat Sri Akal."

Bikram found himself seated next to a muscular Bajigar, a man with an impressive moustache and a handsome face. This, he realized, must be the famous Rustum Mukhia. He nodded, and the man joined his hands and muttered a greeting. The politician in Bikram was alive to the fact that this man was a leader of his people, someone who could introduce him to the other mukhias of the Bajigar deras in his constituency. Eager to be ingratiating, he introduced himself.

The Mukhia shook his hand.

"And this is my father, Masterji Lal Singh. He was Satwant Singh's teacher in Samrala."

Papaji shook hands with the wrestler as well. They made small talk, keeping their voices respectfully hushed. Bikram discovered that the man had retired from wrestling and now owned a butcher's stall at the Adda. His son tended the Zaildar's cattle and exercised the Captain's mare. After spending a couple of hours sharing in the mournful gathering, he rose with Papaji and bowed with joined hands to take his leave.

He was lucky to have met the Bajigar, Bikram thought. *Even in tragedy*, he mused, *one finds blessings.*

Basanti

"That was an army jeep!" someone shouted.

It was the first clue they had that night that something terrible had happened. The Mukhia, Sehba, and Naura hurried to the haveli, and they stayed there all night. Before daybreak, their worst fear was confirmed. The Captain had been killed fighting some tribe in a place far away in the east.

Basanti closed her eyes and prayed, "Laxmi Maa, say it's not true."

In the morning, after Wazeer left to work in the fields, Basanti and Devi tried to lose themselves in their chores, tending the cattle, sweeping, cleaning. Done too soon, they decided to wash all the bedding before sitting down to eat the roti left over from the night before.

"I can't." Devi flung hers to a pariah dog waiting patiently by the hearth, who instantly snapped it up. The rest of the pack converged, and Basanti decided they could have hers, too. She tossed it, and a snarling battle ensued. The biggest dog quickly had it in his teeth and strolled away to settle down under a shade tree, his tail arced in the air.

They did not speak for a long time. Devi was quiet, her eyes red-rimmed and her face smudged with tears. At last Basanti broke the silence. "He was my deity come to life in human form to protect us," she said.

"He was my hero." Devi began to whimper. "Now, I have only misery and pain to look forward to."

"You know, Devi, when I saw him riding towards us on Bakki that day, I felt as if no harm could possibly come to me with him around."

Devi wiped her nose on her sleeve. "Me too."

The Mukhia returned at last that evening, and though he wanted nothing more than to sleep, his clan was clamouring for news of the family at the haveli.

"It was very sad to see the mighty Malik lying on a cot under a blanket, his eyes vacant, his voice slurred." The Mukhia sat down heavily at the kitchen hearth.

Sehba sighed. "I can still hear the wails of the mother, the wife, and Siamo. They were rolling in the dirt in desperate sorrow. How they grieved, how they wept, calling out Satwant's name."

"And Pinki?" Basanti asked.

"She was taken to a kinsman's house."

That was a kindness, Basanti thought. A child should not have to witness such sorrow.

The Mukhia broke a piece of roti and dipped it in dal that Basanti had cooked for the evening meal. He said, "The body will arrive in three days, I was told."

It was the finality of it, the Captain described now as a body, that triggered her tears again. How soon death changed one's perspective, Basanti thought. She was determined to remember him sitting atop his beloved mare, and the wonderfully rich smile on his radiant face.

Wazeer came home. He quickly walked by, turning his face away. But Sehba must have seen.

"Hey, what happened to your face?" she asked. "It's a mess."

"Probably lost a fight," the Mukhia muttered.

Sehba stood up and followed Wazeer.

"Put another spoon of ghee in my dal, Basanti." The Mukhia raised his bowl. "Spoon in some more dal, too."

Basanti always marvelled at how much her father-in-law could eat.

"Take some meat, Basanti." The Mukhia had become very generous upon hearing she was pregnant. "I want you to give me a grandson who takes after me. Grows up to be a Rustum."

Outside, she heard women's voices raised in argument.

"Go mind your own business," she heard Naura yell at Sehba. "Don't come nosing around here any more."

The Mukhia looked up. "Basanti, go drag your mother-in-law home."

As soon as she could be sure they weren't overheard, Basanti asked

Devi, "What is going on with Wazeer?"

"Oh, he took a beating from Lalu the bootlegger."

"Why?"

"For not paying for the liquor he is borrowing."

"He drinks a lot?"

Devi sighed.

On the day that Satwant's body came home, Basanti and Devi stood at the dera gates, where most of the elders had gathered. They veiled themselves and slipped out to stand by the fence. There was a large crowd on both sides of the path and the paved road. One policeman directed traffic while others pushed people back.

"Make way, make way."

"I see it," shouted someone perched high up in a tree. "The army convoy."

People rushed onto the path, and the policemen began to push them back until they were perilously close to the tall acacia fence with its long thorns. Basanti and Devi quickly elbowed their way to the front, and men made way for them, since jostling a woman in public might invite a policeman's ire.

The crowd fell silent as the big truck slowly turned onto the path. She saw the flag-draped box on its flat trailer, with a soldier kneeling at each corner. As the gleaming truck straightened and gained speed, a dark cloud of exhaust fumes spewed out. She covered her nose with an end of her chador.

Someone shouted from behind her as two more trucks full of soldiers passed, followed by a few jeeps and cars. "Look at all those officers."

"That's Aalok Nath sitting in the back," another said.

She saw an elderly man wearing thick glasses and a Gandhi cap peer towards her from the white car. He looked important, as did the others who glided by.

Once the last vehicle had passed, the crowd again filled the path and disappeared in the direction of the haveli. She saw it spill into the fields as more and more people arrived on bicycles, tongas, or on foot, all headed for the funeral of her Captain. Basanti followed, as though in a trance.

She saw the trailer bearing the captain's body pass through the haveli gate, and seeing it floating away from her she gave an involuntary sob. The trailer was followed by army trucks full of soldiers, followed by officers in jeeps. The Zaildar stood at the gates and watched, eyes glazed with tears, as they brought the bier into the courtyard for the ceremonial bathing. The Giyani uttered the verses of comfort as the crowds were pushed out the gates to allow the family to grieve in privacy.

Basanti stood a little distance away, unable to take her eyes from the scene. The Zaildar's wife and Siamo knelt beside him to slowly unfurl the flag and reveal Satwant's face in the midday sun. She heard the heart-rending wails of Amrita, held tight by her mother and sisters-in-law.

Inder wept. "My sweet, sweet son. Why did you leave me alone here on earth?"

"Oh, Waheguru, take me instead of Satwant," Siamo cried.

Amrita wailed, her words incoherent, the tone piercing.

The Zaildar gently caressed his son's cold, blue cheeks, his silken beard. He bent to look closer. Basanti knew that the eyes of the corpse would have been stitched shut. A wave of anguish seemed to wash over the Zaildar. The finality of his loss had overwhelmed him. He looked up to the heavens and gave out a hoarse cry.

Baru Marasi came to comfort him. "Weep, Ajit Singh, weep. Weep until you can cry no more."

Bikram

Bikram and his father returned on the morning of the body's arrival and stood among the village council and the local elders. They listened to the village Giyani offer prayers and watched the box being lifted off the truck and carried into the courtyard.

He cringed as the women wailed and beat their breasts. Their grief-stricken cries sent shivers up his spine. *What a terrible loss of a young life*. He blinked his suddenly teary eyes as the body was lifted onto a bare cot to be ceremonially bathed with the sprinkling of water from a brass urn. The Zaildar stoically performed the ritual as a kinsman patted the wet spots with a towel.

They wrapped the body in a white shroud and placed it on a wooden bier.

The Giyani stood at the feet and read the Ardas prayer.

Next, four soldiers sombrely lifted the bier onto their shoulders and began the slow shuffle to the cremation grounds. Bikram followed with Papaji, who rested a hand on his shoulder. He saw the MLA, Aalok Nath, walking beside the other politicians and officials. A military band began to play. The procession circled the village, and in the distance he could see the Pir's orchard. He felt his legs weaken.

Rustum Mukhia, walking beside him, steadied him with his strong hands. "Courage, Bikram Sahib."

He thanked the Bajigar and saw a look of respect in the man's eyes. *He thinks I am stumbling because of blind grief for the Captain*, he thought—a timely stumble indeed. He forgot about the orchard and made sure to sigh loudly, wipe his eyes, blow his nose at appropriate moments in the presence of the man whom he would need to win the election. The Mukhia had told Papaji that he considered Satwant as his own son. The Zaildar was his malik and his patron, he said, and he had donated the land for his clan to establish their dera. It had earned his and the Bajigars' loyalty.

"Stop." The order was given in a loud voice.

The band ceased playing and the procession halted. They faced the cremation grounds now, beyond which stood a cone-topped temple surrounded by ancient trees. A pond glistened in the sun, and the buffalo floating in it snorted and swam closer. A peacock flew with a great cawing from one tree to another farther away, its plumage twinkling against the sky.

"Waheguru, Waheguru, Waheguru-ji."

The Giyani started the chant, and others picked it up as they laid the wooden bier atop the pyre built of logs, dung cakes, and kindling. Two lines of soldiers carrying rifles moved into place on either side, facing each other. At a command from an officer holding a sword, they raised their rifles and fired three rounds.

Beside him, Papaji winced. The buffalo retreated en masse to the far shore of the pond as birds burst out of trees at the sudden blasts. The military salute was most impressive, and Bikram felt proud that the Captain was receiving full honours. More soldiers and officers formed a cordon around the pyre and formally saluted the body, and an officer marched to the Zaildar and offered the folded flag of India.

Bikram leaned to whisper in the Mukhia's ear. "Wonderful gesture."

"Yes, yes." The man nodded.

Two kinsmen placed a lit torch in the Zaildar's hands and helped him approach the pyre and light it. Bikram smelled burning ghee. They must have poured it onto the fuel to help it burn quickly, he thought. The flames licked the shrouded body.

"Waheguru, Waheguru, Waheguru-ji."

The chant went up and drowned the keening of the women.

A week later, the gurudwara in Raikot was packed for the conclusion of the Sadharan Path, ritual prayers in Satwant's honour, with people spilling out into its spacious courtyard. Inside, Bikram found a spot as close to the Zaildar as possible, and Papaji squeezed beside him in the crowded space, with men standing on one side and women on the other. The Giyani concluded the service before inviting the dignitaries to speak.

The first was the commanding officer of the Captain's army

division. The major-general, a grey-haired Sikh resplendent in his uniform, spoke of the selfless service, the ultimate sacrifice, the pain of the loss, and honoured the Zaildar and his family with words of respectful praise. Next to speak was the local member of Parliament, a burly Sikh with an orator's voice. "I bring condolences on behalf of the Government of India, the President, and the Prime Minister of the nation. I pledge that a suitable monument will be built to honour Captain Satwant Singh's sacrifice."

The MLA, Aalok Nath, had to wait and have the microphone lowered to his height before intoning, in a barely audible voice, "I bring condolences from the Chief Minister and Cabinet of the Legislative Assembly. The Chief Minister pledges that a great memorial will be constructed shortly to honour the Captain's sacrifice. A full scholarship for college studies will be bestowed on his daughter."

The Zaildar had nominated the Captain's father-in-law, Jagirdar Sher Singh, to give thanks to the congregation. "Please stay for the langar," he asked. "We truly appreciate your presence here and thank you from the bottom of our hearts."

The prasad was served.

Bikram lingered by the men of the family and made sure that Papaji was introduced to them by the Zaildar.

"Satwant's Masterji, Lal Singh."

"My son, Bikram Singh."

"My sincerest condolences." Bikram bowed with joined hands, impressed by the Captain's two brothers-in-law, one a judge and the other a deputy superintendent of police, distinguished-looking men with sombre faces, just like their wealthy father.

The servers began to lay long lines of jute sheets on the floor of the courtyard for people to sit on for langar. Bikram was introduced to the elected leaders of nearby villages, and he repeated their names and the names of their villages in his head to remember them better.

"When you visit Samrala next time, come visit me at my shop. I would love to learn more about your village and its needs."

He issued dozens of invitations and wished that he had someone to take down names, set up appointments. His heart beat faster as he discovered a natural ability to engage men in conversation and realized the value of listening to them. They all seemed interested in him, and he worked the crowd.

The Bajigars, recognizable by their tribal clothing, sat in two lines, facing each other, women and girls on one side and men and boys on the other. Some of the women wore veils. He spied the Captain's little daughter wearing a suit with a chador over her head, carrying a rag doll. She was meandering through the courtyard as if looking for someone. Suddenly she stopped and ran through the lines, and plunked herself in the lap of a veiled woman.

"Look at that, Bapuji," he heard the Captain's wife tell the Zaildar. "Pinki found Basanti. Can you believe that?"

A small smile played on the Zaildar's lips.

"Who is that woman?" Bikram asked.

"Basanti is Rustum Mukhia's daughter-in-law. She is Pinki's favourite."

The little girl might have sat on her grandmother's lap, or her mother's, but she sought out a Bajigar woman to feed her. Bikram decided that he really ought to stop by the dera. Visit with the clan's leader.

A few days later, Bikram and Papaji pulled up at the dera in Bikram's Ambassador sedan. There was a shortage of cars in the country thanks to high import tariffs and consequently there were years-long waiting lists for the three domestic brands. The shiny vehicle was immediately surrounded by children. The Mukhia came out to greet them and led them to the centre of the dera, where he called for a cot. A woman brought one and another covered it with a blanket.

"Sit, please, sit."

Bikram had never been to a dera, but this at least looked better than the mud-brick and tin shanties where untouchables and migrants lived. The huts stood wide apart, and the ground was swept clean. People gathered around him, and he was served tea. It was a good place for Bikram to practise his campaign skills.

"Tell me, Mukhia, what is the greatest need of your clan?"

The Mukhia looked surprised, and Papaji clarified, saying, "Bikram is going to run for the seat of the local MLA."

Bikram felt all eyes upon him.

"You are not elected yet. Don't you have to be an MLA to help us?" an elder asked.

"Anyone can help if they want to. Not only an MLA."

An older woman spoke up. "In that case, I will tell you what the women want the most, shall I?"

"Please."

"We have only one water pump for all of us and our animals. Sometimes, we have to waste hours waiting to get a turn."

He waited.

"Would you pay for a second one?"

He smiled. This one was easy. "I will do it in honour of Captain Satwant Singh. In his memory."

The women muttered blessings in appreciation, and he saw Papaji's face light up.

"Not only a pump," he said, remembering how much Jagtar enjoyed the luxury of a washroom. "I will also build a walled washroom with a covered roof so the women can wash and bathe in privacy."

At this, the women started a little celebratory dance.

"Stop!" the Mukhia shouted. "We are still in mourning. No singing, dancing, or hooting."

"You are a god to us, Sardar Bikram Singh," an elder said.

"A true benefactor who donates in our Satwant's memory," praised another.

"I gratefully accept your kind offer," the Mukhia said. He joined his hands and bowed.

Basanti

Rana left her alone at night now, which was a relief. She had not derived a moment's pleasure from all his humping and snorting, which only made her feel like the doomed fly in the grip of a spider. Now he came home and went to bed early, barely speaking a word. He seemed to have taken the news of the Captain's death hard. It had not dampened his parents' ardour, though.

"I think they are trying desperately to make another Rana," Devi said when Basanti told her about this.

"Why?"

"In case you kill the idiot one day."

"But I am now pregnant with their grandson."

"How do you know it's a boy? You could drop seven daughters, one after the other." Then Devi smiled and put a hand on Basanti's protruding belly. "I can feel him moving in there." She gently massaged the spot.

Basanti had noticed a gradual change in Devi. More and more, she seemed to be lost in herself, almost sleepwalking. And one morning, Basanti was horrified to see bruises on her cousin's face. She drew her into her hut, so she could speak to her privately.

"Wazeer is hitting you?"

"It's every day now."

"Why don't you cry out?"

"I have no more tears." Devi shrugged. "What's the point?"

"Naura doesn't stop him?"

Devi shook her head.

A wife had to endure her husband's abuse. That was just how things were. Basanti wished that the Captain were still alive. He would have done something to stop the terror. It was almost three months since his passing, and she prayed daily to Laxmi Maa to grant peace to his soul.

"Girls, get ready. We are plucking cotton, starting today," Sehba called out to them. "Pack something to eat, Basanti. We will draw water at the well for drinking."

They followed Sehba along dry water channels to the fields beside the Pir's orchard. The day was sunny and humid.

"Here, line up." Sehba pointed to the field that had long lines of shoulder-high bushes heavy with cotton.

Basanti lined up beside Devi, knotted a gunny sheet over her fore-head, and let it fall down her back to make a sack. It was open on both sides, so she could pick with both hands and throw the cotton behind her.

"Start," Sehba ordered, and the line of twenty began to move for-ward. Shanti began to sing, and the rest joined in.

Basanti's sack was heavy and full by the time the sun stood above in the middle of the sky, when Sehba called a break. She followed her mother-in-law to the thick shade of the trees circling the well, pulled her load off, and sat down heavily on the cool grass. Now that she was pregnant, Sehba had been generous with food. She would give her a bowl of yogurt with a dab of freshly churned butter every morning, and a tall tumbler of sweetened boiled milk after supper. Basanti saved some of the rich gravy and a few bits of meat to give to Devi when no one was looking, and she'd swipe the odd pinni and share it with her.

Sehba pulled out the wrapped rotis and pickle that Basanti had packed.

"Two for you and two for me."

Basanti looked over to where Naura and Devi were sitting. The older woman took out a wrap but did not offer anything to her daughter-in-law.

"What about her?" she asked the dour woman.

"It's all I have."

"What is she supposed to eat?"

Naura shrugged her shoulders.

A rage began to rise in Basanti. Sehba looked at her in alarm.

"Basanti, we will share with Devi."

Now Shanti took up the fight. "Cruel woman, starving your own daughter-in-law."

Naura told her to shut up and mind her own business.

"This is terrible, Sehba!" Shanti said. "Not good for the dera. I hear Devi being slapped around almost every night."

"What do you want me to do?" Sehba asked.

"You are the Mukhia's wife. All the women look up to you. Put an end to this. Tell the Mukhia to punch Wazeer right in his smirking face. Threaten to break his bones."

Sehba just scoffed. "Wazeer is his nephew. And besides, I have never seen him raise his hand against anyone unless in a wrestling match."

"Tell him to talk to Wazeer, then."

Sehba kept chewing.

"One day, Naura, your boy is going to go too far. There are already ugly rumours about him."

"What ugly rumours, you bitch?" Naura shouted at Shanti.

Devi put down her roti and, burying her head in her knees, began to cry.

At the end of a day of plucking cotton, the women would tie it tightly in their gunny sacks and carry them on their heads to the haveli. In the evening, Siamo would weigh them on a scale that hung from the ceiling. They would be paid in kind with a portion of the harvest. It was the same when they shucked maize or cut sugarcane. Only the men were paid in cash.

When Basanti got to the haveli, Pinki chased her and then stood in front of her, her little fists on her hips. "Basanti, you are not learning any more alphabet. Why?"

"Basanti has to work," Amrita said.

"But I want her to play with me, visit me."

"I will bring Basanti as soon as we finish plucking cotton," Sehba said.

"You promise, Bajigar grandma?"

"I promise."

Pinki gave Basanti a big hug then and rubbed her belly. "You look just like Mummy. You both look fat."

Siamo said, "Pinki, they are pregnant. Soon you will have two boys to play with."

"One boy and one girl. I want one of each."

No one spoke. The Malik badly wanted a grandson, and the Mukhia wanted one, too.

"Sehba, wait, I have some ladoos for you to take," Siamo said.

Ladoos were given as a celebratory treat, but the haveli was in mourning. As soon as they were out of the gates, Naura grabbed the bag of ladoos and started to distribute them.

"Eat," she told Devi. "Take that stupid look off your face."

One evening, as they sat at the hearth, a heavy-set man walked into the dera in the failing light.

"Who's that?" Basanti asked.

The man shouted, "Wazeer!"

"Lalu the bootlegger." Sehba grimaced. "This can't be good."

"Wazeer, come out, you bastard!" Lalu snarled.

Wazeer stepped out of his hut with joined hands, his face twisted in fear.

"Do you have my payment?"

"Sardar, please, don't humiliate me here," Wazeer said.

"No money, then? Bring her to my well tonight, or else!" Lalu shouted.

"Sardar, please. Stop it." Wazeer knelt on the ground.

"Bring who to your well?" The Mukhia came out of his hut, carrying his butcher's axe.

Devi shot out of the hut and fell at his feet. "Uncle, save me! Wazeer promised me to Lalu to pay his debt."

"What?" The Mukhia glared at Lalu. "Is this true?"

People began to gather around.

"Wasn't my idea," Lalu said.

"And you thought you would just walk into my dera tonight to collect?"

The Mukhia looked bigger and brawnier than usual. Basanti expected Lalu to back down right away, but she was wrong. Lalu was going to prostitute Devi, sell her to a Kanjari khanna. She felt like throwing up.

"What're you going to do about it, stupid Bajigar?" the bootlegger shouted.

"Kill you, you bastard! Then I'll kill my stupid nephew," the Mukhia roared, and he raised his axe.

Lalu's eyes widened with terror. He took a few quick steps back, turned on his heels, and ran out of the dera.

Wazeer rolled in the dust. "Forgive me, Uncle. Please forgive me!"

The Mukhia dropped the axe, bent down, and grabbed Wazeer by the throat. He pounded his fist into Wazeer's head and face. "You bring such shame on my dera and my clan, you son of a bitch. I am going to beat you to a pulp."

"Stop him!" Naura shouted. Men grabbed the Mukhia's arms and pulled him off the cowering man. The Mukhia dropped Wazeer and kicked him hard in the ribs.

Wazeer howled like a wounded dog, and Basanti savoured the sound.

"Listen to me and listen well, Wazeer. Now you have gone too far. I am going to be finished with your crap once and for all." The Mukhia was frothing at the mouth. "Sehba, take Devi to our hut."

Sehba leapt to obey her husband's order.

"She stays under my roof until the tribe's council and the Raja decide what to do with Wazeer."

The Mukhia's fury was unrelenting. He sat on a cot in the centre all day and fumed. Even the bravest among them tiptoed around him.

The tribal elders arrived, as did the Raja, and they spent two days smoking hookahs and deliberating. The Mukhia spared no expense in hosting them. Basanti, Sehba and Shanti cooked big meals, while Devi waited in the hut for the verdict.

"At last you will have justice," Basanti whispered to Devi when they went to the fields before dusk.

"I hope they hang him."

On the third morning, after the children had left for school, the Raja called the clan together. Sehba brought Devi out to stand before him. Wazeer remained in his hut.

"Naura, stand with her," an elder said.

The Raja cleared his throat before speaking.

"The council of the tribe and I have reached a decision. Wazeer is to be ostracized and expelled from this dera, and from all other Bajigar deras, forever. He is not fit to be a Bajigar. He brought great shame on himself, his family, his clan, and the entire tribe by trying to stain Devi and offering her, his wife, to another man in payment for his addiction to alcohol."

Naura began to weep.

"That will leave both you women without the support and protection of a man. So, we have decided this. The Mukhia will take Naura as his second wife by placing a chador over her head."

Sehba gasped and began to wail.

"Rana will take Devi as his second wife."

Devi dropped to her knees. Basanti was shocked. Devi was to be her sautaan and share Rana's cot with her. Lives were changing. Wazeer's stupidity was taking a toll on everyone.

When Sehba protested, the Mukhia stepped over and slapped her harshly on both cheeks. "Silence, woman. Let the Raja speak."

"We are done. Tell Wazeer to pack his belongings and get out of the dera. I want to see the back of this despicable man for the last time," the Raja said.

"You will stay to witness the ceremony?" the Mukhia asked.

"I will be happy to. Send for Rana."

Basanti watched as Wazeer came out with his belongings in a bundle—mostly clothes, plus his cane-cutting machete. He bent to touch his mother's feet, turned, and walked out without looking back.

Naura wept loudly, and no one moved to comfort her.

The Mukhia had moved Naura's cot to his own hut, and Rana, Basanti, and Devi shared what had been Naura's.

Basanti sat beside Devi in the glow of the embers in the chullah at her new kitchen and waited for Rana to arrive home from milking the Malik's cattle. They had not exchanged a word, and Devi stared stonily into the darkness. Basanti had seen the excited look on Rana's face throughout the chador ceremony. He'd positively beamed. Had he coveted Devi all along?

Men gathered at the Mukhia's kitchen hearth to celebrate his new wife and sat drinking his alcohol on cots pulled close together. They sang a bawdy song and the women pulled their children inside their doors.

"Make the cot creak tonight!" the men sang, raising glasses. "Creak, creak, creak, creak!"

Basanti had seen the same excitement on the Mukhia's face that she'd seen on Rana's. Naura was the wife of his dead brother and kin to Sehba. Despite her dour demeanour, she was a handsome and shapely woman. Taller and fuller than Sehba, with fairer skin and finer features. Now the two had shut themselves up inside their hut.

"I wonder how those two are getting along," Basanti ventured.

Devi sighed and stirred the embers with a stick.

Basanti stood up and went into her tiny hut. The earthen lamp had a small flame, and the hut seemed dark and claustrophobic. There was just one tiny window here. Two cots were set against the walls with only a little room between them. The rest of the space inside was taken up by the grindstone and a sack of grain. She made her bed and placed her own and Rana's pillows on it. Then she unfolded Devi's bedding on the other cot, smoothed it, and fluffed the pillow.

The door opened and Rana came in. He refused to meet her eyes, but he quickly grabbed his pillow, placed it on Devi's cot, and sat there.

"Bring her in. It's time for bed."

"Your glass of milk is waiting."

"You drink it. I've had a few shots."

Devi refused to budge. Rana came out and dragged her inside. He pushed her onto the cot.

"Blow out the lamp, Basanti."

Basanti did as told and lay down on her cot as the tussle continued on the cot beside her.

"Be calm now," Rana said, his nasal breathing starting to whistle in the dark.

She heard the rustling of clothes, Rana's grunts. The cot started to creak. Before she could fold her chador and wrap it around her ears, he gave the porcine grunt she was so familiar with, followed by the long exhalation of breath. He was spent.

She heard nothing from Devi. Not a whimper or a sigh, much less a moan.

Ajit

Ajit came to the Adda to catch a bus into Samrala, and decided to visit the Mukhia at work. The Mukhia was sitting in his stall, which had steel netting at the sides to prevent flies from landing on the meat. As Ajit entered, there was a goat carcass hanging from a hook. The butcher's tools were neatly laid out on a thick chopping block.

Ajit noticed a change in the Mukhia. The man had bounced back from the defeat that ended his wrestling days and looked younger, more vigorous. His splendid long moustache was waxed and curled.

"How goes the world with you, old friend?" Ajit asked.

"I took Naura as my second wife yesterday, after we ostracized her stupid son."

"Just like that?"

"It's our custom, Malik. The women must live under the protection of a man."

"And business? You're doing well?"

"I am sold out by noon every day. I am getting lots of orders for weddings and engagements now. Sometimes two goats at a time."

"Sounds as though you need a partner to help you."

"Agreed! I am thinking of asking Basanti's father, Changu, to join me. He used her bride price to build a healthy herd, and he owns three dozen goats now."

Ajit was impressed. The clan was slowly becoming entrepreneurial. Two of the Bajigar women were now hawking palm frond mats and fans near the Mukhia's stall. And a young man had set up a dyeing business, bringing colour to the Adda with dyed and starched clothes hanging between the trees. Ajit decided to give this man his turbans to dye, instead of using the dyers in Samrala.

It was a cool, cloudy day, and when he got to town he took his time passing through the bazaar. Men stopped to shake his hand and inquire after his health.

"Trying to be strong," he would answer, with a bow.

"You have a tiny granddaughter to raise, Zaildar, and I hear a grandson is on the way, an heir for the haveli."

He nodded at the man's hopeful prediction of a boy and thanked him. But he wished he could tell the truth out loud: he already had an heir, even if he couldn't find him.

Nasib's recovery from polio had left him with only a slight limp, Ajit was told, but that disability, and the fact that he would inherit only a few acres of poor land from his maternal grandfather, had been enough to blight his prospects. On her most recent family visit, Siamo had learned that the boy had gone with a kinsman to Bengal to find work as a cleaner of trucks. This was a tough life. He had been sending home money but he had not come back from Bengal in the last two years. Ajit was terrified: he had lost one son to the Nagas and he could very well lose another on the dangerous roads of Calcutta and never know about it.

The main reason for his trip today was a visit to Bikram Singh, and when he arrived at the shop, Bikram leapt off his diwan and bent to touch his feet.

"Zaildar Sahib."

"Live long, my son."

"This is an unexpected pleasure, and an honour, Zaildar Sahib."

Ajit looked carefully at the younger man. He was growing his beard longer and fuller, and he wore the blue of the Akali Dal as well as the symbols of a baptized Sikh—the heavy steel kara around his wrist, and the small, sheathed ceremonial kirpan that hung by his side. Bikram Singh looked prosperous, he thought—he'd even developed a bit of a paunch. The skinny, nervous boy he had first met at the recruitment office in Ludhiana almost fourteen years ago was now a big businessman.

"I came to thank you and Masterji for your kindness at the time of Satwant's passing. The Bajigars' mukhia told me you had offered to build a bathroom and drill another water pump at the dera in my son's memory."

"I felt it was the least I could do, after all that you have done for me." Bikram gave an order to his munshi. "Send for the car. Zaildar

Sahib will have lunch at the mansion today. Ask Papaji to join us."

"I don't want to put you to any trouble."

"Zaildar Sahib, I have waited a decade and a half to properly thank you. You are the man responsible for all of this." Bikram gestured around his establishment.

"All right. Well, I had better go over and see my grain dealer first. I'm sure he saw me come in here, and I'll need to reassure him that I have not defected or he'll have a nervous breakdown."

"With respect, Zaildar, your grain dealer is a crook. Did you know the market inspector discovered that he keeps two sets of weights, a heavier one to buy with and a lighter one to sell with? He cheats the Jat and the consumer both."

Of course, every grain dealer the Zaildar had ever met had told him the same thing about the local competition.

Bikram's Ambassador sedan with its dignified turbaned driver pulled up in front to pick them up. And if that were not impressive enough, Bikram's grand mansion certainly was. Everything—starting with the large, brass plate at the gate that read "Hon. Captain Bikram Singh, Ex-Army"—was of the highest quality. The courtyard walls were plastered and whitewashed, the floor cobbled and swept, and the peepal tree had a magnificent canopy. The three-storey building had a wide-columned verandah fronting it. The doors and windows were of hand-finished wood. Ajit stopped at the entrance to admire the exquisitely furnished gathering room, with its imported furniture and cabinets full of crystal.

Bikram's wife and young son came out to greet him, though the boy quickly ran away.

"He is very shy," the mother said.

Bikram called to a servant to bring a bottle of whiskey.

"No, no, no. You are a baptized Sikh and I will not drink in your house," Ajit said.

"Zaildar Sahib, I am an ex-army man. Appearances are for the public. And I live my private life, well . . . privately."

Bikram's father joined them, and over lunch, Masterji told stories of the shenanigans Satwant and his friends had got into during his school days.

"But he was a very good student," he rushed to add. "And respectful, kind, and generous. Enjoyed sports."

The old stories were like a balm to Ajit, and when at last he was on his way home—Bikram had insisted on summoning his driver—he found that the visit had helped to soothe his tightly held grief.

When his summer crops came in, Ajit hired trucks from Frontier Transport to haul them to the market. And this time, he decided to sell some to Bikram Singh. His own grain merchant did not dare complain, but he had a pained look.

"Your father was my father's client, Ajit Singh," he said. "Ours is a generations-old relationship."

Ajit reassured the man. "I had a really good harvest. Only sold the surplus to Bikram Singh."

"You are a good percentage of my business, Ajit Singh. I too have children and grandchildren to feed."

Ajit felt torn. What would Satwant have done? Would he have refused to give some business to the son of his favourite teacher? No, of course not, he thought. And that eased his conscience.

☙

"Save her! Save her!" The woman's cries were desperate. What on earth was happening?

Ajit, home at the haveli, heard the terrified shrieks and ran to the edge of the roof. From there he could see Sehba racing through the fields towards the village.

She screamed at him, "Wazeer is drowning Devi! In your well by the orchard!"

Ajit ran down the stairs and spotted Rana cutting wood in the cattle yard.

"Run to the well. Wazeer is drowning Devi! Hurry! Stop him!"

Rana straightened up and sprinted, the axe still in his hand. When he passed his mother she turned and followed him. Soon there were many men racing with them towards the well.

Ajit, his chest heaving, could do nothing but watch and pray aloud, "Save her, Waheguru-ji, please save her."

A moment later, he heard a terrible scream that made his blood run cold.

Someone shouted, "Rana axed Wazeer in his skull!"

Now the women were flying out of the haveli. Siamo shouted, "What's going on?"

Almost before he knew what he was doing, Ajit was through the gates, following the men racing across the fields from the Adda and the dera. All the while, Sehba never stopped screaming.

At the well, Ajit pushed through a crowd to see Wazeer, covered in blood, lying on the ground. An axe was buried in his skull. Rana was standing over him, looking stunned.

Ajit looked into the well. Two men were holding a limp Devi up above the water line.

One of them shook his head. "She is dead. I'm certain of it."

"Haul her up. There might still be time to revive her," Ajit said. "Hurry, hurry, hurry." The urgency made his voice tremble.

Rana began to wail.

Ajit helped lay Devi on the grass and pressed her sides frantically to get the water out of her lungs.

The dripping man kneeling beside him shook his head. "We were too late."

"No!"

"Malik!" He heard the Mukhia's cry. "Oh, Malik, save her."

But Devi did not breathe again.

Ajit stood up wearily and told a kinsman, "Send for the police inspector."

The two bodies were covered with sheets, and they waited.

Naura fell to her knees beside Wazeer, beating her breast. "Why? Oh, why?"

"The bastard drowned Devi for no reason," Rana said, furious.

"And you, you bastard, you killed your own cousin, your own blood, over a tainted woman!" Naura screamed at him.

"Shut up, both of you," the Mukhia shouted.

It made no difference. Rana shouted at Naura, and Naura screamed obscenities at Devi, accusing her of every possible sin. Unable to silence her, the Mukhia slapped her a few times, and finally she lay down, curled up, and wept.

They waited.

It was three hours before six uniformed men and an inspector arrived
on bicycles. They asked their questions before putting Rana in hand-
cuffs. The inspector directed that the two bodies be carried to the dera
on cots, and he invited everyone who claimed to be a witness to follow
him there. When they arrived at the dera, Basanti came running up.
She lifted the sheet covering Devi. A tortured shriek rose from her
throat and she fell to the ground. Women rushed to her and carried
her into a hut.

"She is pregnant, Malik," the Mukhia said, looking worried.

Ajit put a hand on the devastated man's shoulder.

"Save us, Laxmi Maa," the Mukhia prayed. "Save us."

The inspector held court in the centre, sitting on a cot beside a sergeant, who held a ledger.

"You first."

Sehba sat down on the ground at his feet and told her story.

"Sahib, I took Devi to collect dried maize roots from a field beside
the Malik's well. We were looking down, when suddenly Wazeer's
shadow fell over us. He was carrying his machete. Devi screamed and
ran away. He went after her, threatening to chop her into pieces. I
tried to stop him. He chased her and slashed her back."

"Go on."

"Devi screamed louder and ran to the well. She jumped into it.
Wazeer jumped in right after her. He held Devi's head under the water.
I saw her struggle."

"Then?"

"I ran as fast as I could to raise the alarm."

"And who was the first to get to the well?"

"Rana."

"He had an axe in his hand?"

"I did not see anything."

The inspector glared at her.

"Who arrived next?"

A man raised his arm. The inspector called him to sit closer, and
took his name and address.

"What did you see?"

"I saw Wazeer already out of the well, leaning over it, when Rana closed in. Rana was screaming. He raised the axe and smashed it into the back of Wazeer's head."

"I saw nothing like that, Sahib," Sehba interrupted.

"Shut up," the inspector growled. "Go on, you."

The man swallowed. "Wazeer did not even scream or nothing. He jerked backward and fell to the ground. I have never seen anything like it in my life."

"He's lying, Sahib. Rana did not do that."

"Tell me then how the axe ended up in Wazeer's skull?"

Sehba made a face and looked away.

"No sense lying now," the Mukhia told her.

"I am a mother," she replied.

Ajit could hear Basanti's wails rising up from the hut where she'd been taken. Although he waited with the rest of the witnesses, he was not asked to give a statement. "You are excused, Zaildar Sahib," the inspector told him. "I have all the facts I need."

The inspector sent for a tonga to transfer the two bodies to the Civil Hospital in Samrala. Rana refused to speak, and the inspector ordered a constable to put him on the back of his bicycle and haul him to jail. Sehba wailed as Rana was taken away. The constable pedalled out of the dera, escorted by two of his uniformed men.

Sehba and the Mukhia ran after them, keeping up as long as they could, shouting encouragements to Rana.

Bikram

The twin murders in the dera shocked the countryside; men and women talked about the incident wherever they could, and the newspapers devoted a lot of ink to it. Jagtar read everything she could get her hands on.

"What is this world coming to, Ji? First the Captain is martyred, and then two Bajigars are murdered. Raikot is getting a lot of attention, Ji. And not in a good way."

Bikram sighed. "I am going to go offer my condolences to the Mukhia."

In the dera, scores of Bajigar men sat on cots laid out everywhere, puffing on hookahs and sipping tea. Bikram spied the Zaildar sitting in their midst, the Mukhia beside him, and he began weaving his way towards them. The Mukhia made room for him to sit on a cot.

"There are a lot of visitors today," Bikram said, glancing around.

"Every Bajigar mukhia has brought a mourning party," the Zaildar explained.

Bikram nodded gravely, but he was thinking: *What luck!* Now he would be introduced to the mukhias of all the deras by their champion, the former Rustum! Good thing he remembered his notebook and pen.

"Sardar Bikram Singh gave us the new water pump and built the washroom for our women, in memory of my malik's son," the Mukhia announced loudly, and a buzz started and men squinted in Bikram's direction and nodded approvingly.

The plan had been to have the new pump and washroom inaugurated by the Zaildar after a prayer read by the village Giyani. However, the Bajigar women had started using it as soon as the concrete floor dried, days before the masons installed the roof and the door. He noticed the concrete plaque on which the dedication to the

Captain would be mounted. It was still damp to the touch.

A couple of men, each holding the curved staff of a mukhia, rose to shake his hand.

"Where are you from?" Bikram asked.

"Manki."

"Salaudi."

Villages to the south of Samrala. He had clients there. He mentioned their names, and the mukhias nodded and spoke about the men with admiration. Sometimes, Bikram thought, it was that easy to make a connection.

The bodies of Devi and Wazeer had been brought back after the post-mortems and lay shrouded side by side in the centre of the dera. Most of those gathered stood by with sombre faces, but a veiled woman with a swollen belly wailed terribly and had to be comforted.

The Zaildar leaned over and whispered, "She is the Mukhia's daughter-in-law, Basanti, a cousin of the slain woman."

He remembered the name. She was the one that the Captain's daughter, Pinki, had sought out and sat down to eat with at the langar.

"It's her husband who's in jail in Samrala, is that right?"

"Yes. Rana. The Mukhia's son."

Bikram and the Zaildar walked together in the funerary procession. When the Pir's orchard came into view, Bikram was careful to look away. The last time he had set eyes on it, he'd suffered a terrible nightmare. He'd woken up feeling strangled and his choking noises had terrified Jagtar.

The twin pyres were lit and flames leapt into the sky. He smelled burning flesh, and slightly nauseated, he looked up to see the bones of a knee emerge in the flames nearest to him, and he watched in fascination as the rest of the skeleton slowly, gruesomely, appeared. The Zaildar tapped his shoulder, and he turned to follow the men back to the dera.

Bikram caught up to the mukhias from Manki and Salaudi, and they invited him to sit with them on a cot at the dera.

One of the men pointed to the washroom. "A very generous gesture, Bikram Singh."

The other sighed. "I wish we had a patron like you," he said.

Bikram smiled. "You *have* a patron in me."

"You mean you will consider building one at each of our deras?"

"Why not? I will build this facility at every dera in the Samrala Provincial Constituency. All a Mukhia has to do is visit my shop and ask. Give me details."

"I can give you details now."

"Me, too."

Bikram smiled and took out his notebook.

He stayed at the dera until most of the mourners had left. And he sought out the Mukhia once again.

"Do you visit your son?" he asked.

"Every day. It is a mean place, that fetid jail in Samrala."

"I will try to get him better treatment. The inspector there is a friend of mine."

The Mukhia gripped his shoulder. "Please do whatever you can. Please."

"I promise to do my best. And if you need anything . . ." He slipped a few twenty-rupee notes into the Mukhia's breast pocket.

"May your courtyard sing with the laughter of a dozen sons," the Mukhia said.

The driver stopped in front of the walled police station and Bikram got out. The constable on guard saluted smartly. The inspector met him midway in the sprawling courtyard and led him to his office, where he called for tea.

"To what do I credit the honour of your visit?"

Bikram explained the situation.

"Come, I will show you."

He followed the inspector to the back of the police station. It was lined with dark, dank cells. Several men sat on the bare floor of one and stared balefully at him. The only light was from a high, barred window.

"Rana."

A slight youth slowly stood up.

"Move him to an empty cell," the inspector ordered the jailer.

Bikram patted Rana's shoulder as he went by. "I will send a cot and some bedding for him," he told the inspector.

"Anything else?"

"If you have time today, stop by for a few swigs at the mansion."
The inspector smiled. "I will."

Driving past Aalok Nath's house, where the Indian flag flew on the roof, he realized that neither the MLA nor his greedy son had made an appearance at the dera, despite the widespread reporting of the sensational case. That was fine with him—he got to hog all the limelight as a benefactor of the Bajigars. He had stood shoulder to shoulder with their revered Mukhia in the hour of his suffering.

Basanti

For a month, Basanti would not leave her hut. Sehba brought her meals and slept next to her. And the Mukhia came by often to check on her. Her father had been invited to join the dera, and now he worked with the Mukhia at his butcher stall, while her brother Gulab took over Rana's job at the Malik's cattle yard. They both dropped in every day to see her and sat quietly beside her.

Some days Sehba accompanied the Mukhia to the jail in Samrala and brought back news of Rana.

"He has his own cell. Bikram Singh got him a cot and bedding, and sends food for him, too."

Bikram Singh—Basanti barely remembered him, but she knew he was the benefactor who had built their washroom. She and Devi had enjoyed washing in the privacy of four walls, taking off all their clothes and taking their time to soap their hair and bodies. This was the one thing in those days that would brighten Devi's face and make her smile. And now Devi was dead, along with Wazeer. And Rana, in jail, was lost to them too.

She might as well be a widow. How was she going to raise her child? If she had a daughter, would the Mukhia continue to support her? He was set on having a grandson. That was all he talked about.

"I will bathe all the clan's men in rum when I first set my eyes on my grandson."

"Eat for the boy, Basanti."

"I want a grandson that takes after me. Big and strong."

Unlike his son, the scrawny, pigeon-chested Rana.

Laxmi Maa, please bless me with a boy, she prayed. *Have I not suffered enough to earn a better karma?*

One day, Siamo brought Pinki to visit her, and Basanti rose at last and stepped out of the hut into the sunlight of a cool, clear day.

"I brought the slate and the chalk," Pinki said, and gave her a long hug.

Sehba pulled over a cot and covered it, then Pinki sat in the middle, with Siamo and Basanti on either side, and the other women gathered around to watch the lesson. Pinki scrunched up her face and wiped the slate clean. She handed it to Basanti. "You remember how to draw the letter *ura*?"

Basanti frowned and concentrated. It was a bigger circle atop a smaller circle. She held the chalk firmly and drew them. Pinki watched her.

"There is one more."

"One more what?" Then she remembered that their last lesson had ended abruptly when Pinki had pulled off her chador in the presence of the Malik.

"Oh, Basanti, you are making it hard. Here, I will show you."

Pinki drew a cap on top of the two circles.

"Do it again."

The women tittered and earned a stern look from Pinki. Siamo was silent, but her lips were clamped tight and her sides were jiggling.

"Good. See how easy it is? Want to learn the *ara* now?"

"*Ura, ara*," she recited.

"Good." Pinki clapped. "I will write a letter to you, Basanti, and you send me a reply."

"Knowing just two letters?" Siamo asked.

Pinki thought about that. "Why not?"

"*Ura, ara, ura, ara, ura, ara*." Siamo clapped and sang. The women joined in.

"See, now all of you can say the letters," Pinki said.

"You taught us well, Pinki." Shanti pinched her cherubic cheeks before placing a hand on the child's head to bless her. "Live long, my daughter. Live long."

Little Paso came by. The same age as Pinki, she was too young for school. The two looked at each other, and Pinki jumped off the cot.

"Let's play."

Naura brought tea and pinnis.

"Satwant used to love these," Siamo said.

A pall fell over Basanti. She remembered the days when the Captain had visited the dera. Sehba was convinced that he came only to eat her pinnis.

"Look at them." Siamo pointed to the two girls chasing each other, laughing at the top of their lungs.

"Take a bath, Basanti, and wash your clothes," Sehba told her one day. "You smell, and I won't take you like that to the haveli."

Basanti boiled water and scrubbed the kurti and ghunia she had worn for almost the entire month. Then she asked Shanti to help wash her hair and soap her back with warm water. She sat in the sun to dry her hair, and then Shanti oiled and combed it, and patiently picked the lice from it.

"Your hair was like a weaver bird's nest. All tangled and glued together."

Basanti looked at her image in the square mirror and was pleased to recognize herself. Shanti had braided her hair and tied it with black thread. Her skin was clear, though her eyes were a bit sunken. She had begun to waddle as the baby started to drop. The midwife had just yesterday palpated her abdomen and declared, "Two more weeks at the latest, and I predict a boy from the way it sits so low."

"I will reward you with a beautiful new suit of clothes," the Mukhia told the midwife upon hearing her words.

The saucy woman arched her brows at him. "You'd better."

The Mukhia had bought new clothes for Naura, the current object of his affections. Though the other women muttered that she should have been in mourning for her son, Naura gloried in her finery and sashayed around the dera. She seemed to enjoy especially the fact that she'd put Sehba's nose out of joint by usurping her position. The Mukhia barely looked at Sehba now.

"She has put him in a trance, Basanti," Sehba complained. "Set the evil eye on me. Be careful she does not do it to you, too. Naura is an evil, evil woman."

Pinki had invited Basanti and Sehba to the haveli, and she had insisted that her new friend Paso also come along. The girls played together in the courtyard.

Amrita asked Basanti to sit beside her, and now she turned to the younger woman a little bashfully and said, "Basanti, I was very sorry to hear of the tragedy with your cousin Devi. I know you must miss her, but I hope you are not too terribly sad."

Startled, Basanti gazed into the eyes of the Captain's wife; she saw compassion there. She muttered her thanks and lowered her eyes. Amrita patted her back. It occurred to Basanti then that they had something in common, both pregnant with missing husbands, and in-laws expecting them to produce grandsons, though such a thing was beyond their control.

She gathered her courage and said to Amrita, "If I may ask . . . how is your pregnancy coming along?"

"Well. The midwife said at the most a month."

"Mine predicted two weeks."

"Well, I wish you good health and good news."

"And I pray for you and your baby, too. May Laxmi Maa fulfill your dreams."

They sat and watched Paso chase Pinki as the courtyard rang with the children's laughter.

"It seems like a brighter day today." Amrita sighed. "We have had such burdens to bear."

"Yes. We live our karma."

"You believe that?"

"How else to explain it?"

"I believe in the one and true Waheguru and have placed myself in His hands."

"I pray to Laxmi Maa day and night."

"Basanti, Rana could be gone for many years. I want you to know that you can always come to me for any help you need. I feel that you are like a younger sister to me."

And as Amrita opened her arms, Basanti fell weeping into her embrace.

Basanti's birth pangs began in the middle of the afternoon. Sehba moved her to the Mukhia's hut, which was brighter and more spacious. There was a basket freshly filled with ashes, a bucket of water, a small load of clean rags, and a pair of scissors.

The midwife came in and pulled off Basanti's ghunia and loosened her kurti. After palpating her abdomen, she counted the length of the contraction and the time before the next one. Then for awhile she left her, with Naura and Sehba there to help. For a long time it seemed as though nothing much was happening, although each contraction came a little bit sooner and was a lot more painful than the last.

"Mata!" she cried when she felt her waters break. What a strange sensation, and how silly it felt to wet herself like a little child!

The midwife came back to check on her, and after a few more contractions, there was one that sucked the breath right out of her, leaving her panting. She'd never imagined that anything could hurt so much.

"Breathe, Basanti, breathe," the midwife urged, as Naura held her right hand and Sehba her left.

The midwife spread Basanti's knees and got into position.

Then, "Push, Basanti, push!"

She heard the voices of Naura and Sehba encouraging her as though they were a distant chorus behind the intense pain that rushed at her in waves.

"I can see the head," the midwife finally yelled. "Push, push, push!"

Basanti felt a sudden release just as the women gathered around at her feet. The midwife lifted the baby smeared with blood. It began to shriek. The midwife turned it, and Sehba let out a whoop.

"It's a boy! It's a boy!"

There was a great commotion outside the closed door.

"Congratulations, Mukhia. You have a grandson!"

Relief washed over her.

The midwife helped Basanti deliver the afterbirth and then gave the baby a thorough inspection. Sehba wiped her clean and helped her dress before laying her on a cot with bedding on it, with a pillow under her neck. Naura and the midwife cleaned the baby, swaddled him, and placed him in the crook of his mother's arm.

Basanti looked down at his thick, black, shiny hair before gently manoeuvring him to face her. He puckered his lips, keeping his eyes closed, and she twisted to kiss the pink cheeks. A great upwelling of love filled her, and she began to coo and gently rock her baby.

Sehba hovered over her, before she too kneeled by the cot and kissed the newborn and caressed the head. A boy, an heir. "My little bawa, my life, my sun and moon."

More sounds of celebration drifted in through the open door.

"The Mukhia is happy?"

"Happy? He is dancing in the dera, filling glasses, handing out coins."

Basanti sighed contentedly. The Mukhia had a grandson, and she had a son to hold close to her breast, nurture, and shower with love. In that moment, she felt that Laxmi Maa had fulfilled her, made her whole again.

"I am going to name him after my goddess. I am going to name him Laxman Das."

Sehba frowned. "The Mukhia will hold a naming ceremony, as is our custom."

"I will always call him Laxman Das. The servant of my goddess. It is a good name."

"Don't get too attached to it. The Mukhia has that right. Don't forget it."

You can bark as much as you want, Sehba. My son's name is Laxman Das.

Naura came in carrying a tumbler. "Drink some sweetened milk. It will make yours flow."

Sehba took the swaddled bundle out of her arms and gently danced around. Basanti sat up to drink the milk and watch the new grandmother singing and swaying.

After drinking the milk Basanti felt drowsy and laid her head down. She dreamed.

She was riding a horse, seated behind the Captain, holding on to his waist, her breasts pressed against his back. They rode through fields of flowering mustard, and they seemed to last forever. They dismounted when they came to some woods, and they found two small girls waiting for them there. One of them was Pinki. Pinki looked up and offered her a flower, but the smaller child kept her head lowered.

The Captain handed her the reins.

"Basanti, I leave them in your care."

He moved away, and as she watched, horrified, the earth around him opened and he disappeared into a black abyss.

When she woke, Sehba was looming over her. "Are you all right?"

She shivered and blinked in the darkness.

"I was dreaming. I got scared."

The baby stirred and started to cry.

"Take him to your breast, Basanti. Time to feed him."

She waited for the light of the lantern, opened her kurta, and settled down to her new duty. Sehba lowered the wick.

Two days later, Mata and Dadi arrived and brought gifts of cloth and more milk-cake pinnis. They took turns holding Laxman Das, cuddling and kissing him. The hut was full of love and peace.

"Bless you, bless you, my little one," Dadi said.

"How are you, my daughter?" Mata sat down beside Basanti and pulled her into a hug, and she cried a little in her mother's arms. She wanted to talk about Devi, but when she mentioned her name her father cautioned her, "Now's not the time to speak of the dead."

"Your Bhapa went to visit Rana in jail," Mata told her. "Says he is happy for the birth of a son."

She wiped her face as Sehba and Naura came in with a jug of tea and glasses. They set them down and Sehba went to open the windows, and the air in the hut began to freshen up. But Dadi was furious. "Are you a fool? Watch for evil spirits. Keep the door and windows closed."

"You can burn a stick of incense instead," Mata said. "That will purify the air in here."

Sehba stepped out and returned with one stick and put it into a crack in a wall. She lit it, and a sweet aroma filled the hut.

"Breathe deeply, Basanti," Mata told her. "Fill your lungs with the divine smoke."

Dadi gathered the first piece of ash to fall from the burning stick and rubbed it on Laxman Das's forehead. "Against the evil eye."

"He is a handsome, handsome bawa," Sehba said, gently holding his little hands in hers. "His grandfather has not been sober in three days, drunk with joy."

"Basanti, I am here."

It was Pinki's voice, clear as a bell. Mata opened the door and let her in.

"I came to the dera with my Babaji. Show me the baby, please?"

Basanti opened her arms and Pinki ran to her.

"Show me the baby. I want to see the baby!"

Dadi held Laxman Das towards her, and Pinki looked at him intently.

"Can I touch him?"

"Go ahead."

Pinki wiped his forehead with her fingers and made a face.

"Those are ashes my grandmother rubbed on his forehead for good luck."

"Oh."

"It's all right."

Pinki caressed the baby's cheeks.

On the night of the sixth day, Laxman Das had difficulty holding onto the nipple, and his body shivered and arched. Sehba took off the swaddling and held him up naked to examine him. After she changed his diaper, he relaxed and fell asleep. But during the night he became restless. Dadi checked him for a fever but his skin remained cool to the touch. When he went without a feeding for a night and a day, Basanti began to panic.

"I don't like this."

The midwife came in and unbundled him, and they watched in the light of the lantern as he shivered, his body arching, and his tiny lips puckered. His fists twisted at the wrist. The midwife tried gently to straighten his stiff limbs, then sighed and covered him.

"We'll wait. It might pass."

Sehba lit a stick of incense and muttered some prayers. Still, Laxman Das did not take to Basanti's breast again, and she sat up the whole night.

"Call the shaman," Sehba told the Mukhia in the morning.

"Is something wrong?" Basanti heard the alarm in his voice.

"Just go. Get him."

The dera fell silent except for the lowing and bleating of the animals. They all waited. Laxman Das lay stiff as a board. For Basanti, time had stopped, suspended, like the beating of her heart and the rhythm of her breath.

The shaman arrived just before dusk and set out his paraphernalia on the floor. Sehba brought a glowing cow chip and laid it before him. He sprinkled something on it. It crackled, and smoke rose. He began to chant while slowly fanning the flames with a fly-whisk of peacock feathers. Basanti felt her eyelids get heavy with the hypnotic incantations. Dadi took Laxman Das from her and laid her down on the cot. Sleep took hold.

The light of dawn woke her. She sat up and realized with a start that she had slept through the night. And Laxman Das had not woken her once with his crying. Sehba sat huddled with Dadi and Mata on the cot, holding the swaddled boy.

"Go get the doctor," the Malik ordered.

Sehba came in to explain that he did not believe in shamans and wanted a real doctor to examine the baby. "He got agitated when he heard that my bawa has not suckled in almost three days."

Basanti gazed at the scrunched face of Laxman Das. He seemed to be shrinking. Now her heart, which had seemed to stop, beat faster, and her breath came in short bursts.

Dadi looked at her and her eyes widened. "Basanti, don't panic, my daughter. The doctor will tell us what is going on with the boy. Be calm."

The waiting was agony. The elders took turns holding Laxman Das while Basanti lay down. The hut felt cold and clammy.

The doctor, a tall Sikh wearing glasses, came in at last, carrying a leather bag. He took out a stethoscope.

"Unwrap the baby."

He sat down on the cot beside Laxman Das and listened carefully to his breathing, poked and prodded, sighed, and stood up. He looked at Basanti and bent to pat her on the head before muttering, "Be strong." He closed the bag and walked out.

"What's your opinion, doctor?" The Malik's voice was anxious.

"I should have been called earlier. Too late for me to do anything now."

"Why, what's wrong?"

"Lockjaw. Keep him comfortable."

"We should rush him to the Christian Hospital in Ludhiana?"

"Waste of time, Ajit Singh. He could die any moment."

Wails filled the hut, and the strangled shrieks of the Mukhia drowned out Basanti's own pleas to the goddess, who seemed to have abandoned her once again. She raised her face and cried, "What sins have I committed? Tell me, Laxmi Maa, tell me!"

"He is leaving." Dadi put Laxman Das in her arms.

Basanti pressed the stiff body against her breast and lowered her head to listen to his failing breath, her eyes blinded with tears. The baby's breathing stopped, and Basanti held him tighter against her, trying to capture the warmth still on his skin. Dadi untangled her fingers, took him from her, covered his face, and laid him down on the floor. It was dark, with no sign of light through the cracks in the door or the windows. They chanted holy words, "Om, Hari Om," sitting beside him, and though they held her, Basanti felt herself collapsing.

The Mukhia's cries reverberated in the dera as the men bathed Laxman Das at the pump and ritually bound him in a white shroud. The village Giyani, a kindly, white-haired Sikh, read holy verses in a steady voice as the sun rose. The clan gathered around the small bundle on the bare earth of the dera's common. The Giyani uttered the final prayer, kneeled, and touched his forehead to the ground.

"Bole so nihal!" he shouted.

"Sat Sri Akal," the gathered replied.

Bhapaji looked at Basanti with a tortured gaze before picking up the shrouded Laxman Das in his arms. She was held up to follow the men to the entrance of the dera. She saw Gulab and another man carrying shovels.

"They will bury him by the canal," Shanti said.

Dadi and Mata bathed her in the washroom and let her sit bareheaded in the sun, turned away from the men in the centre who were gathered around the Mukhia. The women surrounded her in silence. No one said a word. She had no more tears to shed. Dadi began to comb her hair and braid it. Then she covered Basanti's head with a chador. As the afternoon sun waned, people began to rise and go to their chores, feed the animals, start the cooking fires.

Suddenly wails arose from the haveli, and someone ran into the dera, calling out, "The Malik lost his daughter-in-law during childbirth."

"And the baby?" someone asked.

"It's a girl. The baby is alive."

"Om, Hari Om," Dadi said.

Mata stood her up and helped Basanti to her hut. Basanti lay down on the cot and curled up as tightly as she could, shutting her eyes and ears to the living world around her. Amrita, her newfound older sister, was dead. She recalled her dream of the Captain disappearing into the dark abyss. She wished she had jumped in after him.

Sehba and the Mukhia were summoned to the haveli at dawn. When Sehba returned later, alone, she sat down heavily on the cot beside Basanti.

"Basanti, the Malik is asking you for a very important favour. He is asking . . . if you will be the wet nurse for his newborn granddaughter."

Basanti sat up and stared at Sehba. What was it the old woman said? Nothing seemed to make sense.

"Basanti, you understand that Amrita is dead. The baby girl has no mother to feed her. The Malik is afraid that the baby won't survive if you will not—"

"I will do it," Basanti said, and she was on her feet in an instant.

They helped her wash and collect a few clothes, and gave her a mug of tea to drink. She felt a strange emotion. She wanted to hold an infant in her arms and take it to her breast. She needed to. As they set out for the haveli, she almost ran ahead of the women.

The Malik's courtyard was filled with people. Mata, Dadi, and Sehba waited there while Siamo led Basanti into a backroom and asked her to sit on a cot. The sounds of women crying somewhere filled the home.

Siamo left briefly and returned with the Malkin, another older woman, and two younger ones.

"Basanti, I am Amrita's mother, and these are my daughters-in-law," the older woman said.

Basanti stood up and bent to touch the elders' feet.

"It is a tragic time—for you and for us—and something good must come of it," Amrita's mother said in a low voice.

"Does your milk still flow?" the Malkin asked.

Basanti undid her kurti and revealed her swollen breasts. She squeezed one and milk erupted.

The two younger women looked at her and then shared a smile.

"What are you two doing, behaving like buyers in a barn," Amrita's mother scolded them, and they lowered their eyes and hung their heads.

"I will get the baby," the Malkin said.

Basanti waited, her heart racing. The Malkin returned with a swaddled infant and placed her in her arms. Basanti looked at the pink face with the thick head of hair. She looked just like Laxman Das. She felt tears running down her cheeks as she brought the baby to her breast. It took her barely a moment to latch on, and soon she gave a contented grunt and started suckling.

"Thank you, Waheguru," Siamo said.

"Thank you, Basanti." The Malkin wiped her eyes and came to bless her.

Siamo followed, as did Amrita's mother, and the two daughters-in-law.

"You must have done some good in your past life, Basanti. Laxmi Maa has filled your lap and your arms again," Dadi whispered, placing both hands on her head. "Live long, live happy, live a life of peace."

BOOK THREE

1951–1952

Bikram

"How much tragedy can one man bear?" Papaji sighed. He was thinking of Zaildar Ajit Singh as they travelled to Raikot once again to attend a final funerary observance, the Antim Bhog, this time for the Captain's wife, Amrita. They were riding in comfort in the back seat of the chauffeured car.

"She left behind a baby girl," Bikram said.

"Another tragedy. A boy would at least have ensured him an heir to carry his name forward. Instead, he is burdened by two little grand-daughters. What does he have to look forward to now? The girls will grow up, marry and go to their husbands' homes. He will live a lonely old age in that big haveli of his."

"Not a great prospect, is it?"

Papaji shook his head.

Bikram and his father paid their respects at the ceremony, and Bikram, ever mindful of his upcoming campaign, kept an eye out for anyone who might be useful. He sought out the Mukhia to offer his condolences.

The Mukhia moaned loudly. "It's a terrible business. I have lost my grandson, my heir, the great delight of my old age. And my son is lost to me as well, in prison, facing a possible death sentence. And all because he tried to stop his sick, perverted cousin from killing his own wife. Was ever a man so tortured?"

Then Bikram and his father went to sit beside Amrita's grieving father, Jagirdar Sher Singh, and his two strapping sons, to eat the langar.

After some time, one of the sons turned to Bikram.

"I read a news report about you and your building project in the deras. Proper washrooms, with privacy and convenience for their women. I compliment you on the initiative."

"The Bajigars need help. I thought, what better way to repay Waheguru for His generosity to me?" Which son was this, he wondered, the judge or the deputy superintendent of police? "I have been happy to offer this project as my sewa. And now I am being asked to do the same for the bastees of the untouchables."

The second brother nudged the first. "We should donate towards the cause."

"I actually built the first washroom at the dera right here, in honour of Satwant Singh's sacrifice," Bikram was quick to point out.

"Is that right?" That caught Sher Singh's attention. "In that case, we thank you from the bottom of our hearts."

"It was my good fortune to be able to honour the Captain in this way," said Bikram, touching his breast as he spoke. "You may not know this, but it was Zaildar Ajit Singh who helped get me recruited as an NCO in the army. I owe him a great deal."

"You are such a humble and good man, Bikram Singh." Sher patted his back. "Call on me any time."

"Yes, let us know what funds you need for the great cause," said the son Bikram thought might be the judge.

"I will. Thank you so much. And please allow me to offer my condolences once more on your terrible loss."

They bowed to him and uttered their gratitude.

Now the Zaildar himself approached.

"Bikram Singh, I want to drop by your shop for a visit soon. I have a need that you might be able to help with."

Bikram bowed to the Zaildar with joined hands. "I look forward to helping you in any way I can."

When the Zaildar did come, he rode up to Bikram's shop on a mare. Disappointingly, though, it was not the majestic horse called Bakki. He handed the reins to a boy in the street, who seemed more than happy to mind the animal for a couple of coins.

"Come in, come in, welcome," Bikram said, beckoning the Zaildar into the front office.

The Zaildar sat down on the cushioned diwan and crossed his legs.

A truck pulled into the grain market, and when Bikram saw Mangal step down from it he waved him in.

"My friend Mangal Singh, proprietor of Frontier Transport."

Mangal made the spacious office feel cramped just by stepping into it. The Zaildar gaped at the giant but proffered his hand. Mangal shook it and offered his condolences. "I was away in Bengal, Calcutta in fact, on business and could not attend the Captain's funeral."

"Calcutta?" the Zaildar asked.

"Yes, I bought a small fleet of trucks there. Now I'm hauling steel from Jamshedpur to Calcutta to be shipped to Japan. Steady work, rain or shine."

"How interesting, and very fortuitous, as it happens," said the Zaildar. "You see, I've been searching for someone lately—that's why I'm here—and I understand that he's been working on trucks in Bengal."

"A relative?"

"You could say that. My widowed cousin's one and only nephew."

"From which village?"

"Naugarh."

Mangal thought for a moment. "I know a man from there. Owns a truck in Calcutta."

Bikram noticed that the Zaildar became rather animated. "Oh, you do? Do you have his address? I need to send him a letter."

"I can get a letter to him through my men. Just leave it to me."

It seemed as if, suddenly, Mangal had become the Zaildar's best friend.

Bikram stood in front of the full-length mirror. How would he appear to voters? His beard flowed past his breastbone now, and he thought it made him look more mature than his thirty-two years. His spectacles added to the sombre expression, and gave him an educated and intelligent air. He was a very credible candidate, he thought.

He started practising oratory under the tutelage of the high school drama teacher. He was taught how to project his voice, how to pace himself, pause for effect, and emphasize key words. He learned to interest and entertain his listeners, fire them up, and earn their applause.

His first speeches were to a few dozen people in the Bajigar deras and untouchables' bastees. Soon he felt comfortable speaking to hundreds at school functions, village fairs, and religious festivals, where he made monetary contributions and bought time on the podium. He handed out awards and prizes, honoured local leaders with garlands of rupee notes, announced sweet rice feasts, and praised the dead.

His brother-in-law Darshan wrote his speeches, and gradually became his personal assistant, after Mangal gave him time off from the bus station. Next Bikram added a publicist to his entourage, and in no time at all local newspapers were carrying small stories about him or his speeches on the inside pages. No photos yet, but the plan was working.

Bikram was called to the school to discuss a discipline problem concerning his son.

"I read about you." Sewa's attractive young teacher smiled and held his gaze.

Wait until you see me on the front page with a splashy photo, he wanted to say.

She let him lightly caress her breast—accidentally, of course. He rushed home and, finding Jagtar in their bedroom sorting out a closet, he grabbed her and took her from behind, violently thrusting and grunting.

"What came over you, Ji?" she asked after they washed up. "You haven't been this passionate for months."

"This politics business can be quite arousing."

"But I thought you went to visit Sewa's teacher," Jagtar said.

"Well, even keeping the brat in school is becoming political. I had to use some persuasive skills to calm the teacher. Luckily, she had read about me in the newspaper and looked a bit intimidated."

"Of course, she's probably thinking about the day you do become an MLA and she needs your help with a promotion or a transfer."

"Whenever, whenever," he said dismissively.

The idea stuck with him, though, and it excited him to think about the woman coming to him for help, meeting in private to listen to her needs, and telling her his. He felt energized and motivated. Money was not the only reward of politics, he realized.

Basanti

Despite a chill in the air, the family was sitting in the courtyard, and Basanti, careful to cover her head first, came out to join them. The Malkin was holding the baby, her new little granddaughter, and the Malik was sitting at the table with Siamo. Basanti came over and touched his feet. He blessed her, and she squatted on the ground beside him.

The baby was called Nikki, the little one. Inder carried her over to the washroom to bathe her, but apparently Nikki did not approve, and she cried, with gusto.

"She is a feisty one, I tell you, Bir," Siamo said.

Pinki came to sit in her grandfather's lap and he mussed her hair.

"Nikki only drinks milk, poops, and sleeps, Babaji," Pinki said.

"Wait until she grows up a bit and begins to crawl. You will be singing a different tune then," he said and turned to Basanti. "Basanti, please get up and sit beside me. And you don't need to veil yourself in my presence."

Basanti wasn't sure how to respond, but Siamo stood her up, pushed her gently on to the chair, and lifted her veil.

She saw the Malik's eyes widen in amazement. Siamo must have noticed his surprise, and she said, "I told you, Bir! Except for the tribal tattoos on her face, she could almost be Amrita's twin."

Basanti kept her eyes lowered, hands on her lap. Inder brought the baby back and handed her to Basanti. Then she took Pinki off her grandfather's lap and headed back to the washroom. Basanti saw her opportunity. In one swift move, she gently placed Nikki in her grandfather's arms. "Hold her, Malik. She wants your love."

Siamo stared at them. A slow smile broke across her face and she patted Basanti's shoulder. "Well done, Basanti. It's about time he held Nikki."

Basanti was not sure if she had been too bold, but the Malik smiled at the baby, whose eyes were wide and bright, and brought her closer. He kissed her cheeks and she made a face.

"You're tickling her with your moustache, Malik!" Basanti said.

His smile grew wider and he crinkled his eyes. "What a pretty, pretty face."

"See?" Siamo turned to Basanti. "Bir is just a big, gentle bear. Full of love and affection. Look at him. He's smitten. I know that look."

Inder came back rubbing Pinki's head with a towel and stood staring at him.

"Basanti did it," Siamo explained. "Just handed him the baby."

Inder shook her head. "I would not have believed it if I were not seeing it with my own eyes. I begged you for five weeks, every day, to hold her."

"Look at him now." Siamo chuckled.

"Basanti," Inder called. "It's your turn to bathe. Make sure to wear fresh clothes. Remember, we are visiting the gods today."

As Ajit kissed the baby again, her little fist escaped the swaddling and gripped his moustache.

"Remember, Bir? Satwant used to tug on your moustache until there were tears in your eyes." Siamo laughed.

"That Nikki is a very naughty girl!" Pinki said.

Inder went with Siamo and Basanti, carrying Nikki, to the Naag Baba temple. It was time to present the baby to the deities. Together they poured milk into the hollows atop the small stupas. Pariah dogs circled, and as soon as they started their circumambulation of the shrine the animals rushed to lick up the milk. Siamo took a handful of grain from the offering tray and spread it on the ground, and birds swooped down from the trees to peck at it.

Next Siamo swept the grounds around the Pir's raised tomb while Inder served prasad to the men who were passing by. Finally Inder put an offering of dried fruit and nuts at the base of the tomb, as that was rumoured to have been the Pir's favourite snack. They knelt and bowed and sought silent benediction.

At the gurudwara, their next stop, the Giyani read the day's lesson, the word of the day, and accepted a donation of cloth and cash. He blessed Nikki by placing his hand over her head. "Live long, my child."

Inder served prasad here, too, and women came out of their court-yards to gaze at the baby. Inder passed Nikki around to be fussed over and blessed with gifts of coins. The older ones blessed Basanti as well, as she bent to touch their feet.

"Live long and un-widowed."

They mussed Pinki's hair.

"She is going to be a real beauty one day," someone said.

Pinki smiled shyly.

During the long winter weeks that followed, Sehba came by from time to time to oil and comb Basanti's hair and bring her news from the dera.

"Naura is a witch, Basanti. Lolls around all day while I milk the buffalo, clear the dung and make dung pies, water the beasts, tether them in the sun. I cook and clean. I wash the clothes. Of course that means I am no longer allowed to visit my son—too many chores to do. I beg the Mukhia to let me go, but he has closed his ears to me. I even have to heat water and lug it to the washroom so his new queen can bathe. Imagine that! And all night long I have to lie silently and listen to his grunts and the witch's moans."

Sehba's woes were unending.

"The only bright light in all this is Bikram Singh. That man is a god. He takes good care of Rana at the jail. Did I tell you he's a close friend of the police inspector?"

The room Basanti lived in had a high ceiling, whitewashed walls, and a big window. A large lantern kept it well lit. Her cot was wide with comfortable bedding. A large wardrobe with shelves and drawers was full of clothes she could choose from, a variety of shoes, tins of talcum powder. On the outside was a mirror large enough to let her see her reflection from head to toe. Jeet Kaur had insisted on giving Basanti most of Amrita's clothes and possessions. "You must wear these. It will calm my heart to see you in them, Basanti," the grieving mother had said. She had even brought her a gold chain to wear around her neck, saying, "I bought this to give to Amrita as a present for the birth. You wear it now."

Books lined a long shelf on one wall. Amrita was a voracious reader, the Malkin had told her. She read all kinds of books in Punjabi, Hindi, and English. Some had pictures in them, and those Basanti leafed through. There were pictures of bridges, houses, boats, and ships, and all kinds of animals, but the ones she really liked had portraits of fashionable women with fabulous clothing, eye-popping hairstyles, makeup, and jewellery.

A tray, heavily laden with food, was brought in for Basanti's lunch. Sehba whispered, "Save some for me. I am famished."

"You eat first." Basanti pushed the tray towards her mother-in-law and watched her devour the food.

Siamo walked in, and Sehba quickly pushed the tray back.

"You can eat at the kitchen, Sehba. Follow me," Siamo said.

Siamo took away the tray and returned with a full one.

Basanti handed her Nikki, who was fussing, and Siamo began to sing her a lullaby.

Life in the Malik's haveli was safe and without the worries of the dera. Basanti no longer woke up with the anxiety of hunger that had been bred into her. There was no more scavenging for fuel, eating berries and wild fruits to fill up, stealing a quick sip of milk or a swallow of soft butter. Now she had tea twice a day, lassi with breakfast and lunch, and a tall glass of warm, sweet milk before bed. She felt utterly spoiled. She dreaded the day she'd have to return to the dera to live under the thumb of two old women constantly at war.

Nikki was a lovable baby. And she was thriving, getting bigger and heavier and more demanding. She filled her diapers regularly. Pinki ran out at the sight of a soiled one, holding her nose.

"Shee, shee! Basanti Maa, her poops are bigger than her!"

"Look at her, Basanti Maa. Just look at her!" Pinki would say.

Being called Maa overwhelmed Basanti's heart with joy. But thoughts of Laxman Das still tortured her at night. In her own home, she had not had a proper chance to grieve. She had not been able to sit in mourning in the company of her kin and hear their kind words, feel their consoling touch. And when Sehba came to visit her, it was as though she had completely forgotten her grandson. She spoke only of Rana, or railed against Naura, or lamented her neglect by the Mukhia.

One morning Basanti woke with a sadness that dropped over her like a heavy blanket. She didn't touch her breakfast.

The Malik asked in a gentle voice, "Basanti, what's wrong?"

Tears filled Basanti's eyes.

"Basanti?" The Malkin leaned forward to hold her hand.

"I dreamed about my son last night," Basanti managed to say. And then, she couldn't help it, the tears ran freely down her cheeks.

"Courage, Basanti, courage," the Malik said, and Siamo rubbed her back. "We have all suffered such tragedies."

"Thank you, Malik. Thank you, Malkin."

"Basanti." The Malik sat down. "Please, call me Bapuji, as Amrita did."

"And call me Maaji, please." The Malkin smiled. "I want to hear that word so badly."

"You are family now," the Malik reminded her. His voice was heavy, and he took out his handkerchief to blow his nose.

Even Siamo agreed, and asked to be addressed as aunt. "Satwant and Amrita called me Bhua. You can too."

"Thank you, Bhua. I feel so fortunate, I don't know where I would be without your kindness."

One day, Pushpa, the Brahmin elder, stopped by to visit. Basanti offered her tea in the courtyard, and the woman promptly sat down beside her, slurping her tea and chewing the biscuits. Basanti spoke of her worries, and of the twists of fate that had brought her to the haveli, the tragedies, the suffering, and the sorrows.

"It's no mystery to me, Basanti, why so many terrible things came to pass. Your mother-in-law is to blame. Sehba is a greedy woman. When you were a new bride, she should have presented you to our deities before hauling you through the village to collect gifts. Look at the bad luck it brought you."

"I have been to visit the deities to present Nikki to them."

"Good. Make sure to pray to them daily. Ask them to protect you."

"How do I do that?"

"Simple. As soon as you wake up, invoke them by name. *O Naag Baba, O Pir Shah, protect me and watch over me.* Do the same before bed."

"That's all?"

"That's all. A second of pure worship is better than a month of fasting. The founder of the Sikh religion, Guru Nanak said that. Make sure you concentrate, though. Don't allow your mind to wander."

"I will."

The elder smiled, and then sighed. "Basanti, I too will pray for you. You seem to be such a pure soul."

Occasionally, Basanti had an unsettling thought. Was she becoming Amrita? Taking her place? She had to shake her head to rid it of the thought, but it kept returning. At night, she dreamed of the Captain, and woke up feeling guilty about betraying Amrita.

Was it a sin to lust after a dead man? She so wanted to ask Pushpa, but fearing the woman's horrified reaction to her confession, she chose to keep her own counsel.

∽

Spring arrived, and with the warm sun came the labourers to harvest the winter crop. Basanti threw herself into the task of helping cook the massive meals required. She would carry a basket full of rotis on her head, following Bapuji, who carried buckets of dal, and they would make their way along canals to the fields to feed the workers. She always veiled her face then.

Naura, Sehba and Shanti were in the fields with scythes, hoping to earn some grain for their families.

Shanti called out, "You look like a Jat woman now, Basanti!"

"She does. Even walks like one," another woman commented.

"It's the shoes. They make you walk differently," Shanti pointed out.

"Give me another roti," Sehba said.

"A bit more dal," Naura demanded.

At midday, Baru Marasi, who tended the cattle, poured cool well water from a goatskin in the thick shade of the sheesham trees surrounding the well. Beyond the shade of the trees, the ground burned as the sun blazed mercilessly in the cloudless sky, and a warm breeze raised dust in the air.

"It must be very nice lolling under the shade of the haveli verandah instead of squatting with us cutting wheat," Naura said bitterly.

"Mind your tongue," Shanti snapped.

Sehba looked up. "See, Basanti, what I have to live with?"

Basanti left them arguing at the well and returned to the haveli. The wide, empty basket on her head was like a shade umbrella. Bapuji trudged ahead of her, swinging the empty buckets, his head covered in a loose turban.

The harvest lasted a month and the days passed in a blur. Nikki slept almost through the night now, so Basanti could sleep for a few uninterrupted hours. During the day she worked at the hearth, stopping only to feed Nikki. When the transport trucks came to take away the wheat, she helped feed the loaders and the drivers. Carrying her basket of rotis to the fields, she came to realize how much land Bapuji owned. It started at the haveli and reached the Adda, ran along the paved road to the canal, then north to the path that ran past the Pir's orchard.

Bapuji returned from Samrala one day, having sold the last truckload. He handed Maaji a thick stack of notes.

"It was a great harvest. One of the best."

Maaji stood up from her chair and went inside to put the money away.

"You were a great help, Basanti." Bapuji smiled.

"I don't know how we could have done it without her," Siamo added.

"Bapuji," Basanti began, "Sehba was asking for a sack of wheat since I could not help her in the harvest."

Bapuji glanced at Siamo. "Oh, I will sort it out," he said.

Siamo snorted. "She gets thirty rupees a month already for your stay here, Basanti, and asks for a bundle of fuel or a bag of jaggery each time she comes over."

"It's all right. Basanti is worth it," the Malik said.

It was news to Basanti that Sehba was collecting cash from the haveli. She was shocked and felt humiliated. She began to cry. Sehba was selling her milk like a cow's!

"Bapuji, I do this to repay my family's and my clan's debt to your son, and out of my love for Amrita, Pinki, and Nikki. Not to earn a wage or a sack of wheat," she said between sobs.

When Maaji returned, Siamo told her, "Basanti is upset that her services are being sold."

"Basanti, my daughter. I know the love and loyalty you have for us, and I understand your frustration. But we too are bound by traditions and obligations. Sehba is doing what she must, since her only son is in jail. We must help her, too. Your feelings for Nikki and Pinki are those of a mother, and I will never be able to place a value on them." Maaji came over to pat her back. "It will all work out, Basanti. Believe me."

"But I want to give without payment. I wish I had something to give you, Maaji."

"You already do, Basanti. You give your love to Nikki and Pinki, honour Satwant's and Amrita's memory, respect us, and care for the haveli." Maaji leaned forward to caress her face. "Because you give these gifts from your heart, they are priceless."

Siamo said, "You are as much a prisoner of your love for us as we are now of our love for you."

One day, Siamo asked for Basanti's help to organize the pantry. Maaji was taking a nap, and Nikki was sleeping beside her.

Basanti stepped into the room, which contained all sizes of brass and glass utensils sitting on deep, concrete shelves built into the back wall. Covered iron drums lined another wall. Baskets of onions, garlic, and ginger lay on the floor, beside ceramic vats that smelled of maturing pickles. Glass jars of spices and condiments sat on the top of a cabinet.

"Don't stand there with your mouth open, Basanti. Help me fill the drum with jaggery from this sack."

Basanti picked fist-sized pieces and handed them to Siamo. Smelling the spices, condiments, pickles, and jaggery made her long to cook with them. Bapuji had been complaining lately about the toughness of goat cooked on the kitchen stoves. She decided to make him a dish of meat and poolis cooked on an upside-down pot. She had prepared it for the Mukhia often, and he had showered her with praise. It was her father's recipe.

"Bapuji, can you buy some meat today? I want to cook it for you."

"The Bajigar way?"

She nodded.

He smiled and left for the Adda.

"This I've got to see," said Chinti, who was in charge of the kitchen and normally cooked for the haveli.

"Give her a chance," Maaji told her.

Basanti crushed generous quantities of onions, garlic, and ginger in a mortar while heating ghee over a low flame. Maaji and Siamo stood and watched over the half-wall.

"Why so much?"

"For meat I use more ingredients."

She added the onion mixture to the ghee and stirred as it sizzled to a golden hue. Next she added pieces of meat, still on the bone, and waited for it to brown.

"When will you add water?" asked Chinti.

"I don't add water."

"At all?"

"At all. I cook the meat in its own juices."

"It will burn, stick to the bottom."

"Oh, just wait!"

Basanti added salt, chillies, ground cardamom, cumin, coriander, whole star anise, cloves, and a stick of cinnamon. More stirring.

"Oh, what an aroma!" Siamo exclaimed.

Bapuji called down from the top of the staircase. "I am already hungry. When will it be ready?"

"By dusk."

"But that's hours away!"

Next Basanti built a bed of dung pies in a corner and lit it. When it was glowing, she put the pot on it, covered it, and sealed the cover with a string of dough.

"I cook it slowly, just let it bubble away inside the sealed pot."

"Now I want to see you make Bajigar poolies," Chinti said.

Basanti placed an earthen pot with a nice round belly upside down on the chullah. They all watched her knead the dough, using more water than they were used to for making rotis. She put the dough in a bowl and covered it with a piece of cheesecloth.

Later, she lit a fire under the upside-down pot, and once it was hot she started quickly rolling out the large poolies, making them thin, and flipped the first one onto the pot. Each one cooked in a minute. Chinti turned them, folded them twice, and placed them in a cloth-lined basket.

While the poolies baked, Basanti took the pot with the meat off the bed of coals and unsealed the cover. Delicious steam spread through the kitchen. She added in chopped fresh coriander and green onions and stirred.

"Get the bowls."

"Fill your Bapuji's first. He is drumming the table," Maaji said.

Bapuji sniffed the dish before breaking a piece of pooli to wrap around a piece of meat dripping in oil. And every one of the women held her breath.

He put it in his mouth and held it for a moment before starting to chew. A moan escaped his lips.

Chinti took a bite and smiled. "Welcome to the kitchen, Basanti."

Bapuji cleared his throat. "You will cook the meats from now on."

"Is it good, Bapuji?"

"Is it good? It is delicious! Better than any meat I've ever eaten in any restaurant in the city."

Bikram

The Giyani of the gurudwara in Raikot pondered his request.

"Ajit Singh is expecting some political luminaries to speak after the services are over. If they take a long time, I can't promise you any time at the microphone."

"I will take that chance," Bikram said, and he bowed to the Giyani.

It was the first anniversary of the death of Captain Satwant Singh, and the Zaildar and his family had arranged for a ceremonial bhog at the gurudwara, followed by the traditional langar. This was a valuable political opportunity, and Bikram planned to take full advantage of it. He had arrived early to make his request of the Giyani, and brought Darshan and his publicist, Rakesh Kumar, with him. Chand and Papaji would join them later to pay their respects to the Zaildar and his family at the ceremony.

The gurudwara had started to fill up when a couple of army trucks arrived carrying men of the Captain's regiment, led by their colonel in full dress uniform. They laid floral tributes at the foot of the dais upon which the Holy Granth was now being read by the Giyani, who held a silver-handled flyswitch to keep insects from defiling the pages of the holy book. The soldiers sat together on the carpeted floor.

Bikram remained standing, the better to see who was arriving and note their importance in the constituency. So far, and much to his surprise, he had not spotted any political dignitaries. The last to arrive were the Zaildar and his family, and Sher Singh, Amrita's father, with his. Bikram bowed and greeted them.

"Sit by me," Ajit Singh said, and Bikram was deeply conscious of the conspicuous honour.

When the reading was completed, the Giyani invited a group of singers to perform. The three men, two playing harmoniums and one a tabla, began to sing hymns. Bikram noticed Ajit becoming a bit anxious, as neither the MLA nor the MP had yet made an appearance. Except for a few official-looking men he recognized as the sub-divisional officer and the block officer from Samrala, Sher's sons probably outranked everyone there, Bikram thought.

The Ardas was said, and the Giyani read the word of the day, translating it from Gurmukhi to modern Punjabi, since not many people would have understood the ancient language of the scriptures. The speeches would start very soon, and yet not one of the expected dignitaries had shown up. Bikram's hopes were flying. He began to mentally recite the speech he had written and practised over and over with the drama teacher.

The Giyani came over and held a whispered conversation with Ajit, who seemed quite agitated and was obviously working hard to maintain his composure. Then the Giyani leaned towards Bikram and said, "I will introduce you next."

"Honoured congregation," the Giyani began, once he'd returned to the dais. "As you all know, today we are observing the one-year anniversary of Captain Satwant Singh's martyrdom. I thank you all for attending. Zaildar Ajit Singh wants me to thank you from the bottom of his heart. He has also asked Jathedar Bikram Singh, from the Akali Dal in Samrala, to say a few words on this important occasion. I invite Bikram Singh to speak."

Bikram took the microphone in his hands and bowed deeply.

"Sat Sri Akal."

Take your time, the drama teacher had instructed him.

"It is my great and humble honour to say a few words about the Captain's sacrifice for the nation, for Punjab, and for all Sikhs. As Sikhs, you must feel great pride in him and continue to hold him close in your hearts and minds, as I do."

All eyes were now on him.

"The greater Punjab that spreads over most of northern India has many monuments and memorials built to the revered memory of Sikhs who fought and died in holy wars to protect the weak and vulnerable, as well as those who went overseas to fight in the armies of the British. An uncountable number. Today, we are gathered here in this holy place to remember a son of this village and a member of our faith."

Keep up the interest, the drama teacher had emphasized. *Make the point and move on. Do not linger.*

"I bow to the father, Zaildar Ajit Singh, and to his wife, Inder Kaur, who gave their only child and son to India. My heart goes out to the Captain's two small children, girls both, Pinki and Nikki. Ajit Singh and Inder Kaur as adults understand the import of their sacrifice and loss, but these two innocents are too young yet to understand what they have lost."

He gestured to the girls and paused to let his words sink in and sympathy build.

"As Sikhs, we rush to defend, to fight for our home, our village, our neighbours, the Punjab, and India. Our blood is spilled first. We are the tip of the spear that protects this great nation."

He saw the look of appreciation in the eyes of the turbaned soldiers, and the colonel nodded at him.

"Yet I am also sad to see that our sacrifices are not always appreciated or honoured."

Some of his listeners frowned; it was the expression he was looking for.

"How many of you were here for the funerary bhog a year ago?" he asked.

Most people raised their hands.

"I am sure you remember the pledges made by our local MLA, Aalok Nath, and our boastful MP. Do you remember their words, spoken in the hallowed presence of the Holy Granth?"

Heads nodded.

"Do you see those two Congressmen here today?"

"No." The answer was loud, and it was angry.

"Do you miss those liars right now? Do we need to listen respectfully while they make more false promises in the holy memory of Captain Satwant Singh?"

"No!"

The Zaildar nodded too.

"MLA Aalok Nath and our MP, Arjun Singh, could not even spare a little time today to commemorate the ultimate sacrifice of a Sikh, the only soldier in their constituency to fall for his nation in the last year."

He had checked that fact out. It was important to what he was going to say next.

"Neither did they arrive at any time in the last year to lay foundation stones for the memorials built in our beloved Captain's honour. Yet . . ." Bikram and his team had been doing their research. He pulled a folded newspaper out of his pocket, shook it, and showed them the columns. "Yet they had time to lay numerous other foundation stones. MLA Aalok Nath attended the ceremonies for the launching of one hundred and eleven new projects, while your MP, Arjun Singh, attended roughly a hundred."

Mutterings of disgust rose from the congregation, and people looked at each other with fiery eyes.

"Remember this when they come to ask for your votes."

Bikram paused to let that thought sink in.

"Please listen to what I am pledging today, here in the presence of the Holy Granth."

At that point, the Mukhia stood up and shouted, "You have already done so much, Bikram Singh—built twenty-seven washrooms and twenty-seven pumps in our deras in memory of the Captain."

"And you've given so generously to us in my bastee right here in Raikot," said a white-haired man that Bikram recognized as an elder of the untouchables.

The congregation applauded, until the Giyani settled them with a sharp reminder that they must observe decorum in the gurudwara.

Bikram continued, "Today I pledge that if I'm elected as your next MLA I will build two health centres, one for the public and one for your animals—a medical centre and a veterinary centre, side by side in this village. This I will do in memory of Captain Satwant Singh, a man who was devoted to public service. I will also promote the local elementary school to a high school, and have all the paths to the village paved."

Once again the Giyani had to rebuke the congregation. "Quiet, please. Quiet."

"Thank you, Zaildar-ji. Thank you, Giyani-ji. And my thanks to all of you here for your patience and for listening to my words. Bole so nihal."

"Sat Sri Akal," they replied, and the cry almost raised the dome of the temple.

Men rose to shake his hand, or pat his shoulders.

"Wonderful speech, Bikram. Thank you, thank you." Ajit hugged him.

Sher followed. "Such true words," he said, and his sons hugged Bikram tightly.

Papaji watched, his eyes aglow with pride.

Bikram was pleased to find his speech on the second page of two dailies, highlighted and spread over two columns. Rakesh had mailed the text to the newspapers in advance, and his friends at the dailies had printed it verbatim, adding an additional paragraph noting the folly of the MLA and MP for not attending and lecturing them on their duties.

"Excellent. Good work," Bikram told Rakesh.

The speech had also caused a stir at the Akali Dal headquarters in Amritsar. Not long after, they sent a senior advisor to meet with Bikram in Samrala.

"I suggest you organize a dharna at the Civil Courts here. Hold a sit-in, a public protest," said the advisor. "Try to get a large number of protesters to join you. At least five thousand."

"That many?"

"That should not be difficult, now that you have the people's attention. And you'll want to do it as soon as possible, before MLA Aalok Nath preempts you by deciding to lay a foundation stone. You don't want to let him steal your thunder."

Bikram looked at the smiling man with increasing respect and interest.

"What if nothing comes of it? What if the government ignores me?"

"Then you threaten something, like a fast unto death."

"What?" Bikram could feel the colour drain from his face.

The advisor said, "I hope you have the courage and conviction of a Sikh, Bikram Singh."

Rakesh coughed, and the man turned to him. The publicist engaged him in a lengthy conversation.

Chand glared at Bikram, and he felt his face flush with shame.

"You need some steel in your spine," his father-in-law whispered.

As soon as the advisor had gone, Bikram gathered his entourage and brought out the whiskey. He was glad to see the back of the man, who had scared him witless.

"No one is going to be foolish enough to let you fast to the death, Bikram," Rakesh said. "They don't want another martyr. The government will race to lay a foundation stone for a suitable memorial in Raikot. You will earn the accolades for forcing their hand, and it will put you on the front pages of the newspapers."

"It's the opportunity we have waited for." Chand swallowed some spicy boar pickle and burped. "Samrala is a Sikh majority constituency, and riling them up around a cause will push your support through the roof."

"All right. Let's get to work, then. Send out messages to all the sarpanches we met and all the mukhias of the deras. The Zaildar alone could get us two thousand men if he raises fifty protesters from each of the forty villages under his zaildari."

It was starting to look promising. He looked at Mangal, who had been listening silently. Mangal took a deep breath before speaking.

"A peaceful dharna will not make news the way a violent one will. I will arrange for some roughnecks to raise a bit of a ruckus."

"And that will bring a charge from the police, and we can level accusations of police brutality on top of government indifference to the Sikhs," Darshan said, pouring himself a stiff shot.

"It will look even better if you get manhandled a bit and actually bleed from a cut, Bikram. It will make you look heroic," Mangal pointed out.

Bleed? Get manhandled? But he was so close to success now. As long as no one broke his bones or caused internal injuries, it would probably be worth it.

Ajit

Ajit received a visit from Bikram Singh, who told him about a plan for a sit-in.

"I need your help, Zaildar Sahib, to round up men. I know, if you ask, that we will have no trouble crowding the Civil Court grounds with protesters. All in Satwant's name."

Ajit was excited, and he shared the news with the Comrade the next time his friend dropped in for a visit. They were sitting at the table playing a game of gin rummy.

"The man is a charlatan," the Comrade said, while deftly arranging the cards he'd been dealt.

"What? How can you say that?" Siamo shouted.

"He is. I know Bikram well. I went to school with him."

"But he served in the army for ten years. In fact, I was the one who got him recruited as an NCO."

"Ten years as an NCO drawing an NCO's wages. So how did he become so rich, so fast? How was he able to buy properties, land, and a huge mansion in Samrala?"

"He must have been a good saver," Siamo said.

The Comrade snorted. "If you meet the ghost of the headless girl, ask her about him," he said.

"The ghost of the headless girl?" Basanti asked in a cracked voice. She was sitting at the table with Pinki in her lap; the little girl was watching the cards intently.

"You've never heard of the headless girl?" The Comrade seemed genuinely surprised.

"I did hear a tale once about a massacre of Muslims at the Pir's orchard. A woman at the dera still has nightmares about bathing and burying the dead," Basanti replied.

"Well," said the Comrade, "I hear that if you visit the Pir's orchard on the night of a full moon, you will see her floating through the trees and moaning, 'Where's my head? O, find my head. Please make me whole again.'"

Basanti trembled and her face went white.

"All right, now, all of you. Pinki has big ears," Inder cautioned.

Nevertheless, Ajit sent Baru Marasi to ride through the forty villages and meet with the numberdars. Each one was instructed to bring many men to Samrala for the dharna. The date was set for a Wednesday in the second week of July. Messages were sent to all of his relatives and friends, and to the men he did business with in Ludhiana, Machiwara, Doraha, Khanna, and Samrala. Ajit visited every house in Raikot to urge its head to show support, and the Mukhia assured him that all the men, including the elders of the Bajigar deras, planned to attend.

"Everyone is aghast at the government, Malik. We will stand with you."

By dawn on the day of the protest, crowds of men had gathered at the gates of the haveli. Mangal had sent buses from Frontier Transport, and before they boarded, the Giyani, who had been invited by Inder, gave them all his blessing. Two more trucks waited, with men packed into their trailers. There was a festive atmosphere about it all.

The Giyani said the Ardas, and with shouts of "Bole so nihal" and replies of "Sat Sri Akal" the vehicles started down the path towards the road, followed by dozens of people on bicycles. All the way to Samrala people stood on the sides of the road to wave at them. When they arrived, the men were driven to the far end of town and then assembled into long lines by volunteers who handed them banners and flags.

"Line up, line up."

Ajit estimated the protesters to be in the thousands, and still more and more buses and trucks arrived.

"You will walk in the first line, Zaildar-ji," Bikram said. He looked very excited.

"You will march with Bikram and the Akali MLAs from Phillour and Kapurthala," Rakesh told him.

"Akali MLAs?"

"Yes, there is province-wide support."

"My God."

"A lot of the press is here with cameras, too."

It overwhelmed Ajit, this expression of solidarity from far and wide. He couldn't help but feel that it all elevated even further the sacrifice of his son.

A tractor hauled in a trailer decorated with bunting in saffron and blue, with two loudspeakers tied atop bamboo posts. Five men appropriately dressed as the Panj Pyaras, the very first Sikh warriors, carried the flag of the Sikhs and held up unsheathed swords. A band struck up a martial tune. A man climbed onto the trailer, picked up a microphone, and began issuing instructions. Finally, when everyone was organized into lines for marching, he shouted, "Bole so nihal!"

"Sat Sri Akal!" The words rose from thousands of throats.

The procession was on.

"Captain Satwant Singh ki jai!" the man with the microphone cried. Victory to Captain Satwant Singh.

"Captain Satwant Singh ki jai!" The marchers pumped their fists in the air. Shouting these and more slogans, they stopped in front of the house of Aalok Nath.

"Aalok Nath, hai, hai." Woe to Aalok Nath.

"Aalok Nath murdabad."

Ajit was silent as they called for the death of the MLA. He couldn't bring himself to go that far.

"Congress Party murdabad."

"Akali Dal zindabad." Long live the Akali Dal.

"March."

As they proceeded through the bazaar, Ajit noticed the closed shutters—not one shop was open. Restaurants were dark, and the vendors' carts were nowhere to be seen. But policemen were very much in evidence, standing widely spaced on both sides of the road. He knew the local constabulary numbered perhaps two dozen men and officers, but it seemed there were more than that. Had they brought in reinforcements from other towns? Two were positioned on rooftops and carried rifles.

They crossed the Machiwara-Khanna Road and marched past the courts to the huge Civil Court grounds, where a stage with a raised dais was waiting. Bikram led him, Sher Singh, and the Akali Dal

MLAs up the five steps and offered them chairs. Ajit decided to stand for the time being so he could watch the marchers arrive, their colourfully turbaned heads bobbing.

The man who had spoken from the trailer climbed up onto the dais and began now to adjust and test the microphone. Ajit watched the police inspector push through the crowd up to the stage.

"Bikram Singh, keep it peaceful, please," the inspector shouted.

Bikram nodded and walked up to the microphone.

"Thank you, thank you, thank you all. Thank you for taking the time to join us today to protest the indifference of the ruling Congress Party to the sacrifice of our beloved Captain Satwant Singh, a son of Raikot and Punjab, a lion of India."

The crowd slowly fell silent.

"On behalf of us all, I bow to and salute Zaildar Ajit Singh, father of the Captain."

Bikram folded his hands and bowed.

"I now salute Jagirdar Sher Singh, father-in-law of the Captain. And I thank all the elected and common members of my Akali Dal, who have travelled long distances to stand with us."

Each time he spoke, the crowd roared.

"Captain Satwant Singh ki jai." Bikram raised a fist in the air.

The grounds reverberated with his son's name. Helpless in his grief and pride, Ajit wiped tears from his eyes.

"This is how we must celebrate his sacrifice, by standing together as one with these two fathers."

Just then a scuffle broke out. From the stage, Ajit thought it looked like a puff of dust erupting amidst the crowd.

"We seem to have Congress Party goons among us trying to sully our protest," Bikram shouted from the podium. He pointed to some brawny men without turbans who were raining blows on a few fallen turbaned men. They were soon grabbed by the police.

"Congress Party murdabad!"

The slogan was carried through the huge, tightly packed crowd and began to grow. The fighting was spreading too, erupting now at the fringes, now breaking out in unexpected eddies. Constables rushed to stem the violence, and Ajit saw the crowds pushing away from the combatants.

"Teach the traitors a lesson!" someone shouted, and the crowd surged angrily towards the policemen, who were hurrying away with their prisoners. Stones were flying—Ajit couldn't tell where they were coming from. One landed on the stage not far from his feet. Ajit cringed, and his hands went up reflexively to protect his head.

Another stone—this one hit Bikram on the forehead. Bikram stumbled backwards and his hands flew up to his face as blood spurted from a cut. Ajit rushed to him with a clean handkerchief to stop the bleeding, and just then Mangal appeared from out of nowhere and jumped onto the stage. He grabbed the microphone and growled, "Stop the stupidity. No more violence!"

The stones stopped flying, but the hotheads continued to manhandle the policemen.

The police inspector fired his gun into the air.

"Stop it!" Mangal screamed again. "Everybody stay calm!"

And then the trouble stopped, as abruptly as it had started.

The inspector approached the stage with two armed constables.

"Bikram Singh, I am placing you under arrest for leading a violent protest."

Bikram meekly offered his wrists as blood trickled down his face and dripped onto his collar.

Cameras flashed.

Basanti

Just as dusk was falling, Basanti heard buses pull up outside the haveli. Bapuji came through the gates, and she nearly gasped when she noticed blood on his white kurta. Maaji saw it too, and ran to meet him.

"It's nothing. I was not hurt. But Bikram Singh was injured in the melee."

"What? Is he all right?" Maaji asked.

"He was arrested. I posted bail so he could go home to his wife and son."

"Waheguru, Waheguru," Siamo wailed.

The men from the village and the dera had been invited to a langar on their return from the protest, and now two hundred or more were spilling into the courtyard. Maaji had been working over the stoves all day preparing food, with help from many of the local women and girls. Servants were pulling down cots, inviting the men to sit.

The Mukhia arrived and he greeted Maaji and Basanti with a big grin. "It was something else. I have never experienced such a crowd, such excitement. My heart hasn't slowed down yet."

Basanti, her face veiled in deference to the elders from the village and the dera, began to distribute thalis to the seated men. Maaji shouted instructions. A few neighbourhood boys were ladling dal and curried vegetables. A few carried baskets of rotis, while others poured water from jugs into steel tumblers. She saw her brother Gulab carrying a case. Bapuji opened it and began handing out bottles to smiling men. Gulab ran up the stairs and brought another one down.

Maaji frowned. "It's langar and your Bapuji is serving liquor. I don't like it."

Bapuji seemed excited and happy.

Basanti found her father and brother enjoying a shot of top-notch liquor.

"I was worried about you," she said. "I hear there was violence at the dharna."

Gulab puffed himself up a bit. "Nothing we weren't prepared for. It's a proud thing to put yourself at risk for a good cause."

"As Bajigars, with no place of our own, we must honour our alliances," said her father. "And the alliance of our clan to the family of this haveli is our most important bond. The Malik has shown great honour and generosity to us. Standing up for the memory of his son, and against the neglect of the Congress Party, is the least we can do to show our respect. A little danger is nothing to our people."

The next day, a man dropped off a stack of newspapers at the haveli. Bapuji ran down the staircase and laid them on the table, and Maaji picked one up to read.

"'Major protest in Samrala.' Another one here, 'Men arrested at protest accused of disturbing the peace.'"

"Congress Party goons," Bapuji said.

Basanti walked over to look at the photos. All of them featured Bapuji standing beside a bloodied Bikram Singh. She listened with Siamo and the women as Maaji read aloud. Over eight thousand men had gathered for the protest led by Akali Dal leaders. There had been some violence but only light injuries. All arrested had met the conditions for bail and been released.

Bapuji's friend the Comrade came by for a visit, and Bapuji was proud to show him the articles.

"Every paper in Punjab. English, Hindi, Punjabi, and Urdu dailies all reported the protest." Bapuji had a satisfied look on his face.

"I see Bikram sustained a terrible scratch in the scuffle," the Comrade said with a smirk.

"He is a hero!" Maaji insisted.

"It certainly makes him look like one, but I wouldn't be surprised if he contrived it just for that reason."

"Do you think so? What foolishness. A man would arrange for himself to be injured?"

"He might if there was enough to gain by doing so," the Comrade said.

"Well, all I know is that Aalok Nath had better wake up if he doesn't want to lose to Bikram Singh," Siamo said.

Basanti, too, hoped for a win for the man who had bled for the Captain, and she said a silent prayer to the deities. *Bless him, Naag Baba. Bless him, Pir Shah. Bless him, Laxmi Maa.*

Every report of the protest mentioned the Captain's sacrifice. Maaji's eyes welled up, and she even smudged a couple of pages with her tears.

"Pinki, come see your Daddyji's picture," Bapuji said. A portrait of the Captain was printed on the front page.

Pinki came over and stood looking at it.

"Isn't your father a very handsome man?" Siamo asked.

"I don't know." Pinki gazed at the photo.

"You remember your Daddyji."

"A little."

Basanti felt her heart break. And even sadder, Nikki would have no memories at all of her mother and father. An image of Laxman Das flashed through her mind, but for once the memory of her child was not as painful or troubling. She felt a jolt of guilt.

All my thoughts and all my love belong to these two now, Pinki and Nikki.

Bikram

The date for the elections was announced, and Bikram went immediately to the Elections Office to file his papers as a candidate for his Akali Dal. He was given a booklet outlining the rules and regulations of the Elections Act, but he put it aside after reading a few of the you-must and you-must-not instructions. Jagtar made prasad and called on neighbours up and down the street, telling them, "Vote for Ji." The fight was on.

Mangal set up camp in one of the second-floor bedrooms, telling Bikram, "I am not leaving your side until after election day." They gathered around the dining room table that night to strategize, and Bikram was gratified to see the astrologer, Pundit Gopal Sharma, arriving to offer his help.

"But you are Aalok Nath's kin," Chand said.

"Didn't stop his greedy son from taking a bribe from me, did it?" Gopal sneered. "And anyway, I have big news. Aalok Nath has taken ill and been admitted to the Brown Hospital in Ludhiana."

"So, he might not be able to campaign?" Bikram asked.

"He might not even live until election day."

Bikram was exhilarated. That would help him tremendously. In spite of the recent protest, Aalok Nath was well known and liked.

"But then . . . his son will step in as candidate for the Congress Party in Samrala?" Chand asked.

"That idiot can never hope to fill his father's shoes."

Bikram's campaigners set out to canvass for him in tongas decorated with posters bearing his picture and equipped with loudspeakers blaring out holy hymns and appeals for votes. They were followed by trucks distributing free flour and lentils in the deras and bastees and, as Mangal had predicted, the poor climbed over each other to grab it.

Each man handing out the gifts from the back of the truck spoke the same words: "Promise you will vote for Bikram Singh." He would not release his grip on the bag until the recipient made the pledge.

Rakesh was in charge of writing Bikram's speeches, which were crafted to appeal to the largely unlettered villagers. Everyone eighteen and older was registered to vote—men and women, rich and poor, high caste and untouchable. In the town, bands playing popular tunes meandered through the narrow streets followed by teenagers hired to shout slogans.

"Bikram Singh zindabad."

"Akali Dal ki jai."

"Congress Party ko harao." Defeat the Congress Party.

Wisely, no specific mention was made of the ailing Aalok Nath.

A month before election day, word came to Bikram that Aalok Nath had passed away. The Congress Party campaign in Samrala simply stopped. Bikram went to the cremation ceremony and offered his condolences to the bereaved family. The Chief Minister attended, along with members of his cabinet, high court judges, other well-known dignitaries, writers, and poets. Aalok Nath's son Prushotam was nominated as the new Congress Party candidate for the Samrala Constituency. His campaigning was of course constrained by the protocol of formal mourning.

"Prushotam has to count on the sympathy vote," Gopal said.

"Because he's got nothing else going for him," Mangal added.

Men stopped by Bikram's shop to submit daily reports and collect their pay from his munshi. Bikram rode around with his entourage and visited every village, dera, and bastee to shake hands with clan leaders, sarpanches, caste elders, and prominent citizens. Bottles of booze were discreetly passed around, rupee notes handed out, demands listed, and grievances heard. Promises were made for government jobs, development projects, bridges and culverts, schools and clinics.

It was no surprise that Bikram won the election by a wide margin. He was over the moon! And Jagtar could not stop singing his praises.

"No one can beat Ji! Didn't I tell you? He is simply the best!"

Mangal opened a bottle of Bikram's whiskey and people arrived to congratulate him. The local magistrate, police inspector, sub-divisional officer, and block officer all came by, followed by the town mayor and ward councillors. By midday, several sarpanches and mukhias had shown up to shake his hand. He thanked them profusely.

Zaildar Ajit Singh came.

"Well done, Bikram. Well done."

Bikram bent to touch the older man's feet, and Jagtar followed suit. The Zaildar smiled. "My blessings on this home."

There was only one cloud in the clear blue sky of Bikram's success. The Congress Party, by a slim majority, would form the new provincial government. Bikram would sit on the Opposition benches, receive a stipend and a living allowance, but he would have no real power. He had blithely made hundreds of promises he could not now keep.

One day, however, not long after the election, a visitor came—a man wearing a handspun cotton suit and a Nehru jacket, the uniform of the Congress Party.

Bikram turned to Mangal. "Now what?"

The man approached and offered his hand. "I am Sat Prakash Verma, President of the PEPSU Congress Party. I have come to discuss an offer from the Chief Minister." The man looked pointedly at Mangal and added, "In private."

"Please come this way," Bikram said.

In the gathering room, Bikram pulled the doors closed, Verma sat down on a sofa and smiled.

"A fine home, indeed."

"Drinks?" Bikram opened a cabinet to display his large collection of liquor.

"No, Bikram Singh. I am a teetotaller."

Bikram sat down beside Verma and waited.

"The Chief Minister is very impressed by what you have accomplished here as a novice politician and worries about the trouble you will cause seated in the Opposition ranks."

"I plan to serve in a most respectful manner."

"I'm sure. However, the CM would like you to know that, should you consider crossing the floor and joining the Congress Party, a ministerial post would be offered to you. Is that an idea you might be open to?"

This came as a thunderbolt. Bikram's mind raced and he decided to stall for time. He walked over to the door and called for tea to be served. He turned to Verma. "Do you need an answer right now?"

"Preferably. The CM is waiting to finalize his cabinet."

Bikram sat down again and gathered his wits. He was desperately wishing that there was someone else in the room he could turn to for advice.

"Can I hear the offer again, please?"

The Congress Party emissary leaned forward. "Look, Bikram Singh. This is a once-in-a-lifetime chance for you to attain a position of power. The CM offers you the post held by our revered, deceased Shri Aalok Nath, Minister for Rural Development. Imagine the good you could do for your people, the Jat Sikhs. You would bring progress to rural Punjab, and better the lives of countless villagers."

In spite of what he might have said during the campaign, Bikram had never envisioned himself as a champion of the Jat Sikhs. He had become a Jathedar purely out of boredom, and that had ended horribly in blood and nightmares. All his ambitions were spurred by the people closest to him, particularly his rapacious wife. Now that he had won, he was being offered an opportunity beyond his wildest dreams. His portfolio would oversee the rural development of the whole of East Punjab, from Delhi to Kashmir, from the border of Pakistan to that of Tibet. It was an area that included vast plains and the highest mountains, rich farmland that made it India's bread basket. How could he possibly refuse?

Jagtar brought in the tea and greeted the visitor.

"Verma-ji," Bikram said, giving his answer, "would you introduce me to my wife with my new title, please?"

Verma smiled. "Of course. Madamji, please meet Bikram Singh, a member of the Congress Party, the MLA for Samrala and the new Minister for Rural Development."

Her delighted shrieks nearly punctured his eardrums.

Basanti

"I just can't believe it," Inder said.

"It's right here on the front page," Ajit replied.

"Still. Bikram Singh has turned his back on the Sikhs, on his own party."

"Yes, yes. He crossed the floor to join the Congress Party."

Inder sighed.

"Listen," Ajit said, "think of it this way. This is a great honour for us. Now we know a minister of the government, and I can perhaps get him to fast-track some much-needed projects in my zaildari."

"And maybe now he can build the clinics in Satwant's memory," Siamo said.

"Bapuji, I prayed every day for him to win," Basanti said. "I so want the Captain to be honoured."

He smiled at her. "See? Your prayers were answered."

One day, Basanti noticed that Bapuji and Maaji had been huddled for a long time, speaking in whispers. Siamo joined them, and Basanti saw the Bhua look towards her and nod.

What are they talking about? Does it have something to do with me?

The answer came that evening when the Mukhia and Sehba arrived.

"O Malik, may you be blessed a thousand ways." Sehba fell at Bapuji's feet and he struggled to raise her. Then she fell at Maaji's feet and wept loudly.

Basanti helped Sehba up.

Maaji explained that Bapuji had taken the Mukhia to Ludhiana, and there they had hired a lawyer, Mehar Singh Mangat, to act in Rana's defence at his upcoming murder trial. The lawyer was not very optimistic—because there were so many witnesses, he expected a severe sentence. However, he promised to do his best to save Rana from hanging. Bapuji had given the lawyer a five-hundred-rupee advance. It was an unimaginable amount of money for the Mukhia. He was a proud man. How would he ever be able to pay it back?

Now Maaji urged them to come and sit at the table.

"Inder and I have talked," Bapuji said. "I have a proposal that will, I believe, serve both our families well."

The Mukhia folded his hands and muttered a prayer.

"Basanti has become like a member of this family." Maaji turned to smile at her. "She already eats with us at the table just like our own daughter. And I would like to keep her here to help us raise the girls."

Basanti was both stunned and elated. She had started to worry that her time at the haveli would soon end, when her services were no longer needed. The little girls called her Maa. How would she ever tear herself away from them?

"Let's say we pay four hundred rupees a year for Basanti to work at the haveli. In that way, the lawyer's fee would be paid in five years," Bapuji said.

Five years! Basanti was overjoyed! She couldn't believe her good fortune!

"With interest, let's say eight years," Maaji added.

"If Rana gets a reduced sentence, then, with good behaviour, he could be released around the same time that Basanti's indenture is complete," Bapuji said.

Sehba and the Mukhia folded their hands and bowed their heads.

"Whatever you think is fair, Malik," Sehba said. "This is more of a blessing than our son deserves, and more than he will ever be able to thank you for. And it is certainly best that Basanti live under your gracious protection while her husband serves his sentence."

Bapuji patted the Mukhia's hands. "I am just trying to make the best of a difficult situation."

"Chinti, bring tea and biscuits, please," Maaji said.

Bapuji was invited to Bikram Singh's swearing-in ceremony, in the city of Simla. Simla was the capital, while the new city of Chandigarh was being built. And instead of bringing Maaji—who would not have enjoyed the cold, or the dizzying ride on the narrow mountain roads—Bapuji decided to take the Mukhia with him for company.

It was funny what a difference it made, Basanti thought, to have the rooster out of the henhouse. But a little peace and quiet certainly felt welcome. So she was somewhat disappointed when she noticed a visitor, a tall man, arriving at the gates. She looked up from her work at the kitchen to see who it was. She could tell from his clothes that he was not a Bajigar, and she didn't recognize him from the village. But Siamo must have known him, because she rushed to meet him and immediately wrapped the young man in a hug.

"Nasib!"

Maaji came and joined Basanti. "That must be Bhua's nephew," she said, smiling. "I think he has been away for a long time in Bengal, working on trucks."

Siamo caressed the young man's cheek. "Let me look at you." The smile on her face threatened to split it.

"Welcome," Maaji called out to him, and the man, who wore the zebra-patterned turban favoured by truck drivers, slowly walked over to greet her. It was then that Basanti noticed that he walked with a slight limp.

Chinti, who was seated beside Basanti at the hearth, nudged her with an elbow. "He's handsome, no?"

Basanti had to admit that it was true. His colour was fair, and he had fine features.

He bent to touch Maaji's feet, and she offered him her blessing.

"Look at him, look at him," Siamo said, obviously delighted.

"Would you like tea?" Maaji asked.

Basanti brought the tea, and when she handed him his mug she looked into his eyes, and her heart skipped a beat. He had the most captivating eyes—soft and kind and bright—and a small smile played on his lips. She quickly lowered her gaze and withdrew.

"That's Basanti, Nasib," she heard Siamo say.

She saw him give her a quizzical look.

Maaji said, "You have never visited us here before, Nasib, have you? What a shame you've never come to see your Bhua Siamo! You are family, and you've stayed away so long."

"I remember the gifts you sent when I was young," he said. "You have always been so kind and generous, Ji."

Perhaps she was imagining things, Basanti thought, but this seemed to make Siamo uncomfortable. Perhaps there was a reason he was so rarely spoken of at the haveli. Had he done something the family was ashamed of? Was he a bad man . . . even a criminal? She found it hard to believe that such a gentle-looking young man could be any kind of ruffian. But you could never tell.

"I heard of Satwant's martyrdom." Nasib spoke softly. "I came to offer my condolences. I wish I could have come before now."

"You got our messages?" Siamo asked.

"That is one reason I came back from Bengal. And also, my grand-parents in Naugarh are in fragile health."

"I haven't been able to visit them for some time, Nasib," Siamo said. "After Satwant, his wife Amrita too passed away in childbirth. Left a baby girl behind. Basanti is Nikki's wet nurse."

Basanti was standing under the verandah, and he glanced up at her. She couldn't pull her eyes away from him. He looked familiar some-how, but she could not imagine why.

Just then, Pinki arrived with her rag doll. He turned to smile at her.

"Say Sat Sri Akal to your Uncle Nasib, Pinki." Siamo pulled the child towards her. "He is your chacha."

"Chacha?" Pinki asked. "I have a chacha?"

Nasib gave her a nervous smile and nodded. Pinki surprised him by hopping onto his lap, and he hugged her to him.

When the young man and Pinki both looked up at her, the penny dropped for Basanti. Their eyes! They had the same eyes. And she could see that he looked a lot like Bapuji—if Bapuji had kept a styl-ishly trimmed black beard, a pencil-thin moustache, and was younger. She could feel her heart drumming in her chest. Only the Captain had ever had that effect on her.

"You will stay for a few days?" Maaji asked. "Siamo has told us so much about you. And of course the Zaildar is away today, and I'm sure you want to pay your respects to him as well."

"Of course he will stay for a while and visit his one and only aunt," Siamo hurriedly declared.

Nasib looked at her. "I borrowed a bicycle from a kinsman in Naugarh to come here, and I must return it today."

"You are back from Bengal for a while, though, aren't you?" Maaji asked. "You will visit again."

"If I can. My employer gave me only a month, and it takes a week just to travel between here and Bengal."

"That's too bad. But you will stay for lunch. I really do insist!"

He nodded.

Pinki jumped off his lap and grabbed his hand. "Chacha, come with me. I want to show you my books."

He stood up to follow the little girl and Basanti studied him from the back. The shape of his neck and shoulders, his slender waist and long legs—he looked so like the Captain.

Siamo caught her eye and told her to get busy right away cooking something delicious for her nephew.

"Cook the cauliflower I bought yesterday," Maaji suggested.

Siamo decided to go with Nasib to Naugarh. She packed a couple of bags with clothes and gifts and a tin of ghee.

"Look how thin he is. Probably from the awful food he has to eat on the roads."

"You fatten him up." Maaji smiled, adding another tin of ghee.

Basanti was holding Nikki, and as they were leaving, Nasib came over to place a rupee in the child's hand. When his fingers touched Basanti's, their eyes met and momentarily held. She could scarcely breathe. He turned around and gave Pinki a rupee too, and then bent to touch Maaji's feet.

"Live long, Nasib. It was nice to meet you at last. We will look forward to seeing you here again soon. How disappointed my husband will be that he was not here."

They followed Nasib and Siamo to the gates, where he swung onto the bicycle seat and waited for Siamo to climb onto the seat behind. Her bags hung from the handles.

"Be careful now, Siamo. Don't get your chador caught in the spokes," Maaji said as he pushed off.

Basanti stood watching until they turned at the Adda.

In the morning, Bapuji came down the stairs. She had not heard him arrive home from Simla the night before. It must have been very late, she thought. He looked tired.

Maaji asked him about the swearing-in ceremony.

"It was so regal, Inder. It took place in this old, elegant building with a lot of pomp and ceremony. Even the governor was there. I was introduced to every important man in Punjab. And Bikram Singh was very gracious."

Chinti served them parathas. Maaji ladled yogurt into their bowls and then placed a bit of pickle onto the plates. She added more for Bapuji, who was very fond of them.

He looked around. "Where is Siamo?" he asked.

"Oh, I forgot to tell you. She went to Naugarh."

"To Naugarh? Why?"

"Her nephew came to visit yesterday and took her with him."

Bapuji sat straight up and stared. "Nasib?"

"Yes. Very nice young man, too. I'm so happy I finally got to meet him. Tall and very handsome. Ask Basanti, she couldn't keep her eyes off him." Maaji laughed, making Basanti blush.

She noticed a tremor in Bapuji's usually steady hands. He looked pale and anxious for some reason, and he could barely finish his meal.

"Something wrong?" Maaji asked as he pushed his chair back and stood up.

He shook his head and just walked to the cattle yard.

"Saddle the mare," she heard him say to Gulab.

The next moment he was running up the stairs.

"What's the matter with him?" Maaji sounded worried.

They waited and watched as he flew back down the staircase and turned to wave.

"I will be gone all day," he shouted, before disappearing through the gates.

Bikram

The first meeting of the cabinet took place the day after the swearing-in ceremony. The Chief Minister began by reading out a long statement on the current status of the government, and followed up by listing the projects he wanted to accomplish during his five-year term.

"The one thing that matters to me," he said, "is that there be no corruption, no bribe-taking, and no lobbying."

Jagtar would be apoplectic, Bikram thought. That was all she and her family had talked about since he'd accepted the offer to join the cabinet as a member of the Congress Party—the lucrative opportunities.

Bikram was very conscious of being the new boy in the cabinet, so he listened and didn't utter a single word. He saw how the more experienced ministers jockeyed for position, and he understood that in the cabinet hierarchy his portfolio ranked in the bottom third. Bikram had discovered, too, that his disloyalty to his old party would not go unpunished. The eight Akali Dal MLAs shot him poisonous looks across the legislature. One even whispered to him, "Bloody traitor. We will settle with you soon."

This legislative session would last three weeks. Bikram's principal secretary, a middle-aged bureaucrat, would be the chief administrator and run the ministry on a day-to-day basis, leaving Bikram lots of time for legislative duties and field visits. He would also have a personal assistant, a clerk and stenographer, a peon to deliver messages, and a driver for his government-issue car. He would be eligible for a government bungalow in Simla with a staff to cook and clean for him. For the time being, he was hosted in a guesthouse with other Congress MLAs, and when the cabinet meeting adjourned, he made his way there to settle in and meet his colleagues.

"The CM does not want any corruption in his ministries." Ranjit, a Hindu Jat from Hissar district, grinned, showing snow-white teeth under his dark moustache. "But I bet, by the next elections, he'll be ten times richer than he is today."

"Oh, obviously," said another. "He'll make a fortune from the construction of Chandigarh alone." This man was, like Bikram, a junior minister.

"Chandigarh? How?" Bikram asked.

"You'd better get in on the ground floor of that project. It's going to make a lot of money for a lot of us," Ranjit said.

Bikram learned that Ranjit was a school dropout from a powerful Jat clan who faced criminal charges for several physical assaults committed during the elections. But by that time, Ranjit had become his drinking buddy and his mentor on the subject of political graft.

"Ten percent," Ranjit repeated. "You take back ten percent from anything you personally do to help someone, be it a government contract, a licence, a bus route, or a job or promotion. The system is already set up so that bribes are collected at the grassroots and come to you via officials. Your birthday, the New Year, special occasions— these are all pretexts for giving you your cut. That is when you get the thick, brown envelopes stuffed with cash."

"But the CM said—"

"You're an idiot if you pay any attention. That's for show only. Just be discreet. Maintain decorum. Let others handle the dirty work. My father collects on my behalf sitting at our verandah smoking his hookah. He even lets the carriers take puffs from it. Says it bonds them to him."

This, it occurred to Bikram, was just the job for Chand.

After three weeks, when the session was over, Bikram was happy to return to Samrala and sleep in his own bed. But on his first morning home, he was awoken by Ramu, calling from the doorway.

"Sahib, wake up, please. People are waiting for you!"

Light filtered through the drawn drapes. Bikram opened his eyes slowly. His head was pounding from the whiskey he'd drunk the night before and he could still smell it on his breath. He raised himself to check the time. It was just eight o'clock, and it was a Sunday.

"Tell them I will start meeting at one o'clock. I am tired."

By the time he had finished bathing, the courtyard was full of men standing around wrapped in woollen blankets. The sun was high and the brilliance of the day hurt his eyes. He stepped back in quickly as the realization hit him. He was in demand.

His father-in-law Chand was there, and was apparently already comfortable in the role of go-between. Darshan was with him, and they ushered in the first supplicant.

"Bikram Singh, you must get my son a job. He has been out of school for two years and he is still idle." This was a fellow he recognized—they had met a few times—and now he was pleading and pointing to a sturdy young man who'd come with him.

"I think he would make a good constable," Chand suggested. "Six feet tall, good kabbadi player, and a matriculate."

When did you become an employment expert? Bikram wanted to ask. But the young man did look right for a policeman.

"Note it down," he told Darshan, who held an open notebook.

"It will be six months' pay up front," Chand told the father.

"What?" Bikram glared at Chand.

"We will pay more if that is not enough, Bikram Singh," the father assured him. "My son will make it back in bribes, I have no doubt."

"That was not my point." He recalled when he had gone for his job interview so many years ago. It was almost as though he were once again sitting on the dusty bench of the bus station, waiting for the manager. *How can I ask him for money when I wept at the demand for sixty rupees up front?*

"Done. Go now, please."

Darshan ushered the father and son out.

"Don't bring anyone else in yet. We need to talk," he told Darshan.

He turned to Chand. "Who told you that you could negotiate bribes on my behalf?" he snarled.

"I . . . I am being besieged in your absence, Bikram. I am just trying to do the best," Chand said.

Darshan stepped in. "Look, we are not doing anything that was not happening already. We went and talked to another minister's people and they gave us the rates they are charging."

"How many men have you demanded bribes from?"

"Hundreds have knocked on the gates."

"Do you know what kind of reputation you are earning for me? I look like a five-rupee whore. Stop. Send everyone away until I have a chance to think this through."

When Jagtar heard later what had happened, she was livid. She waited until the family sat down to dinner, then gave him a piece of her mind.

"What is this, Ji? You become an MLA and then a minister and you are rude to my father, Ji? He devoted a decade of his life to you. Apologize, Ji. Don't set a bad example for your son."

He pushed his plate away and turned to her. "Talk like that to me again and I will make you eat your meals in the kitchen."

Darshan rose to pat her shoulders as she burst into tears. Everyone sat staring into the air. But a grin played on his mother's lips, and Papaji coughed into a napkin.

Sewa crushed a roti in his hands like putty and tried to shape it into a boat.

"Ji doesn't realize all the money is gone." Jagtar wept. "I have had to borrow from Mangal to keep us from starving."

The drama amused him. He waited for more.

Mangal cleared his throat and said, "Just give Bikram some time to sort things out in his mind. Don't rush him."

"What do I do with all the promises I have made?" Chand pleaded, as Beeji stared with pinched lips.

"Hush," Mangal said. "Eat your food and we will meet at the truck stop tomorrow."

"At least someone has sense," Jagtar said, as Sewa looked at his big uncle with adoring eyes.

When they gathered the next day at Mangal's office, Chand had a forlorn look. Papaji had conveniently excused himself as he was volunteering at a bhog. Rakesh, the publicist, freshly shaved and groomed, reeked of strong cologne that made Bikram sneeze.

Darshan opened a ledger.

"Father and I were approached by a total of four hundred and thirty-four men looking for government jobs for their children. The average monthly salary of these jobs is from fifty to a few hundred rupees."

"What kind of jobs?" he asked.

"Anything from peons and clerks to teachers and junior engineers, policemen to inspectors."

"Go on."

"If we receive six months' of wages in advance—"

"In advance?" The words brought a bitter taste to Bikram's mouth.

"Let's say as a fee, then." Darshan cleared his throat. "The total sum comes close to two lakh rupees."

"That much money, you see, Bikram?" Chand said, emboldened by the figure.

"What about the businessmen and merchants?"

"Add another four to five lakh rupees."

Bikram did a quick calculation. In the five years before the next election he could amass millions of rupees, not counting the various opportunities that Ranjit the Jat had shown him.

"I need to think about this," he said.

"But why?" Chand asked.

"Because first I have promises to keep."

"Like?"

"Like laying the foundation stones for the clinics in the Captain's memory in Raikot. I've already got the Chief Minister's approval."

Rakesh straightened up. "Do you mind if I arrange the event?"

"Please do. Make sure it gets me front page photos."

Ajit

As Ajit rode the mare along the road to Naugarh, he felt the oddest sense of déjà vu. So many times before he had started out, rushed off to see his younger son, only to stop himself. This time he was really on his way.

It was Siamo who met him at the gate. She must have guessed he would come as soon as he heard. She was veiled, which added to the strangeness of the scene. She never veiled her face at home in Raikot, but here she would be observing the custom in deference to her elderly father-in-law.

"I've told him," she said simply.

Ajit swallowed a lump in his throat and followed her through to the mud-walled courtyard. He saw his son sitting on a cot with his grandparents. Ajit walked over and placed a hand on Nasib's head and gazed at his handsome face. So like Satwant's, and at the same time the face of a stranger. Nasib stood up, and Ajit was startled to see that they were the same height. He had always pictured Nasib as a boy.

Siamo watched, blinking back tears.

"Live long, my son. Live long," he said.

Nasib's face was impassive. What was he thinking? Surely the news had come as a shock.

"Sit, Bir." Siamo pointed to a loosely strung cot.

Nasib sat down again next to his grandfather.

"I was very sad when I heard about the death of your son, Zaildar," the grandfather said. "My deepest condolences." His face was creased, and his eyes were cloudy now, but Ajit recognized the same hard man who, many years ago, had shown up at his haveli saying, "Palo is pregnant with your child."

Ajit sighed, joined his hands, and looked skywards. "It was His will and I accept it."

"It was also His will to give you Nasib," Siamo said.

Nasib said nothing. The old couple bowed their heads.

Siamo stood abruptly. "I will make tea."

They sat in uncomfortable silence for a while before Ajit turned to Nasib. He had been preparing this speech in his mind for a long time. "Son."

The youth squirmed.

"I want you to understand that my decision to stay away while you were a child was not an easy one. I was respecting the needs and feelings of many people. I wanted to see you desperately, and almost came so many times. And when I heard about your suffering with polio . . ."

Now tears flowed down Nasib's cheeks, and he allowed Ajit to embrace him. They wept in each other's arms.

"You were present in other ways," the grandfather said. "It was a big help."

"We could not have survived without your generosity, Zaildar," the grandmother added.

Yes, there was money. But I should have done so much more.

Ajit reluctantly let go of Nasib when Siamo brought the tea.

"Here, take the glass, Bir," she said.

"You take it first, Nasib. I want to watch you. My eyes have ached for a glimpse of you all these years."

"Bir talked about you every day, Nasib. I know just how much he struggled and suffered. How much he wanted to take you home to Raikot."

"*This* is home." It was the first thing Nasib had managed to say.

"Now you have two." Siamo smiled.

"But I'm not going to live with you. And I'm not going back to Bengal, either. Look at them." Nasib gestured towards the elderly couple. "*They* are my parents, first and foremost."

"And they should be, Nasib, they should be." Ajit nodded. "They stood in for me."

"And my mother."

"Yes, your mother, too."

"I was told my mother died in childbirth. Was that a lie as well? Is my mother still alive?"

Their silence only convinced him.

"What a life I have lived." Nasib said. "Believing I was an orphan when my parents are both alive. I want to go and see her."

"Now, we don't want to open old wounds," the grandfather said. "Your mother has her own life. Let her be."

"My father showed up only after he lost his firstborn son. I wonder if he would have come to me otherwise."

"He had been told not to. We believed it was for the best. You can blame me for that, Nasib," his grandfather said.

This old man, once a strong man, was standing up bravely for Ajit, and he was grateful. But Nasib's accusation stung and spread its poison inside him, nevertheless.

On the long ride home Ajit struggled with a problem. How would he explain to Inder, after all these years of keeping this secret? Telling her about Nasib meant confessing to his affair with Palo, Nasib's mother. It was so long ago—would she still care? How would she weigh that one infidelity against all their years of marriage? Would she still trust him? Or would the admission of one betrayal open her imagination to the possibility of others?

He had so many excuses and rationalizations for what he'd done, and they all raced around his mind. But finally he determined just to be frank with his wife. She could accept the truth or not. He had his son, and it was time to declare it to the world.

Basanti was the first to come running over as he rode through the haveli gates at dusk and dismounted.

"You are limping, Bapuji. What happened?"

"I am saddle-sore is all."

"I will prepare warm compresses."

"No. I just need a good night's rest. I will be fine tomorrow."

In the courtyard, she pulled out a chair for him, but the cot was more inviting. He lay on it and sighed. Pinki ran over and climbed up on his chest. "I missed you, Babaji. Where did you go?"

"I missed you, too. I had to visit someone."

Pinki laughed. "Look at Nikki, Babaji!"

The baby had managed to pull herself up straight by holding onto the leg of the cot.

"You are starting to get around, aren't you, little one?"

"She certainly is." Inder joined them. She picked Pinki up and put Nikki on his chest instead. The imp quickly grabbed his beard and pulled. He grimaced, and Inder had to untangle them.

After dinner, Basanti cleared the table, then returned to get the children ready for bed.

Ajit turned to Inder. "There's something I need to tell you."

She sat down in a chair facing him. "Something troubles you."

He looked at her and sighed. "I have a confession to make."

A wary, pained look came into her eyes. "You want to marry again. For a son."

"No." He shook his head, and gathered all his courage. "Nasib is my son."

He watched her struggle between relief and shock. She started to cry, and wrapped her chador around her face.

"All these years, all these years you knew. Siamo knew too, didn't she?"

"Yes," he said.

"Why did you not tell me before?"

"I was sparing your feelings."

"Oh, God. Waheguru."

"Inder, it was fate. It was His will."

"No, it was your lust. For Palo—am I right? That stupid girl!" she spat. "Don't you dare bring Waheguru into it."

Ajit had nothing to say to that, and Inder began again.

"Tell me the truth, if you're capable of it. Would you have accepted him as your son if Satwant were still alive?"

"I had already accepted him here." He touched his heart. "Shame, and concern for you and Satwant, for the family, were all that ever held me back."

"And now you need a male heir, so you ride off to Naugarh to stake your claim on the poor boy?"

Her words wounded his soul.

"And how are you going to present him to the world, your bastard son? Are you bringing him here to live?"

"No, he has chosen to live with his grandparents. But I need your help, Inder. I am agonizing over it. I need you to stand beside me."

"I am your wife. Do I have a choice?"

"I need you to accept Nasib, take him into your heart, make him your son, too."

"My son is dead, and no one will ever take his place." She dropped her head into her hands and took a deep, shuddering breath. When she looked up again, she said, "But I will accept Nasib, because he's an innocent—he had nothing to do with your betrayals."

She began to cry again, and Ajit worried that she might never stop.

Basanti

An unmistakable change came over the household. At the dining table each night, Bapuji ate in silence while Maaji fussed with her food, barely looking at him, giving all her attention to feeding Nikki.

"Basanti, give your Bapuji another paratha."

"Basanti, tell your Maaji I will be away all day."

Why don't you tell her yourself? Basanti nearly asked out loud.

She could hear Maaji crying in her room at night. When she went to comfort her, and asked why she was so sad, Maaji just said, "I am missing Satwant and Amrita and weeping over my karma," in a broken voice. Basanti wondered if all this had something to do with the visit from the handsome man, and the way Bapuji had ridden away so suddenly and not come home till late.

Bapuji asked Basanti one day to pack two bags of Siamo's clothing. He was going to take them to Naugarh for her.

"Maaji, how long will Siamo be gone?"

"Hopefully forever." Maaji said. Then, seeing Basanti's expression, she added, "I am sorry, Basanti, but life is going to be very different from now on. There are things you don't know yet."

It took a letter in the mail to bring sunshine back into the home. It was from Bikram Singh.

"This is to inform you that I have selected the twentieth of February to lay the foundation stones for the health clinics in honour of Captain Satwant Singh. The Chief Minister has approved the budgets for their construction, furnishings, and annual operational costs. I will share the details with you on that day."

This brought shouts of joy from both Bapuji and Maaji. The air crackled with their excitement, and the icy mood at the haveli thawed just a little.

On that auspicious day, a canopy was strung in the courtyard at the haveli and rented tables and chairs were laid out for the cabinet minister and his entourage. "All very important men," Maaji told Basanti. A caterer from Samrala had been hired to serve the food.

"We are going to make it a grand occasion," Bapuji repeated excitedly to everyone he saw.

A man arrived to climb up a ladder and decorate the verandah, the gates, and the bamboo posts of the canopy with bunting. Maaji took out one of Amrita's finer suits and better sandals for Basanti to wear for the ceremony. The chador was of an exquisite material and dotted with sequins.

"You look so pretty, Maa," Pinki observed with wide eyes.

"So do you, Pinki."

Pinki preened in her store-bought, ready-made suit. With pink ribbons in her hair, she looked like a princess. And Nikki wore a frock, knee-high socks, and blue shoes. Like Pinki's, her hair was done up with ribbons, and she had a lovely sweater that she kept taking off.

"Keep it on, please, Nikki," Maaji said. "Oh, how I wish Siamo were here to help." Then Maaji blushed a bit.

"You miss her too, don't you?" Basanti asked.

Maaji nodded.

That made Basanti feel better. She had become very fond of the simple, outspoken woman. The haveli seemed empty without the doughty aunt grunting and complaining about her old bones and sore joints.

When everyone was ready, they made their way to the cleared plot of land where the path met the paved road, across from the dera. This was the land that Bapuji had donated for the clinics.

The women of the dera surrounded Basanti when they arrived, and Nikki was passed around to be hugged and kissed. Pinki was soon clutching her friend Paso's hand and holding court herself with the younger girls, all wearing the Punjabi suits that were their school uniforms and doubled as their visiting clothes, while their mothers wore kurtis and ghunias.

Basanti noted that Naura's clothes were noticeably newer than Sehba's. Sehba was trying to hide a small patch sewn on her ghunia, and she looked dowdy standing beside her sautaan. In spite of everything, just then she felt sorry for her mother-in-law.

The sound of cars honking startled her, and people rose and turned to look.

"The minister is here," someone said.

Basanti stood on tiptoe to see Bikram Singh stepping out of the car. As he straightened up, Bapuji placed a garland of marigold flowers around his neck before embracing him. Other men garlanded the guest of honour, and then he was led past the seated people to the spot where a great hole had been dug. A large rectangular stone lay beside it, and a man waited with a shiny new spade.

"Today, I am grateful to Waheguru-ji," the minister began. "Today, I am privileged to keep the promise made by my revered predecessor, Shri Aalok Nath. Today, I honour the sacrifice made by Captain Satwant Singh."

The Giyani stepped forward and said the Ardas.

Basanti watched through her fine veil as the formality of laying the foundation stone was completed.

Bikram Singh stood at the microphone and made a very good speech full of praise for her Captain. He spoke also of Bapuji and Maaji and their sacrifice, and mentioned the girls by name. He thanked everyone for attending and again for voting for him.

Afterwards, he came forward to bend and touch Maaji's feet. Then he stood before Basanti and put his hands out for Nikki. She could feel the intensity in his eyes as they fixed on hers, and he pursed his lips with the flick of the tongue. She watched as he rocked Nikki and made her laugh, kissed her on the cheek, and handed her back, his fingers lingering on Basanti's.

She remembered how men had stared when she and Devi were younger. She had felt then like a lamb being eyed by a wolf, and she was startled to get the same feeling now from Bikram Singh. She thought so highly of him, of his honour for the Captain and for Bapuji and Maaji. But his eyes . . . those dead, staring eyes showed life only when he spoke into a microphone. They reminded her of the eyes of the guard who had raped her. A shudder ran through her.

That night, after the crowds had been fed and the delegation had left and the men had arrived to take down the canopy, Bapuji gave a full report of what he had learned from Bikram Singh. Amrita's family sat with Bapuji and Maaji at the dining table, and since there was no room for her there, Basanti pulled a cot closer to sit and listen.

"The health clinic is going to be large and manned by a doctor, a pharmacist, and a nurse. It will be able to handle minor surgeries. The medicines will be given out free of cost. The veterinary clinic will be well equipped too."

"You gave almost two acres. Is that much land necessary?" Amrita's father asked.

"Yes. In addition to the clinics there will be quarters for the staff to live in with their families. Both the doctor and the veterinarian will have separate bungalows. It will be a first-class facility I was assured."

"Good, very good."

"It will take a while, maybe two or three years, to construct. The tenders have been issued."

"At last, at long last." Maaji folded her hands and raised her face to the sky. "My son's legacy is secured. I am so grateful. Thank you, Waheguru-ji. Thank you."

Watching Nikki and Pinki sitting on their uncles' laps, then moving onto their grandfathers', Basanti admired the protection they had from such regal men. How could any harm ever come to them? She felt safer herself as a pride of lions sat near her at the table.

"Stay for supper," Bapuji was pleading as the chairs scraped back and Amrita's family stood up.

"Thank you, Ajit." The father bowed. "You know our customs. But thank you for your kind hospitality. I am so happy that the clinics are going to be a reality. I know how much you agonized over the memorials to Satwant."

Basanti stood up. Jeet Kaur came up to her and handed her a bag, and her husband and sons all followed suit and gave her money. She accepted humbly with a bowed head.

"Live long, daughter. We pray your husband wins his case."

She looked at Amrita's brother, the judge, but he had turned and was walking towards the gates where their car stood. She wondered if she could run after him and ask his opinion, but she restrained herself. She was happy here at the haveli, her lap blessed with two girls who called her Maa and showered her with their love. What difference would his thoughts make? She was staying here for another eight years at least, whether Rana was acquitted or hanged.

The haveli was her home.

BOOK FOUR

1952–1963

Bikram

Bikram was having trouble sleeping.

His campaign strategy of buying votes with philanthropy had been effective, but it had also been extremely expensive. His wealth had been depleted. And Jagtar had begun to harangue him.

"Ji. Think of your son, Ji. Better start filling your safe, Ji. All you have is five measly years to do it, Ji. What if you are not re-elected then?"

As she never ceased to remind him, he had even borrowed money from Mangal. His friend was not pressing him for repayment, but Jagtar was right to be concerned. Mangal was the kind of man you wanted to have in your debt, not the other way around.

There was no comfort for Bikram in bed, either. His love-making with Jagtar the night before had to be interrupted because it was just too painful for her. She had been experiencing bad cramps and bleeding. And when he had suggested she consult a doctor, she had dismissed the idea, because she didn't want a strange man to "look at her down there." She blamed him for her troubles—"You almost ripped me apart, Ji. You are like a bull, Ji!" She waved the bloody sheet in his face and moved to another room, pleading illness and dread.

He drank another full bottle of whiskey hoping it would help him sleep. His mind was in turmoil, and the new powers he had as a minister of the government worked like an aphrodisiac, inflaming his passions. He wondered about the teacher with the hard nipples, then settled on his memory of the beautiful Bajigarni, Basanti, conjuring fantasies. His mind went blank as he finally passed out.

He experienced a vivid, frightening dream. He was walking in the woods in the greyish light of the full moon, pushing aside the black shades of twisted bare branches. A strange voice was calling him urgently, compellingly, and he ran towards it. Suddenly a pale figure loomed up before him. Now the voice was female, it was a scream, and the figure fell forward, headless, blood spurting out from its neck. He tasted salt.

He woke up, his lips glued tight, and rushed to the washroom. In the mirror he saw that he had cut his tongue, there was blood in his mouth and beard. He washed it away and dried his face. He gargled away the taste of blood. But his tongue was swollen, and when he tried to speak his words came out garbled.

"Bad dream," he explained to his wife later. "Bit my tongue."

"You drank too much, Ji," Jagtar said.

A doctor was called to examine him. "It's stress, a normal reaction," he explained.

Bikram was given tablets to help him sleep. He took double the dose. The dreamless, medicated sleep was like a cocoon he was afraid to leave.

"He did what?"

They were in the headmaster's office, and Sewa sat on the floor, his head lowered.

"Yes, Bikram. He told me that he would have me fired by you. Dismissed."

"You did that?" He turned to glare at the miscreant.

The boy kept his head down.

"He said that he will have you get rid of me, and get rid of Miss here for complaining to me about his disruptive behaviour."

The teacher, seated next to Bikram, stared straight ahead.

"What did he say to you?" Bikram asked her.

She turned to meet his gaze, and he realized just how pretty she was. Tears started to trickle down her cheeks.

He patted her shoulder. "I am sorry. I'm planning to move Sewa to a convent school in Chandigarh when the legislature moves next year. I hear they won't spare the rod on him there. For now, I'll have to handle him myself."

When the meeting was over, Sewa was sent to his next class, with warnings ringing in his ears. Bikram thanked the headmaster, and he and the young teacher stepped out into the hall, where she stood for a moment composing herself.

"Would you like a transfer to a school in Chandigarh?" he asked softly.

She looked up with wide eyes and smiled faintly. "But . . . isn't it expensive to live there?"

"No, no, you won't have to worry about rent or anything. Do you . . . understand?"

She nodded, gave him another quick smile, and walked away.

His loins felt like they were on fire, and he rushed back to the mansion to find Jagtar. She would no longer sleep with him, but she could be talked into satisfying him in other ways she knew.

"Oh, Ji. You get really aroused when you go to talk to that young teacher."

"Just do it, Jagtar. By the way, I only met with the old headmaster, and he does not arouse me."

"Okay, Ji. Just this once."

Ajit

Ajit had big plans for his son. He had been putting money aside for Nasib for years, which he now felt would be best spent building a brick house for the young man and his grandparents in Naugarh. He instructed Nasib about what a Jat Sikh should know about land management, and there were personal issues he wanted to address as well. Although Nasib did not smoke in his presence, he stank of tobacco.

"Look here, we are Sikhs. We don't smoke or chew tobacco. It's a dirty habit and I want you to stop it."

"I picked it up in Calcutta," Nasib said. "Helped me stay awake."

"You are no longer in Calcutta. You should stop it."

Siamo mentioned that Nasib also went out drinking with local louts. "He has money now, Bir."

Ajit confronted him, and Nasib said he would stop.

"My plan is to cede Nasib the zaildari when he is ready." Ajit made the announcement one night after dinner.

Inder looked up from her knitting. "Are you going to breed him too, like Bakki?"

Baru Marasi had recently suggested it was time to breed the beautiful mare, and he had a stallion in mind, a Marwari, like Bakki, in Sahnewal. The offspring would fetch a good price.

"Oh, for God's sake, Inder!" Ajit shouted. He stood up and turned to leave the room.

"I know you are looking for a bride for Nasib, Ji," Inder said stiffly. "I am sorry if I offended you."

"Comparing him to an animal. That is low."

He retreated to his rooms to read his mail, but he could not concentrate. Inder's words had cut him deep. She had never spoken to him that way before. Recently she had become remote, her expression bitter. Pushpa, the Brahmin elder, visited her more often now to comfort her. But wasn't he grieving too? Was his loneliness any less than hers? And all this snideness because he was trying to do the right thing for the one son he had left. Was that so wrong?

Ajit spent most of his time in Naugarh now. Inder said nothing.

The house in Naugarh went up quickly, and Nasib planted some acres of the land with saplings of fast-growing softwood lumber. When he earned his commercial driver's licence, Mangal hired him as a bus driver on local routes. Soon a numberdar arrived with a proposal of marriage. Ajit was delighted; his heart ached for grandsons, and he could not wait for a bride to arrive.

Siamo went to visit the girl and came back with a glowing report.

"Good family, big family, father has lots of land and cattle. Bholi has such nice features and a temperament to match. She is educated, too, a five-pass. You will be very happy with her, Nasib."

But it was not to be.

The engagement ceremony took place at Nasib's newly built house, and a month later the wedding party set off for the bride's village for the wedding—fifty men, plus one of Punjab's best singers to entertain the guests. But the bride, Bholi, refused to sit in front of the Holy Granth for the ceremony, despite desperate pleas from her father and brothers.

"I was not told he is a cripple," she said. "I won't wed a cripple."

They returned empty-handed, and Ajit could not bear to look at his son's humiliated face. Siamo wept for a week. Everything that had begun with such promise ended in grief and humiliation. Nasib's grandmother, heartbroken, breathed her last within the month, and his grandfather followed her a fortnight later.

"I can't live here any more," Nasib said after the funerary rites. "People pity me. They laugh behind my back."

Inder had declared that Nasib would never live under her roof, but now Ajit swallowed his pride and begged her to reconsider.

"I will be devastated if Nasib takes off for Bengal again."

Inder said nothing at first, and Ajit had the distinct impression that she was, at least a little bit, relishing the fact of having the upper hand for once. "All right," she finally conceded. "But he stays at the cattle yard, not the haveli, not in my home."

There was a small building beside the barn that was used to house guest workers, men who came from the city to paint or make repairs and needed overnight accommodation. Siamo and Basanti cleaned and prepared it. There was just one room, large and airy, with two windows. A wide cot and bedding went in, as well as a wardrobe. Nasib would wash at the pump until a washroom could be built for him.

"She is behaving like a vengeful stepmother, Bir," Siamo said. And Ajit could not disagree.

Basanti

It was the handsome man, Nasib, who seemed to be at the centre of all the drama at the haveli. First came the news that he was getting married—Basanti had felt a bit foolish in her disappointment. But fate had its say, because Nasib's betrothed had refused to be wed to him.

Foolish girl, Basanti said to herself. *What's a slight limp compared to all the other ways that a man can be damaged?*

And now Nasib would stay with them, with Maaji's reluctant consent.

At this time, Rana's trial started, and every day for two months Bapuji accompanied the Mukhia to Ludhiana for the hearings. One day he returned home with a sad look on his face. A lump rose in Basanti's throat. Had her husband been sentenced to hang?

"Rana got twenty-five years of hard labour." Bapuji sat down heavily on a chair and asked for a glass of cold water.

This was good news. But she realized that now she would be in a virtual prison herself. To have a missing but living husband was a sort of widowhood.

Bhapa brought Mata, Dadi, and Shanti to commiserate with her in their ancient language.

"It's karma, and we must bow to it." Dadi sighed.

Mata wept into her chador. "The fates have not been kind to Basanti."

"Be strong, my daughter," Bhapa said.

The days and weeks passed, and Basanti was busy from the moment she woke up until bedtime. Every day she got Pinki ready for school and Nikki changed and washed; she fed both girls breakfast before she herself could eat. The mornings were spent toiling in the kitchen. She sorted dals and beans, washed and chopped vegetables, kneaded dough. She washed and ironed the clothes and put them away.

Nikki was now quite a handful, more full of mischief than her sister had ever been. Her favourite place was the cattle yard—she loved the horses. One day Bapuji sat her on the old mare's back and taught her how to hold on to the mane. Nikki started kicking her heels and hopping on the horse's back as if she were riding. Bapuji untethered the animal and walked her around the cattle yard in a wide circle. Nikki came alive then, with such a look of joy on her face as she chortled and urged the mare on.

"Look at her, Maaji. Look at her." Basanti laughed.

"She is a natural," Inder said. "Just like her father. I remember he started at the same age. You couldn't peel him off the mare."

It took all four of them to lift her off, wailing in protest.

"You woke a sleeping monster, Ji," Inder said to Ajit with a smile.

People continued to visit the haveli, and no one was ever turned away empty-handed. The Comrade and Pushpa were regulars and honoured guests. The Mukhia and Sehba, and sometimes Naura, showed up every few days. Occasionally, Bhaga the snake-catcher came by when he'd run out of rations, and Siamo or Maaji would give him a stack of rotis and fill his empty bowl with dal. He was an odd-looking man with a pockmarked face and a lazy eye, but he had stories to tell, for he was called everywhere to remove snakes big and small from homes and barns. As a devotee of the Naag Baba, the cobra god, he had never been bitten.

As for Nasib, he rarely ventured into the haveli. He would leave for work before daybreak to get to Samrala in time to drive the first route of the day, and he wouldn't be back until after dark. And then one day Basanti learned that Nasib had left. Bapuji said he had gone to the Middle East to work on a five-year contract. Bapuji was terribly upset, grieving almost as though there had been a death. He blamed Maaji.

"Happy now, are you, you evil woman? You drove my son out of here. You were determined to humiliate him by making him live in the cattle yard like a hired hand."

Maaji covered her mouth and ran into the haveli, followed by Bapuji. Siamo watched in shock before collapsing onto a chair.

"I should have married his mother instead of abandoning her!" Bapuji shouted. "I did not, to spare you the agony, and this is how you repay me. Get out of the haveli and go live with your brothers! I don't want you here any more, you useless, cruel woman! Go, now!"

Basanti couldn't believe what was happening. The poison in Bapuji's words burned in her veins, and Maaji's howls deadened her senses. The girls started to cry and she quickly took them to her breast, as the thought raced through her mind: *Nasib is Bapuji's son!*

Bikram

The day came when the government was at last ready to move to its new, modern home in Chandigarh.

Jagtar stayed at the mansion in Samrala, while Bikram lived in an air-conditioned room at the MLA hostel until the new bungalow assigned to him was ready. He packed most of his belongings then but left a few crucial items at the hostel, which he continued to rent since it offered a convenient and discreet place to conduct his late-night trysts with Sewa's young teacher. Her name was Krishna Kumari. Coming from a poor family, she had been living in a rented room in Samrala and sending most of her money home to help. Bikram had found her a teaching job in Chandigarh, as he'd promised, and a room to live in. It was an arrangement that suited them both.

Bikram came home to Samrala frequently to deal with his own business interests and problems. One of those problems was Mangal. The big man had seized control of the main truck stand in Ludhiana as well as the local union. The union president had not given up without a fight, and shots were fired. The president and his supporters fled, and Mangal became the transport czar. He now faced several charges of assault.

"You'll help me, won't you, Bikram? Remember everything I have done for you."

The superintendent of police for the area, Jorawar Singh, was a brother-in-law of the late Captain Singh, and Bikram remembered meeting him in Raikot. He went to see him at his office in Ludhiana and put his cards on the table.

"I take my duties very seriously, Minister Sahib. Mangal Singh faces charges that I must investigate."

It took three months but a deal was finally reached, with mediation provided by the superintendent's brother, Sub-Divisional Magistrate

Kulbir Singh. Mangal agreed to cede a quarter of the routes to the former president of the trucking union. Charges were dropped and all parties pledged to keep the peace. Bikram sent each of the Singh brothers a case of imported whiskey.

Jagtar was still having what Bikram thought of vaguely as "female problems," and finally she agreed to visit the Post-Graduate Institute of Medical Sciences in Chandigarh.

Her parents were visiting, and Bikram announced, "We will all go to the city. It will give you a chance to see the bungalow and decide if you want to move to Chandigarh. Think about it—we could send Sewa to a good convent school there." It pleased Bikram to think that his son would be educated in English, that being the language of instruction in all convent schools, which were the choice of elected politicians, bureaucrats, judges, and army officers.

Beeji and Chand were thrilled to stay at the long, low bungalow in a prestigious part of the city. Beeji couldn't believe the modern facilities. She flushed every toilet and turned every tap on and off and marvelled at the fact that there was running hot water available twenty-four hours of the day.

Chand sat behind the desk in Bikram's home office. "Seat of power." He held a goblet of scotch in one hand and pretended to sign documents with the other.

The headmaster at All Saints School had agreed to a provisional admission for Sewa to see if he could be fast-tracked in English. But after only three days, he sent for Bikram.

"You son will not fit here. He is extremely rude and disruptive. I cannot see a way to admit him on a full-time basis."

Before he could even begin to object, a male teacher hauled Sewa into the office by his collar. The boy had swollen eyes and a cut lip.

"What happened?"

"Minister Sahib, your son did a very bad thing. He lifted up the skirt of a girl and tried to rub himself against her. The girl's older brother found out and beat him up in the washroom."

"I am going to punish that boy," Bikram shouted.

"That boy is the grandson of the Chief Justice of the High Court."

Bikram sighed. That was a different story. The Chief Justice was a severe Sikh who came from a regal lineage. He could not afford to be in that man's bad books. He apologized to the teacher, thanked the headmaster, and left the office, shoving Sewa ahead of him. They had to walk a long hallway, being stared at by smirking students. It was humiliating.

As soon as their car pulled out of the school grounds he started beating Sewa.

"Motherfucker, you." He slapped the right cheek, then the left.

'Minister-ji, please," the driver said, alarmed.

"You have no idea what a rotten shit this boy is."

"Stop, Papa, stop," Sewa snivelled.

When they got home, Bikram pushed the boy towards Jagtar. "Take the brat back with you," he said. "Today."

Chand watched with a creased forehead as Beeji put cold compresses on Sewa's eyes and cheeks and cried. "My lovely boy, my little lion," she cooed.

"My sad fate." Jagtar moaned. "My sad fate."

Ajit

Inder went to live with her brothers under a cloud of disgrace, and a pall once again fell over the haveli. Days and weeks passed, and then months. One day, Inder's five brothers came to see Ajit. They assured him of Inder's regret and begged him to forgive their only sister and let her come back.

"She is tortured too, Ajit. You have to understand."

No mention was made of Nasib. It was all very proper, and he assented.

The little girls almost choked her with hugs when she got out of the car he had hired to bring her home. Basanti embraced her and Siamo practically mauled her, and for long minutes they all cried. Pushpa ran over to sit with her, and the women of Ajit's kin stopped by to embrace her.

Nasib's departure had brought into the open all the emotions Ajit had struggled with for so long. Painful secrets had been brought to light, punishments had been meted out, and life now returned to something like normal.

Word soon got around that the Zaildar had a son born out of wedlock, but no one said a bad word. Many of the men still felt sorry for him because of Satwant's death, and they were relieved that Nasib would carry on his name and inherit the zaildari.

Nasib had shown some spine. Rather than live as an outcast, he had proudly gone away to stand on his own two feet. Now Ajit stood every day at the haveli gates anxiously waiting for the mail. One day his patience was rewarded.

"From Nasib!"

Siamo stood up and hurried over as he waved the letter.

All stood around as he read it quietly first, to make sure there were no hurtful words, then he read it aloud.

"'Bapuji, I am doing well in Lebanon and my health is good. It is a very beautiful country with lots of pretty places, and I go to sit by the sea a lot. I am sorry that I left without notice, but I knew that you would have tried to make me stay. I could not go on being a cause of conflict between you and Maaji. Please tell her I bend to touch her feet and seek her blessing.

"'My employer is an educated man, and his brother is a bone doctor. I have been fitted with a special shoe and brace and I can walk normally now. It also makes it safer for me to drive. People here are very kind and respect my turban. I live in a rented house with other Punjabi drivers.'"

"Bless him," Siamo said.

Ajit continued, "'Time will go quickly, and I promise to visit as soon as my contract is completed. Give my love to Pinki and Nikki. Tell them their chacha thinks of them every day. My regards to Maaji and Aunt Siamo. Tell Basanti that I miss her cooking. No one makes curried meat like her. Write back to the address below. Your respectful and loving son, Nasib.'"

Ajit sighed, a great burden of worry lifted off his shoulders. Now he had to steel himself for the long wait to see his son again.

"How does he remember me?" Basanti asked, blushing. "We barely met."

"Well, he certainly remembers your cooking," Siamo said.

It was nice that he'd said that, Ajit thought. It showed his good manners.

"Babaji, can I keep the stamps? They are so colourful."

He gave Pinki the envelope, and Nikki stomped her feet.

"I wanted it too!"

"You can have the next one," he said as she pouted.

"Nikki has to have everything Pinki has," Inder said, shaking her head. "Pinki has to hide her satchel as soon as she gets home from school."

"Nikki already tore pages out of my reader!" Pinki added.

"Well then, why don't we go to the Adda to celebrate," Ajit suggested. "You can each have something sweet!"

One day men arrived to install a wooden sign on the side of the paved road outside the Adda. It read:

SITE OF CAPTAIN SATWANT SINGH HEALTH CENTRES
RAIKOT (LUDHIANA)
A PROJECT OF THE GOVERNMENT (PEPSU)
BY ORDER OF (HON.) BIKRAM SINGH, MINISTER OF RURAL
DEVELOPMENT

Work began, and the Adda became a thriving marketplace. The Mukhia's butcher stall, the tea stall, and the dyer's set-up were joined by hawkers selling vegetables, fruits, plastic bangles, and all kinds of knickknacks.

Basanti

The seasons turned, and the little girls were growing up. Nikki was as busy as ever, demanding to "help" Basanti at the hearth by kneading the dough, flipping the rotis on the griddle, stirring the dal. Basanti often had to chase her away.

Pinki was studious and earned good marks. She and Paso did their homework together at the haveli. She was losing her baby fat and growing into a lovely long-legged colt of a girl with a mane of dark-brown curly hair. It seemed as though every six months Maaji was taking her to the tailor for new clothes and buying her bigger shoes. The clothes she outgrew were washed, folded, and put away, waiting for Nikki to catch up.

One thing that hadn't changed was Pinki's fascination with card games.

"I win." Pinki laid down the winning card and raised her arms in delighted victory.

Bapuji lowered the newspaper he was reading and grinned. "Too, too smart. Now you know why I don't play against her."

Maaji had Nikki in her lap and was combing her hair. "Nikki, how many times do I tell you not to undo your braids before bed? Your hair gets all jumbled up during the night."

"Nikki is a wild little junglee." Pinki laughed.

"I can ride the mare," Nikki said.

"No you can't," Pinki taunted. "Gulab still has to hold the reins."

"I will show you and ride her by myself, you watch," Nikki said.

Siamo groaned. "You will be banned from the cattle yard, I promise."

"Babaji would never do that to me."

"Oh no? And why not?"

"Because I am his pride and joy, his Jat girl."

"So am I," Pinki insisted.

Bapuji was still reading the newspaper. "Elections next year," he reported.

"Yes?" said Maaji. "Now watch them rush the building of the health centres. Bikram will want to inaugurate them before the voting."

Basanti lay awake in her cot, thinking about the letter from Nasib, and how she'd blushed when Bapuji read the part where she was mentioned. When Siamo had grinned at her, she'd blushed even more.

She wondered about her husband, and what life in prison was like for him. It would be like living in a cage, she thought. The Mukhia and Sehba visited Rana once a month with food, fresh clothes, and sundries, but they had never brought back a word for her. She had no reason to believe that her name came up at all. Sehba was always whining about her "poor Rana." The most recent complaint was that poor Rana was being harassed by rough men, one of whom had attacked him.

"We complained to the superintendent, and the Mukhia told him that he was a personal friend of Bikram Singh. That's when the officer paid attention."

Basanti sighed, rolled over on the cot, and wondered what the next twenty-odd years would be like. Would Sehba keep bringing Rana's sorrows home for her to listen to? What could she do about them? She was already indentured to the Zaildar for another five years to pay for the family's legal costs. She loved staying at the haveli. But what would happen when the debt was finally paid? Would Maaji and Bapuji still need her at the haveli, or would she have to return to the dera?

"We will cross that bridge when we come to it," Bapuji had said to her once, when the subject came up.

Basanti hoped and prayed.

Bikram

Jagtar wore black sandals and a silver suit sparkling with sequins. Her face was powdered and her mouth was highlighted with a lush red lipstick.

"How do I look, Ji?"

"Ravishing."

Done up fashionably, she looked almost seductive, Bikram thought. He hadn't seen his wife in that light for some time, but the school-teacher, Krishna, had returned to her family home in Manali, and he had yet to find a replacement. He wondered if his wife would offer him relief for his lust. It would have to wait for tonight, though. First, he had to keep his promise and inaugurate the Captain Satwant Singh Memorial Health Centres in Raikot.

"Papa, how do I look?" Sewa was outfitted in a western-style suit, and the dyer had tied his turban smartly.

"You look like an officer, Sewa. Very handsome indeed."

Jagtar gave him a grateful look. The compliment seemed to puff up Sewa's chest.

The boy was fourteen years old and taller than Jagtar, and already he stood past Bikram's shoulders. But, lazy and addicted to sweets, he looked rather soft. He now went to school in Samrala and still got into trouble, but Bikram had bribed the headmaster with a case of rum to promote the boy to the next grade. Bikram was not worried about Sewa's school marks, so long as he did not shame the family by failing to graduate.

Recently Bikram had been introduced to a new method of making money. It was the practice known as land banking, and his partner in this venture was Ranjit.

"You muscle in on undeveloped land by using your political influ-ence. You buy it for pennies, then turn around and sell it later to some ordinary citizen for pounds. Instant riches, my friend. Instant riches."

Everyone was doing it, Ranjit told him, even the Chief Minister. It was technically legal, Bikram was assured, but of course he understood that to mean that it was, from an ethical standpoint, highly questionable.

Ranjit was his partner in a commercial centre in Chandigarh that boasted twenty shops with apartments above, a high-end hotel in Ludhiana, and a cinema in Rohtak. He also owned a string of liquor vends that were managed by Darshan. It was Chand's job to collect rents and lease payments. This was the empire that Sewa would inherit.

Today they were on their way to the dedication of the health centres. Chand rode in front with the driver and Bikram sat in the back with Sewa and Jagtar. A police jeep pulled in front to escort them as they exited through the gates of the mansion. Darshan followed in his own car with Bikram's publicist, Rakesh, and Gopal, the former astrologer. People stopped and waved as they recognized Bikram's official government car with the flag on its hood. The constable at the traffic circle blew his whistle shrilly and stopped traffic in all directions to let them pass.

As they approached the Adda, Chand pointed. "Look to your left," he said. "All that land belongs to the Zaildar. Three hundred acres of some of the richest soil in Punjab."

"Thanks to the floods laying down rich sediments," the driver, a Jat, said.

Chand sighed. "I would love to own land like that."

The Adda itself was festooned with bunting and streamers for the occasion, and a large crowd had gathered. People were shouting slogans of praise as Bikram's car turned into the huge courtyard.

"Bikram Singh zindabad!"

"Congress zindabad!"

The Zaildar opened the car door and Bikram stepped out and into his embrace. His wife did the same on the other side and took Jagtar into her arms before garlanding her and blessing Sewa.

"Welcome, Bikram Singh. Welcome."

Men crowded around him to shake his hand and garland him.

"This way, Sahib."

And there were the new buildings, clean and modern, freshly painted. They didn't look like much compared to the grand buildings of Chandigarh, but still, they looked like the future of Punjab.

The police inspector led them to a ribbon strung between two flag-poles each flying the Indian flag. A school choir, looking very neat and tidy in their uniforms, began to sing the national anthem, and of course Bikram stood at attention. The Giyani then stepped forward to say the Ardas.

"Bole so nihal."

"Sat Sri Akal."

Bikram and the Zaildar were each handed a pair of large, shiny scissors. Newsmen crowded in front of them with their cameras poised.

Rakesh counted down—"Three, two, one . . ."—and Bikram and the Zaildar cut the ribbon together.

Bikram, enjoying the crowd's applause, was led to a raised dais and stepped up to the microphone.

"Today I am so happy, so happy to see these buildings and read the sign above each of them. It gives me great pleasure and pride to have a hand in honouring our revered and beloved martyr, Captain Satwant Singh, whose ultimate sacrifice can never be forgotten. It must continue to inspire us in defending our nation against its enemies, one and all."

Bikram glanced out at the crowd to see the Zaildar sitting in the front row with his family, glowing with pride. The beautiful Bajigarni was sitting between the Captain's growing daughters, Pinki and Nikki—Rakesh had reminded him of their names. The older one was very pretty. He complimented the girls and blessed them in his speech. Also in the front row, standing out in their fine clothing, Jagtar looked proudly at him and Sewa had an adoring look on his face.

When the speeches were over, the medical centre's young Hindu doctor gave Bikram and his entourage a tour of the facilities. They were well furnished and spacious; the faint smell of turpentine lingered in the air, since the paint was barely dry. He complimented the staff for joining the centre.

He toured the grounds and looked at the freshly painted staff quarters and doctors' bungalows and nodded in satisfaction. "Very well done," he told the contractor, who had slipped him ten percent of the construction estimate as soon as he had approved the tender. The whole exercise had been a rich one for Bikram, in both money and votes.

After the official ceremonies were over, Ajit hosted Bikram and the men of his entourage at a private celebration, catered and served grandly by men in livery, in his rooms atop the haveli. Sher and his sons, the superintendent of police and the sub-divisional magistrate, joined them. They sat and talked and chewed on delicious bits of tandoori chicken, lamb kebabs, and fried fish. Ajit served a rare imported black-market whiskey.

The newspaper men had been invited by Rakesh to stay for a drink under a canopy on the roof of the haveli. Bikram was called out for an impromptu interview, and while responding to the flattery, his eyes fell on the orchard in the distance. He quickly turned his back to the disturbing view.

Downstairs in the courtyard he spied Sewa crossing the path from the haveli to the cattle yard in the company of the Captain's young daughters. The three of them headed straight for Satwant's magnificent mare. When she swished her tail and neighed, Sewa stepped back so quickly he nearly fell over.

Jagtar was smiling beatifically when they finally got into their car to return home, once again with an escort from the police jeep, which tooted its horn importantly.

"That was a wonderful day," she said. And then she added, wistfully, "I wish I could have this every day, be fêted and honoured, kow-towed to."

"How was your visit to the cattle yard, Sewa? I saw you there with Pinki and Nikki."

"You saw me?"

"I was on the roof. You can see the whole yard from up there."

"It was Nikki's idea. She was boasting that she can ride the mare all by herself."

"She can?" Jagtar frowned. "She's just a twig of a girl."

"She is also bloody rude." Sewa scowled.

"Rude? How?"

"Well, I followed her and Pinki, and Nikki asked me to pet the mare. It's a huge beast and it snorted and neighed. I backed away. Nikki called me a darpoke, but I'm not a coward."

"Yes, but she wasn't lying, now, was she?" Bikram challenged him.

"Ji, how can you say that? Sewa is a lion."

"A jackal more likely."

"See, Ji? See, you have to spoil the day with your crude remarks about our son."

"I was just joking."

Sewa gave him an angry look. "I wanted to punch Nikki right in her ugly face."

"Sewa! She is just a little girl! And she is not ugly. In fact, I think she's going to be prettier than Pinki," Jagtar said.

"I like Pinki. She was nice to me and apologized for her sister."

"Yes, Pinki seems well-mannered and polite. So respectful," Jagtar said. And then a thoughtful look crossed her face that Bikram knew all too well.

"Ji. Listen to me, Ji."

They were lying in bed, and Jagtar had reverted to her little-girl voice. Something nice always happened when she spoke in that tone. It raised his hopes. The doctors at the hospital in Chandigarh had performed a procedure that Bikram didn't understand, but he knew it had helped somehow with her "female troubles," and she had been much more welcoming lately in bed.

"What?" He started to massage her nipples.

"Stop, Ji. Listen to me."

"My ears are open."

"I was thinking, Ji."

The nipples hardened in his fingers.

"I was wondering, Ji. Sewa really seems to like Pinki. I do, too."

"Juvenile crush, Jagtar."

"No, Ji. I think he is sincere."

"Hunh." His hand moved lower.

"Ji. Concentrate, Ji. I am thinking of something very important."

He undid the cord of her salwar.

"What do you think of asking for Pinki's hand for Sewa?"

"Are you nuts? She is just a child."

"She is ten years old, Ji."

"So?"

"So, Ji, she will grow up into a woman before you know it."

He slipped in a finger. Jagtar moaned.

"I would like you to start working on that, Ji. Chances like these don't come every day."

I like my chances right now. In the dark, he was grinning.

Jagtar sat up. He pushed her back onto the cot and mounted her.

"Look, Ji. Please listen to me. I want Pinki as a daughter-in-law."

"I agree," he said, without breaking rhythm. "She will improve our breed."

"You are so vulgar, Ji."

He let her beg for a full week—he was enjoying the physical relief before the start of the final legislative session and the looming two-month hurly-burly of the elections—but finally he agreed to her proposal.

"You know the uncles, Ji. Start with them," Jagtar said when he told her he feared rejection. The Zaildar was from old stock, a family with a long history as stewards of great expanses of land, while he was just a common Jat, son of a poor schoolteacher.

Her suggestion made sense, though. He could talk with Sher's sons, hint at the benefits of a union with his family. After all, he was already being mentioned in the press as a man to watch, star material, and the Chief Minister had promised to promote him to a senior portfolio after the election. Why, he felt, he could be the number-two man in the cabinet, and one day he might even be the CM. Royalty didn't count for much in India these days—the royals had already been turned into mere figureheads. Who wouldn't want to be related to the new democratic rulers of Punjab?

His confidence grew, and he looked forward to the challenge. He could always count on Jagtar to spur him on to greater heights. A zaildar and a jagirdar's granddaughter would grace his mansion, bear his grandsons, and they could grow up to the same physical stature as the bride's father and uncles. The thought gave him satisfaction. It was a worthy pursuit.

"I love you, Ji." Jagtar embraced him as he got ready to visit the two brothers in Ludhiana. He had invited them to dine with him at Kwality Restaurant there.

"Easy now, easy, save it for tonight."

Jagtar smiled.

The men were ushered into a spacious, curtained booth at the back of the restaurant.

"This is an honour, Minister Sahib." Kulbir Singh, the sub-divisional magistrate, bowed.

"It is indeed." The superintendent of police bowed as well.

"The honour is all mine," Bikram said.

The waiter brought a jug of ice water. Bikram pulled out a bottle of Glenfiddich single malt whiskey that he'd brought with him and ceremoniously opened it to pour three shots.

"Cheers."

"Cheers, Sahib. Cheers."

"Look, we are all almost the same age. No more Sahib. I am Bikram, and I would like us to know each other by first names."

That brought smiles.

"Kulbir, what is your choice tonight?"

"I like their saag meat."

"Jorawar?"

"I like the lamb kofta with rice pulao."

The waiter stopped by and he ordered the meal after pouring another round of shots.

"To a long association and friendship."

"To friendship." They clinked their glasses.

"I must tell you that inaugurating the centres was one of the proudest moments of my life."

"It made us very proud, too, Bikram." Kulbir smiled. "You did a great honour to our families."

"The honour was all mine. After all, I owe everything to the Zaildar. He got me recruited as an NCO in the army when I had no other real prospects."

They listened as he told them a whitewashed version of his life story. He had rehearsed it well and often and had come to almost believe it himself. They nodded politely, made all the right noises.

"So here we are."

He knew that they were astute men, and they had let him set the stage for the meat of the meeting.

"Jagtar was very impressed by the haveli and truly honoured by meeting your mother and wives. She is charmed by Inder Kaur. And she loves the girls, particularly Pinki. Won't stop talking about her. How pretty she is, how well-mannered and polite. Jagtar is completely taken with her."

The brothers exchanged quick glances.

"My son Sewa is fourteen and of the right age."

The cards were on the table.

Kulbir cleared his throat.

"We feel a fatherly responsibility towards our nieces and want them to wed into good homes."

Bikram was well launched into his humble approach. "And dare I imagine that you would consider mine a good home?"

Jorawar nodded. "Yes, of course! A truly great one."

"So . . . you like my idea?"

They nodded. "We will have to speak to our father first, get his approval, and he will take it to the Zaildar."

"Your father has half the decision-making power for Pinki. I think, if he agrees, he will convince Ajit Singh."

Jorawar poured shots all around. They toasted each other.

The food arrived piping hot.

They had not quite exhausted the agenda for the evening, because the brothers had their own axe to grind.

"Promotions are very political, Bikram. Well, I hardly need to tell you that. Look at me, for example—I've been stuck with the same title for six years," Kulbir said.

"And I have been a superintendent for the same amount of time," Jorawar said.

Bikram lowered his voice, and they leaned forward. "Don't say a word about what I am going to tell you."

They nodded.

"The CM has promised me a senior portfolio. He's going to make me a member of his inner circle after the next elections."

Their eyes widened.

"It will give me a lot of influence, if you know what I mean."

"My lips are sealed," Kulbir said. "I pray for your success."

"My success, brothers, is our success."

A week later, the silver rupee arrived confirming the promise of Pinki's hand to Sewa. Maaji joined Jagtar and Beeji in dancing as the men raised their glasses and congratulated Bikram.

Papaji's smile was radiant for the entire evening. "I never even dreamed of this day, Chand," he said proudly.

"Bikram has accomplished a lot. This is a miracle. Imagine, an alliance with a big house like theirs!"

Sewa came home after watching a film in Khanna with his friend Jung. He stood in the doorway.

"What is going on?"

Papaji stood up, walked over, and hugged Sewa. "I am very happy today, Sewa. We accepted the Zaildar's silver rupee. He offered his granddaughter's hand to you in marriage."

"Which one?" Sewa asked.

"The older one, of course. Pinki."

"Good. I would never marry her sister. She is terrible."

"Come on, my son." Bikram took him in his embrace. "Are you happy?"

"I don't know." Sewa blushed.

"Come in, Jung. Have a drink," Darshan said.

"Thank you, but I will have sweets only. My father will kill me if he smells liquor on my breath."

"Here." Beeji filled a plate for him.

"Let's go upstairs." Sewa pulled his arm.

"No, let's stay," Jung insisted.

"We are celebrating your promise, Sewa. Join us." Papaji pushed him down by the shoulders to sit beside Jung, and he reached for a sweet.

Maaji came over to bless him and gave him a gift of rupee notes. Everyone else followed suit. Jung looked at the fattening bundle in Sewa's hand and smiled.

Sewa smiled back. "Enough here to go watch a film every day for a month."

"I hope you don't neglect your studies," Papaji said.

Darshan poured another round. They raised their glasses to Sewa.

"I don't know if you remember, Sewa, but Pinki's father once lifted you onto the back of his beautiful mare."

"What a sight it was." Jagtar smiled. "I often think of that day."

"You should ask for a mare, one of Bakki's fillies, in dowry for Sewa," Papaji said.

"I think I will. I always dreamed of Sewa riding through the bazaar one day on the back of a mare like Bakki, people stopping in their tracks to admire him."

"That would be a sight to behold," Beeji said, joining her hands.

Basanti

Basanti was giving the girls their lunch before they went back to school for the afternoon. They were chattering away as usual, when suddenly they heard wails coming from the dera.

Siamo sighed. "Someone must have died."

Gulab came running through the gates. "It's Rana," he said, out of breath. "He was killed during a riot at the jail."

Basanti's mind went blank.

"Happened last night," Gulab continued. "They say it might have been political—somebody paid off some of the inmates to start trouble and make it look as if the jail was out of control. Looks very bad for the Congress Party. Basanti . . . they will bring the body home tomorrow."

No tears filled her eyes, and her heart did not sink. It was almost like hearing about the death of a stranger. Maaji rose to comfort her. Siamo stroked her arm. The girls stared with open mouths.

"He was a good man," Siamo said with a sigh.

"Waheguru, Waheguru, Waheguru-ji. Grant peace to his soul," Maaji said.

Gulab placed a gentle hand on Basanti's shoulder. "Sister, follow me to the dera."

Maaji got up. "I will come with you."

"I will get a chador for Basanti," Siamo said. "Finish your lunch, girls."

Maaji walked Basanti to the door, and Siamo brought her a white chador, the shroud of widowhood. The women followed Gulab, and the wails got louder as they approached the dera. The white chador was thick and Basanti could barely see, but she could hear the Mukhia's heart-rending cries and Sehba's screams. It was Sehba whose grief counted the most, Basanti thought. A mother will always grieve her son, no matter what.

Maaji sat Basanti down on the bare ground and several women joined her. She sat in silence listening to the weeping. She was grateful for the heavy chador because, try as she might, she could not shed a tear. She had never loved Rana, and she had never been taken to see him in jail. She had felt like a widow for so long, the fact that she truly was one now came as something like a relief.

"Basanti, I am so sad." Mata hugged her and Dadi put her bony arm around her neck. They both wailed in her ears and rocked her between them, as she wondered just why they were grieving this man who had never even tried to make her happy.

It was dark by the time Gulab escorted her back to the haveli and her waiting girls, who clung to her all evening and slept on either side of her under the quilt.

"I love you, Maa," Pinki whispered.

"I love you, Maa," Nikki said, kissing her cheek.

Basanti walked in the procession to the cremation grounds and watched from a distance, seated among the women, as men placed the bier on the pyre, adjusted it, and waited until after the Giyani had uttered the Ardas before setting it alight.

"The Mukhia is a shadow of himself," she heard Naura say.

Looking at the flames consuming Rana's body Basanti joined her hands. "O, Laxmi Maa, send his soul to a calm place full of cows for him to tend to and milk. Show me the path that I can walk to my destination. Guide me, Laxmi Maa."

Then she looked into the flames. "Goodbye, Rana. You lived your karma, and now I will endure mine."

She felt at peace.

The Mukhia spared no expense on the funeral rites for Rana. He had always leaned towards the Sikh faith and his wishes were respected. Basanti attended each ceremony, with Mata and Dadi. She did not hear Sehba cry, and guessed the suffering mother's tears had dried up.

"You will observe a year of bereavement," Maaji said to her, back at the haveli. She would not wear makeup, braid her hair, wear anything colourful, or sing or dance at a celebration. She didn't mind, because she had no prospects or hopes for herself beyond her dedication to the haveli and the girls. They gave her purpose and a reason to wake up each dawn.

"But you can still play cards with me, can't you, Maa?" Pinki asked.

"Sure," Maaji replied on her behalf. "Just . . . without too much gaiety."

Bikram

Bikram won his seat in the 1958 elections, once again by a very healthy margin. The Chief Minister kept his word and awarded him the Ministry of Justice, making him the senior-most legal authority in the province. As one of his first acts, he promoted Pinki's uncle Kulbir Singh to become an additional district magistrate in Ludhiana. Later, during a review of senior police officers, he appointed Jorawar as senior superintendent of police, giving him charge of a quarter of the Ludhiana district, so that Samrala came under his watch.

The Justice portfolio put him at the forefront in matters of the law. Accordingly, and with coaching from Rakesh, he adopted the demeanour of a thoughtful and sophisticated man, spoke in even tones and a calming voice, quoted famous lawmakers and case law. The Punjabis were a feisty lot, he soon discovered, quick to anger. Their fights frequently ended up in the hands of the police and clogged the courts. People tried to circumvent the system by knocking on his door in the company of prominent supporters from his constituency, and he was obliged to give them a hearing, offer tea and samosas, spend time with them. They left with promises, which of course were never fulfilled.

One day Bikram and his publicist were meeting behind closed doors in his office at the Secretariat, which had a magnificent view of the hills.

"On a personal note, I have another Krishna Kumari in mind for you," Rakesh told him.

"Who?"

"Providentially, another teacher, a widow with a son."

"Good-looking?"

"Absolutely gorgeous."

"Well, I trust you, Rakesh."

Jagtar was back under the care of the specialist in Chandigarh, and they had not made love in at least a month. A woman's touch and affection were sorely lacking in Bikram's life.

"So I will arrange a meeting."

"Make it soon, please."

Rakesh's discovery turned out to be a college lecturer with expensive tastes who could no longer afford her spacious third-floor apartment, the scooter she drove, or the private school fees for her six-year-old son on her own salary. They were introduced over dinner in a private booth of a classy restaurant. Anita was beautiful, with large, almond eyes, a small nose, and full lips. She also had an ample bosom, and he couldn't keep his eyes off her belly, bare from the bottom of her high-cut blouse to the top of her low-tied sari. Her colouring was fair, and she had a charming habit of sprinkling English words into her sentences.

"Can I invite you to view my quarters at the MLA Hostel?"

She lowered her eyes and demurely nodded.

"Now."

"Now?" She glanced around the restaurant.

"Now. My car is waiting."

"I can only stay an hour or so. My mother is living with me and she will worry if I'm late."

It was eight PM. The night was young.

"Sewa will not pass his matriculation examinations."

The headmaster had called Bikram, along with the science teacher and the mathematics teacher, to a conference in the office.

"But he can repeat the year, can't he?" Bikram asked.

The science teacher shook his head. "Won't help. He is not a good student at all."

The math teacher was even more emphatic. "His math is abysmal."

Sewa *had* to matriculate. Bikram had heard that Pinki was doing very well in high school and was considered a rising scholar. Sewa's failure would not look good to the Zaildar or the Jagirdar, or even to his own exalted circle of politicians and high officials. But the matriculation examinations were conducted under the auspices of Punjab University. The candidates were assigned numbers, and papers were marked by anonymous teachers from another district. The headmaster had no influence there.

"So, that's it." Bikram stood up.

The headmaster offered a way out. "I have a nephew who is a records clerk at the university. He might . . . be of help?"

"Give me his name, please. I truly appreciate it."

The headmaster looked as relieved as the teachers. It was obvious they could not wait to see the back of Sewa, who had tested everyone's patience.

The boy had started to spend more time in his room. His mother claimed he was studying, burning the midnight oil. But when Bikram got home one evening and knocked on his son's door, Sewa took time answering. There was some rustling before he opened the door.

Bikram pushed past his son and stood in the room with the windows shut tight and smelled the musk.

"What were you doing?" he asked.

"Nothing. Reading."

"Let's see." He bent down, looked under the cot, and pulled out a stack of pornographic magazines. He started to read aloud from one.

"'She turned round and round and he unfurled her sari until he could see her thick dark bush and—'"

"Papa, please. Papa!"

Bikram dropped the magazine and punched Sewa in the head. "This is reading? You dirty bastard, you son of a bitch!"

Both Jagtar and Ramu rushed into the room. They pulled him away from Sewa, who whimpered and cowered.

"Stop, Ji. Stop, I say. Don't you dare lay a finger on him!"

"Shut up, you stupid woman," he shouted. "Want to see what he is reading?"

He opened the magazine and stuck it under her flaring nostrils.

She looked down and gasped before covering her eyes. Ramu pushed Sewa out the door.

"See?" Bikram snarled. "You have raised a fucking wretch, a pervert."

Jagtar sat down slowly on a chair, her face drained of colour, her lips moving silently.

"I am through with this crap. I am going to marry again. I need intelligent sons. This bastard is only going to pour ashes on my head anyway. I am done."

He stormed out. She followed and pulled him into their bedroom.

"Listen, Ji. I beg you, Ji. Never say those words again. I will kill myself."

"Go ahead," he said.

Her eyes went wide with fear.

"Go ahead, Jagtar. Go ahead. It will make things easier for me. Yes, much, much easier for me."

"You don't love me, Ji. You hate me!" she shrieked, and she started pulling her hair out.

Beeji chose that moment to run in and take Jagtar in her arms.

"Why are you saying cruel things to my daughter, Bikram? Why?"

"Ask her."

He slammed the door behind him.

In the gathering room he found Chand cowering on the sofa. He walked out into the courtyard and shouted, "Start the car. I am getting out of here."

A few days later, an urgent call from Ludhiana had Bikram racing to Brown Hospital. Jagtar had been rushed there from Samrala, bleeding heavily, and the doctor feared for her life. He did not want to chance the much longer ride to the PGI in Chandigarh. Now Jagtar was undergoing emergency surgery. Bikram sat in a waiting room in an older wing, separate from the modern hospital, with Chand and Beeji. They prayed with joined hands and intoned holy verses.

Finally the surgeon, an older, bespectacled British woman wearing a green hospital gown, waved them into a hallway and told them in a heavily accented voice, "Jagtar has been given a hysterectomy. The operation was successful. Not to worry. Perhaps a long recovery, but she'll be fine."

Beeji and Chand looked stricken and covered their faces with their hands before collapsing on the hard, wooden benches in the waiting room. Bikram resolved to have his wife moved to a private room in the main hospital with round-the-clock nursing. He was taken to see Jagtar in the recovery room, and when she woke up he murmured kind, encouraging words to her. She squeezed his hand and wouldn't let go, until a young nurse came and gently loosened her fingers.

"She will be fine, Sahib."

"Thank you."

Once outside, he took deep breaths to rid himself of the strong odour of Dettol and the suffocating smell of Jagtar's chloroform-laced breath. He sat down on a rickety chair at a tea stall. Chand soon caught up with him there. His eyes were red, and he buried his nose in a handkerchief. They ordered tea.

"It's a tragedy, Bikram. It is. So young, and now she will not be able to bear you more children."

Bikram looked at Chand. "That's hardly news. In fifteen years she hasn't borne another child. For all I know, she has been barren for years."

"Now, Bikram, please don't do anything rash." Chand was clearly agitated. "I know Gopal is talking about finding you a match."

"Gopal? He hasn't mentioned a word of this to me. What are you insinuating?"

Chand collected himself and sat up straight. "I just want you to know, Bikram, that your affairs are very much entangled with Jagtar and us, her family."

"Are you threatening me?"

"No, no, no. I was just making an honest observation, Bikram. Before you make some rash decision to remarry."

Bikram was furious, but he kept his mouth shut. He stood up, turned on his heels, and went looking for his driver.

When he got back to the mansion he found Mangal and Sewa sharing a bottle in the gathering room. Sewa quickly gulped the last of his drink and slipped out the far door, closing it softly behind him. As annoyed as he was at his son, Bikram was just too tired and upset to bother. He sank into the sofa, and Mangal poured him a double shot.

"Jagtar will live," he said.

Mangal folded his hands and raised his broad face and muttered thanks.

"They took out her bachedani."

Mangal quickly gulped his shot and burped.

"So Sewa the pervert is my one and only heir. What would you suggest I do?"

"Accept your fate, and put more energy into making Sewa into a fine young man."

"Do you think I can? I'm afraid he's a lost cause."

"Look, Bikram, you're being too hard on the boy. Spend time with him. Listen to him. Become his confidant."

"You know what I found in his room?"

"Some adult magazines, big deal. Sewa showed them to me. I leafed through the muck. It's adolescent stuff, Bikram. The boy is struggling to find himself, grow up. It's just a stage. Think of yourself at his age. How much did you jerk off?"

"There was no privacy in my home, and I slept next to my father. I had a book under my nose every waking hour."

"I feel sorry for you, Bikram. Sincerely I do." Mangal raised a glass.

∽

Jagtar stayed in the hospital for two weeks to recuperate, and when she returned home Beeji moved in to help care for her. She was still in pain, and the local doctor gave her injections of morphine to help her relax. She slept most of the time.

Bikram returned to Chandigarh to work on the final stages of the Second Five Year Plan for the province. He was involved in numerous meetings and presentations, and now that he was a senior minister he was called on to help make momentous decisions involving vast amounts of money for the economic development of Punjab. Thousands of tubewells—wells in which a tube or pipe is bored into an underground aquifer—were approved to increase irrigation. The massive Bhaghra Nangal Dam had been completed, and electric power would be taken to every corner of the state. New schools, colleges, and health centres would be built, and modern improvements would be brought to animal husbandry. Increasing its literacy rate was the nation's number one priority. Enormous sums of foreign-aid money were flowing in. Bikram was invited to join delegations to major foreign capitals, and in turn he was constantly hosting foreign dignitaries. They were a heady couple of years, and they passed in a whirl.

Sewa had been admitted to the college in Khanna after Bikram bribed the headmaster's nephew in the records department of Punjab University to alter the results of his matriculation examinations. The boy received a respectable second-division pass. He was now floundering in college.

A police inspector from Khanna came to visit Bikram one day, wearing civilian clothes.

"Minister Sahib, Sewa is in bad company. They drink, tease girls, and create scenes. We have had to remove him from dangerous situations. I suggest you find another college and move him away from Khanna." Sewa was not the only political princeling giving nightmares to his father. "It's the father's power that they get drunk on. Can't help showing it off," the inspector said.

Bikram didn't know what to do. But Jagtar had a suggestion. "Talk to the Zaildar, Ji. Get him to move the wedding forward."

"I think we need to let Pinki finish high school first. At least one of them must have a bit of real education. It is Pinki who will be our salvation. It will be up to her to save Sewa."

Mangal made a suggestion.

"Get Sewa admitted to a college in Ludhiana. He can stay at my bungalow there, and my men and I will keep an eye on him."

Bikram had doubts about the wisdom of that arrangement. Mangal was not his idea of a guardian. On the other hand, there was a lot to be said for Sewa living in Ludhiana. He would be anonymous in the big city, and away from the prying eyes of people in his constituency.

"All right, then. I will do just that," Bikram said warily.

Mangal grinned.

"But please, I beg you, my brother. I need you both to stay out of trouble."

Ajit

Ajit buried himself in his work. There was much that had to be done. The modernizing of agriculture was bringing about a lot of change. He was in the process of re-drilling his wells with bigger pipes so that water could be drawn with a powerful engine. He had a tractor now, and this rendered both the camels and the three pairs of oxen redundant. He needed fewer field hands from the village, which came as a relief to the women at the hearth.

And there were rumours that the zaildari would be eliminated to make way for a more efficient system of tax collection. It was seen as a feudal remnant of India's inglorious past. Ajit had no intention of yielding his responsibilities, and unless he was forced to stop, he planned to go on making the traditional tours of the villages in his jurisdiction, checking in with his numberdars and hearing the concerns of the locals.

The Adda was thriving because of the health centres. Predictably, a chemist had set up shop nearby. Most people did not trust the free medicines offered at the health centre and preferred to buy their own. There were two tea stalls, one on either side of the road, busy from morning till night. One of them served meat and fried fish, and its patrons tended to be the men who visited the liquor vend. No untoward incidents of drunken behaviour had occurred, and the place was still considered safe for women and children.

The local elementary school had been upgraded to a high school, and Pinki and Paso were in the first class of ninth-graders. Pinki usually had a book in her lap. Nikki was in the sixth grade, and she could truly ride Bakki all by herself now. Baru Marasi was instructing her in proper horsemanship. While Basanti looked after the girls, Ajit was more than happy to keep her at the haveli, even after the debt the Mukhia owed for Rana's legal bills had been fully paid. However,

Basanti's father was pestering her to remarry.

"What am I going to get from marrying an uneducated, widowed Bajigar?'" she would say. "And anyway, I won't ever leave my girls."

Basanti had lived so long at the haveli that one day Siamo teased, "Basanti, when will you ever learn to speak Punjabi properly, like the rest of us?"

"When you learn to speak Gauri, like me."

"I might do that. But wear a kurti and a ghunia? Never!"

Pinki laughed. "You would look beautiful in Bajigar clothing, Bhua!"

One day, Sher brought Jeet Kaur to spend a day at the haveli. Pinki's wedding was still a long way off, but the women began to make a list of items to be included in her dowry. Ajit made the mistake of sticking his nose in.

"It's too early to be thinking of such details, no?"

"With respect, Bir, men should stick to what men know and leave the gathering of the dowry to the women."

Sher laughed. "That puts us in our place, Ajit!"

But there was one item on the dowry list that Ajit knew he was responsible for.

"Bakki is carrying again, and I hope it's a filly."

Ajit told Sher what Bikram Singh had told him: "I have never forgotten the sight of Satwant riding that beautiful mare Bakki through the bazaar. Please give Sewa a filly from Bakki in the dowry. It would make me the happiest man in the world."

Sher pondered that. "I hear that Sewa is a bit of an oddball. Can't even ride a bicycle and has to be driven to college in a car. What is he going to do with a mare?"

"Bikram has his heart set on it. He is going to build a stable for it at his dairy."

"It is kind of an old-fashioned custom. Even my boys wanted motorcycles instead."

"I like keeping up the old traditions. As it is, we lose another one every day."

"Will you want a mare for Nasib when he gets married?"

"Certainly."

"Well, you'd better check with him first." Sher took a long breath and went on. "You know, Ajit, Bikram has done well for Kulbir and Jorawar, and I feel as though I owe him something for it."

"What's on your mind?"

"I want to buy a car for Pinki's dowry, to honour Bikram's status."

"A car?"

"Yes. It will set a new standard, and he will feel very honoured."

It was a startling and expensive proposal, but Ajit knew that Sher could afford it. And it was true, his sons had been promoted twice to more powerful positions. A car seemed like a generous way of saying thank you. Still, he couldn't help thinking, *What on earth is the world coming to?*

Bikram

The police report lay on his desk, and he closed his eyes after reading it. His PA waited.

It was worse than he had feared, or could ever have imagined. Mangal had taken Sewa to a Kanjar khanna, presumably to treat him to a whore's pleasures. According to the detailed report, something happened and Sewa had almost broken the woman's jaw. The pimps had rushed in to lay a beating on him, and Mangal had charged in and broken bones before dragging Sewa away. A First Incident Report was filed by the madam, the owner of the brothel; her own son claimed to have suffered a broken arm and a busted nose.

The problem was that the brothel fell within Jorawar's jurisdiction, and it was he who had signed the report. He'd attached a note, saying, "No action has been initiated and I have stopped any further investigation until I receive instructions from you."

The note gave him hope, and shamed him, too. Jorawar was Pinki's uncle.

"I should never have put Sewa under Mangal's care. What the hell was I thinking?"

"Be glad you have only one son, Sahib," said his PA. "Imagine the headaches the CM has with half a dozen. There are lots of nasty rumours about them."

Bikram sighed. "Imagine for a moment. Here I am, the father, working day and night to build an estate, and there is the son, Sewa, busy burning my political capital and destroying my reputation."

"You are afraid Pinki's family might cancel the engagement?"

"That would be the ultimate humiliation. And who could blame them? Tell me what I should do here."

The PA sat down and scratched his chin. "For one, I would simply buy off the injured, pay them off, and then coerce them to drop the charges."

"Second?"

"I would get Sewa wed as soon as possible."

Bikram managed to keep Jagtar completely in the dark about the incident. He waited until he was alone with Mangal to ask questions.

"Sewa has so much curiosity—I thought it might be a good idea to let him experience the real thing instead of looking at smut all day," said Mangal.

"He's still buying those magazines?"

"Yes, and I do believe they have caused some damage. Sewa could not control himself. The whore barely opened her knees and he shot it on her belly. She was mighty amused and taunted him. That's when he punched her in the face."

"Oh, God."

"He's very worried. I want to take him to a good Hakeem who treats these kinds of men's maladies."

"You're not taking him back with you, are you?"

"What's he going to do here? Jagtar can't control him. Were you planning to take him to Chandigarh with you?"

Bikram cringed at the thought.

"All right, go ahead and take him. Just get him treated. Keep Sewa on a tight leash. And keep him out of Kanjar khannas, please. I beg you with joined hands."

He stood up to fetch a bottle and call for ice water.

"Listen, another thing. Sewa drinks a lot. I find empty bottles under his cot."

Bikram sat down heavily and winced. Could it get any worse?

"He is very sneaky, Bikram. Might need more than a short leash."

"Like what?"

"Like a wife, and fast."

"He drinks, he ejaculates prematurely . . . how will a quick wedding help that? I already feel for Pinki."

"A loving wife can change a rogue."

"Like your wife changed you?"

"My wife doesn't know the meaning of the word *loving*. She's no Jagtar."

Aren't you lucky. "Just take him to the damned Hakeem as soon as possible. Get Sewa treated. I will fix the wedding date when you tell me he is under control and cured."

As Mangal left, it crossed Bikram's mind that he barely knew his own son while, to Mangal, Sewa was an open book.

The Zaildar remained adamant. At sixteen, Pinki was still too young to be wed. Finally, at Bikram's urging, Ajit promised to consult his wife and Sher's family.

Bikram had spoken to Jorawar as well, who had laughed off the incident at the Kanjar khanna as just a young man sowing his wild oats. So Bikram was not worried about the story reaching the Zaildar's ears.

Bikram had another worry.

Since her hysterectomy, Jagtar had been taking painkillers, and she was becoming more withdrawn and lethargic. Her skin had turned sallow, her waist had thickened, her eyes were marked with dark circles, and her face looked swollen.

"Jagtar is addicted to those damn pills," Bikram complained to her parents. "She doesn't even look after herself now, she has a live-in maid who waits on her hand and foot, does everything but piss for her."

"We are beside ourselves, Bikram. What can we do?"

"Watch her. Let her take only the recommended dose of her pills. Ramu tells me she goes through her prescription much too quickly. She's probably doubling the dose."

"Her doctor should stop her, then."

"I talked to him. He says Jagtar must be bribing the chemist to get more pills."

"Have him arrested."

"Easier said than done. The man will sing like a nightingale. The whole town will know what goes on in the mansion. I might as well be carrying a sign saying, *Does anyone know who is selling narcotics to my idiot wife?*"

Beeji winced at his derisive tone, but Bikram was past caring.

Mangal phoned from Ludhiana.

"Bikram, I took Sewa to the Hakeem in Malerkotla. Would you believe it? The fucker is a midget." Mangal chortled over the phone.

"Tell me what happened." He wouldn't give a damn if the Hakeem had two heads as long as he could fix Sewa's problem. Anyway, a midget was considered good luck.

"Well, Hakeem Abdul Latif Lahori is a godsend. He sat us down and explained in detail to Sewa why he has the problem. Too many nerves on his knob."

"That's a problem?"

"Yes, a big one. They are extremely sensitive and arouse him too fast."

"I see."

"He gave him something that will deaden them."

"Deaden them? What if he becomes impotent? That will be the end of it!"

"No, Bikram. The nerves will be less sensitive, not dead. Listen, in ten days Sewa should be back to normal. Ten days of applying the ointment twice a day."

"Make sure it works."

"Yeah, sure, do you think I'm going to slop it on *myself*?"

"What if it doesn't do what it's supposed to?"

"In that case, the Hakeem mentioned that a sunnat is a permanent solution."

"What?" A circumcision was one anatomical factor that separated the Sikhs from the Muslims.

"Don't get upset. I think Sewa got the message. You should have seen him cover his groin with his hands when the Hakeem suggested it."

Basanti

After almost a dozen years of living at the haveli, Basanti was feeling more and more removed from her people. She rarely visited the dera, and when she did, she often arrived with gifts. While the women of the dera were mending their tattered clothes with scraps of fabric and worrying about having enough fuel to cook with and enough flour or rice to feed their families, Basanti, with permission from Bapuji and Maaji, would bring them hand-me-down clothes, dried sugarcane for their fires, jaggery to sweeten their tea, or a bag of grain to grind for roti.

"You become more like a villager and a Jat every day," Naura told her, and Basanti felt the sting.

Truly, Basanti had no worries about her own well-being. Bapuji had raised her wages to five hundred rupees a year, but each time he sat her down to count the notes onto her palm she refused, insisting that it was better that he save them for her. Bhapa did well as a butcher and was still in demand as a drummer. Gulab had earned a huge raise once he learned to drive the tractor. She had nowhere to go and no one to spend her money on.

Maaji treated her as always to new clothes, bangles, sundries, sandals and slippers, just as she did for Siamo. Each harvest brought a bounty of gifts. Bapuji kept her sweet tooth satisfied, and the girls filled her heart and soul with their love.

It still annoyed her that her father wanted her to remarry. When she remembered her husband, it was mostly his sneering looks and his nightly grunting. But it was not true that her heart had been turned to stone. The thought of Nasib caused Basanti heartache. Some nights she dreamed of them being together and did not want to wake up when the cock crowed, wishing that she could wring the bird's neck and shut it up. When her urges grew too much she took to the privacy of the washroom for a long bath. She knew that he would return one day, but then a suitable bride would be found for him—a woman she would have to welcome as a sister at the haveli.

She turned to Pushpa for guidance.

"Seek solace from the deities, my child. I know you worship Laxmi Maa and pray to her. I want you to add Naag Baba and Pir Shah in your daily prayers. They will help you, Basanti. You will see. Wake up early every day and bathe. Sit in Samadhi."

"Samadhi?"

"Sit in the lotus position. Breathe deeply and empty your mind of all thoughts and distractions. Then repeat the names. O *Laxmi Maa, O Pir Shah, O Naag Baba*. Do it one hundred and one times."

"I can't count."

"Count with your fingers, ten times plus one."

"Show me."

"Here, like this."

The hundred and one repetitions had a calming effect on her; they brought peace to her soul and gave her strength of mind. She asked Siamo to accompany her to the Naag Baba temple and Pir Shah's tomb. She took offerings to the Holy Granth at the gurudwara. She always remembered Nasib in her prayers.

The planning of Pinki's dowry was a revelation to Basanti. She had attended weddings in the village and admired the dowries, but this one was shaping up to be the mother of all dowries. Maaji wanted eleven nimari cots with bedding, twin hope chests with carved lions' feet and brass fittings, a complete set of silver cutlery and fine china, as well as a set of brass cooking pots made in Kanpur.

Each set of bedding would include a cotton durrie woven with colourful scenes of daily life, a mattress stuffed with fluffed cotton, embroidered sheets and pillow covers, a thin cotton summer cover, and a thick winter quilt. The cots were to be constructed of hardwood frames and carved softwood posts, and tightly strung with cotton bands. It would take a year and a half for everything to be made and delivered.

There was one more important part of the dowry, and it arrived right on time.

"It's a filly, with great markings," Baru Marasi shouted at midnight after midwifing the delivery. They had waited under the verandah while the girls slept inside.

Bapuji did a little dance and followed him to the cattle yard.

"Thank you, Waheguru-ji," Maaji said.

Bapuji made a deal with Pinki. If she won a provincial scholarship, he would let her study at the Home Sciences College for Women in Chandigarh. Her cousin Jeetan, the judge's daughter, would go there too, so she would not feel alone.

Pinki held up her end of the bargain, and Paso bettered her by earning an even higher mark. The headmaster was ecstatic, and he was showered with praise. Bapuji invited him and all the teachers and staff to the haveli for a formal tea attended by the village elders; the Mukhia came as well, accompanied by elders from the dera.

Paso wanted to become a nurse, and she had won admission to the Christian Medical College in Ludhiana. But her mother was distraught. Paso was promised, and she was afraid that any delay would cause her fiancé to abandon her.

"He doesn't need to. I am rejecting him," Paso's father said. "The fool is no longer a match for my daughter. He never went to school."

"But you can't go back on your word! It will blacken our faces in the tribe!" the mother cried.

The Mukhia interceded. "It's different times, a new age now. We have to move with the world. I approve the decision to send Paso to nursing school."

Not long after, a letter arrived from Bikram Singh. Bapuji read it aloud.

"I am very proud of Pinki's scholastic achievement. I hope she achieves more in college. I approve of her decision to attend the Home Sciences College. It has a fine reputation. Some of my fellow ministers have daughters studying there and they sing its praises. It is with pride that I tell you that Sewa is moving to the Government College for Men in Ludhiana and changing his subject to Civic Studies, with a view to a future career in politics. I hope he walks in my shoes someday soon."

"There you go," Maaji said, smiling. "Both will earn degrees."

"What's a degree?" Nikki asked.

"It is what you get for finishing college," Pinki explained. "I will be a Bachelor of Sciences. I can use the letters B Sc after my name."

Nikki shrugged. "Big deal."

Maaji looked at the younger girl and frowned. "Suddenly you are interested in college? I thought you had no interest in life except for the mare and the filly."

The filly was called Toofan. Nikki had chosen the name, meaning typhoon, because of the horse's stormy temperament.

"I want to keep her for *my* dowry," Nikki had said. "What is that darpoke going to do with Toofan? Toofan will be wasted on the city boy."

"Nikki, you will have a filly for your dowry," Bapuji said patiently. "Toofan is going with Pinki."

When the day finally arrived for Pinki to leave for college, Nikki became morose, cried, and clung to her.

"I am going to be so lonely without you."

Siamo too had tears in her eyes.

Basanti felt as though something had been torn out of her. It was all she could do to keep from flailing out herself and weeping aloud. She urgently prayed, "Laxmi Maa, Naag Baba, Pir Shah, Waheguru-ji. Please protect my child."

When her uncle arrived in a car with her cousin Jeetan, Pinki clung to Basanti.

"I love you, Maa. I promise to visit often. And I will write, too."

The car drove away with her, and they watched until it disappeared up the road.

～

One day, a letter came with news that they had all been longing for. It was from Nasib—he would soon be coming back from the Middle East. Bapuji was thrilled. Siamo was both relieved and grateful, as was Inder, who had been hoping that Nasib would stand in Satwant's place to give Pinki away. Basanti felt that her prayers had been answered, but as a Bajigarni she could not expect anything more than just to be able to see him.

Basanti spent the day before his arrival cleaning and airing Nasib's room. On the day, Bapuji went to fetch his son from the railway station.

As they waited at the haveli, Siamo watched Basanti fussing and said with a smile, "You look lively."

"It's a happy day. Did you see the smile on Bapuji's face?"

"It is a happy day indeed, and I pray it is the end of our trials," Maaji said with joined hands.

When Nasib arrived home with Bapuji, Maaji and Siamo took him in their arms and cried happy tears.

Basanti admired the chiselled face and the brown eyes and pearly teeth and felt short of breath; she escaped outside to the kitchen to gather herself. His time away had stretched to seven years.

"You look well, Nasib," she heard Maaji say.

"I will look even happier when I've tasted Basanti's cooking again."

"Look what her cooking has done to me." Siamo laughed and patted her belly.

Nasib brought out the gifts he had brought for the family: beautiful fabrics for Maaji and Siamo, dolls for the girls, and a Swiss watch for Bapuji. And then there was one more.

Nasib turned to Basanti. "They have people in Arabia that remind me of Bajigars. They are called Bedouins. Here is your gift." He handed her a wrapped package.

She was shocked. A gift for her? She opened the package and held up a colourful chador.

"How beautiful," Inder gushed. "Look at all the needlework."

Basanti's face glowed. "I will save it for a very special day."

BOOK FIVE

1963–1965

Bikram

Bikram's PA came into the office one day, waving a newspaper. "Did you see this?" His face shone with excitement.

"What?"

"Here, read this. They found the headless girl's skull."

Bikram was dumbstruck. His throat had closed entirely. He sat perfectly still.

"Remember? The girl whose head went missing after the massacre in the Pir's orchard in Raikot? That's near your home, isn't it? Happened years ago. Almost everyone knows about her. Her ghost wanders around looking for it, they say. Lots of people claim to have seen her on full-moon nights."

A trickle of icy sweat ran down Bikram's spine. He glanced at the Hindi newspaper. There was a large black-and-white photo of Baru Marasi cradling a white skull in his hands. The empty sockets stared right through Bikram, and he felt his heart pounding in his ears.

"Sahib, are you alright?" the PA asked.

"Get me a glass of water."

"Right away."

He began to shiver as darkness descended upon him.

Basanti

"I was scared," Nasib said, "and I don't mind admitting it."

They were sitting in the courtyard—Bhaga the snake-catcher, Baru Marasi, Bapuji, and the women—sipping tea and discussing the day's sensational news. It was Nasib who had found the skull, and he told them every detail about his discovery.

"There were a bunch of baby cobras coiled up inside, peering out of the eye sockets."

Basanti shivered. "I would have been terrified."

"Next time, Nasib, remember that a baby cobra is just as deadly as a full-grown one," Bhaga said.

"Waheguru-ji, Waheguru-ji," Siamo moaned.

"Can I see the skull again?" Nikki asked Baru. It was wrapped in cloth and sat in his lap. Baru was going to reunite the skull with its skeleton in the grave he'd marked with a mulberry bush.

"Nikki, enough!" Maaji scolded her. "It's not a curiosity to be stared at."

"Go ahead, here, you can hold it." Baru had a soft spot for Nikki, his disciple in horsemanship.

Nikki proceeded to unwrap the skull very carefully. Then she held it up for everyone to see.

Siamo immediately put her hands over her eyes. "Cover it, child!"

Basanti took one look and shut her eyes as well.

"Give it back to Baru!" she heard Bapuji shout.

"I am not scared," Nikki insisted.

"Oh, God," Maaji prayed, "give this child some sense!"

When Basanti dared to open her eyes again, Nikki had slipped away, and the skull was once again wrapped and sitting in Baru's lap. Siamo had spilled her tea and her mug had rolled under the cot. She bent over to retrieve, groaning with the effort, and Basanti picked it up for her.

Clearly there would be no more work done that day. They had talked in hushed tones of the famous headless girl, and traded ghost stories. Bhaga's were the best, because he travelled to all parts of the region to master the snakes and knew the history of every village and its legends. The sun slowly dropped and they were feeling lazy and pleasantly distracted.

And then came a distant scream.

They rushed to the gates.

There was Nikki riding Bakki, galloping back to the haveli followed by the filly Toofan. Nasib quickly opened the gates. The pounding of hooves shook the earth under their feet as the mare turned into the cattle yard, with Nikki barely hanging on, and came to an abrupt stop. Nikki flew through the air, did a somersault, and landed on a pile of maize stalks.

"Nikki!" Maaji ran over to where the girl lay still.

"Save us, God. Save us," Bapuji whispered.

Basanti ran and pulled Nikki up, her mind filled with all kinds of horrors.

"Speak, Nikki. Say something," Siamo urged her.

Nikki opened her eyes and pulled away from Basanti. "That was amazing!" She stood up and dusted herself off.

Maaji scolded her, tearfully, "You almost killed me, you silly girl! I thought I was going to have a heart attack!"

"You were flying through the air, child," Nasib said, holding her sternly by the shoulders.

"Chacha, you should have seen it. It was huge. Scared both Bakki and Toofan, and I almost soiled my shorts." Nikki did not look frightened at all. She smiled.

"What? What did you see?" Bapuji demanded.

"Naag Baba. It rose out of a furrow in the field, spread its hood this wide." Nikki lifted her arms above her head and joined her fingers. "Then it hissed. Froze my blood. Bakki panicked and galloped, with Toofan right behind. I hung on to her mane for dear life."

"Look at the filly. Her eyes are almost popping out of her head. And her skin is rippling. That animal is scared stiff," Baru said, calm as ever.

"What were you doing riding bareback on Bakki in the first place?" Bapuji asked Nikki.

"I just wanted to go look at the spot where Chacha found the skull."

"And you ran into the father cobra," Bhaga said.

Siamo said, "Naag Baba appears only when he is asked. Someone has prayed to him. Inder, we must go pray at his temple."

Basanti still had her hand over her chest, and Nasib asked, "Are you alright? Take deep breaths and calm yourself."

"It's your fault, Nikki. You took years off my life, too," Siamo said.

"And mine," Bapuji said. "You are banned from riding."

"What?" Nikki shouted. "I didn't ask Naag Baba to come and scare the mare. I am being unfairly punished!"

Maaji's eyes flared. "Oh, shut up, Nikki."

Three days after the skull was found, news reached them that Bikram Singh had been hospitalized. Bapuji went with Sher Singh to Chandigarh to visit him at the hospital and returned shaking his head.

"Family visits only. Doctor's orders."

"Is he very ill?" Maaji asked.

"We talked to Jagtar and to Bikram's parents. They say he is improving."

"Well, in any case, he will know that you were concerned and went to visit," Maaji said.

"Since we were there, of course, we stopped by to visit Pinki and Jeetan."

"The college girls! I wish I'd been with you. How are they doing?"

"They look very happy. Showed us the school and fed us at the cafeteria."

"How's the food?"

Bapuji shrugged. "It's . . . edible."

"That bad?"

"Pinki was upset that Bikram was in the hospital and wanted to know if she should try to visit him. I suggested she send him a card wishing him a quick recovery instead."

"Quite right. Was Sewa there at the hospital?"

"No."

Maaji frowned. "Strange."

It was clear to the entire family that Bapuji was keen to see Nasib dressed as a groom as soon as possible. Nasib, however, had his own ideas.

"I believe I will wait until after Pinki's wedding to find a bride. I don't want to steal the spotlight from my niece."

Basanti knew that Bapuji was opposed to rushing Pinki's wedding, but obviously this meant that he might have to relent.

"Then I will get Pinki married off tomorrow!"

"Two more years, I said, for Pinki," Maaji insisted. "And you, Nasib, are just making excuses."

"You are not getting any younger, Nasib," Bapuji said. "I have already started looking for a match for you."

"Jeet Kaur had proposed a couple of girls," Siamo said.

"That was ages ago. Those girls are now long wed, I'm sure," Nasib countered. "I promise, Maaji, I will get married after Pinki."

"So, if we get a suitable proposal, you will let us accept it."

"*After* Pinki is wed."

"Stubborn, aren't you?" Maaji teased.

Nasib glanced her way, and Basanti averted her eyes. As long as he was single, she could indulge her fantasies about him. It would be a different story the day another woman owned him and joined her at the hearth, trying to be her friend. She would be tested. She prayed.

Maaji had a list of things she wanted to buy in Ludhiana for Pinki's dowry, and she insisted that Basanti accompany her. Bapuji would escort them.

Basanti boarded a bus for the first time ever. She sat between Maaji and Bapuji, watching with fascination the other passengers getting in and out, the harried conductor cutting tickets, and the driver deftly wheeling the bus. Dark, oily smoke came in through the windows whenever the bus stopped, choking her. They slowed as they entered the city, the roads now clogged with traffic. The driver blew the horn incessantly and leaned out the open window to berate pedestrians.

Finally, when the bus stopped again they stepped down into the midst of a crowd. Basanti was shocked when someone pinched her buttock, and when she whipped around to confront the culprit, someone else squeezed her breast. Who was it? Everyone looked so intent and innocent. So this was the city.

She let Maaji drag her by the hand to a rickshaw stand. "Chaura Bazaar," Bapuji told the man as they climbed aboard. The driver eased them into the traffic and rang his bell, yelled warnings, and his scrawny legs pedalled mightily. They finally turned into a narrow street into the bazaar.

"Look at Maaji!" Bapuji turned to Basanti with a grin. "Such a big smile. This is her favourite place!"

"It will become Basanti's favourite, too," said Maaji, who did indeed look delighted. "Wait and see!"

The shops overflowed with goods, the sidewalks were piled up with even more merchandise, and shoppers hustled about as vendors shouted their wares. They spent most of the day ducking in and out of shops until it all was a blur for Basanti. They settled on one cloth merchant as their favourite. So much colour! She walked around and let her fingers drift over the many different fabrics to feel their textures—chenilles and satins, cottons and silks, wools and blends. She was flattered that Maaji would ask her opinion about colours and patterns.

The merchant heaped praise and flattery on Maaji and called for cups of spiced tea. His assistants smiled broadly and shook or nodded their heads on cue. "Great choice," they would affirm once she'd made a selection.

The huge pile of fabric was sorted carefully and the assistants tied it into a tight bundle with a rough cloth and thick string. The merchant added up the bill, and Basanti watched wide-eyed as Bapuji counted out the notes to pay.

"I will have it delivered tomorrow," the merchant said, and he bowed them to the door.

They came out and ate gol gappas on the street. Then they sat down inside a restaurant for snacks and tea—Maaji made her try different things, fiery hot or very sweet, steaming or freezing—and finally they stood outside it and had fresh jelebis. All these were exotic delicacies for Basanti and her head swam from the indulgence.

On the way back, she fell asleep in the bus.

Ajit

Lal Singh, Bikram's father, was almost begging them. "Bikram is in poor health. Jagtar is suffering. Sewa needs to get married, and soon."

Bikram and his family had invited Ajit and Sher Singh to the mansion to plead their case for an early wedding.

"We need Pinki here to help run the household," Chand said. "Sewa has quit college, he is so worried about his parents. He is managing the grain shop and helping me with the properties."

"I want nothing more than to have Pinki here to grace my home. I don't want silver or gold or anything." Jagtar sighed. "I need my daughter-in-law to take over. Only then will I be able to recover."

Ajit saw that Jagtar did look unusually tired and subdued.

Bikram sat quietly next to his mother, who had her arm around his shoulders.

Ajit sighed. "My ambition was always to let Pinki study for as long as she desired. She is a good student, as you all know. It is going to be hard telling her that she must quit college."

"I see your dilemma," Bikram finally said, speaking in a soft voice. "But this is an unexpected situation. We didn't know we were both going to suffer with health issues."

"Well, Inder and Jeet Kaur have almost put together the dowry. Toofan is being broken to be ridden."

Ajit was relenting, and he wondered how much the erosion of his initial reluctance had to do with Nasib's insistence that he would not marry until after Pinki was wed. Was he betraying Pinki because of his selfish desire to have Nasib sire grandsons for him as soon as possible? Pinki would be only seventeen at the time of her wedding. Was he letting her go too young, and robbing her of an education? Or was he looking after her best interests by doing everything he could to see her settled with a good family, facing a happy future? Which was the right path for his beautiful granddaughter?

He nodded.

"That settles it then." Lal Singh smiled.

Too late now for any qualms, Ajit thought.

Some colour came back to Jagtar's cheeks. "I can't wait to welcome Pinki to her new home."

"This autumn?" Bikram sat up straighter. "I realize you will want the summer crops harvested first."

"Agreed." Ajit stood up and accepted their embraces.

"Ramu," Bikram shouted. "Ice water and glasses. Bring a plate of boar pickle, too."

"Ladies." Chand motioned for the women to leave.

Jagtar bent to touch Ajit's feet.

"Live long and un-widowed," he said.

When the women had gone, the men settled back into their seats, drank smooth imported whiskey, and bit into the fiery pickle. And they made plans for the grand wedding to come. Of course, since Bikram was a cabinet minister, they could expect many dignitaries— Bikram thought at least three hundred would attend, including the Chief Minister. A military band would lead the groom's procession, with Sewa riding on a white horse.

Ajit could see it in his mind's eye. Caught up in the grandeur of the event he felt elated now, and very sure. He nodded vigorously.

Sher patted his back and smiled. "Now that will be a sight to see."

"Trust Bikram to rise to the occasion." Chand was glowing.

"I have but one son and one grandson. We will spare no expense. It will be first class all the way," Bikram's humble father said.

"And I promise you we will be good hosts." Ajit was nodding enthusiastically. "This wedding will be unforgettable."

Pinki was not happy.

"Babaji, why are you rushing this? I really want to get my degree."

"Sewa's parents are not healthy. They need you to run the mansion."

"But I have other ambitions," Pinki said.

She was home for two weeks of holidays.

"I pushed it as far back as possible, Pinki."

"And we have to go to Ludhiana tomorrow to have you measured for your wedding suit and dowry clothes. Also, we have to visit the jewellers so you can select your gold sets," Inder said.

"Babaji, none of my friends are even engaged yet," Pinki said.

"We are rural people, Pinki. We follow the old ways."

"What old ways? Everything is changing. Only we seem to be stuck in the past, Babaji."

He let her carry on, get it out of her system.

"Even Paso's father cancelled her promise. She will probably become a nurse long before she even considers being married. And me? I have no choice?"

Her lips trembled, and Basanti stepped closer to her.

"Maa, speak up. Support me, please!"

Basanti wiped her tears and hugged her.

Siamo was still against the rushed wedding, and of course she had no trouble standing up to him.

"So, what would Satwant and Amrita say to this, Bir? You know they believed in education. They would have wanted Pinki to have choices!"

He reminded her of Nasib's stubbornness. "I am caught in a dilemma. What does a year matter for Pinki, one way or another?"

But guilt overcame him, and he quickly sipped his tea and stood up. "I am going to the cattle yard." As he hurried his steps, he could still hear Pinki's wails behind him.

When he heard the news, Ajit's old friend the Comrade came over to the haveli to deliver his verdict.

"I told you once before, Ajit—Bikram Singh is a fraud. And now he is rushing Pinki into marriage for selfish reasons of his own. Such a lovely girl, your granddaughter, so smart, and you are content to see her leave college and live under that man's roof? It saddens me to say it, but I have lost respect for you, my friend."

He did not come to the haveli again after that.

Basanti

Nikki insisted on tagging along on the next shopping trip to Ludhiana, and Jeet Kaur, the girls' maternal grandmother, picked them all up in her car. The driver would do double duty by carrying their parcels all day.

First, they visited the goldsmith's shop. Jewellery sets—necklace, earrings, bangles, and rings—were brought out in satin-lined boxes for their inspection. Some designs were plain and some were jewel-studded. Basanti was amazed to see that some sets cost more than her yearly wages.

"Maaji, I want to buy Pinki a set myself." She had been saving her money for five years now.

Bapuji, who was sitting reading a paper while they shopped, looked up and shook his head. "You already gave something more valuable than gold to Pinki, a mother's love and devotion."

But Maaji looked at her sympathetically and said, "All right, Basanti, but only one piece of jewellery, not a whole set."

"What would you like from me, Pinki?"

Pinki thought for a moment. "A necklace, Maa. I will always wear it, never take it off."

Though Pinki had set out with a cloud of resentment hanging over her head, she now seemed to be warming to the idea of being a bride, stepping into the spotlight, and offering her family an occasion for celebration.

"What about me? What do I get?" Nikki asked.

"Basanti will buy you one for your wedding, Nikki. How's that?" Maaji said, and she mussed the girl's hair.

"Maaji, why don't I buy identical necklaces for them? You can put Nikki's away until her wedding."

"Spoken like a mother."

The jeweller started bringing out a variety of simple necklaces.

"I have one design that we have carried in this store for generations. It will not be changed, at least in my lifetime." He disappeared behind the curtain and emerged with a sturdy necklace made with a series of small filigreed gold balls in graduated sizes linked together with beautiful chain work.

Pinki tried it on. "I love it."

Nikki tried it on next and made a big deal of looking at herself in the mirror from various angles, batting her eyelids.

"All right, all right, Miss Film Star," Pinki huffed.

At the cloth merchant's shop, the tailors took measurements by draping the selected fabrics around Pinki. Suddenly she looked like a bride, and this took Basanti's breath away. In the electric light of the store, Pinki's features looked stunning, and everyone—including the merchant, his assistants, and the elderly tailor—complimented her lavishly.

Nikki made faces.

"You are next, little sister. I will see you here in a few years," the merchant teased.

Pinki's hope chests arrived and stood side by side in the main hall. Maaji kept them covered with old sheets. The beautiful new bedding was carefully sorted, rolled, and tied with twine before being stacked inside. New items commissioned for Pinki's dowry were arriving almost every day. Maaji kept her list handy and struck them off one by one.

When something heavy needed to be moved, Basanti would sometimes find herself close to Nasib, holding on to the handles of a trunk or pushing a heavy box alongside him. They couldn't help touching each other. Once, while pushing a heavy chest, they paused for breath. For a moment their eyes locked.

"It's not just your cooking I like," Nasib whispered.

She dared not breathe.

"I like you."

O Laxmi Maa, she prayed. They were alone in the hall, but she could hear Maaji and Siamo talking outside.

He gently caressed her cheek.

The voices came closer. As if on cue, they both attacked the hope chest again and pushed it, it slid, and they had it where Maaji wanted it. Perspiration ran down their faces, and she saw his eyes drop to her heaving bosom, then rise again to gently meet her own. She felt herself blush and lifted her chador to wipe her face so no one would notice.

Things started to change after that. When they passed each other Nasib would smile at her. When they worked together, he would make it so that their arms or fingers would brush. She did not want to encourage him, make him see her as a loose woman. She was a widow, and a Bajigarni. He was of another world. And what if he were not serious? Could it be that he was just playing a selfish game? Eventually, when she didn't reciprocate beyond a shy smile, he stopped, and after that he went around with a sad look, like a kicked puppy. Her heart went out to him then.

It was especially hard for her whenever another proposal came for Nasib. The girls would ask a lot of questions and prolong her misery by discussing the candidate's age, height, wealth, and looks.

"What do you think, Chacha?" Nikki would ask. "I like this one."

Usually Nasib managed to remain impassive, keeping his feelings to himself. But one day he exploded.

"Do you remember Bholi? Everyone liked her, too, but do you have any idea how humiliating that was for me? Change the subject, please. I want to eat in peace."

The family was startled into silence, but Nikki would not be hushed.

"Who's this Bholi, Chacha?" she blurted out at last. "Tell me and I will go rip off her braid."

"You will what, Nikki?" Maaji glared at her.

"No one insults my family, nobody!"

Bapuji looked at her with narrowed eyes. "I am still alive, Nikki. It is for me to decide whom to fight."

The mood was tense, but Pinki found a way to lighten it.

"Don't you know, Babaji, we have our own warrior queen, Jhansi ki Rani?" she asked.

"That's right. People do call Nikki Jhansi ki Rani when she rides out on Bakki." Siamo grinned.

"I won't use a sword, you know," Nikki said. "I will take Babaji's rifle and shoot them."

"My rifle?"

"Yes, Babaji. I found it in your steel wardrobe."

"Nikki!" Bapuji shouted. "I keep that under lock and key. Nikki, don't ever do anything like that again," Bapuji said.

"I was just curious." Nikki pouted.

"You had better keep the key with you at all times from now on," Maaji said.

Bapuji stood up. "I am going upstairs to check my rooms."

"Lock the rum in your wardrobe while you're at it, Ji," Maaji said. "Nikki just might decide to check that out, too, one day."

Nasib started to laugh.

"Let's arm-wrestle, Chacha. I will beat you." Nikki moved over to sit opposite to him.

"I love you, my Nikki, my dear niece." He reached over the table and embraced her.

"I love you, too, Chacha, and no Bholi is ever going to humiliate you. I will never let that happen to you."

Siamo watched them lock hands and set their jaws. "She drank your milk, Basanti."

"Yes, I am a Jat Bajigarni," Nikki shouted, and she nailed Nasib's hand to the table.

Bikram

Bikram was worried. What was happening to him? First, just seeing a photo of the skull in a newspaper had provoked a seizure, and now he felt his mind dulled by heavy medications. Was he falling apart? Back in Samrala to recuperate, he knew it was crucial that he regain his health, both physical and mental. But first he had to set his own household in order.

He took away Jagtar's pills and doled them out to her exactly according to the prescriptions—no one else, it seemed, had been able to do this. After a couple of weeks, Jagtar seemed to regain her energy. She even began to take pleasure in planning Sewa's wedding.

Sewa, however, didn't last long in Ludhiana. One day Mangal dragged him by the collar and brought him back to the mansion. Apparently the Hakeem's treatment had not worked, and Sewa had misbehaved once again. Mangal was furious.

"The idiot tried to test himself on my maid. She resisted, screamed bloody murder, and he almost beat her to death. It's all I could do to convince her to be treated by a private doctor and stay away from the police."

Sewa sat with his head bowed.

"What is wrong with you?" Bikram asked.

Sewa said nothing.

"I think his hormones are running amok," Mangal said. "I can't help you any more, Bikram. I am done. He is an animal."

Bikram turned to Mangal. "I will take it from here. He will stay and work with me."

The new rules were simple. Sewa had to be at the grain shop when it opened in the morning. He would sit there and watch the munshi and learn the details of running the business. He would return home in the company of his grandfather and not stop anywhere in the bazaar.

A half bottle of whiskey awaited him to be drunk, in company, before dinner, and then off to bed. Bikram personally checked Sewa's bedroom regularly for smut. He hoped that a few months of clean living under strict watch would bring some sanity and discipline to the youth.

But two weeks later, while he was at the shop, Sewa, on some pretext, went into the warehouse. Soon there came a scream. Bikram ran into the warehouse to find Sewa atop a young girl who worked there with her family. Her skirt had been hiked above her hips and Sewa was struggling feverishly to spread her knees. The girl's father arrived on the scene and he and Bikram together pulled the crazed Sewa away from the screaming girl.

"What the hell were you thinking?" Bikram shouted, raining blows on his son.

"I will kill him!" The girl's father said, frantically searching for something to hit Sewa with. The warehouse filled with people from the market, and the munshi smuggled Sewa out the back door.

The labourers immediately announced a dharna to close the market until the grievous act was punished and justice served. And Bikram felt the sting of acute embarrassment—the sneers on people's faces, the fire in their eyes, and the poison of their words.

"Settle it," the head of the grain dealers' association told him. "And fast."

It took long, hard negotiations to keep the matter under wraps. Money changed hands. The girl was compensated with a full year's wages and sent to her home village in Uttar Pradesh. Sewa became a prisoner inside the mansion.

Bikram was now an outcast in the grain market. He began to realize that his son could very well be a monster—a rapist, and a psychopath without an iota of conscience. Thank God, he would soon be wed. It was the only way to save him from himself.

ॐ

Preparations for the wedding were in full swing. Beeji and Maaji spent their days at the mansion making lists of guests and sending invitations. They shopped for three full days in Ludhiana, returning late in the evening, loaded down with fabrics and gifts. The best tailor was summoned from the city to measure Bikram and his whole family for their wedding outfits. Gifts of clothing and shoes were bought for the servants.

Gifts started to arrive from builders, contractors, merchants, and businessmen for whom Bikram had approved jobs, subsidies, and licences. Cases of liquor, stacks of cash, and gold were delivered by car. Jagtar accepted each and every offering, then stored them in a room under lock and key. In the evening, she gave Bikram a detailed description of each gift, calculated its value, and cross-referenced it to the status of the giver. She made a list on a ledger for later reference.

It amazed him when Sewa agreed to riding lessons. Papaji accompanied him to the police stables and brought him back with glowing reports of Sewa's efforts at horsemanship.

"He even went to the dairy to see the stall for the mare he is going to get in his dowry."

"Toofan."

"Yes, Toofan."

At dinner, Sewa's uncle, Darshan, told him, "I saw Toofan being ridden past the Adda by Baru Marasi the other day. The Zaildar's granddaughter, Nikki, was right behind him riding the filly's dam, Bakki."

"Is that so?" Beeji asked. "The Zaildar lets her behave that way, like a wild child?"

"Yes, Beeji," Darshan said. "He is an erudite and broad-minded man. On top of all that, Nikki is also very pretty. She looks very regal riding the mare. People call her their Jhansi ki Rani."

"What's Pinki like?" Beeji asked.

"I only see her getting on or off the bus. She is very feminine, not like her sister, and so, so beautiful," Darshan said.

"We got you a good one, Sewa." Beeji cheered.

"Pinki will improve our breed," Bikram said.

Sewa reared his head in anger. "What is that supposed to mean?"

"Look at you, look at your mother, look at me. Do you see much in the way of physical beauty, height, or fair colouring? Next to us, Pinki looks like a memsahib."

Sewa got up and stormed out.

"You must stop putting him down, Ji."

"Jagtar, the day he starts behaving, I will start praising him."

"But, Ji, at least stop humiliating him in front of other people. Imagine how that makes him feel."

"I couldn't care less."

On the day of the wedding, everything went according to plan. It was just as Bikram had long imagined: the military band, the white police gelding that Sewa rode to the haveli gates, the hospitality of the Zaildar, the elegant settings, and the exquisite food and drinks. He could not have asked for more. Even the November weather co-operated, and it was pleasantly cool and free of troublesome bugs.

Pinki had insisted that she would not wear a veil, which had made Bikram slightly nervous, but many of his guests seemed to admire her for it. Even the Chief Minister approved.

"We are Sikhs. Why are we following old Mughal traditions of purdah?"

The ceremony itself was conducted by the Raikot Giyani, assisted by a team of pious-looking elders. The hymn-singers hired from Amritsar mesmerized the congregation. The Sikhya was read by one of Jorawar's daughters and offered advice to the newlywed couple as to how they would become two souls in one.

The poet laureate of Punjab read a poem specially written for the occasion, and the guests rewarded him with a shower of rupees.

Sewa was resplendent in his wedding suit. Papaji and Chand smiled constantly, impressed by the flower arrangements, the decorations, the attentive servers and waiters. They were even more impressed when Bikram told them that the catering was done by the Gulmohr Hotel in Ludhiana.

"The Zaildar is loaded," they said.

The showing of the dowry was a breathtaking affair. The sheer opulence, quality, and quantity cried money, and lots of it. Gold sets glistened in the mid-afternoon sun. The heavy brass pots, polished to a brilliant sheen, stood lined up on a long table. The eleven nimari cots and bedrolls were admired, as were the magnificent twin hope chests. People lingered over the suits, blankets, and stoles.

Bikram had kept one thing secret. He hadn't even told the grandfathers about it.

A shiny, new Ambassador car was driven in, its roof draped with a colourful sheet called a fulkari, and there was pin-drop silence as people stared with open mouths. No one had ever heard of a car being given or received in a dowry. It was unprecedented. Even Sewa rushed over to admire it. Papaji and Chand insisted on sitting in it.

"You've set a new standard, Zaildar," the Chief Minister said to Ajit Singh.

"No, the car is a gift from the bride's maternal grandfather."

The Chief Minister patted the Jagirdar's shoulder.

The guests were now invited to step outside the haveli gates for a performance. They stood lined up on either side of the newly paved path, which now looked like a proper road. A drum roll sounded from around a corner at the junction where the path joined the village ring road. People strained to see.

The drum picked up a toe-tapping beat, and the first drummer was joined by others, who spread out to let a party of exotically dressed Bajigar dancers shimmy by. The dancers led the way to the Adda, followed by a group of men performing the Baji. The wiry-looking men jumped high, performed somersaults, walked upside-down on their hands, and formed a breathtaking human pyramid. The onlookers clapped and shouted their praise.

Suddenly the drums stopped, and Bikram heard the thunder of hoofbeats as a rider came around the haveli atop a galloping mare, its nostrils flared and ears flat. The sight of the handsome, muscular beast brought a crescendo of applause. It slowed down before the Adda; then the rider, a slim, turbaned figure, made the mare turn in tight circles, backstep, and twirl on its hind legs—a feat most of the audience had never seen before. The drums began a slow, rhythmic beat. The rider stopped in front of Bikram and the Chief Minister, and jumped off the saddle in one graceful motion.

The turban came off and a long braid unfolded to reveal a young woman. She bowed, and Bikram noted a look of both surprise and admiration on Sewa's smiling face.

"Jhansi ki Rani, Jhansi ki Rani!" many in the crowd cried, and soon the chant was picked up by all the spectators.

The Chief Minister stepped forward and took the girl into his embrace, placed a hand on her head, and announced, "I present to you all a daughter of Punjab. A princess of Punjab. A Kaur of the Sikhs!"

Someone hurried over and whispered in the Chief Minister's ear.

"A daughter of our revered martyr Captain Satwant Singh," the leader announced. "I am honoured by your performance, Nikki. May Waheguru-ji bless you."

"Stole the show, she did." Mangal shook his head in wonderment. "I have never seen anything like it. That girl was fantastic. I hope one of my daughters grows up to be just like her. I think I will buy them a mare and get them trained on it. I have neglected them enough."

There was a wistful tone to his voice that surprised Bikram. Mangal barely ever mentioned his daughters at all.

They were riding to the mansion in Samrala in a car right behind the new Ambassador, which was now decorated with garlands and carried Sewa and Pinki in the back seat. The military band preceded them. People waited on the road to gawk. Some waved.

"Did you see the mare she was riding?" Chand still had a stunned look on his face.

"Toofan. What did I tell you? She's a beauty, a majestic beast," Bikram said.

"It will now grace our household." Papaji joined his hands to mutter a quick prayer.

"That was a wondrous day," Chand said for what seemed like the hundredth time at least.

Bikram sat back and soaked in the words, the looks, and the sheer satisfaction that filled his soul with joy. He felt as though he was finally reaching his destiny after a journey down a long, winding, and often rocky road. The euphoria made him light-headed.

Mangal opened a bottle and passed it to Papaji, who took the first sip before handing it to Chand. Bikram got it next and took a swig as Papaji watched anxiously. The doctor had strongly advised him against drinking alcohol.

"It's a very special day," he said. He took another swig before passing it to Mangal.

The gates of the mansion swung open and Jagtar led the women to open the new car's door and help Pinki out. The women sang a song of welcome, and Bikram's mother poured oil on the posts to welcome the bride to her new home. Pinki was escorted through the courtyard and into the mansion. The courtyard was lit with colourful electric lights strung in rows from every direction. A dozen round tables were arrayed on one side. Bottles, jugs of ice water, and glasses stood on the tables. Waiters were poised to bring out steaming trays of fritters and samosas.

"Sit," Bikram said to all.

"Cheers!" Mangal raised a bottle.

"Cheers," the men said.

Inside, the women kept up their singing.

Sewa sat with his father and the other men. The suhaag raat was scheduled for the next night, Jagtar being concerned that the showing-the-face ceremony for Pinki might last until late into the night—too late to set up the new marital bed.

Bikram looked at his son and smiled. "Now you are married, Sewa. And tomorrow you become a real man."

The next morning, the men went to the dairy, where Toofan was shown to the townsfolk and greatly admired. The women took Pinki to pray at the local gurudwara and offer prasad at the Hindu temple, then they returned to the mansion for a showing of a portion of the dowry—the jewels and suits only. Neighbourhood women cooed and gushed before blessing Pinki and dropping notes into her lap.

"Bikram Singh, your mansion will glow from your daughter-in-law's beauty. No need for candles and lights," an older woman said loudly, and others nodded.

"Sewa is a very fortunate young man!" This from the woman who lived on the street behind the mansion, whose husband owned a guard dog that barked all day at passersby.

After lunch, Bikram went to rest on the roof, where it was quiet. When he woke up around four he felt refreshed and rested. On his way downstairs he heard Jagtar speaking in Sewa's room. He poked his head in.

"We are preparing for their suhaag raat," she said, as other women hung bunting and moved furniture.

"Who's with Pinki?"

"Your Maaji."

In the gathering room he found Mangal and Chand lying on sofas, snoring. Papaji dozed in an armchair, an open newspaper at his feet.

Darshan was counting money. Bikram sat down beside him and waved at the stacks of notes. "I've never seen such generosity at a wedding." He hoped it was a good omen.

The evening was inevitably an anticlimax after the boisterous celebrations of the day before. Bikram sat with Mangal sipping a small shot and enjoying a bit of peace. He could hear the women talking in the dining room and sometimes laughing. They were probably teasing each other, and Pinki. Later, he heard them climbing up the stairs.

Ramu came to announce that the meal was ready, and Sewa joined them at the table. He looked flushed and his eyes were red.

"What's with you?"

"I just woke up."

"You slept all evening?"

Sewa did not reply. He played with his food.

"He's probably nervous," Mangal said with a grin.

"Now you be good, Sewa. Be gentle and loving," Bikram said.

"You wait this long to give me instructions?"

His insolence was infuriating, but Bikram controlled the urge to lash out at his son.

"All your father is trying to tell you is to create a good first impression," Mangal said. "It's very important, Sewa, in establishing a solid foundation for the future."

They heard the women coming down the stairs singing a racy ditty.

"She should have veiled herself," Sewa said.

Bikram looked up, frowning. "Pinki has the right to refuse to veil her face. This is not old times."

"I hated the way everyone stared at her bare face."

"I stared, too. Not because her face was bare but because she looked so beautiful sitting beside you in front of the Holy Granth. I was so proud that my son got this lovely match. I was happy."

"So was I." Mangal nodded. "I think Pinki is a very well-brought-up girl. Very humble and respectful. She touched my feet twice today. I absolutely adore her."

"She'd better touch my feet tonight."

"Now, now, Sewa. Calm down. Be patient."

After seeing the other women off, Jagtar came in and sat beside them.

"How's my sweet boy?"

"I am all right."

"Listen, after you eat, make sure to wash your hands and face and clean your teeth before you go upstairs for your suhaag raat."

"I will."

"Don't stay up too late with these old men."

"This old man is going to go to bed now." Mangal wiped up the last bit of curry with a finger and licked it.

"You should sleep tonight in one of the bedrooms downstairs," Jagtar said.

"All right. I get it. The newlyweds need their privacy."

Sewa looked up. "Good night, Uncle."

Bikram and Jagtar were alone with their son for the first time in many days.

"I am so happy, Sewa." Jagtar rubbed his back. "You are married to a beautiful wife. I have someone now to help with the household. Your father can go back to Chandigarh with his mind at rest."

Those words rang true to Bikram. At last, his life might start to feel right again. When his head finally hit the pillow that night, a sense of calm settled over him. All was well in his world.

Bikram woke with a start. Someone was shaking him.

"Wake up, please. Wake up."

The light came on and he searched for his glasses. Sewa stood beside the bed.

"Help me, Mummy. Help!"

"Why are you shaking? What's going on?" Jagtar got up in a panic.

"It's Pinki. Something is wrong with her!"

"What's happening?" Mangal loomed in the doorway.

Sewa ran to him and fell at his feet. Loud sobs rose from his throat.

"Help, Uncle. Help. It's Pinki."

"Is she sick?"

"No, she is not moving. Just hanging there."

Bikram leaped from the bed. He pushed past the others and ran up the stairs. Outside Sewa's open door, he came to a dead stop. It was a nightmare vision he saw.

Pinki was hanging against the wall, her feet a foot above the floor. Her eyes were closed, her mouth agape, and her arms and legs dangled limply. She almost seemed to be levitating.

"Oh, God."

Mangal pushed past him, followed by Jagtar.

"What the hell?" Mangal pulled her a bit and then leaned to look behind her head. He stepped back in shock.

"She is impaled on the keela. It's all the way into her skull."

Jagtar began to scream, and Mangal quickly put his hand over her mouth.

"Shush. No one say a thing, don't make any noise."

Bikram felt his world collapsing. As Sewa crawled past him, he felt a powerful urge to kick his son's head in.

"It's not my fault, believe me," Sewa pleaded with joined hands.

"Shut up." Mangal glared at him with red-rimmed eyes. "Shut up. You don't want to wake up the neighbours."

Bikram stumbled to the marital bed, which was still covered in rosebuds. The sheets were barely wrinkled.

"What happened? Tell us, Sewa. The truth!"

Sewa lifted his face up. Tears ran down his cheeks.

"I just wanted her to touch my feet. That's all. She started to shake her head. I was angry, and I cursed her for keeping her face bare for everyone to see. She tried running past me to the door, and I pushed her—I must have pushed her hard—and flung her against the wall. She just hung there. She shook for a while and went still. I kept calling her name but she—"

"A push?" Mangal said. "A push that lifted her almost two feet in the air and slammed her into the wall with enough force to drive a six-inch keela into her skull?"

"Oh, God. Oh, God," Jagtar moaned.

Blind anger rose up in Bikram. "You will hang for this, you animal."

Sewa started to whimper and hid his face in his hands.

Jagtar shook, her eyes wide. "No, no, Ji. My son cannot hang. It was not his fault."

"No one has to hang," Mangal said. "Shut up, all of you." He pushed Sewa towards the bathroom. "Go wash your face."

Mangal thought for a minute, then turned to Bikram. "Remember what I told you on the roof, Bikram?"

His mind raced, and then it came to him. That time they had gone up there with Gopal. Mangal had offered to toss Jagtar over the balustrade to the cobbled street fifty feet below so that Bikram could marry again. He held his breath.

"I can take Pinki up there and drop her head-first onto the street below. Make it look like an accident."

"A suicide," Jagtar whispered. "A suicide. Nothing will happen to Sewa then."

Bikram dropped his head between his knees to keep from throwing up.

"We will need some plausible story about why she felt compelled to jump," Jagtar said, her voice terrifyingly smooth and cold.

They sat in silence. Sewa came out of the washroom and looked from one face to the other.

"Help me lower her, very carefully now," Mangal said. "You clean up here, Jagtar. Leave no trace."

Jagtar leapt up and found a towel. There was blood on the keela, but none on the wall or the floor. She began to wipe furiously. She went into the washroom and came back with a damp cloth. Soon the keela shone clean.

"Stay silent. Turn off the lights."

They sat frozen, listening to his footsteps as he laboured up two flights of stairs with Pinki in his arms. When all was quiet, they hurried downstairs. Sewa stayed in his room.

A few minutes later, a dog started to bark.

Ajit

The pounding on the gates and the shouting outside awoke Ajit and he looked at the radium dial on his watch. It was four in the morning. He switched on the light, found his sandals, and stepped out his door just as Nasib came rushing out of his room.

"Turn the light on. Be careful on the stairs," he cautioned Nasib because of his weak foot.

Ajit hurried to open the gates and shielded his eyes from the headlights of a jeep. It took him back suddenly to the night he'd heard of Satwant's death. Only this time there was no soldier; it was Jorawar who stood in front of him.

"Pinki had an accident. She is at the Civil Hospital in Samrala. We have to get there."

"What? Pinki?"

"Please get dressed. I will wait here."

Ajit turned and hurried back upstairs just as a light came on in the haveli downstairs and Inder shouted, "What is happening?"

He dressed with shaking hands. Nasib was at the gates with Inder and Basanti, talking with Jorawar. He felt their fear and panic.

"That's all I know," Jorawar was saying. "I received a call from the police station. We will know more once we get there."

Ajit clambered into the jeep and saw the eyes of all three staring at him as the driver shifted gears and they lurched forward, the noise of the engine amplified in the still night.

They raced up the road, over the Nilon Bridge, towards Samrala. Ajit had a dozen questions, but there was nothing more Jorawar could tell him. There had been an accident, and Pinki was in the hospital.

The jeep came to a stop inside the hospital gates. They elbowed their way through the considerable crowd that had gathered there, and Jorawar led him through the main door into a waiting room.

350 SOHAN S KOONAR

A man in a white coat greeted them and pulled them into an office. Bikram was there, sitting on a bench with Jagtar. He rose, collapsed into Ajit's arms, and started to cry.

Ajit's heart fell. He could barely breathe. His mind went blank.

"Pinki is no more, Zaildar. Pinki is no more."

Pinki? *Pinki is no more?* He had sent her off in her bridal finery barely a day before!

Jagtar joined them. "I am so sad, so sad. I am inconsolable. It hurts so bad."

"No," Ajit heard himself shout. "No, no, no!"

Jorawar's strong hands pushed him down into a chair and pulled his head into an embrace, cradling him as he wept, muttering words he couldn't understand. Through a fog he heard the wails of Jagtar and Bikram.

Ajit was still in a daze when the white-coated doctor led him into a hallway and down a few yards to a closed door, where he knocked. It opened and a familiar face appeared. It was Paso, dressed in her nurse's uniform. She turned to reveal a draped figure on a gurney and began to peel back the wet sheet. Ajit screamed at the sight of Pinki's matted hair and bloodied face. Her twisted body lay on a slab of ice in the fetid, airless room.

What violence has been visited on her? A sickening rage rose up in him.

He heard the voice of the doctor. "She was found on the street behind the mansion. Looks as though she jumped off the roof."

Impossible! he wanted to scream. *Impossible! A lie!*

"We will investigate," Jorawar whispered in his ear. "Thank you, doctor."

He was led out and back into the office. Bikram and Jagtar were gone.

The doctor sat down in front of them. Offered water and tea.

The police inspector arrived and saluted Jorawar, then bent down to offer condolences.

"We scoured the street, went up onto the roof, inspected the mansion. Nothing suspicious. Nothing at all."

"Sewa?" Jorawar asked.

"Dead drunk. Passed out in his room. We couldn't wake him up."

"Servants?"

"According to Minister Singh, the servants sleep in rooms he built for them at the dairy. They would not know anything."

"Was there anyone else?"

"There was a guard, retired army, outside the gates all night with a shotgun. He claims he heard nothing from his position and wasn't aware anything was wrong until neighbours alerted him that they had found the bride on the street behind the mansion."

"Anyone else at the mansion?"

"Mangal Singh was sitting in the gathering room when we got there. Kept talking about how Pinki respected him by twice touching his feet. Denied hearing any noise. He said he had slept on the ground floor to let Sewa and Pinki enjoy privacy on their suhaag raat."

"Where are Bikram Singh and his wife?" Ajit asked. It seemed odd that they had disappeared.

"Gone home to bathe and change clothes, I'm told," the police inspector said.

"Look," said Jorawar, "my brother is a sessions judge. He will be here soon with my father. Get the sub-divisional magistrate to cancel court for today and hold an urgent hearing into this tragedy. Bring the parents and Sewa there by eight sharp. Wake him up, even if you have to slap him awake."

"Yes, Superintendent Sahib. It will be done."

"Zaildar-ji," the doctor said, "I can give you something to help."

Ajit looked up and his eyes met those of the kind young man.

"Give me my Pinki back," he said.

The sub-divisional magistrate held the hearing in his court. The clerk closed the doors to the crowd gathered outside. Ajit sat between Sher and Kulbir. Jorawar stood with the police inspector. Jagtar and Bikram sat holding each other. The civil surgeon, the doctor who had spoken to them at the hospital, sat alone.

"Can you tell us what happened last night?" the magistrate asked Bikram.

"We had a very pleasant evening. Jagtar and the women prepared the marital bed. They escorted Pinki upstairs. Mangal went to bed early, downstairs. Jagtar and I sat with Sewa and gave him advice.

Then we went to bed as well."

"Did you hear any commotion, any noises upstairs?"

"No."

"How did you find out that Pinki had fallen off the roof?"

"The neighbour who lives behind us told us that his dog started barking and woke him up. He went outside onto the street with a flashlight and found Pinki lying on the cobblestones."

They waited to let him compose himself. Jagtar cried into her chador.

"The neighbour got help and they rushed Pinki to the hospital. A couple came to pound on our gate to wake us and we rushed over to the hospital and found out that she was dead on arrival."

The magistrate turned to the civil surgeon.

"I can confirm that there was no pulse, no heartbeat. There was considerable trauma from the fall."

"Was the fall the cause of death?"

"Yes. I can perform a post-mortem to ascertain the clinical details."

There was a knock at the door. A constable came in with Sewa, dishevelled and looking around wildly.

"Come here, you," Jagtar shouted. "Tell us what happened last night. What made Pinki so distraught that she had to jump off the roof?"

"Tell us, son," Bikram said.

"I was just told that my wife is dead," Sewa said, his lips trembling.

"Something happened, I am sure of it." Jagtar slapped Sewa. "Tell me!"

"Give him a glass of water," the magistrate said.

Sewa calmed down a bit, coughed, wiped his face, blew his nose, took another gulp from the glass.

"We argued. I said bad words. Accused her."

"Accused her? Of what?"

Sewa quickly glanced at Ajit and hung his head again.

"Pinki was not pure."

A stunned silence fell across the room. Ajit felt blood rush to his face.

"You scolded her, threatened her, Sewa?" the magistrate asked.

"I said a lot of bad words. I was angry. Disappointed."

"That's enough," Kulbir shouted.

"Leave us," Sher ordered everyone. "Please, the family needs a moment alone."

The courtroom was cleared, and only Ajit, Jorawar, Kulbir, and Sher remained. The four of them sat staring at the walls.

"My God," Jorawar said, holding his head in his hands.

Sher too looked shocked.

Kulbir finally spoke. "The post-mortem won't reveal anything about the cause of death that the civil surgeon can't already tell from looking at the body. The only point would be to confirm Sewa's statement."

Ajit felt as though he was going to throw up. The thought of the doctor's fingers violating Pinki in her death shook him to his core.

"I can't allow that."

Kulbir let a minute go by.

"We have to think about the stigma that will follow. We have young girls still to be wed. The post-mortem report would be filed all the way to Chandigarh and read by men we know and who respect us. No. I think you've made the right decision. There is no use in having Pinki . . ."

Cut up. The unspoken words stabbed at Ajit's heart. He felt his chest tighten, and Jorawar brought him a glass of water. The accusation of Pinki's impurity made him feel so ashamed that he wanted to die on the spot.

"Call the magistrate in, Kulbir. Let's get this over with and take Pinki home," Sher said.

The magistrate came in, followed by Jagtar and Bikram. The policemen stayed outside with Sewa.

"I don't want the word 'suicide' used," Kulbir said sadly. "Classify the death as a misadventure. No post-mortem. We accept Sewa's version of events. Officially, at least."

"As you say, Judge Sahib. That classification seems appropriate. I will prepare my report."

"I will arrange to have Pinki's body taken home," Jorawar said, and he walked out.

Ajit staggered home to give the terrible news to his family. He wished he could turn the clock back, because from here on, there would be no joy at the haveli, ever again.

Basanti

Basanti collapsed on the floor and started wailing, tearing her hair out.

"No, no, no, O Laxmi Maa, no. Take me instead! Give me my daughter back! Give me my Pinki back."

Women rushed to restrain her, held her so she would stop flailing. She could hear Maaji's wails, and Nikki's cries. After that, she felt as though she was aware only in flashes of consciousness.

Sehba and Mata had rushed over from the dera and took her to lie on a cot. Sehba held her as Mata wiped her face. Her screams were strangled, and her eyes burned with hot tears.

"Courage. Courage, my daughter. Courage," Mata whispered.

The speakers from the gurudwara crackled and the Giyani started reciting holy verses.

Basanti sat up, and now Pushpa was with her. The older woman leaned over her and muttered something she couldn't make out. She caressed Basanti's forehead, and her hand felt cool.

Someone shouted for Baru Marasi then, telling him to get fuel collected. They were already preparing the pyre for Pinki, to turn her to ashes! Terrible, impossible visions crowded her mind.

"Calm, Basanti. Calm," Pushpa said.

"The body is here," someone else said.

"Collect yourself, Basanti. There are rites to perform."

She reached deep down into her soul, struggled to find courage. She knew that she had to be strong for Nikki, Bapuji, Maaji, Siamo, and Nasib. They were Pinki's blood. She had to find the courage to face the inevitable.

She watched as four men carried Pinki's shrouded body and laid it on a cot in the centre of the courtyard. Jeet Kaur arrived, wailing loudly, and kneeled to take Pinki in her arms. The women moved to surround her as the men left and closed the gates behind them.

"I will perform the bathing," Pushpa said.

"I will help," Basanti said, her strength returning to her as she realized these would be the last few precious moments she would get with Pinki.

Pushpa gently unshrouded Pinki. Basanti gasped at the sight of Pinki's broken body, and the other women too cried out. With all the strength she could muster, choking with grief, Basanti lowered herself by the cot and slowly began to caress Pinki, the dear child of her heart.

The other women made way as Nikki approached, almost in a trance, drained by grief. Her voice was strangely quiet and sweet.

"What happened to you, my beautiful sister? What happened to you? You went away in your wedding finery and returned broken in a sack."

The grandfathers took the ashes to the holy city of Haridwar.

Maaji and Siamo sat with relatives and friends who came to mourn with them. Basanti held Nikki in her arms as much as she could. Nasib sat with the men for the seven days before the final prayers and the bhog at the gurudwara.

Bikram Singh and his wife stopped at the haveli with their usual entourage. Basanti served them tea. She was surprised that Sewa did not come with them.

His mother explained, "He is too distraught. Inconsolable."

He was inconsolable? And yet he had known Pinki for such a short time. Surely he could have pulled himself together long enough to pay his respects to the family that had raised and loved her.

They grieved in silence, didn't know if they were still alive. Weeks passed in this dazed state, then months. Siamo's hair went white quickly; Maaji's began to turn grey. Bapuji kept to himself upstairs and rarely ventured out. Nasib took over all his responsibilities.

"Can you send for the doctor, Basanti?" Siamo asked one morning. "I don't feel well at all."

"I think you might have a heart problem," the doctor said. "I can hear something." He put away his listening device.

"My heart is broken, Doctor." Siamo sighed.

"I will try to fix it." He gave her a packet of pills to take, one every morning. "Come to the centre in a week so I can examine you again."

A day later, Maaji fainted, and he was back.

"You need to start eating," he told her. "You can't live on an empty stomach."

It was only then that Basanti realized that Maaji had barely touched her food since Pinki died.

All of them needed to be watched. Siamo was dying of a broken heart, Maaji was starving herself to death, and Bapuji was drinking himself into oblivion. Nikki and Nasib were the only ones who had some life in them.

The haveli had to be maintained, and she would not fail in her duties. No matter how much she hurt.

Bikram

"They owe us a virgin bride."

When Jagtar's mother had demanded to know why Pinki had "jumped off the roof," they had of course given her their invented story: that she was not pure.

"Have you gone mad?" Bikram asked.

"Don't speak to my mother in that tone," Jagtar admonished him.

"Then tell her to keep her bloody nose out of our affairs."

"What's so bad about what she said, Ji?"

He closed and opened his fists. They had come within a hair's breadth of disaster. If not for Mangal's presence of mind, Sewa would have been rotting in prison right now. He and Jagtar would have been run out of Samrala. The Chief Minister would have fired him from the cabinet and the Congress Party. But Beeji and Jagtar were both smitten with Pinki's younger sister, Nikki. And here was the old bitch trying to resurrect the ancient tradition of a younger sister taking her deceased sister's place by marrying the widower. Did she seriously imagine that the Zaildar would offer Nikki as a replacement for Pinki?

"She is mad, completely mad, and you have lost your senses," he told Jagtar.

"Beeji is only asking for our rights."

"Rights to what?"

"A virgin bride. The other one was impure."

Oh, my God, he thought. *She's heard the lie so often, she's starting to believe it.*

"You are tempting fate, woman," he said.

"Fate favours us," Jagtar said.

"For how long?"

"Forever."

"Bitch."

Beeji stood up in a huff. "I won't sit here and listen to you abusing my daughter, Bikram."

"Then get the hell out, and stay out!" he shouted.

She turned and left, and Jagtar ran after her.

"Beeji, please."

For three days following that fateful night, his heart had not stopped racing. It was only after he'd learned that Pinki had been cremated, and her ashes collected, that he knew no further evidence existed of Sewa's crime. Since then he'd been working hard to have the sub-divisional magistrate, the police inspector, the civil surgeon, and anyone who had handled the body transferred to faraway places. The nursing student who was doing a clinical placement had gone back to her school in Ludhiana.

Going to the haveli and attending the bhog for Pinki had taken its toll on him. Even now, the guilt was soul-crushing. At home they had been discussing the business of what to do about Pinki's dowry. He was in favour of returning it in full, including the extravagant gifts that Jagtar's parents had received—the magnificent set of gold jewellery that Beeji wore, the thick gold kara that Chand kept on his wrist and his splendid imported watch.

He hadn't the slightest wish to pursue a relationship with the Zaildar, who remained ignorant of the real story of his beloved grand-daughter's death. Punjab was rife with blood feuds that spanned generations. An eye for an eye was a long-held Punjabi tradition, and specially bred in Jats.

Jagtar kept him awake three nights in a row weeping and crying for him to listen to what her mother suggested. They already had the dowry, and all that was needed was the Zaildar's blessing for Sewa to put a chador over Nikki's head. There was no need for a wedding, either. That was how it was done in the old days, how it was still done in the villages and among some lower castes. It was a blessing for poor fathers with too many daughters.

"Listen, Ji. Have courage, Ji," Jagtar said.

Tired of her voice droning in his ear, he nodded. "I will run it by the uncles."

"I love you, Ji. You are my hero, Ji."

Bikram went to visit the uncles in Ludhiana. He presented his proposal as an honoured tradition he wished to continue, so that a tragedy could have a meaningful end. The family bonds would remain cemented. It was to everyone's benefit. They listened to him and agreed to seek their father's support.

When he told Mangal, the big man's reaction was alarming.

"Have you gone mad, Bikram? Have those seizures burned some wires in your brain?"

"It was Jagtar's mother's request."

"That old hag is evil. You know it, Bikram. She is playing you. Look here, since that fateful night after I carried poor Pinki—"

"Stop. I don't even want you to say that out loud."

Mangal blinked and his Adam's apple bobbed up and down. He looked more haggard than Bikram could ever remember seeing him.

"Since then, I have been unable to sleep. I have nightmares. I know that I have done a lot of bad, dark things in my life, but that night changed me. I will never forget it, never." He paused, and when he spoke again it was in a whisper. "Such a sweet girl . . . that awful sound of her body hitting the cobblestones . . ."

The words Bikram never wanted to hear. He too couldn't help imagining the scene, running it over and over in his mind, and his stomach revolted. What was almost worse was to hear this confession from Mangal, the giant who, he had once believed, had no weakness, no conscience. A man who, in his own words, had been capable of countless dark deeds that never troubled his sleep. That shook him, more than almost anything else. He knew that the subject had to be taboo, never spoken of again. There was too much at stake, including, possibly, their own souls.

Ajit

Sher came with Jorawar and Kulbir to visit, and Ajit hosted them in his rooms upstairs. Nasib sat with them and they made small talk while Basanti served tea and biscuits. Once she went downstairs, Sher cleared his throat and began.

"Bikram Singh visited Jorawar and Kulbir. He expressed a desire for the relations to continue."

They did not have to spell it out to him. Ajit understood that Bikram must have asked for Nikki's hand for his son.

Nasib leaned forward. "Continue how?"

"Nasib, you might not understand, but it is an ancient custom to replace one daughter with the other," Sher explained.

"Is that so? Well, as the man who stood for Pinki in place of her late father, I say no."

Ajit was surprised by Nasib's firmness.

Sher sighed and looked to his sons for support.

"Listen, Nasib. Our family honours traditions," Kulbir said.

"It is not an unreasonable request," Jorawar added.

Ajit looked at Nasib, and he saw Satwant in his eyes. The same inquiring gaze, the same persistent quest for truth, the intelligence and strength of character. He felt proud, and decided to let Nasib have the floor.

"Did Bikram Singh guarantee Nikki's safety?" Nasib asked.

"Safety?" Jorawar frowned. "I don't understand."

"Yes, you do. Will Bikram guarantee that Nikki, too, won't feel compelled to jump off a roof to her death on her suhaag raat? Explain that to me." Nasib stuck out his jaw, daring them.

They sat in silence.

"Nasib," Ajit said gently. "There was a reason."

"What reason?"

Could he say it? Ajit had found it impossible to accept. All that seemed to matter, though, was that the husband had declared it.

"Sewa said she was . . . impure."

Nasib's eyes spat fire.

"And you paper lions believe that brat's accusation about a daughter of your house?"

Ajit felt both shamed and grateful that it was his son who had the strength to say this.

"Sewa is not a brat," Jorawar said, obviously stung by Nasib's insult.

"You are the big policeman. Did you know that just a few months before his wedding Sewa was caught red-handed trying to rape a young woman working in his father's warehouse? The labourers threatened to shut the market down. Bikram Singh paid a fortune to bury the story."

Ajit was stunned.

"Why didn't you tell us before?" Sher asked, his face suddenly pale.

"I found out only two weeks ago. I drove to Samrala to have a tractor wheel repaired. Got talking to a few drivers who were waiting to get their trucks fixed. Apparently, the whole town of Samrala knows the idiot is violent, twisted, and spoiled."

Sher looked at Jorawar, who looked away.

"Do you know anything about this, Jorawar? Did you hear anything?"

"Nothing."

"Are you sure?" Sher asked.

"I am." Jorawar stood up.

Sher and Kulbir followed.

"So, what should we say to Bikram Singh?" Sher asked.

"Tell him it's out of the question," Nasib said.

"Ajit?"

Ajit, shocked, could not find words.

"My father stands by my decision," Nasib said. "Nikki is not available as a replacement for Pinki. They failed to protect a daughter of my dead brother. They are not entitled to his only remaining memory."

"I think you might be mistaken, Nasib," Kulbir said.

"In that case, Kulbir, offer Sewa your daughter Jeetan. She is of marriageable age."

Kulbir was stunned.

"Let's leave, brother." Jorawar took Kulbir by the elbow.

Ajit would recall Sher and his sons scurrying from the haveli in their haste to get away.

Bikram

The answer came within a week. Both the wife of the Jagirdar and the wife of the Zaildar were accusing Bikram and Jagtar of failing to protect Pinki under their roof. There was no way that they would allow Nikki, the only living memory of their son, Satwant, to be given as a wife to Sewa. Please return the dowry and put the past to rest.

Jorawar and Kulbir were contrite and apologetic. They had done their best. Jagtar, however, became hysterical. She tore her chador and unbraided her hair, making a show of her utter humiliation.

"What do they think we are, Ji? Monsters? If we had known, we would have died saving Pinki! They've poured ashes on my head, Ji."

"Jagtar," he said. "Cut the drama and thank your lucky stars. One day, if you are fortunate enough to have granddaughters, you will appreciate how they feel."

"And how am I to have grandchildren now, Ji, when the whole world—including my own family—is turning against my lovely son?"

In the midst of all this, Sewa arrived home from the grain shop and sat down.

"What's going on?"

"We are returning the dowry in full," Bikram said sternly.

"Not the mare."

"Yes, the mare, too. Toofan came with the dowry and back she goes."

Sewa stood up. "I will not let you return the mare."

"Why not?"

"I want to keep it, I have to keep it."

"Why? When was the last time you rode her?"

"I will start riding her now. Give them back everything else, but not the mare."

"I can't do that."

"You know something, Father? You've sung that song too many times. *My son Sewa riding on a magnificent mare through the bazaar and stopping people in their tracks to stare in admiration and envy at him. Oh, that is my dream.* It's burned into my brain. Do you remember your own words?"

"I do," Jagtar said. "I remember the exact words you said to me, Ji. The day the Captain rode through the bazaar, Ji. You said, *I watched him in admiration but mostly in envy.*"

"I said that?"

"Yes, Ji. You did. Your words still ring in my ears."

Chand cleared his throat. "Bikram, offer to pay for the mare. Buy the beast and let's move on."

Bikram agreed. That made sense.

"See, Sewa?" Jagtar said triumphantly.

"You father is a very reasonable man, Sewa," Beeji said.

Bikram went to the dairy the next morning with the police sergeant to take another look at the mare and discuss a price. The sergeant remarked on the horse's glossy bay coat and the white star on her forehead, the white socks above the hooves. Just like her mother, Bakki.

"Remarkable, Minister Sahib. Perfect colour and markings. When you breed Toofan, lots of wealthy men will pay whatever you ask to have one of her offspring."

With that in mind, Bikram decided he would simply have to pay the market price for the mare, no matter how exorbitant it was. So he was very pleasantly surprised when the Zaildar allowed them to keep Toofan at no cost. He later learned that the Jagirdar had insisted on that. It was apparent that Sher Singh wanted to maintain a family connection, even if Ajit did not.

That night Bikram had a dream. In it, the mare raced along a dirt path straight towards him, churning up clouds of dust with every stride. When it reached him it reared up, pawed the air menacingly with its hooves, and began to transform itself into beastly malignant shapes. The last was a fire-spitting cobra that burned him to a cinder. He woke up drenched in sweat.

At the dining room table the next night, Bikram noticed that Sewa looked a bit leaner. His skin was clearer. He sat straighter, talked sensibly. A hope began to rise in him. Perhaps the tragedy had really put him on a better path.

"I hear you went riding with the sergeant the other day."

"It was good," Sewa answered his father, before turning his attention back to his food.

Chand and Beeji were having dinner with them. Beeji had invited herself back to the mansion, snivelling and insisting, "It's my daughter's home. I am entitled to visit here."

"Maybe you will ride even better than that Jhansi ki Rani," Chand chuckled.

"Yes. The bloody Zaildar did not even have enough sense to give her to you as a bride," Beeji said.

"What?" Sewa looked up again, his eyes narrowing.

"Well, we did not want to tell you, Sewa, but apparently Beeji can't keep her mouth shut." Jagtar glared at her mother.

"Tell me what?"

"Beeji really likes Nikki, so she suggested that we ask for her hand for you. It's an old custom, in circumstances like yours."

"And?"

"The Zaildar refused."

Sewa's demeanour changed, his face twisting with rage.

"Calm down, son," Bikram said softly.

"Calm down, you say? You, the big government minister?" Sewa fumed. "You are like a king and I am your prince. How dare a lowly zaildar defy you?"

"He has every right to."

"No. He does not."

"See what your loose lips have wrought?" Chand shouted at Beeji.

"I was only looking after my grandson's best interests, his right to the younger sister."

"Sewa, be careful now. I warn you. Be very careful. Don't try to stir a hornets' nest."

Sewa took a deep breath and let it out slowly. Then he calmly finished his meal and went upstairs.

"Keep an eye on him," Bikram told his wife.

"He is just reacting to an insult," said Jagtar. "He'll get over it."

Basanti

She took the clothing down from the line strung on the roof and dropped it into a basket. It was a hot, sunny afternoon, perfect for laundry. The next chore would be the ironing. She turned towards the stairs and her eyes narrowed. Against the bright sunshine she saw a rider approaching from the Adda. There was something familiar about the horse, and she soon realized what: it was Sewa on Toofan. *What is he doing here?*

As he passed below her, Basanti raced to the other side of the roof, and she watched him turn right and gallop towards the orchard. Soon he was out of sight.

She decided not to tell anyone that Sewa had ridden by the haveli. Five months after Pinki's passing, things were finally settling. She didn't want to stir up any emotions. But then two days later Sewa rode by again; he looked up at her and shouted something that might have been an obscenity. She watched him disappear, and it took a lot longer this time for her heart rate to return to normal.

She said nothing at the haveli, but decided to stop by the Adda. Her father was sitting at the meat stall.

"Did you see Sewa riding Toofan today?" she asked him.

Bhapa looked closely at her and frowned. "I did. He stopped at his uncle's liquor vend, got a fifth of rum, and drank it before remounting and heading towards Raikot. He did the same thing a couple of days ago."

"Why is he doing that?"

Bhapa took her by the elbow. "Look, Basanti, these are big people. No matter why he is riding by, I want you to stay out of it. Let the Malik worry about it."

"He doesn't know."

"He will if the idiot keeps riding by. The Mukhia was not too upset the first time he rode towards the village, but he looked a bit alarmed today."

"And what can he do?"

"Like the rest of us, not much. Just be careful, Basanti. Know your place."

She left for the dera to talk to Sehba, but before she could find her she saw Paso. The young woman looked nervous.

"Can I talk to you privately?" Paso asked.

"Of course. Come walk with me."

They walked along the path to the village, and Paso waited until she was sure they would not be overheard. Then she said what was on her mind.

"Basanti, did you know that I was working at the hospital in Samrala when they brought Pinki there?"

"No."

"Babaji didn't mention it? I guess, under the circumstances, he probably forgot." She sighed. "I wish *I* could forget that night, but I can't. And there is something I want you to know. It's confidential. If anyone finds out that I told you, it could ruin me."

Basanti was alarmed. "Then don't tell me. Paso, I don't want anything bad to happen to you."

"No, I must tell you. My soul is tortured by what really happened to Pinki."

"What do you mean, what *really* happened to Pinki?"

"Basanti, do you believe Pinki was impure?"

"What?" She had no idea why Paso would say such a thing. Bapuji had told her that Pinki had jumped from the roof, and no one knew why. What was all this about?

"Well, the story I heard was that Pinki jumped off the roof because Sewa threatened her after finding out that she was not a virgin. But Basanti, he was lying."

Basanti had to stop walking, her legs were buckling. Of course Sewa was lying. She had no doubt about that. Pinki was innocent. Unless something had happened to Pinki, the way it had happened to her and Devi when they were children. No, it was an unbearable thought.

Paso took her elbow to steady her.

"Basanti, I have to tell you. Pinki was dead before she fell off the roof."

She wanted to scream. Paso put a finger on her lips.

"The grandfathers and the uncles did not allow a post-mortem because they were afraid of the stigma it would bring. But if they had allowed the post-mortem, Sewa would be in jail today."

"How do you know?"

"I know because I found a deep hole in the back of her skull. A hole like that can only be made by a large-bore bullet or something like an iron rod hammered into the skull."

"Why didn't you say anything?"

"I found it while cleaning her up to be shrouded. Her death certificate had already been signed and accepted."

"O, Goddess."

"Remember, we are lowly Bajigars. We cannot stand up to these powerful people. Sewa's father was able to cover up Pinki's murder. What else is he capable of? Think about that."

Basanti closed her eyes, hoping this was a nightmare. She blinked, scrunched her face, pounded a heel into the ground to wake herself up.

"Basanti," Paso said, "I am so sorry. I just wanted you to know what I know."

Little, innocent Pinki. What did she ever do wrong to deserve such a fate?

Bapuji had been in his room all afternoon, napping and faintly snoring. So it wasn't until a kinsman came by at the end of the day to borrow some tools that he heard about the day's events.

"Maybe he was just riding through," Maaji said.

"Three times in a week?" the kinsman asked. "I am at my well resting for a bit, and he always shows up at the same time."

"Now why would Sewa do that?" Siamo asked.

"Next time, I will stop him and ask him," Nasib said.

"No, don't!" Basanti was frightened by the menacing tone in his voice.

Nasib looked at her, and she lowered her eyes. She realized that she would have to be very careful and honour her promise to keep Paso's secret. If Bapuji and Nasib found out the truth, they would surely do something to Sewa and then end up in jail. *Basanti*, she told herself, *seal your lips*.

After watching Sewa ride by again one day, Bapuji sent for the Jagirdar and the uncles. They sat under the verandah, surrounded by the anxious women.

"My advice is to not say or do anything. Just ignore him," the judge said.

"Brother is right. Sewa can ride by a dozen times daily, and as long as he minds his own business he is not breaking the law," the policeman stated.

"I will go visit Bikram Singh to complain," the Jagirdar said. "I do not like Sewa's attitude at all. He is taunting us, and that is not to be tolerated."

"Or I could just pull him off the mare and beat the crap out of him," Nasib said.

Bapuji looked at him. "What will that accomplish?"

"What if he runs into Nikki coming home from school on the ring road and does something?" Basanti asked. If he did, she thought, she would kill him herself with her bare hands.

Siamo snorted. "Nikki will kick him silly."

Everyone glared at her.

"If he tries something, then we will deal with him." The policeman set his jaw.

"If he tries something, I will shoot him dead myself," Bapuji said evenly.

"No, you will not!" Maaji shouted. "I will die if you end up in jail."

"I told you, *I* will go talk to Bikram Singh. Tell him to put a stop to his son's idiocy," the Jagirdar said.

"I hope he does." Bapuji sighed. "I hope he does."

Bikram

"Jagtar, your stupid son is riding through Raikot every other day."

Bikram had just had a humiliating visit from the Jagirdar. Sewa's behaviour was upsetting the family, he was told, and the Jagirdar was clearly not in a forgiving mood.

"Perhaps he has a purpose. Needs to go through there for a reason."

"Don't make excuses for him. You will have to stand with me this time. I want to give no more rope to Sewa. He is tempting fate again, I tell you."

"You are just getting upset over nothing."

He looked at her pasty skin, the big, dark circles under her eyes, her slack mouth. Was she taking too many pills again?

"What do you think that cowardly Zaildar will do?" Jagtar asked. "All we had to do to send him scurrying off with his tail between his legs was suggest that his granddaughter wasn't pure. You should congratulate Sewa, Ji. At least he has his pride."

Bikram held his head in his hands. "Oh, God."

When Sewa returned to the mansion that night, Bikram and Jagtar were already eating supper with Beeji and Chand. Bikram got up from the table and followed Sewa into the gathering room, where he was leaning into the liquor cabinet. He told him about the Jagirdar's visit.

"What you are doing is not right, Sewa. It is upsetting the Zaildar very much."

"Then let him try and stop me."

"Sewa, if you take on the Zaildar, it will end very badly for you. The Zaildar is a proud Jat. Beware of him, I warn you."

"He wouldn't dare come after me, and you know it."

"Sewa, if the Zaildar wants to, he can call upon his kin to lynch you."

Sewa sat down. "He touches me and Uncle Mangal will break every bone in his body."

"Talk to Uncle Mangal, then. He is coming through the gates right now."

When Mangal came in he looked at the two of them. "What's going on here?"

Bikram told him the story. Mangal closed in on Sewa, grabbing him by his shirt.

"Look here, Sewa," Mangal snarled in his face. "I still get nightmares from that night. You do remember that night, don't you? You spineless idiot."

Sewa cringed, clutching the bottle.

"Bikram, these are my final words to you and your cowardly son. I am through getting you guys out of trouble. If I find out that Sewa has done anything to harm Nikki or her family, I will personally tear him limb from limb."

Mangal grabbed the bottle from Sewa's hands, lifted him by the collar, and shoved him out the door.

"I am never again raising a finger to help him. He is a loser. Sorry to say that, Bikram. You'd better do something, and soon, to save your son from himself."

Beeji burst into the room.

"Sewa is crying. Who upset him so much?"

"I did, Beeji," said Bikram. "He is being an idiot."

"Look here, Bikram," Beeji said, "I am warning you. You have to leave Sewa alone."

"Oh, you're one to give me warnings!" he shouted. "We wouldn't be in this mess if it weren't for your greedy, conniving family, you stupid old bitch. I never should have married, and then I never would have had this disaster of a son!" Bikram could feel his blood pressure climb, could hear his own voice ringing in his ears. He was out of control. "You and your crazy daughter and your whole family have brought this humiliation down on me. You have ruined my life!"

"Oh." Beeji sat down heavily on a chair, cowering, and tried to hide her face by pulling her chador over her head.

She lifted it, it ballooned out behind her, and Bikram saw instead the hood of a cobra rising menacingly towards him, with the snake's

deathly beady eyes staring in the middle. His mind snapped, and he
started raining blows on her head.

"Die, you serpent. Die!"

"He's seizing," Mangal shouted, lifting Bikram in his massive arms.
"Call the doctor."

"What have you done, Ji?" Jagtar shouted. She sounded so far away.

He looked out the window of his fifth-floor hospital room in
Chandigarh. The hills shimmered in the distance and the scene, framed
by the window, looked like a photograph.

At least, this time, he hadn't bitten his tongue. He was only there
because the specialist wanted to run more tests.

He heard voices at the door. Jagtar came in with Chand.

"Beeji needed stitches, Ji," she said indignantly.

"But she will survive," Chand added.

"Where is Sewa?" Bikram asked.

"At the bungalow here."

"Good."

"We just heard some horrible news. Some truck owner got shot,
half his head blown off," Chand told him.

He frowned. "Any more details?"

"No, just a news report on the radio."

When Bikram's personal assistant arrived, he had the full story, and
it came as a terrible shock.

"I am very sorry, Sahib. Your friend Mangal Singh was shot by a
sniper with an elephant rifle. He is dead."

Bikram felt cold. Mangal? "Who did this?"

The PA shook his head. "The report said police suspect it was a hired
assassin. He had lots of enemies, Sahib. You know that. He was not an
easy man. Very, very aggressive. I guess he would be, a man that big."

Mangal, his protector since their army days together. Somehow
Bikram had assumed he would live forever.

"When is the funeral?"

"Once they finish the post-mortem. Maybe tomorrow."

Jagtar wept a few tears, but Bikram was sure they were just for show.

"You have to go with Sewa and Chand to the funeral," he told her.
"I don't think I will be discharged by then."

"Yes, Ji. I will, Ji."

Sewa came that evening and sat with him for half an hour. They talked about Uncle Mangal and shed some tears.

Sewa hugged him. "Uncle was like another father to me."

"He treated you like a son. Protected you, always."

"I know."

"Sewa, listen. Stay away from Raikot. It's the last thing Uncle asked you to do."

Sewa's lips tightened. Then he said, "You know, Father, it is time that I stand on my own feet, be my own man."

"Sewa, what are you babbling about?"

After his discharge from the PGI, Bikram returned to his bungalow and cried over photographs of himself and Mangal together. Pictures of them in the army, or at a wedding or a family celebration. They always had big smiles on their faces. They looked good together— Big Mangal and Little Bikram. No one had dared to threaten him with Mangal looming in the background. Now he was alone.

He decided to have a drink in Mangal's honour, despite his doctor's strict orders. Mangal's family would observe all the religious and funerary rites, without alcohol, and he wanted to honour his fallen comrade in a way that would be true to their long history together, going all the way back to Chittagong. He poured a shot for himself and filled a glass with four or five more shots for Mangal. He clinked Mangal's glass and raised his own.

"Cheers, my brother. Cheers."

He called for his cook.

"Sahib?"

"Can you pour out this glass on the ground in the back, in honour of my dead friend? Let Mother Earth drink them on Mangal's behalf."

"Now, Sahib?"

"No. When I go to bed."

"Sahib, you are not to drink."

"Mangal is watching over me from up there. I will be all right."

He woke up lying on the sofa, a bright sun streaking through the window, stinging his eyes. He struggled up and shuffled to the washroom before going to bed for the day.

Basanti

For a fortnight, Sewa was not seen riding through the village. Bapuji said it was because the Jagirdar had paid Bikram Singh a visit. Whatever the reason, they all felt they could let their guard down at last. Bapuji said it was a wonder that the young man would be so bold, so reckless. If he hadn't been the son of a cabinet minister, he would have been dealt with very harshly by Bapuji's kinsmen for daring to offer such an insult to the family. Basanti thought that Sewa was lucky he had not crossed paths with Nasib. It would have ended disastrously for the soft city boy.

The family was sitting at the kitchen when Bhaga, the snake-catcher, called from the gates.

"Come in." Siamo got up to pull over a cot for him.

Bhaga sat down and glanced not very subtly at the cooking pots. Basanti understood. She stood up and fetched him a full plate.

"I don't know what's going on. The Naag Babas are all staying away from barns right now, and I have run out of rations." Bhaga was rewarded only for his catches.

"You are always welcome at our kitchen, Bhaga," Inder told him. "Come over every day. Basanti will send you off to work with rotis and dal. Then it won't matter so much if the Naag Babas are hiding."

Nikki shivered. "Please don't talk about Naag Babas. I have had more than my share of scares. Remember, Bhua, when Naag Baba scared Bakki and Toofan?"

"Oh, yes! You almost gave me a heart attack!" Siamo said.

"You think you were scared? The horses lost their minds completely. There was no controlling Bakki. If I'd been a less-skilled rider, I don't know what might have happened."

"Tell me, Bhaga," Basanti said. "Which Naag Baba is the biggest and scariest?"

"I think the same one that panicked Bakki. Over four yards long. It can raise its hood to half its length, straight up in the air."

"Could you catch it?"

"It lives in a burrow at the orchard. I've seen it. I could catch it if I wanted to. But why?"

"No reason," she said.

Bapuji left to go on a final long tour of the villages before the new year, the festival of Baisakhi, and the start of the harvest. Now that Sewa was no longer lurking around, he wasn't quite so worried about leaving.

But on that very same day, Sewa rode through the village again. From the roof, Basanti watched his smug face as he trotted past the haveli. And as he turned onto the ring road, Nikki turned onto it too on her way home from school. Basanti felt a scream rise to her throat. This was her nightmare happening right before her eyes!

Sewa stopped the mare and leaned down as Nikki got closer. He said something to her, and Nikki stopped to glare at him. Then he bent lower and extended a hand towards her. Nikki swung her heavy satchel at his head. Sewa straightened up fast and kicked the mare's flanks. A few seconds later, he was racing past the orchard.

Basanti ran breathlessly down the stairs and out the gates.

"Stupid fool," Nikki said.

"What did he say to you?"

"Maa, why are you so frightened? You are shaking like a leaf."

"Nikki, what did he say?"

"Something like 'I love you. Must have you.' Rubbish from a blithering idiot. Lucky for him I missed him with my satchel. If I had dropped him off the saddle, I was going to smash his skull in."

"Nikki, don't say anything about this to Nasib, please. He will run to Samrala to exact revenge."

"I know, Maa. I can take care of myself. I'm not afraid of that stupid darpoke."

Basanti decided she was ready to set in motion a plan that had bubbled up in her mind. It was time to put the fear of God into the stupid, arrogant young Sewa. But first, she had to bring the men into her scheme. She knew she couldn't do it alone.

She asked them to meet her in the cattle yard—Nasib, Gulab, and Bhaga—and they talked about what should be done about Sewa.

"So, I think we all feel the same," Basanti concluded. "Whatever the Jagirdar might have said to Bikram Singh, Sewa has no intention of leaving us alone."

"He needs a good beating," Nasib said, and Gulab seemed to agree.

"I can't say you're wrong," Basanti said. "But wouldn't it be foolish to provoke Sewa's father and all his powerful allies in that way? I was thinking of something a little less obvious. A terrible fright, a warning to stay away."

Now she turned to Bhaga.

"Do you think Toofan could be startled the way Bakki was by the Naag Baba?" she asked.

Bhaga nodded. "Surely."

"Can you catch the big Naag Baba by tomorrow afternoon?"

"What do you have in mind, Basanti?" Nasib asked warily.

"I want to throw Naag Baba in Sewa's path."

"Just like that?"

She frowned. Perhaps she hadn't quite thought this through.

Bhaga said, "Look, Basanti. Naag Baba, especially the big one, weighs a lot and wiggles in the sack. You will not be able to handle it. It will probably bite you and kill you before you get anywhere near Sewa."

"I will carry the bag," Nasib offered.

Bhaga glared. "No, no. Don't be ridiculous. If you are determined to go through with this, I will have to carry the bag myself. But first, I want to hear this plan that Basanti has been hatching."

"It's simple. Sewa is sure to come riding past the orchard, as he always does. You could wait in the trees and step out as he approaches."

"To fling Naag Baba in his path."

"Yes."

"And how will we know when he is on his way?" Nasib asked.

They thought for a while.

"What if I get Bhapa to warn us?" Basanti said. "He can play a drum beat that tells us Sewa is approaching the Adda. That will give you time to get to the orchard with the Naag Baba. Then he will play a different beat to let us know that Sewa is coming towards the haveli."

Gulab smiled. "I can't believe my own sister is so clever."

"Because your sister must protect Nikki and the family," Basanti told him.

"I will go with you," Nasib said to Bhaga.

"I can do it on my own."

"No, he must see me there. He has to know that it was a punishment and a warning, not an accident."

Basanti did not like that one bit. If Bhaga were alone, he could always explain later that he'd been startled by the rider as he left the orchard, and the sack slipped out of his grip.

"Nasib, please listen to me. Let Bhaga do it. You will be recognized and get into trouble." She hoped he wouldn't hear the worry for him that she knew was in her voice.

Nasib caught her eye, and for a moment he held her gaze. Then he said, "Basanti, your concern is sweet to me, and your heart is kind. But this is my decision. It's my own father he is challenging. I have to stand up to him."

O Laxmi Maa, save him, protect him, she prayed.

That evening, when Bhaga had left and Gulab had closed up the cattle yard and gone home to the dera, Basanti and Nasib stood together alone on the road in the starlight. Nasib placed an arm gently around her waist, and she looked up wonderingly into his soft, dark eyes.

"I care, Basanti. I care for you."

At last, the longed-for words. She so wanted to return them. But instead her heart sank as she found herself saying, "You are a Jat, Nasib. I am a Bajigarni."

He looked away for a moment, then right at her.

"Love is blind," he said.

Basanti woke up restless and kept busy to quiet her mind. She washed all the winter bedding and trooped up the stairs a few times to the rooftop clothesline with the wet sheets and blankets in a basket atop her head. Then she dusted the haveli and rearranged the pantry, scrubbed the brass pots and utensils.

Just when the sun dropped to the right spot, she told Maaji, "I am going upstairs to clean Bapuji's and Nasib's rooms."

Maaji nodded, and then let her head drift onto the pillow for her afternoon nap.

The drums started. She saw Nasib follow Bhaga out of the barn, where the Naag Baba had been housed in a large earthenware vat since the day before. Gulab had fed him a huge rat that he'd caught in a trap. Bhaga looked up and waved with his stick hand, and the sack undulated in the other. Gulab opened the cattle yard gates wide for them. She watched Nasib and Bhaga make their the way to the orchard. Gulab stayed behind at the gates, chewing a twig.

The drums started again and she spied Sewa approaching on Toofan. She ducked into a room and watched through the slats of the wooden blinds. Sewa rode the mare past Gulab at a walk, and Toofan neighed seeing her mother through the open gates. Sewa kicked her flanks and she lurched forward into a trot. Basanti stepped out then and hurried over to the far side of the roof, just as Sewa approached the orchard.

Nasib and Bhaga stepped out of the trees. The mare stopped, and Basanti watched, breathless.

It was a few moments before she saw Bhaga open his sack. The mare reared back, and then there was an ear-piercing scream as Toofan suddenly jumped up high and turned in midair to break into a gallop. She watched in horror as Sewa fell off and was dragged screaming along the ground. Behind him the men melted back into the trees, and Naag Baba slithered into the ditch.

People ran out into the street from their courtyards, and in a few moments Toofan was pounding down the path below her. She saw Sewa slammed hard against the corner of the haveli and then flung against the gate post before Toofan came to a stop, still heaving with fear, in the cattle yard.

Basanti raced down the stairs and saw that Maaji had been woken up by the commotion. and was sitting up on her cot. She ran out through the gates, across the road, and into the cattle yard. Basanti pushed her way to the front of the crowd and stopped in horror. Sewa hung with one twisted, bloody foot caught in the stirrup, his turban lost and his hair filling with blood.

Someone elbowed past her. "Get a cot. Help me get him out of the stirrup. We must rush him to the medical centre."

When they lifted him onto the cot, his body was loose, his legs were twisted, and his face was bloody. Four men grabbed the cot by the corners and raced out onto the road. They turned towards the Adda, the crowd following. Basanti ran along too and watched as they set the cot down in the yard of the medical centre.

The doctor ran out and bent over him. He straightened up, shook his head. "Nothing I can do. Brought dead."

A man she had seen before with Sewa's father ran over from the Adda, took one look at the cot and then at the doctor's face. He fell to his knees, his body shaking.

"My nephew is dead. Oh, God. Oh, God."

In the cattle yard she saw Gulab unsaddling Toofan. Her heart was pounding, and her mind was racing. What was going to happen now? Would they be caught?

Basanti walked slowly back to the haveli just as Nasib and Bhaga turned the corner.

"He's dead," she told them.

"Serves him right. The fool should have stayed away from here. He kept coming back. We had to do something," Nasib whispered.

"But I never meant to kill him!"

Nikki came through the gates, dropped her satchel, and ran to Toofan. She hung fondly on the horse's neck.

"You are home, you are home."

Bikram

"What the hell's going on now?" he asked the driver as the car turned onto his street. The gates of the mansion were wide open and filled with people. Bikram stepped out of the car and heard crying. His heart began to race and his legs shook.

He froze when he saw Jagtar wailing in the courtyard.

"Oh, my cruel God! You have taken my only son! My Sewa!"

Bikram felt faint. Strong hands gripped his arms and dragged him inside, forced him onto the sofa, and held him down.

He heard Darshan's voice. "Get the doctor, just in case."

"What happened?" he managed to ask.

Darshan loomed over him. "The mare must have been startled. She threw Sewa off the saddle and dragged him into Raikot."

"From where?"

"From the Pir's orchard."

"Oh, God!" he shouted. "Is this retribution? I am the one who desecrated the Pir's orchard. I killed a girl there, cut off her head. An innocent Muslim girl. I sinned! *I am the demon!*"

"He is seizing, talking nonsense. Hurry."

"No, I am speaking the truth . . . Another innocent girl died under my roof. I had her dropped from the roof to save Sewa. Sewa was a demon, my demon seed."

A hand covered his mouth and pressed it closed.

He felt the sting of a needle, a surge of euphoria, and then he lost consciousness.

I warned you. I warned you, Bikram Singh, never to enter Raikot again. A bald man wearing a holy man's robes and holding prayer beads admonished him, murmured in his ears. *Atone now for your sins and your son's sins. Atone.*

A body lay on a big slab of melting ice, covered in a sheet that was stained with pink. A uniformed nurse pulled the sheet back. They were there to identify Sewa's body.

Bikram approached and bent his head towards his son's face. Sewa's features were broken and swollen. Stitches criss-crossed a cheek, a red line ran over the bridge of his nose, and his eyes were closed. The mangled body reminded him of Pinki's—twisted, unnatural. A foot seemed dislocated, misshapen, the skin purplish blue.

Beside him, Jagtar wailed, "My son, my son. Who did this to you? I curse that soul to burn in hell. I curse that soul!"

"Sewa." Bikram tried to turn the face towards him. The neck was stiff and the skin cold. "Sewa, why did you defy me? Why?"

"Stop, Ji. Even in death you are scolding him!"

"Bloody bitch," he shouted. "Bloody bitch. You slept while he rode to his death."

"Courage, Bikram." He was in his own home, and Papaji sat beside him on the sofa. "Please don't become unhinged. I can only bear so much, my son. Courage, please. Courage."

He wanted to pour his heart out, confess everything. He wanted to atone.

Sewa's soul had been judged, and Pinki's death would have weighed heavily against it. He had begun the celestial journey, Bikram was sure, from the simplest form of life—a journey that was to span eight million, four hundred thousand progressive lives that would be lived in the air, in the waters, and on land. Only after that would he be born a human again, the highest form of life created by God—a human with the power and ability to learn, have a conscience, distinguish between good and evil, conquer sin, live a life of devotion and sacrifice, to be freed of the cycle of life.

His own soul would be judged one day, and the same journey awaited him, if he did not atone for his sins.

The body was brought home to the courtyard. A Giyani waited for Sewa to be bathed and shrouded and laid out on the bier, before he started the prayers of comfort, uttered the Ardas to beg Waheguru's mercy and grace. Darshan walked Bikram to the cot and handed him a dripping towel. Bikram gently wiped his son's rigid face, his neck, then the rest of his body up to the broken feet. The civil surgeon had pulled Sewa's arms and legs straight, corrected the twisted spine and cleaned the wounds.

Bikram watched as Sewa was shrouded in crisp, white cotton and lifted onto the bier. The body was soon covered with garlands of flowers. The Giyani began the recitations.

"Bole so nihal."

"Sat Sri Akal."

Four strapping, youthful cousins lifted the bier onto their shoulders. A bugle sounded, and the hired band struck up a familiar tune, "Amazing Grace." He had heard it played a thousand times in Chittagong as bodies of soldiers who died on the battlefields were shipped out for cremation or burial.

He followed, supported by Darshan and Sukha, the saintly brother-in-law who had ridden in his Jatha, stood in his path all those years ago, begged him not to attack the camping Muslims and defile the hallowed grounds of the Pir's orchard. Sukha had married a fallen woman who'd gone on to bear him four sons, two of whom now carried Sewa's bier on their broad shoulders.

Sukha's was a truly humane soul. Bikram turned to kiss the man's cheek.

"I should have listened to you. I should have listened to your pleas."

People stood at their gates and on roofs, calling out the names of the dignitaries in the procession.

"There is the CM in the parrot-coloured turban and dark glasses."

"See over there, that's the Chief Justice."

The curious were out in force. None pointed to him, to the grieving mother, or to the numbed grandparents being carried in a rickshaw, clinging to each other. No one called out Sewa's name. It was a rare event, an opportunity to eyeball the rich and the powerful gathered by the dozen to support a colleague in his time of loss.

Bikram felt detached from his own grief. His mind was clear, uncluttered, incapable of anger. As they came onto the ring road, he could see the cremation grounds beside a glistening pond, where buffalo floated with only their snouts visible in the sunshine, under a clear, blue sky.

The band finished playing with a loud flourish of drums. A startled peacock flew from a field towards a banyan tree, its loud protests sending the smaller birds tweeting and chirping into the sky. The buffalo swam towards the far side of the pond and scrambled onto the sandy shore.

"I ordered a maund of sandalwood to perfume the pyre and had it soaked in two drums of ghee, to burn fast and hot," Darshan whispered. The bier was laid on the pyre and men settled it straight.

The Giyani stepped forward and began to recite the holy verses.

"Here." Darshan handed Bikram the blazing torch.

Bikram found himself pushed towards Sewa's shrouded form on the massive pyre.

"Drop it." They shook it out of his hands, and as the blast of hot flames burst, they pulled him back and away.

He watched the angry flames spread, the plume of thick smoke rise to the heavens. The aromas of sandalwood and ghee filled the air. A shape began to form in the flames, and Bikram narrowed his eyes to focus on it. The headless girl held the severed head of Sewa in her hands. The eyes opened and the lips moved.

"Atone, now." The urgent whisper in his ear.

Screams rose as he charged towards the pyre and leapt in.

Ajit

In the matter of Sewa's death, the police, Ajit knew, had to go through the motions. He followed them—along with half the village—as they retraced the events from the edge of the orchard to the cattle yard, with witnesses being interviewed once again.

A neighbour whose gates opened onto the ring road claimed to be the first on the scene.

"I saw Toofan, still at a distance, dragging Sewa beside her. The screams. Oh, those terrible screams."

"Did you see anyone behind the mare, maybe a cyclist or a pedestrian?" asked the inspector-general.

"No, the path was clear."

"I cringed at that terrible sound of the skull striking a brick wall," another said.

"I saw it too," a third person added. "She dragged him right into the post."

"I helped unhook Sewa Singh and lift him onto a cot."

"I helped rush him to the medical centre."

"We already talked to the doctor," Jorawar said.

"Close the case," the officer ordered. "I will sign the report right now."

"You are not going to interview the mare?" a smartass called out.

The inspector-general glared at him and sent him scurrying away.

Basanti looked edgy and jumpy while the policemen were at the haveli. When they left, she asked him, anxiously, "End of case, Bapuji?"

"End of case. It will be classified as a misadventure, just like Pinki's."

"Bapuji, can we talk? Alone? I have to get something off my chest."

They walked into the cattle yard and sat on the cot under the tree, where no one could hear.

"I have something to confess. But first, please do not blame Paso. There was nothing she could do. Pinki's case had already been closed."

"What are you talking about?"

Basanti told Ajit what Paso had explained to her about Pinki's death, how she had been killed before she was dropped onto the street. How the story of Pinki being impure was a fiction designed to keep him from investigating further.

"Sewa got away with murder, Bapuji. And then he kept riding by the haveli, taunting you and Nasib. I was so afraid one or both of you would try to fight him and end up in jail. Or he would try to do something to Nikki, Bapuji. As a mother, what choice did I have but to take matters in my own hands?"

He stared at her.

"I asked Bhaga to catch the biggest Naag Baba, and Nasib went with him to the orchard to throw it in Toofan's path."

He could not believe his ears or utter a sound.

"I did not mean to kill him, Bapuji. I just wanted to scare him enough that he'd stay away from Raikot. Nasib and I wanted to teach him a lesson. Bapuji . . . do you think I will be cursed for what I did? Should I go to jail?"

Ajit struggled to find the right words. It was very important at that moment that he speak his heart.

"No, Basanti. You are a mother. I understand. And so will God."

They sat in silence then as he digested the information. A great sense of shame rose in him and he began to weep.

"Pinki. My sweet Pinki. I failed you, I failed you. And so I failed Satwant, too."

"Bapuji," Basanti said to him through sobs. "I do not want you to think that Pinki would ever shame you. She was pure, Bapuji. Pure. Please remember her as I do."

"Thank you, Basanti, for opening my eyes. Thank you. I have so much to atone for."

Basanti

A month later, over supper, Siamo brought up the latest proposal for Nasib.

"The girl is eighteen, a matriculate, and she has done basic training. She can teach primary school. Good family."

"Bhua." Nasib stopped her.

Siamo folded her arms, ready to argue, and Inder said, "We have to start listening, Nasib. You have to be married."

"But why? If Basanti can stay a widow, why can't I stay a bachelor forever?"

Basanti wished that Nasib had left her name out of it. The last thing she wanted was someone suggesting it was about time she return to the dera as another man's wife. At the same time, she hoped that Siamo would listen to Nasib and stop trying to find him a bride, so she was in favour of any argument that Siamo might listen to.

Nikki raised her arm as though she were in school. "Chacha, I have an idea."

"Quiet, girl," Siamo said with a glare. "Let the grown-ups talk."

Nikki pouted.

"All right, let's discuss this proposal," Nasib said. "I am thirty, and the girl is eighteen. I am eight pass, she is ten pass and finished basic training. I have been lamed by polio, she is healthy. Tell me, where's the match?"

"You are the son of a zaildar, owner of this haveli and hundreds of acres of land," Siamo declared.

"So, that is what makes me qualified in her eyes?"

"She has no say. It's her father who decides."

"Have you told her about my limp, my age, my past?"

"I will make sure this time that is not an issue, Nasib," Siamo said.

"Well, I say she is not suitable. I want to marry someone who wants me for me," Nasib said, clearly hoping to end the discussion.

They were all at a loss for words. Except for Nikki.

"I know who loves you for you, Chacha."

"What are you babbling about, Nikki?" Inder asked.

"Chacha, Maa loves you for you, and I know you like her too. If you marry her, she will no longer live like a widow, and you will no longer be a bachelor."

Basanti gasped and quickly covered her head with her chador. She got up from the table and went to sit at the hearth, hiding behind the half-wall, rather than be seen listening to the conversation that would surely follow.

Maaji glared at Nikki.

"I'm only speaking the truth," Nikki said, folding her arms across her chest.

Nasib looked as guilty as a bootlegger caught with the goods by a policeman's flashlight.

"Look at it this way," Nikki continued. "I have my Maa. If Chacha marries her, he will be my Bapuji. See? I win."

Inder and Siamo had their mouths wide open. Nasib had his head lowered and his hands pressed tightly between his knees. Basanti listened, holding her breath.

"So, Babaji?" Nikki asked her grandfather.

They were all waiting for his reaction. He looked confused, flummoxed, but then he spoke at last.

"What you are proposing, Nikki, makes sense to me. If it's what Nasib wants."

"It is, Bapuji," Nasib said softly.

Basanti felt her heart race so madly she thought she might pass out.

"But Bir, what will people think?" Siamo said. "Basanti is a Bajigarni. We are Jats."

"Times are changing, Siamo," Bapuji said. "Maybe now we can think more about our own happiness, and not worry about people's opinions. We uphold Basanti as the mother of my grandchildren. Nasib is Satwant's brother and has loved the girls as though they were his own. Why should we invite a stranger to come into our home as a stepmother to Nikki when she already has a mother? People will talk, certainly. But then, I think, they will accept."

Basanti peeked over the half-wall and saw Nasib give his father a grateful smile.

"I just don't know how I missed it," Bapuji said. "Does Nikki have better eyesight? Or maybe better foresight?"

Siamo said, "You will have to speak about this matter to the Mukhia and to Changu."

"I will go with you, Babaji. Bajigar Nana will not refuse me anything," Nikki said confidently.

"The Mukhia has never said no to you either," Inder pointed out.

Nikki looked radiantly happy.

"Makes sense." Siamo looked over to the kitchen and caught Basanti's eye and smiled.

"More than anything," Bapuji said, "I want you all to be happy. Nasib is the heir to my name and my titles. Why burden him with a loveless marriage when he has chosen so well for himself? I apologize if I have been blind, wallowing in my own pride and self-pity. Basanti," Bapuji called. "Come back here. I will ask you only one question."

Basanti tiptoed over.

"Basanti, will you marry Nasib?"

"Of course she will," Nikki said. "Won't you, Maa?"

"I will, Bapuji!" Basanti said. "He is my Nasib, my Fate."

Bhapa stuck to his Bajigar ways.

"How much should I ask for the bride price?" he wanted to know.

Basanti had asked to move back to the dera until the arrangements were finalized rather than live scandalously under the same roof as her promised. The wedding was to be held at the gurudwara in the village rather than the dera or the haveli as it was God's house, a holy place that welcomed everyone, rich or poor, high-born or untouchable. It was the only place where a lowly Bajigarni could sit as an equal beside her high-born groom and no one would dare invite Waheguru's wrath by questioning their union.

Also, Basanti was determined to be presented as a bride to the deities before being dragged through the streets by Siamo for the showing-the-face ceremony. This time around she was not going to take any chances. Pushpa promised to guide her through all the rituals for the appeasing of the gods, goddesses, and spirits. And in her heart, she would be walking hand in hand again with her beloved cousin Devi.

"What bride price?" Dadi asked. "You were paid by the Mukhia already."

Bhapa did not blink.

"I know that Nasib owns a bicycle. Maybe you can get that, Bhapa," Gulab said.

Bhapa glared at him. "Be serious now."

"You be serious," Mata told him. "Looking for a bride price for a widowed daughter?"

"You think the Malik can't afford it?"

Basanti had to stop the bickering. Until Bhapa agreed, there could be no wedding.

"I have almost five years of my wages saved with Bapuji. I will pay my own bride price."

"What? Five years of wages? Saved? That must be over two thousand rupees. I can build a two-room brick hut with a tin roof."

"And buy a buffalo for milk. Don't forget that," Gulab said with a grin. He seemed mightily amused by the discussion.

"Have you no shame, Changu?" Dadi asked.

Bhapa stood up and retied his dhoti before putting on his turban and moccasins. There was an urgency in his voice.

"Gulab, let's go give Nasib the silver rupee."

"At this hour?"

"They must still be awake."

"Oh, just go." Mata waved them off, but shouted after them, "Changu, take the Mukhia with you."

And Dadi called, "Wash your hands, Changu, before you hold the silver rupee in them. And bow to Laxmi Maa's shrine on your way out."

"I will go get the ladoos," Gulab said. The feeding of a ladoo by the girl's father to her promised was customary. "The tea stall is still open." He rushed out.

Basanti had a vision of the family gathered for supper under the verandah at the haveli, and Bhapa sailing through the gates holding the silver rupee in his sweaty hands, the sum of two thousand rupees stuck in his head. She stepped out the door to watch the three men of her engagement party, followed by some elders, gather at the dera's entrance. People left their huts and hearths to see. Mata and Dadi were still shouting instructions in the dim light of the lanterns.

Keep it simple, she wanted to say. *Make it quick.*

The Jagirdar came to the dera with his wife and sons, and the Mukhia hosted them on covered cots laid in the centre. Sehba served tea and pinnis.

"Basanti, come here, sit with us," Jeet Kaur called.

Basanti walked over and sat with Jeet Kaur, facing the Jagirdar and his sons.

"Changu."

Bhapa stepped forward.

"Changu, your daughter replaced our daughter as a mother to Pinki and Nikki," the Jagirdar said. "Thus, she became our daughter, too. She is as dear to us as Amrita."

"That she is," the judge said.

"You are my sister, Basanti," the police superintendent said.

Tears filled Basanti's eyes. She was overwhelmed.

The women of the dera, some dressed in their hand-me-down kurta-salwars, squatted around them. Mata and Dadi began to sing songs of praise for the visitors. Bhapa sat on the ground beside the cots. He looked stunned. Naura made an appearance, but slipped away again to watch from a distance, her face twisted with envy.

"This is not the dera Basanti was born in, so I am proposing that her wedding be held at my haveli in Palampur and her doli leave from my courtyard," the Jagirdar said.

"It's only right." Jeet Kaur hugged Basanti and kissed her on the cheek.

"You are all invited as our guests to attend the ceremony," Kulbir said.

"She will need a dowry, Jagirdar," Bhapa said.

"It will be my pleasure. In fact, I am going to give the new car I bought for Pinki in Basanti's dowry, and more."

"Much more," Jorawar said.

Sehba gasped.

"May your families be blessed, Sardars. May you prosper through the ages," Dadi said.

"So you agree, Changu?"

Bhapa was speechless and could only nod vigorously.

"That was a brave thing you did, Basanti," Jeet Kaur whispered in her ear. "Getting rid of that murderous Sewa. May his soul rot in hell."

Nasib had ordered the rath to be repaired, she heard. He wanted his bride to be brought back in style. She was going to wear the fine chador that Nasib had brought her from Arabia. She had saved it for a special occasion, and what better time to wear it than her wedding?

Selected Glossary

Adda – Bus stop

Akali – Member of Akali Dal

Akali Dal – A Sikh political party

Akhara – Wrestling ring

Bapuji – Father

Bet – Wetlands along the Sutlej River

Bhapa – Father

Bhog – Celebration by a complete reading of the Holy Granth

Bastee – Collection of shanties; a settlement

Birri – A cheap cigarette made of rolled tobacco leaf

Bole so nihal – Who so utters, shall be fulfilled.

Chador – Head cover for women

Chullah – An oven made of mud or bricks, using wood and cow dung for fuel

Chotta Malik – Young sir, lord

Darpoke – Coward

Dupatta – Punjabi-style head cover

Giyani – Sikh priest

Haveli – Traditional farmhouse with a large, walled courtyard

Jat – A Farming community of landowners

Jathedar – Local leader of the Akali Dal

Keela – An Iron rod sticking out of wall to hang clothes on

Kabila – Clan

Kanyadaan – Paying for or contributing to a girl's wedding

Langoti – Loincloth worn by wrestlers

Langar – Communal meal

Malik – Lord or Master

Mohur – Gold or Silver coin

Mukhia – Head of a clan

Numberdar – Village tax collector

Pinni – A sweet made of milk cake, nuts, sultanas and sugar

Rath – Decorated, ceremonial ox-cart

Sehra – Face covering for grooms. Usually made of flowers
Sarpanch – Head of an elected village council (panchayat)
Sat Sri Akal – God is truth
Sewa – Voluntary service
Sunnat – Male circumcision
Suhaag raat – Wedding night
Zaildar – Government-appointed tax collector of many villages. Local leader.

Acknowledgements

First of all, I would like to acknowledge New York novelist Naomi Regin for pointing out that there was little she could find about Sikhs in English literature and encouraging me to write about what I know best. There is a paucity of Sikh characters in popular fiction and I have only read three novels in my life based on Sikh protagonists, *Train to Pakistan* by Kushwant Singh, *What the Body Remembers* by Shauna Singh Baldwin, and *The Runaways* by Sandeep Sahota. As a Sikh in changing times I hope my effort contributes to the list.

My special thanks to my father Mr Sukhdev Singh for his numerous stories and history lessons on Sikhism, the greater Punjab, and the Partition of 1947; my childhood friend, the late Shri Surinder Agnihotri, without whose help from India I would not have been able to develop Basanti, a Bajigar, as a narrator; my pre-editors Dan Varrette, Jessica Bowden, and Laurie Smith; and Brian Henry, Lara Hinchberger, and Diane Varrana for their manuscript assessments.

My thanks also to my readers Alan Berger, Curtis and Cathy Fedoruk, Ida and Norm Komaranski, Sara and Robert Mattachini, Mena Train, Josie Pellizzari, and my sisters Swaranjit Sidhu and Sudesh Kent. A bow to my writing buddy Pam Goldstein.

Also thanks to my daughter Sara for suggestions for the cover design, Catherine Marjoribanks, my editor extraordinaire, and my literary agents Sam Hiyate and Kanishka Gupta.

Thanks to Renuka Chatterjee of Speaking Tiger in India and Nurjehan Aziz of Mawenzi House in Toronto and their staff.

My unending gratitude to the eminent author M G Vassanji who edited this final version.